The Return of
SIR
PERCIVAL

The Return of SIR PERCIVAL

BOOK I: GUINEVERE'S PRAYER

S. ALEXANDER O'KEEFE

GREENLEAF
BOOK GROUP PRESS

Published by Greenleaf Book Group Press
Austin, Texas
www.greenleafbookgroup.com

Distributed by Greenleaf Book Group

For ordering information or special discounts for bulk purchases, please contact Greenleaf Book Group at PO Box 91869, Austin, TX 78709, 512.891.6100.

Design and composition by Greenleaf Book Group
Cover design by Greenleaf Book Group
Cover images: ©iStockphoto.com/Nneirda, ©shutterstock.com/amir bajrich

Cataloging-in-Publication data is available.

ISBN 13: 978-1-62634-309-2

eBook ISBN: 978-1-62634-310-8

Part of the Tree Neutral® program, which offsets the number of trees consumed in the production and printing of this book by taking proactive steps, such as planting trees in direct proportion to the number of trees used: www.treeneutral.com

TreeNeutral

Printed in the United States of America on acid-free paper

16 17 18 19 19 21   10 9 8 7 6 5 4 3 2 1

First Edition

Preface

even years have passed since the death of King Arthur and all but one of the Knights of the Round Table at the battle of Camlann, and Albion, the home of the Britons, has descended into a maelstrom of violence and chaos. A savage Norse warlord has seized Londinium and made it his personal fief, bands of brigands roam the roads and countryside, and the people in every town and village throughout the land live in perpetual fear. Morgana, the woman who wrought this nightmare of pain and suffering by destroying the Kingdom of Arthur the Pendragon, has one more life to take before she leaves Albion's shores—that of Merlin the Wise, her hated enemy.

The destruction of the Pendragon's legions and the fall of Camelot has forced Queen Guinevere, and two loyal retainers, to take shelter in a remote abbey in the forests to the north. There the Queen lives, all but bereft of wealth and defenses, under constant threat from mercenary bands, foreign raiders, and Morgana's assassins. Yet, despite these hardships, the Queen valiantly struggles to keep hope alive for her people and to preserve some small vestige of Arthur's dream.

In the midst of these dark times, Guinevere receives word that Sir Percival, a Knight of the Round Table who was thought to have died in the land of the Moors seeking the Holy Grail, has returned to Albion. As the faithful Knight travels to Guinevere's distant sanctuary, he and his companion, a mysterious Numidian soldier, are drawn into the web of violence and intrigue that has descended upon the land.

Sir Percival's return is like a ray of hope from heaven for the oppressed people of Albion, bringing back memories of a time of peace and prosperity that now seems so distant as to be just a dream. The Knight's return also brings to the fore feelings that Guinevere and Percival held for each other but faithfully suppressed while Arthur was alive.

In time, Guinevere, Merlin, and the scheming Morgana will come to realize that Sir Percival is not the same man who left a decade earlier. The horrific trials the last Knight of the Round Table endured in the land of the Moors have forged him into the deadliest of weapons, and those unwise enough to take his measure will not find him wanting.

This Arthurian tale takes place in a fictional Briton roughly two hundred and fifty years after Rome relinquished control of the land. The cities and towns in the tale are referred to by their Roman place names or by their older Briton names, where possible. I have also made liberal use of the old Roman road system, based upon the assumption that these roads would have remained the best available in this time period. The map on the following page provides a guide for those who may desire to place the sequence of events in the story within their general geographic context.

When possible, I have used ancient landmarks that remain today as key locations in the story, such as the ruins of Abbey Cwm Hir in Wales; the tower at Pen Dinas in Wales; the site of the former Walton Castle in Felixstowe; and the Roman signal station in the town of Filey. In those instances where a historical or geographic fact was an impediment to the story, reality yielded to fantasy.

—S. Alexander O'Keefe

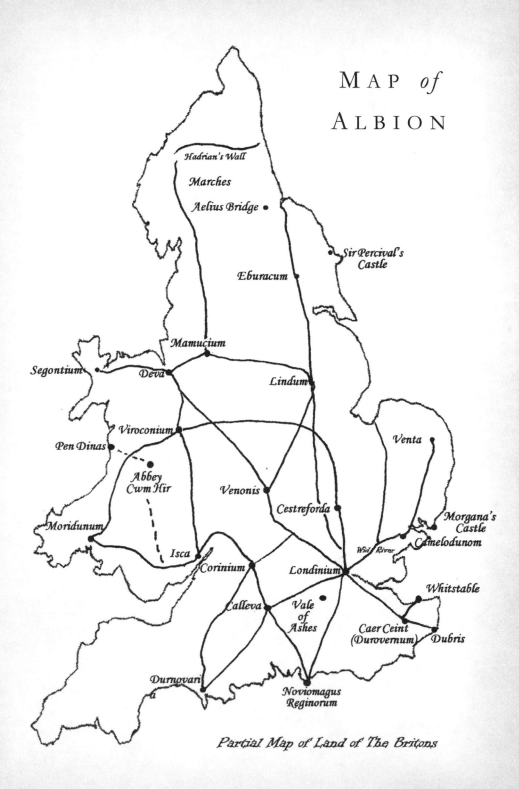

MAP *of* ALBION

Hadrian's Wall

Marches

Aelius Bridge

Sir Percival's Castle

Eburacum

Mamucium

Segontium

Deva

Lindum

Viroconium

Venta

Pen Dinas

Abbey Cwm Hir

Venonis

Cestreforda

Morgana's Castle

Moridunum

Camelodunom

Widi River

Isca

Corinium

Londinium

Whitstable

Calleva

Vale of Ashes

Caer Ceint (Durovernum)

Dubris

Durnovaria

Noviomagus Reginorum

Partial Map of Land of The Britons

Acknowledgments

I want to thank my wife and children, my mother, and my brothers and sisters for their love and support. I particularly want to thank my now deceased father for insisting that I read *A Tale of Two Cities* by Charles Dickens, *The Count of Monte Cristo* by Alexandre Dumas, and *Scaramouche* by Rafael Sabatini when I was ten years old, which I reluctantly did. Thousands of books later, those are still three of my favorites.

CHAPTER 1

THE PASSAGE TO ALBION

Aldwyn Potter stared at the Frankish coast from the stern of the Mandragon, his eyes fixed on the walled settlement drifting in and out of the morning fog a league to the south. Despite the cold breeze, a river of sweat flowed down the old mariner's weathered cheeks to the point of his chin, before falling to the deck below. Like a man in a trance, Potter murmured a prayer over and over again, in cadence with each sweep of the galley's oars.

In each fervent chant, he thanked the Almighty for the fair wind and following sea and begged deliverance from the threat on the receding coast. The twenty rowers amidships, sensing their captain's disquiet, pulled together in a strong, silent rhythm, seeking, with each stroke, the safety of Albion's shores to the north. They, like Potter, lived in mortal fear of the men within those dark walls—the Norse raiders known as the seawolves.

When Potter had first gone to sea, three decades earlier, the Norse had raided the coasts of Albion and Francia from the late spring until the early fall and then returned to the northland until the next season. Alas, even this brief respite was now a thing of the past. In recent years, the seawolves had established settlements on the islands off western Hibernia and along the Frankish coast—settlements allowing them to prowl the surrounding seas from the first day of the sailing season to the last. In these fell times, a sailor from Albion was far more likely to die by a Norseman's sword, or worse, to serve as a slave under his lash, than to die in the cruel embrace of the sea.

On this voyage, Potter had left his Frankish port-of-call to the south well before dawn, intending to sail past the seawolves' settlement in the early hours of the morning. The day before had been a Norse feast day, and he knew the raiders would be slow to rise after a night of drinking and wenching. Thankfully, in this he had been right. The settlement was as quiet as a grave, and with each stroke of the oars, the threat from the savage men within its wooden walls receded.

After taking a last look at the coast, Potter allowed himself a moment of hope. On this, his last voyage, the bones had mercifully rolled his way again, as they had so many times in the past. As he turned and started toward the bow of the ship, the Mandragon passed through a patch of fog reluctantly yielding its grey cloak to the rays of the morning sun. The moment the ship emerged from its shelter, the sailor on watch in the ship's prow screamed a warning.

"Seawolves!"

Potter scanned the sea and seized upon the long galley off the Mandragon's port side. For a moment, he stood there transfixed by the sight of the black dragonprow cutting through the waves toward the Frankish coast and the wall of armed warriors standing amidships, returning his stare. As the captain watched, the galley wheeled in a slow and sure arc toward the Mandragon, and the cadence pounded out by the raiders' oarsmaster—a red-haired giant in the stern—grew louder and more rapid.

As the ship drew closer, a desperate rage came over the old captain, and he broke free of the ice-cold tendrils of fear that were binding his feet to the deck. *They will not take my ship without a fight.* Seizing the iron-tipped cudgel lying on the deck a pace away, he ran toward the bow of the ship.

"Cadeyrn, Drust, Seisyll, Wade, and Ninian, grab your steel and make ready! The rest of you men, pull for your lives!" Potter roared.

Before Potter and his men could reach the forward rail, three Norsemen were already aboard. The leader was a fair-haired mountain of a man, easily twenty hands tall, clad in a foul-smelling bearskin. In one hand, the giant held a wooden shield nearly half as tall as Potter, and in the other, a short, wide sword designed for cutting flesh and smashing bones in close quarters fighting. The web of cuts and gashes in the thick leather helmet atop the giant's head, along with the scars on his face and arms, marked him as a seasoned warrior.

As Potter and his sailors traded blows with the first wave of Norsemen, the old captain could see the growing stream of raiders climbing over the rail behind them, and he knew the battle for Mandragon was being lost. In a desperate effort to turn the tide, Potter dropped beneath the sweep of the blond giant's sword and swung his cudgel at the man's exposed knee.

A moment before the iron tip smashed into the bone, the giant realized the danger and raised his leg. The blow smashed into the primitive iron greave protecting the Norseman's calf, drawing a howl of pain, but otherwise leaving him unharmed. The enraged giant retaliated by smashing his upraised heel into Potter's chest, hurling him backward against the starboard rail.

As the dazed captain struggled futilely to stand and get back into the fight, a man sprang out of the starboard cargo hold. A second man followed on his heels, and the two raced across the deck to join the battle. For a moment, Potter stared at the men, bewildered, and then realized it was the two passengers who had come aboard at Lapurdum, a port in southern Francia. Potter had paid the men little heed, assuming they were wealthy merchants, based upon the quality of their traveling cloaks and their plentiful supply of silver coins. Now, he could see his judgment had been wide of the mark.

The first man out of the hold was nineteen hands tall, but he moved with the ease and speed of a man half his size. His chiseled face was framed by a mane of black hair that flowed past the ropes of muscle in his neck to the formidable shoulders below. He wore a mailed shirt over his torso, steel gauntlets on his forearms, and a gleaming steel buckler shield strapped to his left forearm. The steel sword he grasped in his right hand seemed merely a part of the far more lethal weapon that was the man, rather than a separate instrument of war.

The second man was a bald African, similarly clad. He was a head shorter than the tall man, but had the arms and chest of a blacksmith, and his sword was curved like that of a Moorish warrior. As the African ran across the deck with his companion, he wheeled his sword in a blinding circle, as if performing a ritual, and then his powerful hand enclosed the pommel in an iron grip.

When the two men waded into the Norsemen flooding the deck behind the blond giant, it was as if something terrible and magnificent had been unleashed. The pair weaved among their opponents like wind-borne scythes, working in unison, both masters of the same lethal dance. In moments, the second wave of raiders lay either dead or dying, and the third wave attempting to board had been driven back into the sea.

As the Norse giant and a second raider pressed forward to kill the last of the five sailors who had answered Potter's call to battle, the scream of a dying companion drew his attention. The blond warrior glanced over his shoulder at the carnage on the deck behind him, and then he wheeled around, dragging his companion with him.

The tall, dark-haired man moved forward to engage the giant, leaving the African to hold the rail against further boarders. As soon as the man was within striking distance, the leader of the Norsemen shoved his smaller companion in front of him, using him as a shield. He then leaped forward, intending to strike his adversary down. His gambit failed. The dark-haired man sprang to the right with blinding speed and smashed his buckler shield against the smaller man's head, dropping the stunned raider to the deck.

The blond warrior bellowed out a roar and swung his sword in a slashing blow at the other man's neck, but his enemy dove under the strike, rolled, and came to his feet behind the giant. There, he struck the giant down with a single fluid stroke and stepped aside as the body fell heavily to the deck.

When the sailors threw the giant Norseman's body over the rail, the oarsmaster on the dragonship roared out a command and began to pound out a different beat. As Potter watched, the galley moved away and once again headed toward the settlement on the Frankish coast. The captain of the raiders had decided the blood price for taking the Mandragon was not worth the expected treasure.

An hour after the battle ended, Potter walked the length of the raised quarterdeck, surveying the worn oak planks that ran the length of the ship. After a long moment, he nodded his silver-haired head in satisfaction. The crew had swabbed away all traces of the blood and gore, and the cold sea air had swept away the odor of death. Sadly, neither toil nor wind could resurrect the four sailors who'd breathed their last only steps away from where he stood, nor render the memory of the attack that had taken their lives any less painful.

Potter's gaze scanned the rest of the ship and came to rest on the two passengers who were standing in the prow talking quietly, now innocuously clad in their traveling cloaks. He started toward them, intending to thank them once again for saving his ship, when he noticed Bede, the youngest sailor, staring at the two men as if they were monsters from the deep.

"Quit your gawking, boy, and get on with it," he ordered. "We're an hour out of port, and I want those ropes and barrels stowed."

The young sailor jumped at Potter's growl.

"Aye, Captain. I'll be hard at it."

The exchange drew a grin from Fulke, the bosun, as he lugged a barrel of wine up from the hold on his shoulder.

"You do that," Potter said as he turned to Fulke. "And you, Fulke, don't spill a drop of that wine. That barrel will go for a king's ransom in Caer Ceint."

"Not a drop, sir," Fulke said, the grin on his hard, sea-worn face widening.

Potter slowed as he approached the two men and stopped a respectful distance away. The dark-haired man turned to face him, and for a moment, the captain stood in silence, transfixed, as the memory of the battle with the Norsemen replayed in his mind yet again. Potter suppressed the recollection as he stared thoughtfully into the taller man's face.

Potter was a trader, and a successful one. He'd bargained and parleyed with the Franks, Moors, Greeks, and yes, even the cursed Norsemen, from time to time. He prided himself on being able to quickly take the measure of a man from his mien—in particular, from his eyes—and to use those insights to gain an advantage. In this instance, the dark-haired man's face remained a mystery. The confluence of the strong jaw, aquiline nose, and prominent forehead, all of which had been bronzed by the sun in some distant land, was more noble than handsome, but the enigma lay in the contrast between the eyes and the rest of the man's face.

The striking blue eyes staring back at Potter were those of a man who had waded deep into the cauldron of life and borne the pain of its most scalding waters; the eyes of a soldier who'd oft engaged in battle and felt the near touch of death; and most surprising, the eyes of a man who had found, in spite of the ordeal, a path to the rarest of gifts—wisdom. What troubled Potter was the rest of the man's face: His mien was unscarred and bereft of the burdens of age, and yet he was skilled in battle and wise in years.

The tall man waited patiently for a moment and then stepped toward Potter and extended his hand, revealing a web of scars running over the back of his hand and continuing across much of his heavily muscled forearm. The hand that closed upon Potter's own was like a piece of worn iron, but at the same time, there was an honest warmth in the man's grip and in the words he spoke.

"Captain Potter, it seems our voyage together will yet have a peaceful end."

"That it will," he said with a nod. "And I will thank the Lord and all his angels from this day until my last for sending you and your friend on this voyage. If not for your bravery and skill, we . . . we would all have been killed or sold into slavery, for that is the way of the seawolves."

"So I have heard, Captain." The man turned to the silent African by his side, whose face was hidden within the hood of his dark grey cloak. "I would have you know my friend and brother-in-arms, Capussa."

The African drew off his hood and nodded solemnly to Potter, revealing a square jaw, a wide, prominent nose, and brown eyes that radiated power, confidence, and more than a hint of mirth. Unlike his friend's face, the African's bore the marks of battle; a scar ran from his right ear to the cleft of his jaw, and a second marred his left cheekbone.

The dark-haired man gestured to the approaching shore. "Captain, you seem to be coming in short of the Tamesis. Is Londinium not your port?"

Potter shook his head. "It was my home port, until Hengst and his raiders came."

"Hengst?" the tall man asked.

Potter raised both brows. "Surely you have heard of Hengst the Butcher?"

"No, Captain. I have not."

"Sir, may I ask how long you have been away from Albion?"

The man exchanged glances with the African and then stared at the approaching coast for a moment before turning his attention back to Potter. He slowly shook his head, as if reaching for a distant and painful memory.

"I sailed from Londinium nearly ten summers ago."

Potter let out a slow breath. "Why, the Pendragon was—"

"Still on the throne, and the Table yet unbroken," the man finished.

The captain paused at the quiet anguish in the man's voice and then continued.

"The war began a year after you left. That foul witch, Morgana, and her band of brigands—may she burn in the bowels of hell—were never a match for the Pendragon and the Knights of the Table. But then . . . somehow she found the gold to hire an army of sellswords from the lands of the Norse and Saxons. Those hell-spawn became the scourge of the land. The things they did were truly the devil's own work." Potter's breath rasped in his throat, as if it had become as dry as a bone in the sun.

The African drew a metal flask from his cloak and handed it to the old man. "Drink," he ordered in a voice like the growl of an old bear.

Potter took the flask and drank. For a moment, he thought he'd swallowed a hot coal, but then the burning eased and he could taste the flavor of the fiery brew, a taste he found pleasing.

"That . . . it is noble mead," Potter said with a gasp, returning the flask to the African. "Like fire at first, and yet it has a fine taste once you take the full measure of it."

"That's not mead, Captain," the African said with a smile, "but I'm happy you find it agreeable."

Potter took in another breath. "It is indeed. Now, where was I . . . Oh yes, the war." He frowned. "It raged for two, maybe three years. The King nearly drove the raiders into the sea during the last year, but then the witch brought in a fresh army of Norse and Saxons—Picts too— and the tide began to turn. Then came the last battle . . . Camlann."

He hesitated and drew in a heavy breath before continuing in a voice filled with heartfelt regret. "It was a terrible slaughter. The witch and her foul army were driven from the field, but the price was high . . . too high. The Pendragon was killed, and the Table died with him."

"All were lost?" the tall man asked, his voice hushed.

"Sir?"

"Do you say that all of the Knights of the Table fell that day?"

Potter lifted his shoulders in a weary shrug. "Some say one might have survived the battle, and others claim Sir Percival is still in the Holy Land." He shook his head. "I cannot say. I—"

"And Galahad?" the tall man interjected. "Are you sure that he fell at Camlann with the rest of my . . . with the rest of the Knights?"

Potter eyes widened, surprised at the intensity in the tall man's voice. "That is a true mystery," he said. "They say his body was never found, but he was in the very thick of the battle. I just can't say, sir."

Potter shook his head, and his eyes grew distant. "It . . . it seems like it happened so long ago. Sometimes, well, the younger ones, when they talk of the Pendragon, the Queen, and the Table, it's as if they were legends, people who lived in a far distant time."

"You were speaking of this Hengst," the other man prodded gently.

Potter felt a rush of fear and hate, in equal measure, at the mention of the name.

"He was the leader of the second band of sellswords, who came from the north. After the battle, he took the remnants of his men and began to raid the smaller villages. In the first year, he looted, raped, and killed. Then, as more brigands joined his band, he started to besiege the towns. Several years ago, he made a surprise raid on Londinium in the early morn. He attacked from the landward side and his brother, Ivarr the Red, from the river. A traitor within the city opened one of the gates, and by the time the guards realized the peril, it was too late."

The ship dipped sharply into the trough of a wave, unbalancing the old sailor for a moment. The African put a hand on his shoulder and steadied him. Potter nodded his thanks and went on with his tale.

"The devil himself would have been shocked by the slaughter that followed. My uncle was a cooper there, he . . ." The captain's voice trailed off and he hesitated for a moment, anger welling up inside of him, but he suppressed it and continued.

"Well, here's the way of it now—any ship that lands at Londinium is seized by Hengst's men and forced to pay a tax, or so he calls it, and then his men take whatever they like from the ship as well. Sometimes they leave something, sometimes not. On a bad day, when they've drunk too much, they'll take your ship and sometimes your head. Few ships port there now, other than slavers. Hengst is respectful of those curs—he needs them to buy the men, women, and children he seizes and sells every month."

The tall man's face darkened when Potter mentioned the slaves, but he didn't question him further on the matter.

"Where will we make landfall?" he asked.

Potter pointed to a knoll in the distance, on the port side of the approaching estuary.

"Whitstable, a small village on the other side of that point. I'll sell my goods there. Much of what comes in goes to Caer Ceint by caravan, but some of the braver traders take a load or two upriver to Londinium in smaller boats. They travel in the black of night. It's a dangerous voyage. If you need a boat to Londinium, I know a boatman, an honest one. It's the least I can do for you."

"That will not be necessary, Captain. We travel to another place," the tall man said.

Potter pointed at the approaching shore and said, "I must leave you sirs. There's a nasty shoal on the way in, and I like to man the steering oar myself."

The two men nodded to Potter, and he started back across the deck. As he walked by the mast, he realized that the tall man had never given his name. For a moment, he thought about going back, but a gust of wind began to push the galley off course, forcing him to make his way quickly to the stern.

*　*　*

AFTER POTTER LEFT, the African pulled the hood over his head again and pointed toward the shore. "So we journey to a land of witches and butchers," he said, a hint of mirth in his voice. "A pleasant place. I'm looking forward to this new adventure."

Sir Percival stared out at the dark green forest covering the approaching hills, momentarily awash in the sea of memories evoked by his conversation with Captain Potter. He nodded and turned to his friend.

"Butchers, yes, we have those aplenty, but Morgana is no witch. Her real name is Megaera—she's an assassin from the City of Constantinople. The Roman emperor in the east sent her to kill a man called Melitas Komnenos."

"What did this man do to draw the wrath of the Roman king?"

"That, I don't know," he admitted. "Melitas is also a man of Constantinople—a man of great learning and wisdom, and some say a conjurer as well. Here, the people know him as Merlin the Wise. I believe it was he who persuaded the Pendragon to send me on my ill-fated quest ten seasons ago."

"Do you bear him ill will for this?" Capussa asked, his gaze still on the shoreline.

Percival shook his head.

"No. Yesterday is gone. I seek no retribution for its loss. I will tell the Queen of my failed quest, since she is my liege, and then, if she has no further need of my services, you and I shall return to my family estate in the north. There we shall live as men of peace, who tend the land and their flocks, and fish for the bounty of the sea."

"And so it came to pass that two former gladiators lived out the remainder of their days as peaceable farmers, shepherds, and fisherman, no less, in a land of assassins, slavers, butchers, and conjurers. Why, our luck has surely changed for the better," Capussa said, chuckling softly.

Percival nodded but remained silent. This was not the homecoming he had prayed for on a thousand lonely nights, in a hundred distant lands. His King and brother knights were dead, the Kingdom was broken, and the fate of his Queen was unknown. It seemed he could not end his long quest without first embarking upon another—a quest to find Guinevere.

CHAPTER 2

ABBEY CWM HIR, WALES

Guinevere, Queen of the Britons, stood before a tall, arched window gazing out at the lush green hills in the distance. Her golden tresses, blue-silken dress, and hourglass figure were silhouetted by the last rays of the August sun. In the fleeting moments before nightfall, she allowed herself the luxury of remembering life before the fall—a time that now seemed so distant as to be merely a dream.

On the good days, only the treasured memories would come to the fore, bringing her the respite of happiness and the refuge of hope; but on other days, the memories of the dark times would break free of the fetters she had carefully forged over the years and demand their painful toll. On those days, she would remember the tale of suffering and death that had been the bitter fare of the last years, a tale that always came to a close with the memory of the grief-stricken face of the young messenger, bringing the ill tidings from Camlann.

Thankfully, today's remembrance had been of the good times, although its taste had been bittersweet. It seemed like yesterday . . . a morning ride through the hills surrounding Camelot accompanied by a tall, raven-haired knight with striking blue eyes and a heart as pure as gold—a knight who'd left on a Grail quest a decade earlier and never returned.

As the sun disappeared behind the hills, leaving the alcove in darkness, Guinevere reluctantly relinquished her hold on yesteryear and turned to the modest sitting room behind her. The light from the fire crackling in the room's modest hearth illuminated all that remained of her royal court—Cadwyn Hydwell, her young handmaiden and secretary, and Sister Aranwen, her spiritual advisor.

Cadwyn sat on an old wooden bench near the fire, poring over a parchment delivered an hour earlier by one of Bishop Verdino's guards. The light from the flames danced over the petite young woman's flowing red tresses and her pretty face, with its dimples and button nose. The parchment detailed the rents and grazing fees collected from the tenants occupying Guinevere's lands and the few remaining royal preserves, and the expenses paid from these collections. In the past, the bishop's accountings had sparked more than a few fiery outbursts from her young friend, and it seemed as if another storm was on the horizon.

Eighteen-year-old Cadwyn had served Guinevere since her arrival at the abbey, six years earlier. Guinevere recalled with a smile the abbess's admonition when she'd introduced her mesmerized niece to the newly arrived queen.

"My Queen, Cadwyn is the most precocious child I have ever taught. She can speak, read, and write in the languages of the Greeks, Romans, and Britons, and more often than not, she knows what I am going to say before I say it, which I am not always happy about. On the other hand, she has . . . somewhat of a temper. However, all in all, I believe you will find her to be very helpful."

The abbess had been right. Cadwyn had been more than helpful—she had become indispensable. As for the girl's temper, Sister Aranwen had made it her mission to curb this vice, but despite her frequent scoldings, there was still plenty of fire left in her young handmaiden.

The diminutive Sister Aranwen sat in a rocking chair across from Cadwyn, contentedly knitting a woolen blanket. The pious and reserved nun had been in her fortieth year when her order had assigned her to escort Arthur Pendragon's young bride-to-be to Camelot. Guinevere remembered their first meeting, almost fifteen years ago, as if it had been yesterday. The two women had become friends during the weeklong trip, and Sister Aranwen had remained after the wedding as her spiritual advisor and self-appointed guardian.

As Guinevere watched the two women, she wistfully thought, *My friends, I fear you have become prisoners of my past.*

Sister Aranwen feared yesterday's minions would imprison or kill her royal charge if Guinevere tried to restore the lost kingdom. For the quiet nun, a life of obscurity was a small price to pay for peace and safety. Cadwyn, in contrast, would never relinquish the dream of a glorious restoration. For her, resurrecting Camelot had become her sacred duty.

As Sister Aranwen leaned forward and reached for another ball of yarn, Cadwyn exploded from her chair, holding the bishop's report aloft, her face nearly as red as her russet locks. Wide-eyed, Sister Aranwen dropped the ball of yarn and fell back into her rocking chair.

"That pompous old thief is stealing the fruit of the Queen's lands!" Cadwyn hissed in fury as she paced back and forth in front of the fireplace. "Why if ever a man deserved to be flogged—"

Sister Aranwen gasped. "Cadwyn Hydwell, you go too far! Bishop Verdino is a man of God! I . . . I grant you that he may take with a heavy hand, but—"

"Why, I wish—"

"Dearest friends, please remember, these walls have ears," Guinevere said quietly as she stepped into the room, repressing a smile. Both women turned to the Queen in unison and bowed respectfully as they responded, "Yes, Milady."

A knock on the outside door interrupted the renewal of Cadwyn's tirade, and Sister Aranwen quickly made good use of it, pointing to the door.

"That would be the cook's assistant with dinner, Cadwyn. Please be so kind as to bring in our repast, and please say a prayer of penance on the way."

Cadwyn swallowed her retort and turned to Guinevere. "Milady, where would you like your dinner tonight?"

"On the table, in my chambers, Cadwyn. I have much to do tonight."

"Yes, Milady."

Two hours later, Guinevere heard Cadwyn's familiar knock on the door to the library, which served as the anteroom to her private chambers.

"Come in, Cadwyn," Guinevere said.

The handmaiden entered the room carrying a cloth-covered basket under her arm and closed the door after her. Guinevere patted the open space on the wooden bench beside her. The bench was pulled up close to the small table serving as her desk and, often, the place where she took her meals. The two candles on the table illuminated a small, windowless room whose walls were lined with half-empty bookshelves and locked wooden boxes in varying sizes.

As she sat down, Cadwyn said in a whisper, "I checked on the two guards the bishop left behind. They are dicing in their quarters, and both have had more than a fair share of mead, so we need not fear eavesdroppers tonight."

Guinevere nodded as she glanced toward a nearby window to make sure the shutters were closed. Bishop Cosca Verdino had arrived at the abbey six months after she had taken refuge there, dressed in full liturgical regalia, accompanied by a cadre of four guards wearing outlandish uniforms.

According to the bishop, he'd been appointed by the Holy See to serve as both the Bishop of Albion and as the papal legate to the Queen of the Britons "in her time of need." Guinevere had been skeptical of the pompous little man, whose face was rendered nearly invisible by his bushy beard and the overly large alb and miter he wore whenever they met; but the abbess had vouchsafed for the official-looking documents he bore.

At first, Guinevere had ignored the wheedling little man's oft-repeated warnings regarding the dangers of leaving the abbey's grounds, but over time, it had become more difficult. Verdino had proven to be both persistent and clever, and his authority over the Abbess and the other sisters had given him the means to enforce his will.

Unaccountably, the abbey's horses would be unavailable on the days when the Queen had scheduled a ride. When the horses were available, Verdino would order his guards, along with the unhappy abbess and a flock of sisters, to accompany her on the ride. The tactic was as galling as it was clever. The devious prelate knew she wouldn't countenance the imposition of such a burden on the abbess and the sisters solely to accommodate her own pleasure.

When Guinevere had confronted the bishop regarding his interference, he'd politely offered her a surprising compromise, one she'd felt compelled to accept. Somehow, Verdino had discovered that the tide of chaos and violence sweeping over Albion had deprived her of the ability to collect the rents due from the tenants farming or grazing livestock on her lands and on the lands of the crown. Verdino also knew that without this source of income, Guinevere had no means of maintaining her own modest household; nor could she provide relief to the loyal subjects who continued to serve the needs of what was left of the kingdom.

Verdino had professed to have the means to collect these rents and tithes, through the "power of the church," despite the land's dark times. He promised to collect them if, in return, she would agree not to leave the abbey's grounds unless accompanied by a sufficient force of guards. Although Guinevere had been incredulous of Verdino's claim, the bishop had been true to his word, and so, in the main, she had been true to hers. At times, she found the bargain she'd struck to be oppressive, but it was a burden she had to bear, like so many others, for the good of what was left of the kingdom.

Cadwyn, on the other hand, was not one to bear the bishop's restrictions without complaint. As far as she was concerned, the bishop was a loathsome scoundrel whose sole objective was to find and steal the hidden trove of treasure Arthur was rumored to have left to fund a restoration of Camelot. Although Guinevere suspected this treasure might well exist, its whereabouts were unknown to her. So even if Cadwyn's suspicions were correct, the bishop's avaricious plans would, in the end, come to nought.

"What did the messengers bring today?" Guinevere asked.

Cadwyn sat on the wooden bench, placed the basket in the middle of the table, and drew off the cloth, revealing twelve scrolls of parchment, each encircled by two restraining pieces of twine.

"Quite a lot, Milady. The sparrows have much to report."

"Then let's get started, my dear."

Cadwyn untied the strings on two of the parchments, handed one to Guinevere, and opened the second herself. "Mary, in Camulodunom . . . a cobbler's wife, yes," Guinevere said as she rolled out the parchment.

"Milady, do you know all of the women? How many are there?" Cadwyn asked.

"No, but I do remember most. At one time or other, I have exchanged letters with all of them. As for how many, I can't say. Before the fall, there were about five hundred."

"Did the King know you had all these spies?"

Guinevere looked up from the parchment, a thoughtful look on her face. "No, but then I never really thought of them as spies. I wanted to have a friendly set of eyes and ears in every city and town in the kingdom . . . people who could tell me about matters of import to them."

"How did you know whom to trust?"

"Some were people that I knew, but most came to me through others that I trusted, people like . . . say, Cadwyn Hydwell."

Cadwyn smiled at the compliment and asked, "Why just women, Milady?"

Guinevere smiled. "If you wanted to know what was really going on in the Abbey, would you ask Ferghus, the stablemaster, or Rowena, the cook?"

"Rowena for sure. That woman knows things . . . ," Cadwyn said, her voice trailing off in embarrassment.

"Indeed, she does," Guinevere said as she reached for another parchment. "Men and women talk when they eat and drink, and most of the people serving them are women. So they hear, as you say, many 'things.' I wanted the Rowenas of this land to be my little sparrows . . . to tell me about anything that was important in their city, town, or village." Her smile faded.

"Before the fall, those tidings enabled me to save innocent men and women from unfair punishment by a dishonest lord, to reward the good, to punish the bad, to be a better Queen—at least that was my hope."

"You are a wonderful Queen, Milady," Cadwyn said with a smile.

"Why, thank you, my dear. Can you hand me another scroll?"

"Yes, Milady."

As she read through the missives, each writing wove another thread into the tapestry of pain and suffering that was now Albion. Londinium was the worst. Hengst and his raiders had turned the population into virtual slaves, leading many to secretly leave the city in the dark of night. Of late, the Norse warlord had banned these departures by branding people to mark them as his subjects. Those caught attempting to escape, or found outside of the city, would suffer torture or death in the monthly games Hengst held in Londinium's old Roman stadium.

When Guinevere put down the last letter, she closed her eyes, and the shadows from the flames flickered and danced across her beautiful face.

"Sometimes . . . oftentimes," Guinevere began, in a voice laden with regret, "I feel that I . . . Arthur, the Table . . . we failed them. We were supposed to protect them. That was our charge, our promise to the cobbler, the baker, the farmer, and their wives and children. We were supposed to keep them safe from monsters like Hengst the Butcher—and we did not honor that sacred duty."

"Milady," Cadwyn said in a heartfelt tone, "I am not a wise woman, nor, as I'm sure the abbess has told you, a very pious one, but God cannot fault you or the Pendragon and his Knights, for the fall. I have heard the tales, my Queen. Every man and woman gave their all in those last days and hours. It was . . . it was not to be, but, as you always say, Milady, tomorrow is another day, and we must work to remake what was broken."

Guinevere turned to the younger woman, took Cadwyn's face in her hands, and kissed her on the forehead.

"You are right, my precious young friend. But it is late, so that work must wait until the morrow. Tonight, let us rest."

"Of course, Milady," Cadwyn said as she rose and curtseyed. "Good night, Milady."

After Cadwyn left, Guinevere knelt by the fire and burned the letters from her flock of faithful sparrows, one by one. When the last letter burst into flame, she closed her eyes and prayed, in silence, for the people of Albion.

CHAPTER 3

MORGANA'S CASTLE

Megaera Igaris watched Admiral Phokas walk down the stone dock, followed by ten legionnaires marching in perfect order. The cold morning breeze ruffled his long white tunic and the red cape draped across his right shoulder. Unlike the legionnaires, the only weapon carried by the short, portly Roman was the gold baton signifying his rank, but that was all the protection he needed. Ten imperial galleys and a thousand soldiers stood ready to answer his beck and call.

The legionnaires halted ten yards from Megaera, in response to a gesture from Phokas, and the admiral continued forward, stopping a pace away from her.

"All of the silver is aboard, Lady Igaris," Phokas said with a gesture toward the galley at the end of the dock.

Megaera nodded. "Then you should be on your way, Admiral. The tide is full, but it departs quickly."

"We shall make the tide," Phokas said, glancing at the receding water line on the nearby beach. Then he turned his attention back to Megaera, a smile coming to his face. "I have a present for you. It was forged from the very silver that you so loyally ship to the emperor each season."

Phokas made a slight gesture with his baton. One of the legionnaires stepped forward and handed him a square object covered in a white silk. The soldier retreated to his place as Phokas drew off the silken cover, revealing a magnificent silver mirror, four hands tall and three wide. The admiral held the mirror up to Megaera's face, and for a long moment she stared at the reflection of the woman the people of Albion knew as the feared Morgana.

Her long auburn hair and strikingly beautiful face were just visible within the hood of her black cloak, a garment made of the finest Anatolian wool. She unconsciously caressed the flawless ruby hanging from the golden chain around her neck as it sparkled in the morning sun. The jewel was worth more than the Roman warship moored at the end of the dock, but then the man who had given it to her, the Roman emperor, could well afford the excess.

Megaera looked at the mirror for another moment and then gestured to a young female slave waiting submissively three paces behind her. The young woman stepped forward and took the mirror from Phokas and returned to her place. Megaera turned to her fellow Roman and smiled, mentally assessing what Phokas was attempting to gain from the gratuity. She knew even the smallest kindness was a means to an end in the deadly game of power played within the imperial circle.

"It is beautiful, Admiral. I thank you."

"You deserve that and more," Phokas said, waving off her feigned gratitude. "You know, Lady Igaris, the emperor would welcome you with wealth and position if you were to return home. With a little scheming, a woman of your beauty and cunning might even marry into the royal family."

Megaera looked eastward for a moment, as if considering the idea, but when her eyes returned to Phokas, she spoke in voice that was as cold as it was implacable.

"Your words are kind, Admiral Phokas. However, I would not return to wed the emperor himself, without the head of Melitas Komnenos."

The admiral laughed and raised an eyebrow. "And how will you bring him out of hiding? This land is a sea of forests. A man of Melitas's skill could hide forever in any one of them."

Megaera eased back the hood of her cloak and turned to face him.

"You forget, Admiral, it was I who sent the mighty Arthur Pendragon and his Knights to the grave. Rest assured, I will find Melitas, and I will kill him."

Phokas raised an eyebrow at the cold certainty in her voice and then gestured to the walled castle on the hill overlooking the estuary that was her home in Albion.

"I am told that the knight called Lord Aeron was once a Knight of the Round Table. This man lives within your walls. Why not put him to the torture? Surely he knows something of Melitas?"

"Lord Aeron," Morgana said coldly, "knows nothing of Melitas. If he did, you can be sure I would know of it. And as for torture, that would avail me nothing. Each day that noble fool endures a far greater pain, by choice, than I could inflict upon him by force."

Phokas gestured with his baton, as if casting aside his own suggestion. "I do not mean to question your judgment, Lady Igaris. As I have said, you have done well. The silver from this land is a boon to the empire during this time of war. You can be assured I will tell the emperor that I find your loyalty to be unfailing."

"You are too kind, Admiral Phokas," Megaera said with a smile that never reached her eyes. "I look forward to seeing you in the spring."

Phokas nodded and walked to the warship at the end of the dock, followed by the ten legionnaires, and boarded without looking back.

For a moment, Megaera watched the galley's two banks of oars flash rhythmically up and down, propelling Phokas's flagship toward the nine sister ships weighing anchor in the estuary; then she turned and started up the path to the castle on the rocky knoll above. As she strode up the slope, Megaera's hand closed on the knife inside her cloak, and she spoke in a soft but certain voice. "Rest assured, Admiral Phokas, the head of Melitas Komnenos will await you when you return in the spring."

WHITSTABLE, ALBION

Thomas the farrier said a prayer as he watched the group of traveling merchants and farmers embark upon the road to the market in Caer Ceint. The passage was a dangerous one, and he wished them well. Two mounted men joined the rear of the group, bringing a smile to the farrier's face. The likelihood of the caravan gaining safe passage through the forest had just improved.

An hour earlier, Thomas had sold the two riders a pair of black destriers, warhorses only the wealthy could afford. He had driven a hard bargain for the steeds, maybe too hard, but the men hadn't complained. Better still, they'd paid for the horses in silver coins struck by the metalsmiths in Eburacum, during the reign of the Pendragon. After the fall, and the breaking of the Table, these coins had been hoarded and used sparingly, for their purity was assured.

He ran a hand through his thick brown hair and started back toward the stable, intending to finish shoeing the miller's old bay before the midday meal.

"Thomas!"

The farrier turned and watched Ada, his wife of ten years, bustle down the short slope that separated their cottage from the stable. The top of her coarse woolen dress was dusted with flour dust, and there was a fine white sheen on her pretty round face as well. As she approached, Ada brushed an errant strand of dark brown hair from her face and seemed surprised at the ivory patch that appeared on the back of her hand.

"Don't say a word, Thomas," she said when she saw her husband's smile. "You married a lady's handmaiden, not a baker."

"And a pretty one at that, even if she looks the part of a ghost today," the farrier said with a chuckle.

Ada smiled and then pointed at the two mounted men disappearing up the road. "Who were those men?"

Thomas glanced up the road and ran a hand across his bearded jaw.

"Two travelers. They came ashore on Aldwyn Potter's boat. I made a pretty penny selling them the two destriers that I bought from Ademar a month ago. Paid in good coin, they did."

"Coins! Thomas, you know—"

"Ada, the coins are true. They're from the King's mint in Eburacum."

"Show me."

"Ahhh, woman, don't you—"

"Show me, Thomas," Ada said, putting her hands on her ample hips.

"As you wish. Come into the stable."

Thomas led his wife into the humble stone structure where he spent most of his days and closed the door behind them. He walked past the four wooden horse stalls to a small forge at the far end of the building and dropped to one knee beside the smoldering fire. After glancing back at the closed door, he pulled a rock from the wall behind the forge and drew out a small cloth sack.

"Here they be."

Ada opened the sack, pulled out several of the coins, and examined them closely. A slow smile came to her face.

"You're right. I haven't seen many of these in a good while, but when I worked for Lady Evelynn in Londinium, I handled them aplenty. That's the coin of the Pendragon, for sure."

"I said it was," Thomas said gruffly.

Ada walked over to her husband and kissed him lightly on the cheek. "And so you did, Thomas. Now tell me of these two men. You know how I like to know everything about everyone."

"Well that's surely true," Thomas said wryly. Ada put her hands on her hips, and he raised a placating hand.

"I'll tell you what I know, woman. Hard men, they are, but decent and honest. The tall one, I make him for a knight and . . . well, I swear that I—"

Ada's eyes widened. "A knight? Thomas, why would you say that?"

"It's the way he stood and moved. He . . . well, I just think he was, Ada."

"That's all? Nothing more? Thomas, that makes no sense," Ada said in exasperation.

"Now listen, Ada . . . well, there is a bit more to it. I spoke to Aldwyn Potter down at the dock. Had quite a time of it, he did. His ship was attacked by the seawolves. Said it would have been taken, had it not been for those two men."

"The seawolves! May God protect us," Ada said, quickly making the sign of the cross before demanding. "Tell me of this."

"I'm getting there, woman," Thomas said with mock exasperation before continuing. "Potter said the tall one and the black man . . . well, you should have heard him, Ada. The two of them came on deck dressed in the finest armor and attacked the seawolves like two avenging angels. Struck them all down, they did. Why, Potter said the tall one killed a giant near as big as Hengst the Butcher!"

"Thomas, they must be sellswords. There's plenty of those about these days," Ada said, shaking her head.

"No, Ada, I . . . I know this man, I do," Thomas said in a quiet voice. "I've seen him before."

"What? Who do you think he is?" Ada said, lowering her voice to a whisper.

Thomas sat down on a wooden bench and scratched his beard for a moment. Ada sat down beside him.

"I don't know his name," he said, "but I know where I saw him. It was in the last year of my apprenticeship to old Gildas. His farm was just outside Londinium. When I heard that the Pendragon and his Knights would be riding through the city, I begged the old man to let me have the day off so I could see them. He growled a bit but let me go. I set out early that morning. The sky . . . the sky that day was as blue as your eyes, Ada. Another farrier in Londinium, a friend of the old man, he let me get a view from atop his stable along the parade route."

Thomas slowly stroked his chin, as if to remember the day exactly as it had been. "I watched them ride by, Ada. The Pendragon himself and the Queen, followed by the Knights of the Table, then the lesser knights, the bowmen, and the foot soldiers. I can see it like it happened yesterday. It was a sight to see," he finished, opening his eyes.

"I was there, Thomas, on that very day!" Ada said in an excited whisper, taking her husband's hands in her own. "I watched the parade from Lady Evelynn's balcony. They rode right past us. It was indeed a sight! It was wonderful."

Thomas nodded. "That it was, and the tall man, the man I sold those horses to today, he was there."

"What do you mean? You saw him in the parade? Where?"

"He rode beside Sir Galahad. It was he."

Ada's eyes widened, and her grip on Thomas's hands tightened. "Thomas, how could you remember that? It was so long ago."

"I remember. The tall man and Galahad—they were different. The others, they all looked straight ahead, you know, like lords and ladies do, never seeing anyone below them, but those two, they waved to the people as they rode by."

"Thomas, you still haven't told me how you know it was him."

"Ada, he saw me on the roof, watching. He looked right at me. I saw his face as plain as day. He raised his hand to me in a greeting, like this, Ada."

Thomas raised his right arm and held it out, his palm open.

"You cannot be sure," Ada said, shaking her head.

The farrier looked across at his wife and said with quiet certainty, "Ada, I am sure. I remember faces. The man I saw today had the same face as the man on that horse those many years ago, and he raised his open hand to me, the same way, just before he rode off today."

Thomas shook his head. "For a moment, Ada, it was like I was a young lad, back on that roof all those years ago."

When he opened his eyes, Ada was staring at him, her eyes wide. Then she stood up quickly, kissed him, and ran toward the stable door.

The farrier stood up and started after her. "Ada, what is it?"

"I . . . I smell the bread burning."

Thomas walked over to the stable window, pushed open the heavy wooden shutter, and smiled as he watched his wife rush into their small cottage twenty paces up the hill. The kitchen window was open, and he could see into the room. The farrier was surprised when his wife walked past the stone oven on the far side of the room, took a parchment and a quill from a cabinet, and sat down to write.

CHAPTER 4

THE ROAD TO LONDINIUM

Percival's eyes roved over the group of men, women, and children trudging down the dirt road twenty paces ahead of him, accompanied by a motley caravan of horse-drawn carts. Some of the carts held grain, others fruits, and still others livestock. Most of the men were farmers hoping to trade their excess crops and livestock for clothes, knives, candles, and other wares available in the larger town of Caer Ceint, two and a half leagues distant.

The Knight had traveled the road years before in what now seemed like another life. He knew it wound its way through a deep forest and intersected with the Roman road north of Caer Ceint.

Five of the younger farmers had formed an uneven perimeter around the column, but Percival could tell by the way they held their primitive cudgels, swords, and bows that none were skilled in their use. One of the men guarding the column on the right, a tall, thin man carrying a bow, glanced back at Percival and Capussa for a second time. The unease in the man's eyes was plain to see, an unease shared by the other guards as well. Percival gave the man a friendly nod. The man returned his nod and turned his attention back to the verdant green wall of trees on his right.

Percival suspected the guards feared an attack by brigands, and he scanned the forest ahead, seeking a sign of movement that might betray a waiting ambush. Capussa, riding on his right, seemed unconcerned by the threat. The Numidian gestured to the ancient stands of trees hemming in both sides of the road and spoke in a voice filled with awe.

"I have plied the trade of war for more than two decades, in more lands than I can remember. Yet, in all my travels, I've never seen a place so green and full of life."

Percival nodded, his eyes returning to the forest wall. "Aye, it is that. At the end of each day in the arena, I would seek the Lord's forgiveness for the lives taken and give thanks that mine had been spared. Then . . . then I prayed he would allow me to return home that I might one day ride through a forest such as this before I died. Now that I'm here, I fear I shall awake from this dream and find I must take up the sword once again to put coins in the pocket of Khalid El-Hashem."

Capussa shook his head. "It is no dream. We are free, and whether we die today or in a hundred years, we will die free men, my friend." He glanced over at Percival, his dark eyes dancing with humor. "And as for your prayers, they didn't keep you alive in the arena—my training did, and, maybe, some of your own limited fighting skills."

Percival raised an eyebrow. "I seem to recall that I learned a thing or two from Batukhan as well."

"Bah." Capussa made a dismissive gesture with one hand. "He was good with the bow, and he knew his horses, but no more." As if echoing his master's umbrage, Capussa's mount snorted and shook its head.

For a moment, Percival recalled the hard, flat face of the indomitable Mongol warrior who had shared their fate in the gladiatorial arena— until he was killed trying to escape.

Twenty paces ahead, a small blond girl in a brown woolen dress tried to dart into the forest, only to be thwarted by a stout woman wearing a larger version of the same dress. The woman shook her finger at the little girl and pointed toward the forest, as if it were a dark and dangerous place. As the caravan continued on, the little girl looked longingly at a patch of purple flowers just outside her reach.

"Speaking of horses, Knight," Capussa said, affectionately patting his black destrier, "you paid for these fine steeds with silver coins—coins that the stablemen recognized, no less. Surely the wealth that Jacob of Alexandria left for you, ample though it was, didn't hold the coins of this land?"

"No, the coins that Jacob left for me were gold solidi—the coin of the Romans in the east."

A guard on the right side of the column suddenly raised his cudgel to a striking position, and Percival instinctively reached for the hilt of the sword at his side. The man lowered his weapon a moment later as a rabbit raced from the protection of a nearby bush and into the forest beyond.

"Then where," Capussa said, raising an eyebrow, "did you find those fine silvers?"

Percival hesitated for a moment, as if gathering his thoughts. "Do you remember when we passed through Aquileia?"

His friend nodded.

"It was there. Before I left on the Grail quest, Merlin told me to visit Maximus, the Bishop of Aquileia. I was told he had knowledge of the cup and would aid me in my search. Maximus died before I arrived. His successor, Bishop Severus, gave my quest his blessing and made a large donation, but he knew nothing of the cup's whereabouts. He asked that I visit him on my return voyage and tell him of my search, and so I did."

Capussa nodded. "Yes, now I remember. He gave you coins from this land?"

Percival shook his head. "No. Severus died a year after I left. It was his successor, Bishop Stephen. He said the King had left something for me. It was a small wooden chest."

"And?" Capussa said impatiently.

"It was the same chest that Arthur had instructed me to give Bishop Maximus when I first came to Aquileia," Percival said, glancing over at Capussa. "In the note, Arthur had asked the bishop to give me that same chest when I returned from my quest."

The Numidian nodded his approval. "A wise man, this King Arthur."

"Yes," Percival said, "one would have to be wise indeed to predict one's own death."

"What are you saying?"

"There was a second note in the box, a note Arthur left for me," Percival said quietly. "It had an unbroken wax seal. In the note, Arthur said he would be dead when I read it, and that I should return to Albion in haste, for his Kingdom was in need of my sword."

Percival looked into the distance; his eyes clouded before continuing. "I don't know how he could have known . . . but in the end, it doesn't matter. I have come too late. There's no kingdom left for me to fight for."

Percival fell silent, and the two men rode on in the uneasy quiet for another furlong. As they rounded a bend in the road, Capussa glanced over at the compact bow strapped to Percival's back.

"When we left the village," the African said, resting his hand on the Mongolian horse bow strapped to right side of his own horse, "you suggested that I string the Mongol's bow, which I have done, and I see you have strung yours as well. Tell me, are we hunting game, or men?"

Percival scanned a wooded rise to the west, his eyes focusing on a faint wisp of smoke hovering above the trees.

"A man watched us leave from one of the hills overlooking the village. Once we started up the road, I looked back and he was gone. It may be nothing, but if he was a local brigand then—"

"We shall meet him and his brethren up ahead. If so, once again my training will stand you in good stead," Capussa said, gesturing to Percival's bow.

"I seem to remember that it was Batukhan who taught both of us how to use these bows."

"Bah! I just pretended to let him teach me. I am a humble man, as you know."

"Indeed?" Percival said, raising an eyebrow. "I must have missed that trait."

"That's unfortunate. It is one of my finest," Capussa said with a smile as he raised a warning finger. "You need to be more observant, my friend. Otherwise, you could well overlook both the good and the bad, such as that fellow hiding behind yonder tree, the one that looks like many trees growing into one."

Percival nodded without looking at the tree. "It's called a yew, and I did see him some time back. I just happened to be more concerned about the rest of his band. I suspect they will spring their trap around the next bend."

Capussa's face stiffened slightly, and his grip on the reins of the horse tightened.

"How many?"

"Eight, maybe ten."

"Then we should attack them, now, before they strike. With the horses and the bows, we can cut them down with ease."

Percival shook his head. "Your plan is sound, friend, but I've taken far too many lives already. I will not take any more unless I have to. They're probably just hungry peasants who've been led astray by one or two truly bad men. If I can—"

"Cut off the head of the snake?" Capussa finished for him. "A risky strategy. It would be a shame to see a man who has killed a hundred champions in single combat die from a lucky blow struck by a wayward peasant."

"My fate is in God's hands," Percival said.

"I would prefer if it were in mine," Capussa growled under his breath.

Percival slowed his horse as a band of eight men on the far side of the bend in the road ahead fanned out, blocking the travelers' way. Four more men walked out onto the road behind him and Capussa, barring their retreat. The men to the rear were armed with clubs, cudgels, and long knives, as were the men in front, with the exception of the square, stout man in the center. He was carrying a rusty sword with a broken point.

Capussa nodded toward the men behind them. "I will scatter these vermin and join you at the front. Wait until I get there, Knight. I would not have you striking down more men than I this day."

"I shall endeavor to leave you the greater share of the work, if it comes to that," Percival said dryly as he cantered toward the front of the caravan.

Capussa guided his horse in a slow turn and confronted the four men standing in the road behind him. The men were dressed in coarse, old woolens so filthy he could smell their foul odor thirty paces away. For a moment, the four brigands stared at the man, motionless, and then the largest of the four wiped his nose on his sleeve and stepped forward, waving a cudgel.

"We'll have the horse and whatever else ye got there, or kill you, we will."

Capussa reached over his left shoulder with his right hand and slowly pulled a long, curved sword from the sheath on his back, as if easing a lethal animal from its cage. When the sword was free of the sheath, he raised his arms, and the sleeves of his cloak fell away, revealing a gleaming pair of mailed gloves and gauntlets. He drew back the hood hiding his ebony features, and as the hood fell away, he wheeled the sword in a circle, in a movement as quick as it was effortless.

"Come then, my friends," he said, smiling down at them, "and take that which you seek."

As the four men watched this performance, their bluster was replaced by fear, and after a moment of hesitation, the man with the cudgel backed up slowly. When Capussa bared his teeth and urged his giant mount forward, the four men turned and sprinted into the forest. Capussa followed, swinging his sword over his head, as his horse pounded behind them.

While Capussa took care of the rear guard, Percival rode past the terrified women and children and pulled up twenty paces short of the eight brigands barring the column's passage. One of the brigands had struck down a young farmer, and their leader was poised to plunge his sword into the prone man's chest.

"Hold!" Percival roared.

The brigand froze in midstroke, a look of shock on his broad, ugly face.

"Kill him, and I will surely kill you," Percival said in a voice that a wiser man would have both feared and heeded.

For a moment, the man stared at the Knight and then rage flared in his eyes. "Will you, now?" he snarled. "There's twelve of us and one of you." He glanced scornfully at the four young farmers standing to the right of Percival's horse. "Those sheep won't help you any more than you can help this one."

"Take your leave," Percival said, "and I shall ask these good people to leave some food on the road for you and your men. That is the only offer I will make."

The leader bared his blackened teeth and tightened his grip on his sword. "We'll take it all, and your horse as well, if you don't ride off. Move forward, boys, don't mind—"

An arrow suddenly sprouted from the man's chest, and a second shaft appeared beside it an instant later. The man stood there for a moment, his eyes wide in shock, and then toppled backward, like a tree felled in the forest.

Capussa drew his horse alongside Percival's steed. "Your leader should have taken the offer," he said in a cold, hard baritone.

The other brigands stared in shock at the Numidian, as if he were a demon spawned from the bowels of the earth itself.

"Now, would the rest of you like to make a wiser choice? If not, I will kill those that the Knight leaves alive after his first pass, although I wager there will be none." Capussa leaned forward in his saddle, the promise of death in his eyes.

The man standing beside the dead brigand stammered, "W-We take the offer; we take it!"

"You are a wise man," Percival said with an approving nod. "Now leave, and give thanks for the generosity of these good people."

The brigands backed away with shuffling steps before turning and running into the forest as one.

"You men, see to this man," Percival said, pointing to the thief lying in the road.

Two men standing by a cart filled with apples ran forward, and a young woman followed them.

Percival glanced over at Capussa and raised a questioning eyebrow.

"What?" Capussa said indignantly as he stowed his bow in a leather sleeve beside his saddle. "Just the head of the snake, as we agreed, no more," Capussa said.

"I suppose it had to be done," Percival said. "But if Batukhan were here, he would tell you that your bow pulls slightly to the right."

"Bah!" Capussa scoffed. "I hit exactly where I aimed."

Abbey Cwm Hir

Guinevere stood by the window overlooking the southern end of the abbey, where the church, convent, and the great hall were located on the east, west, and south sides of a broad green. The abbey held a special place in her heart. A century earlier, one of her ancestors had donated the gold needed to build the convent and the first chapel, and she had spent several summers here learning under the tutelage of the abbess, Beatrice Cynwood. After Camlann and the fall of Camelot, the abbey's remote location and stout walls had offered her what she had thought would be only a temporary refuge. Alas, now it seemed as if she would spend the rest of her days here as a powerless and forgotten relic.

In her first week at the abbey, Guinevere had sent out hundreds of messengers with orders directing the remnants of Arthur's army to assemble at the small town of Tywyn, on the coast, in a month's time. A third of the messengers never returned. Those that did make it back described a land awash in a maelstrom of violence.

The coffer of gold Morgana had drawn upon to raise her disparate army of Norse, Saxon, and Pict sellswords had either been exhausted, or the death of the Pendragon and the breaking of the Table had slaked the witch's seemingly unquenchable thirst for blood. Whatever the reason, Morgana had severed the golden tether binding her army together, and unleashed this disparate pack of human wolves upon the people of Albion.

In the face of this kingdom-wide threat, Arthur's surviving liegemen had returned home to defend their own estates and homes, leaving few to answer Guinevere's call. In the end, less than one hundred men had trickled into Tywyn. Only five of these men were knights, and none were members of the Table. It was only after she'd seen this tattered remnant of what had once been Arthur's proud and seemingly invincible legions that the Queen had come to fully understand the depth of disaster that had befallen the land.

In the end, she bid the small group of faithful stalwarts to return to their homes, pledging to call them together again when the time was right. After returning to the abbey, Guinevere's grief had been so great she'd wept until she was spent.

The pain had ebbed with the years, but her impotence had spawned frustration. Her kingdom was now limited to the grounds of the abbey, and each month, she was forced to verbally joust with the insidious Bishop Verdino to protect even that modest dominion. Although Verdino would have welcomed a suspension of these monthly inquisitions, Guinevere knew they were important. She needed every excess farthing from the rents he collected on her behalf to support her small household and to pay the hundreds of informers and messengers serving as her lifeline to what remained of the kingdom. Each meeting was also an opportunity to remind the bishop that she was still Albion's sovereign.

A knock on the door to the library interrupted Guinevere's reverie, and a moment later, Cadwyn slipped inside.

"Milady, the bishop is here."

The undercurrent of loathing in Cadwyn's voice was palpable. Guinevere nodded.

"Thank you. I shall be there in a moment."

Before leaving the room, Guinevere looked in the mirror above her desk and touched her right cheek with her hand. She knew that she was in the last hours of her beauty, and that time would quickly leave her with nothing but memories of a time when—

"Milady?"

Guinevere turned to Cadwyn, who was peering through the partially opened door.

"Are you well? We can—"

"I am fine, Cadwyn. Let us greet our guest."

The Queen walked into the sitting room, where three chairs faced a fourth that was noticeably closer to the fire burning in the hearth.

Sister Aranwen bowed respectfully and gestured to the chair near the fire. "Do you think the bishop's chair is too close to the fire, Milady? We don't want him to be uncomfortable."

"As far as I'm concerned, it should be placed in the flames," Cadwyn said.

Sister Aranwen's face turned a shade of red, and Guinevere, repressing a smile, intervened before the nun could scold the younger woman.

"It's fine, Sister," Guinevere said as she sat down in the middle chair. "The bishop will appreciate the warmth after his journey. Please invite him in."

"You are so kind, Milady," Sister Aranwen said, giving Cadwyn a reproachful look as she walked over to the door. The unrepentant Cadwyn sat down in the chair to Guinevere's right.

The stooped figure waiting outside the door was dressed in a traditional black alb of fine Umbrian wool almost reaching the floor. The black wimple covering Verdino's head was so large and deep that it was difficult to see his facial features. Much of what could be seen was obscured by his bushy grey beard and huge mustache. The only clearly visible feature within the hood's recess was the bishop's modest, falcon-like nose.

Verdino hesitated for a moment and then took an overly long step into the room. Cadwyn put a hand up to her mouth to smother a giggle at the bishop's comical arrogance. Verdino gave her a hard stare, but said nothing.

"Bishop, please come in and warm yourself," Guinevere said, gesturing to the chair by the fire.

"Thank you, Your Highness," the bishop said in a querulous whine as he walked over to the chair. He bowed his head toward the Queen before sitting down. "May the Lord be with you."

"And also with you, Bishop," Guinevere answered politely.

He glanced over at Cadwyn and Aranwen and spoke in Latin instead of the common tongue.

"Milady, we may discuss things of consequence today, and although I suspect your retainers are not versed in the language of the Romans, in these villainous times . . . well, it might be prudent if we spoke alone."

"Indeed," Guinevere replied, "we cannot be too careful, but I trust Sister Aranwen and Lady Cadwyn with my life, and, as you say, your grace, they are deaf to our words."

Verdino sniffed in disapproval but nodded his head in assent.

"Of course, Your Highness."

"Now, Bishop, I am told you have visited my lands and those of the crown. Please tell me how the people fare and whether the land prospers. And, being the able steward that you are, I am sure you have a more detailed accounting of the rents than what appears in the report delivered this morning."

Verdino nodded and wrung his bony hands together in an odd motion that habitually preceded his prevarications.

"Alas, times are hard, Your Highness, and it is the nature of peasants to be slothful. Although I have gently chastised them for their indolence in the past, they remain unrepentant."

"But surely you must have collected something, Bishop."

The pace of Verdino's nodding and handwringing became more hurried.

"Of course, Your Highness. However, the men who guard your person must be paid, the horses fed and quartered, and the abbey is in need of support. After paying all of these debts, there is little left, I fear."

"If, as you say, so little was collected, your grace, then surely it would be a small matter for you to fully account for this pittance and then to promptly return to me what little remains. After you have paid all of these . . . expenses."

"Yes, yes, of course, Your Highness. But, well . . . it is not an easy task. You see, parchment is scarce, so we try to give you a less burdensome accounting than we might otherwise."

"Parchment is indeed in short supply, Bishop. However, the Lord has blessed me with an ample supply. Cadwyn will be happy to give you an extra scroll when we are finished."

Cadwyn made a small smile as she said in Latin, "It would be my pleasure, Milady."

Verdino stiffened. "That won't be necessary, Your Highness. Of late, I have been able to find a scroll or two, at some expense, of course."

"Then we can expect a more complete accounting next week?"

"Uh . . . well, it may take a little longer. Old Ferris my clerk, why, his eyes grow dim, and as you know, he lost an arm in the service of the King. So the parchment, why, it is difficult to keep it laid out. The rolls tend to . . . well, roll back up. As I say—"

"Well, we can't have that, can we, Bishop?" Guinevere gestured to her companions. "I am sure that either Sister Aranwen or Cadwyn could spare several hours a day to assist this man with his work. Sister, do you think you could assist the bishop's clerk on the morrow for an hour or two?"

Aranwen looked up from her knitting. "Of course, Milady, I will—"

Verdino sat up straight as an arrow and raised both his hands in an appeasing gesture.

"That will not be necessary, dear Queen. I could not bear the thought of taking either the good sister or dearest Cadwyn from your hearth. No, I shall assign one of Captain Borgia's men to assist Ferris. It shall all be well."

Guinevere raised a questioning eyebrow. "Captain Borgia's men have clerical skills? How interesting. Then, I am sure that a more detailed report will be completed apace."

"Yes, apace, Your Highness, apace."

"Now, Bishop, is there some other service that I can provide the church today?"

Verdino wrung his hands before answering, as if reluctant to speak of the matter. "Yes, Your Highness, there is . . . a matter of some importance. I . . . I am told that you insisted on walking outside the walls of the abbey in my absence, Your Highness. This is not wise. The kingdom has suffered too much already. It cannot afford to lose its queen."

"Your concern is most kind, Bishop. However, the guards accompanied me, and I was always within sight of the walls. I also think your fear of brigands is unwarranted, Bishop. I am told by the hunters that none have been seen in the surrounding forests for some time now."

Verdino leaned forward and spoke with an intensity that surprised Guinevere.

"It's not the brigands I fear. You remain a potent symbol, despite the passage of time. There are those who may see you as a means to legitimize the fiefs they have carved out of the old kingdom with their swords, and others who would do far worse. Please promise me that you will be more careful in the future."

Guinevere hesitated, staring into Verdino's eyes, visible in the firelight for the briefest of moments, before the bishop leaned back, once again shrouding his face. Somewhere in the recesses of her memories, there was the suggestion that she'd seen those eyes before, in a different place, on a different person. She frowned, the memory fading as quickly as it had appeared. When she spoke again, Guinevere's voice was quiet but firm.

"Bishop, your concern is appreciated, and I will take care, but today I am only a memory, and a distant and faded one at that. I don't believe there are any who would come so far to do me ill, or for that matter, who would come so far to support my cause."

The room was deathly quiet for a long moment, and then Verdino spoke in a voice that was so soft as to be barely audible.

"As to the first, there is surely one. As to the second, have patience, Highness. He comes."

Guinevere blinked at his cryptic statement, and Verdino stood abruptly, bowed, and walked to the door. He stopped at the threshold, bowed again, and then hurried away.

"The man speaks in riddles," Cadwyn said with exasperation. "Do you know the meaning of his words, Milady?"

The Queen leaned back in her chair, surprised by the cryptic exchange. "No, Cadwyn, I do not."

CHAPTER 5

THE ROAD TO LONDINIUM

apussa sat on a long stone bench, his back resting against the wall of a two-story stone tower that looked as if it had been abandoned for many years. A fire was burning a step away, in the bottom of a dry cistern. The light from the flames illuminated a small courtyard and the ruins of an encircling wall.

The Numidian reached into his cloak and drew out an apple, a gift from one of the farmers they had left in Caer Ceint the day before. He rotated the rich red orb in his hand, weighing whether this was the right time to savor this new and unknown taste. After a moment's reflection, he decided to defer the pleasure until the morning and returned the apple to his cloak.

Several minutes later, Percival entered the courtyard through a gap in the wall, carrying a load of dry branches. After piling the branches near the edge of the cistern, the Knight walked over and sat down beside Capussa.

"You have camped here before, my friend," he noted.

Percival nodded. "I was assigned to a force under the command of Sir Gawain, one of the Knights of the Table. We were tasked with destroying a force of pirates and brigands harassing Caer Ceint and the surrounding ports." He gestured toward the crumbling walls encircling the overgrown courtyard. "On the way, we stopped here for a night. This place was once a way station for the Roman legions and for the imperial post traveling between Dubris and Londinium."

"You thought well of this man?"

Percival hesitated a moment before answering. "I did. Gawain . . . he was a wise and good man. I had hoped to see him again . . . to thank him for his wise counsel. It saved my life more than once during my quest."

Capussa nodded. "You must speak to me of this another time. Tonight, I would have you tell me of your Queen. Is she young, old, tall, short, beautiful, or not?"

"I have already spoken of this," Percival said.

"Not so, my friend," Capussa said, raising a hand in protest. "We have lived, trained, fought, and traveled half the world together, yet in all that time, you have rarely spoken of this Queen Guinevere. You have told me of King Arthur, your fellow Knights of the Table Round, and of your home, but Guinevere . . . this you have kept to yourself. If that is your will, I shall respect it."

"Indeed?" Percival said skeptically as he leaned back against the wall, a hint of amusement in his eyes

"However," Capussa continued in a lecturing tone, "remember, you have tasked me with finding your Queen and giving her your last report in the event the gods take you before your long quest comes to an end. Unless I know—"

"You are right," Percival said quietly. He reached inside his shirt and gently drew a silver chain over his head. A gold medallion was affixed to the chain. The Knight stared at the medallion for a moment before handing it to his friend.

Capussa cradled the gold medallion in his palm and stared at the image of a woman's face that a craftsman of consummate skill had imprinted on one side of the coin. He gazed at the fine details of the portrait and then turned the pendant over, revealing an oak tree with a crucifix on the broad trunk.

"It was made by one of the finest craftsmen in the land," Percival said as he stared up at the stars beginning to appear in the night sky. "It is a likeness of Guinevere when she was twenty-one years of age. She will be ten years older now, if she still lives." He turned toward Capussa and gestured to the gold medallion. "If I die before my quest is finished, I would ask that you bring this to her. It will identify you as the holder of my last testament."

Capussa turned the gold piece over again and stared at the image of the woman for a long moment before handing the chain and medallion back to Percival. The Knight gently lifted the chain over his head and returned the gold likeness to its resting place.

"Your Queen will recognize this medallion?"

"Yes, she will surely remember it," Percival said as he stared into the flames of the campfire.

Capussa looked over at his friend for a long moment and then said quietly, "She gave it to you."

"She did," Percival said, nodding slowly as if remembering the moment. "The likeness . . . it does not do her justice. She is . . . a most beautiful woman."

"I see. So, in the event you find yourself upon the wrong end of a sword, my mission is to relieve you of this remembrance and then find a 'most beautiful woman' in an unknown land?" Capussa said as he made a sweeping gesture toward the distant horizon. "Unless every other woman in this land is a hag, that task may well be beyond even my abilities. Might you add a few more brush strokes to the picture?"

"I suspect I must," Percival said in feigned exasperation as he glanced over at Capussa, "or seek refuge in the nearby swamp to obtain a night's rest."

For a long moment the Knight was silent, as if drawing a memory from a distant well, and then he spoke in a quiet, reflective voice.

"Her hair is the color of the last rays of the autumn sun, and it flows like a river from her head almost to her waist. Her face is . . . unforgettable. There is no one feature I can point to, but taken together, the blue eyes, the full red lips, the way that she smiles, it's . . . magic. Trust me, my friend, you will know Guinevere when you meet her."

Capussa frowned slightly. "Knight, you go to a different place when you speak of this woman. Was there—"

"I was one of her guardians. That is all."

Capussa waited a moment for him to continue, and when he didn't, the Numidian stood and made a sweeping gesture encompassing the land to the north.

"And where, in this green isle, shall I find this beauteous woman?"

"I cannot say for sure, but I believe she would have taken refuge with her people in the forests to the northwest, about ten to twelve days ride from here. Her ancestral lands are there, and any invader who sought to harm her would find a bowman waiting behind every tree."

"Show me the way to this place, in the dirt, here," Capussa said, pointing at a patch of bare ground directly in front of the bench. "Use that stick as your quill."

Percival picked up the nearby stick and drew an oblong shape in the dirt and then added a series of circles connected by lines. Leaning back to observe his work, he tapped the stick on one of the lines that ran north.

"Here is the Roman road to Londinium. We are just about here," he said, touching a small circle, "two days' ride from Londinium. We will pass by the city on the high road. It runs along the south bank of the Tamesis River. From there, we travel northwest to Venonis and then on to Viroconium. We shall seek word of Guinevere there."

"Very well then," Capussa said, returning to his place on the bench. "On to Viroconium, and after that . . . we shall see your home. Tell me of that place. I would know where we shall live out our days in peace, or so you say."

"I have already spoken of this as well," Percival said, leaning back against the tower wall and closing his eyes.

Capussa made a gesture with his hand, waving off Percival's objection.

"So speak of it again. The night is long, and I have only my blanket and a patch of grass to look forward to."

Percival raised his hands in mock surrender. "As you wish. There is little enough to tell. Where would you have me start?"

"From the beginning," Capussa said, folding his arms over his chest. "How else would you tell a tale?"

"So be it," Percival said and picked up the stick he'd dropped on the ground a moment earlier. He tapped one of the circles on the map. "This is Londinium."

Then he drew another line to a spot on the edge of the shape, to the north. "The lands of my family are here, ten to twelve days' ride north of the city along the coast. The land and the castle were originally a Roman signal post. When the last Roman commander departed, he awarded the post to the senior centurion, a native-born soldier who'd faithfully served the empire—my distant forbear."

Capussa nodded. "And the surrounding country? What of that?"

"The castle is located on the point of a headlands. It is surrounded on three sides by the sea. A town of a thousand souls lies just to the south. Beyond that is virgin forest, with an abundance of wildlife. My father and I spent many a day riding and hunting there," Percival said as he tapped the spot on the map with the stick.

"So how did you come to join this Table that you speak of?"

Percival sighed, "I have—"

"Spoken of this before," Capussa finished. "So you have, but that was when we were prisoners of that foul creature Khalid El-Hashem. Now that we are free men, and you are in your homeland, your memory will be clear and the story will be so much better."

Percival slowly shook his head and leaned back against the tower wall. "Very well, my inquisitive friend. When I was a boy, my home was a peaceful and prosperous place. Sometimes, pirates and the wilder inland clans would raid our lands, but my father and his liegemen, supported by the men in the town, were always able to repel them. All of that changed in my fourteenth year."

Percival was quiet for a moment. Then he stood up and walked over to the edge of the cistern, picked up a branch, and dropped it into the fire, raising a small cloud of sparks.

"That was the year the Norsemen began to raid in their dragonships, in force. At first the raids were small, and the raiders only came once or twice a summer. Four or five ships would come ashore at dawn, and the raiders would seize as many young women and men as they could before we counterattacked. Slaves are the Norsemen's gold, although they will gladly take the real thing if they can find it. Over time, the raids grew more frequent and the number of ships more numerous. In my fifteenth summer, it seemed as if my sword was only sheathed long enough to bury the dead."

After a long silence, Percival glanced back at Capussa and said wryly, "I'm waiting for the 'and then.'"

"And then?" Capussa asked obligingly.

"And then . . . I remembered something my grandfather had told me. He said that the Roman coastal forts to the south had used a string of signal towers to alert them to the coming of seaborne attacks by the Saxons. I convinced my father we could do the same thing. That winter, my sixteenth year, we built wooden watchtowers on every hill along the coast for three leagues on either side of the town. Then we assembled a force of men to stand ready at all times to take the field against the attackers when the alarm was raised."

The Knight's hand closed on the hilt of his sword as he continued the tale.

"When the first raid came the next summer, over forty ships, we were ready. We met the raiders at the shore and drove them back into the sea, setting many of their ships alight with fire arrows. Only half of the ships escaped. More fleets of raiders came, but with each attack, we grew stronger and more deadly. Over time, the raids became less frequent, and then they stopped."

"You made the price in blood too high," Capussa said with an approving nod.

"Yes, but we paid a price as well," Percival said quietly. "My father was killed in a raid. We . . . I misjudged the point of their landing, and by the time we arrived with the relief force and threw them back into the sea, my father was dead. A year later, my betrothed, the daughter of the liege lord to the south, was killed in a raid."

Percival paused for a moment and stared out at the dark horizon. When he spoke again, his voice was tinged with regret.

"I was many leagues to the north, so there was nothing I could have done. Yet, when I came to know of her death, I felt as if I had failed her. Today, I would see the truth of it."

"Would you, Knight?" Capussa questioned, a knowing look on his face. "I suspect not. You are particularly good at shouldering burdens that are not yours to carry. It is a good thing I am here to save you from yourself."

"I am truly blessed," Percival said wryly.

"Indeed, you are. Now, tell me how you came to be a Knight of this Round Table."

"It seems I will indeed have to sleep in yonder swamp to get a moment's peace," Percival said over his shoulder as he walked over to his horse, drew out a skin of water from his traveling bag, and took a long drink.

Capussa stood, walked over to the fire, and nudged a flaming ember back over the edge into the stone pit. Then he lifted his hands to the night sky in mock supplication.

"Alas, I must surely have offended a powerful god in one land or another to have been condemned to cross the world with a companion who is as talkative as a rock."

"As you wish. The rock speaketh again, but for the last time tonight," Percival said with a smile as he returned to the stone bench.

"Over time, I was able to persuade the lords who held the lands within twenty leagues to the north and south to adopt our tactics and to maintain a force ready to come to the aid of the others, in the event of an attack in force. In my twentieth year, come it did. Over a hundred ships sailed past one of the most northern watchtowers. The fire and smoke signals raised the alarm along the coast, moving from tower to tower, as the raiders continued to sail south.

"The size of the enemy was so great that I rode south with half of my liegemen and picked up additional forces as we passed through the lands of each lord. The outriders I'd sent to shadow the raiders came back at the end of the day and reported our enemies had sailed up the Humber River. That would be here," Percival said, leaning forward and drawing a line from the coast to an inland circle.

"Once I heard this, I knew that Eburacum, a wealthy city along that river, was the most likely target," Percival said, tapping the circle with the stick.

"I sent a rider to warn the city of the raid, but the mayor ignored it. At that time, people were unaware of how powerful the Norse raiders had become. Once I knew Eburacum was the target, I told the other coastal lords we had to march inland to protect the city. Some agreed. Some did not. In the end, I was able to march inland with only seven hundred men, but they were good men. Over the previous three years, I had trained them to march together, to form battle lines, and to move as one during battle, on command."

"I hope," Capussa said with a frown, "you were a better teacher than I found you to be a student. Otherwise, this tale could have a sad ending, and that, of course, would mean another tale. No soldier should end his day with a sad tale."

"Then you can be assured this tale will end well," Percival said with a small smile. "When we arrived at Eburacum the next day, there were over a thousand Norse raiders at the walls, and they'd managed, through stealth, to get a part of their force inside. The city's guards were able to stem the tide for a time, but the weight of the enemy's numbers was taking its toll. A part of the Norse raiders stayed to hold the breach in the wall, and the rest, about nine hundred men, turned to engage my force. After several hours of hard fighting, the raiders decided to take what loot they had and return to their ships."

"Where was the Pendragon and his army during this attack?" Capussa interrupted. "Were there no royal forces available to take the field?"

"Arthur and the kingdom's main force were far to the south, awaiting an expected attack by a major force of Saxons. I was later told that the Norse and a powerful Saxon warlord had planned the raid together. The Saxons agreed to draw Arthur's forces south by threatening a raid on Londinium, in order to give the Norse a free hand in the sack of Eburacum. I suspect they'd agreed to split the takings, which would have been very great indeed if they'd succeeded. All of the realm's gold and silver coins were struck in that city."

"So, your reward for this great deed was a seat at the Round Table."

"Well . . . it just so happened that the Queen was visiting the city when the attack occurred. That might have tipped the scales in my favor."

"I suspect so," Capussa said with a chuckle. "Is that where you first met her?"

"Yes."

"Then you must tell of this!" the Numidian demanded.

"No, no," Percival said. He stood and stretched his arms over his head. "It has been a long day, and I have told enough tales for tonight. I'm going to sleep."

"Tomorrow night, then."

"Good night, Capussa." Percival crossed to his horse, opened the leather travel bag tied to the saddle, and drew out a blanket. Moments later, he was asleep on a patch of grass on the far side of the fire.

Capussa leaned back against the wall of the tower behind him with a rueful smile on his face.

"We have both lived by the sword for a long time," he whispered, "a very long time indeed, my friend. So I shall pray that you find the peace you seek. However, I do not believe fate will allow you to sheath your sword just yet."

Morgana's Domain

Finn walked slowly down the dusty street, staring at the bodies lying in the road and strewn about the central square of the modest village. Many were headless and one was cut near in half. The sellsword's gaze came to rest upon Lord Aeron, the leader of the force Morgana had dispatched to destroy the raiders—the man who'd wrought much of this slaughter.

He sat on a stone wall near the well in the center of the village square, cleaning the blood from his sword with a white cloth. Finn had watched this ritual before. Lord Aeron would cleanse the sword of every drop of blood, gore, and dirt with great care. Once this task was finished, he would rinse and wring out the cloth, sometimes three or four times, before returning it to its place beneath the saddle of his great black steed.

Finn had plied the bloody trade of a sellsword for many a master, but he'd never served under a man like Lord Aeron, Morgana's most feared soldier. Unlike the other men in her force, who, like Finn, wore a motley array of mail shirts and breastplates scavenged from one battle-field or another, Lord Aeron was clad in a full suit of armor forged by a master smith—the battle dress of a knight.

Finn knew enough of metalworking to know that Lord Aeron's armor had once gleamed like the blade of the deadly sword the knight was diligently cleaning. That finish was no more. From the helm cover-ing Lord Aeron's head to the greaves protecting his legs and shins, the metal had been scorched a darker, colder hue by a smith with far less skill than its original maker.

The rest of Morgana's sellswords were on the far side of the square, drinking a round of beer served by the local tavern keeper. Like the rest of the people in the village, the tavern keeper was grateful for their timely intervention. Finn knew Lord Aeron had paid for the rounds, which was odd. There was no need to waste the coin. The innkeeper wouldn't dare to complain.

Odder still was Lord Aeron's rule that no one could take anything from nor inflict any harm upon the villagers. The rule rankled some of the newcomers. As far as they were concerned, looting and raping was a part of the wages they were due after a skirmish or a battle like this one. The two men who'd been foolish enough to break this rule a month earlier had lost their heads to Lord Aeron's sword. After that, there were no further transgressions. Finn hadn't found the rule to be much of a burden. The witch paid them well for their services.

The now-dead band of brigands responsible for raiding villages within the borders Morgana claimed as her domain had greatly out-numbered Lord Aeron's force. Before the battle, Finn could tell that some of the newer men feared for the outcome. Finn had not shared their trepidation. He had served under Lord Aeron's command for more than a year and knew what was about to be unleashed upon Ein-arr, the Norse raider leading the brigands attacking the village.

Lord Aeron, along with Finn and the more experienced men, had served as the hammer in the attack, slamming into the flank of the raiders. The rest of the men had served as the anvil upon which the brigands had been broken. As always, Lord Aeron had led the charge and attacked the opposing force like an invincible demon king, one that grew stronger with the taking of each life. In moments, even the stoutest of the brigands had been frantically trying to escape the terrible fury of the gleaming sword wielded by the blackened knight wading through their ranks.

The survivors had raced down the narrow lane that ran through the village, seeking safety in the forest beyond, only to have their way blocked by the rest of Lord Aeron's men. No prisoners had been taken. Morgana had forbid it. A message was being sent.

Finn waited until Lord Aeron had finished cleaning and resheathing his sword before approaching him. Although he had served under the man for more than a year, he'd never seen his face. No one had. The reclusive knight lived and trained alone in the castle's most remote tower, and whenever he emerged, his face was either hidden within the cowl of his black cloak, or obscured, as now, by his steel helmet. All Finn could discern beneath the helm were a pair of piercing blue eyes, pale skin, and a strong jaw.

Lord Aeron stood as Finn approached, but his gaze was on a little blond girl watching him from the shadow of a darkened doorway. He placed something on the wall behind him before he turned to Finn.

"Your orders, sir?" Finn asked from a respectful distance.

"Is Einarr's body displayed on the border as I requested?" Lord Aeron asked in a flat, emotionless voice, without turning in his direction.

"Yes, sir, I put it there myself. Hengst's men will recognize it . . . even without the head," Finn said.

Lord Aeron nodded. "Good, then we ride for the castle. With luck, we will be there before dark."

"Yes, my lord." Finn bowed and then turned to give the signal to the rest of the men, still drinking outside the tavern. They quickly drained their tankards and hurried to their horses.

As the mounted column of men left the village square, Finn glanced back at the wall beside the well. The little blond girl was reaching for something on the wall, the object placed there by Lord Aeron. Finn watched as the little girl lifted up a straw doll and clasped it to her chest, as if it were a child.

Lord Aeron must have found it on the ground and left it on the wall for the child.

CHAPTER 6

THE ROAD TO LONDINIUM

"We have traveled almost ten leagues since we left the waystation," Percival said, glancing up at the sun. "We should give the horses a rest."

Capussa nodded. "Should I assume we are sleeping under the stars again tonight?"

"You should."

"Then let us choose our resting place with care," Capussa said, lowering his voice, "or it could be our last. We are being followed."

"Where and how many?" Percival said, his gaze fixed on the road ahead.

"One, maybe two. I can't be sure. I saw one on the crest of that hill to the left a moment ago," Capussa said, brushing a fly from the back of his horse. "Could it be that the good people of this Londinium have come to welcome you home?"

"I think not," Percival said wryly.

"Let's find a spot on the right side of the road ahead. There's a shallow river behind that tree line," Percival said, gesturing to the forest on the right. "We can water the horses there and see if our shadows mean us harm."

Capussa nodded. "Good, but let us find an open space. I would see the enemy before they are upon us."

A few furlongs farther, Percival pointed to a broad clearing on the right side of the road. As they drew closer, the remains of a lonely stone house, burned and abandoned years earlier, became visible.

Percival drew his horse up across from the charred ruin and stared at the remains of the small house for a long moment.

"I rode by this place with Sir Gawain. It was a farm," Percival said in a quiet voice. He gestured to the overgrown field that was bordered on one side by the road, and on the other by a shallow river, a half furlong distant. "Back then, all of this . . . it was plowed and ready for planting. It was a hot day, and the farmer's son, a mere boy, offered us water from the well."

For a moment, Percival could see the boy in front of him, eyes wide with awe, as he gazed up at the two knights and the fifteen mounted archers behind them.

"We accepted the lad's kindness and stopped for a moment. Gawain spoke to the farmer and his wife, while the men filled their water skins. I remember looking back at the three of them as we rode away . . . this was their home. They would not have abandoned it willingly," he finished in a voice tinged with anger and regret.

"I fear we may find more like this as we cross this land of yours," Capussa said as he stared at the ruined homestead. "You would be wise not to dwell on such matters."

"Alas, that is a wisdom I do not possess," Percival said quietly.

Capussa pointed to a small rise that ran alongside the river and formed a pocket around the far end of the field.

"Let us make camp there. It will shield our fire from the forest on the other side of the river."

Percival nodded, and the two men rode across the field, dismounted, and tied their horses to a large oak tree. After tending to the horses and building a small fire at the foot of the rise, the two men sat down a pace away. Percival reached in his pack and handed Capussa a share of the dried fish, bread, and fruit he had bought in Caer Ceint. Capussa offered him a drink from his silver flask, and Percival waved it away.

"I have tried your liquid fire before, my friend. Once was enough."

"Alas, I shall have to drink your share. Now, tell me of this Table . . . this company of knights. How did it come to be?"

"I remember asking Merlin that very question a long time ago,"

Percival said as he stood and pushed a branch into the center of the fire with a long stick. "Surprisingly, he actually told me the truth. But of course, at that time, he desired something from me."

"And what was that?"

"To undertake the Grail quest."

"A fool's errand," Capussa said, shaking his head.

"I cannot gainsay that. I couldn't understand the reasons for it then, with war on the horizon, and I cannot now, after all that has come to pass. And yet, I know that Merlin the Wise is anything but a fool. One day, if he still lives, I should like to speak of this matter with him."

The Numidian raised an eyebrow but said nothing.

"As for the Table," Percival continued, "everyone in the kingdom knows the tale of its founding. King Arthur Pendragon brought together the finest knights in the land in order to forge a unique brotherhood—a brotherhood of men proven in battle, noble of purpose, and willing to do the work of Christ. The reality, according to Merlin, was somewhat different."

"Good works are rarely paired with good intentions, my noble friend," Capussa said with a chuckle.

"I fear you see the world as too dark a place. I shall pray for you," Percival said, feigning concern as he returned to his seat on the slope of the hill.

"I see it as it is, Knight, but I do not hate it for its wickedness," Capussa said, raising a hand in a conciliatory gesture.

"Well, I shall have to take comfort in that at least," Percival said, drawing a chuckle from his friend.

"The true objective of the Table," Percival continued, after a moment's silence, "was to lure the most invincible warriors in the land away from their liege lords and to wed their allegiance to a higher purpose—one that just happened to be under Arthur's control. And it worked. Knights came from all over to seek the honor of a seat at the Table, and in so doing, they bound themselves to Arthur.

"Yet, despite that reality, over time, the founding principles . . . that ethos . . . it became a force in itself, a dominating force. Each member of the Table felt bound to strive for the good and to resist evil . . . both that within themselves and in others. Maybe it was Arthur's leadership or the nobility of men like Sir Kay, Sir Tristan, and Sir Gawain, or divine guidance. I cannot say, but over time, the power and the reputation of the Table came to symbolize all that was good and noble in the land—a thing that could not be broken."

Percival paused and looked up at the canopy of stars in the clear night sky before continuing. "Perhaps . . . perhaps, that wasn't a good thing, for when it was broken, the will of the people may well have been broken with it. I don't know."

There was a long silence, and then Capussa spoke with quiet conviction.

"Anything that inspires a man of the sword to do good . . . to rise above his baser instincts . . . is a good and noble thing. So this Table, although it is no more, should be held in honor, and perhaps, one day, it shall be remade."

The Camp of Cynric the Archer

Keil ran along the narrow trail just below the low ridge that paralleled the road to Londinium, soundlessly leaping over the errant tree roots and puddles along the path. Although he was only seventeen, the young man was already one of the best hunters and archers in the small band of men who followed Cynric the Archer. One day, he hoped to be able to match Cynric's skill, but he knew that day was a long way off.

Keil slowed as he approached the camp and waved in the direction of his uncle Tylan, hidden atop the small wooded rise to his left, taking the fourth watch. Keil heard a low growl from behind a tree as he crested the rise.

"Give the signal next time, boy, or you'll end up with an arrow in your chest."

"Yes, sir," Keil said with a smile.

Keil's mother had died shortly after his birth, and his father had been killed by Hengst the Butcher's men five years ago. Tylan, his father's brother, had taken it upon himself to look after the then twelve-year-old boy. Although Keil didn't believe that he needed looking after, he knew Tylan thought otherwise.

Keil jogged into the camp, drawing quick glances from the fifteen men sitting on rocks or logs, eating their evening meal. He knew tonight's modest repast was smoked rabbit, a slice of hard bread, and water or mead, since no one had spotted any deer or wild pigs in the last week. Keil slowed as he approached a tall, lean man sitting on a rock near the edge of the river, staring at a small eddy of water swirling just beyond his feet.

The man was clothed in the same coarse brown woolen shirt, pants, and leather boots that Keil and the other men wore, but his boots were of a finer cut, and he wore a black leather jerkin. A faded red dragon, with an arrow of the same color beneath it, was sewn into the right shoulder of the jerkin, marking the wearer as a former soldier in the Pendragon's elite core of archers.

The young man stopped several paces from Cynric and waited respectfully. Keil had grown up hearing the tales of the King and the Knights of the Round Table, men who'd kept the peace in the land for over two decades. When he thought of the Knights, he envisioned a band of invincible men clad in gleaming armor, riding massive black chargers and bearing mighty swords—men who might one day return and cast the hordes of invading Norsemen and Saxons back into the sea.

Although Cynric never spoke of it, Keil knew from Tylan and the others that Cynric had often marched into battle in support of the Knights; some even said he'd fought at the battle of Camlann.

Without looking up, the tall, lean man gestured to a large, flat rock beside him. "Sit, Keil, and tell me what you will."

"Yes, sir," Keil said as he sat down and tried to catch his breath. "Sir, those two sellswords we've been tracking, they're camped by the river, near old Ogden's farm."

Cynric lifted his gaze and turned toward the young man, a weariness in his blue-grey eyes. "I see. Well, we shall have to pay them a visit in the morning. Have Tylan assemble the men two hours after dawn."

"Sir, may I . . ."

"Yes, Keil, you may come," the bowman said, a hint of amusement in his voice. "If you follow your uncle's orders."

"Thank you, sir!" Keil said as he jumped up from the rock in excitement, turned, and jogged across the campsite to tell a friend.

Cynric watched the boy for a moment, then his gaze turned to the sun setting behind the hills in the distance and said in a quiet voice, "Don't thank me, my young friend. You will one day grow weary of killing other men, no matter the cause."

* * *

PERCIVAL STOOD ON the bank of the shallow river and finished washing the sweat from his body. The brutal training routine he and Capussa engaged in each morning had ended moments before. As he stood up, a flock of birds took flight from the top of a distant hill to the east. After listening for a moment, the Knight walked back to the campsite.

Capussa was stoking the fire, vainly seeking a live ember from the night before.

"The fire will have to wait," Percival said. "Those who have been following us come."

"I will assume we should dress for a fight, this being such a peaceful land," Capussa said with a smile.

"That would be wise."

The two men donned their mailed shirts, gauntlets, greaves, helms, and swords with long-practiced ease and mounted their horses. Percival eased his mount up the rise to the point where he could see the river and forest beyond, but where most of his body, and that of his horse, remained shielded. Capussa's rode up on his left.

Percival came to a sudden halt as a half score of men emerged from the forest on the far side of the river. They formed an uneven line and walked to the edge of the water.

The men were armed with bows of varying sizes and quality, and every man wore a hunting knife at his belt. Their clothes were a motley collection of coarse woolens and animal hides, but unlike the band of brigands he and Capussa had encountered earlier, their clothes were passably clean. The men by the river moved like woodsmen and hunters, instead of city dwellers who'd taken to the wood to become outlaws.

The tall, lean man in the center of the line spoke quietly to the shorter, stockier man beside him. The man nodded and made a hand signal. A moment later, the men moved toward the river, spacing themselves two paces apart.

Percival stared through his helm at the man in the center of the line, who was clearly the leader of the band of archers. His hair was short and streaked with grey, as was his full mustache and neatly trimmed beard. The man's facial features were not clearly discernable, but Percival could see the long white scar on the left side of his face.

The Knight leaned forward on his horse and stared at the tall man, his brow furrowed. He knew a tall, lean man with a wound like that, an archer as well. The man had received the wound a lifetime ago, in a battle on a bridge outside a besieged castle, far to the north. Percival's sword had killed the man who'd struck the blow, and he'd defended the wounded bowman against Morgana's mercenaries, with Galahad by his side, for over an hour, until help had come.

Percival stared at the four-foot-long bow the tall archer held easily in his right hand and the faded red marking on the right shoulder of his worn black leather jerkin. He recognized the mark. It was the emblem worn by the Pendragon's archers. Percival nodded toward the approaching line of archers. "I would speak with one of them before this turns into a fight."

Capussa glanced over at him. "You can speak to whomever is left after we break their line."

Percival shook his head. "I may know the leader of these men. I will not shed his blood."

"The archer in the middle?"

"Yes."

"And if you're wrong?" Capussa asked skeptically.

"Then I will ride toward their line at full speed, and you will cover me with Batukhan's bow."

"It's my bow now, not Batukhan's," his friend reminded him, "and that's not much of a battle plan."

The Knight eased his horse forward and spoke over his shoulder. "I agree."

As he came over the rise and rode down the other side, Percival raised his left hand in a peaceful gesture. Two of the men in the line nocked their arrows and raised their bows as he approached, but a word from the tall archer stayed their hands. When the Knight came to within fifty paces of the river, the man to the right of the tall archer called out.

"Not another step, Norseman, or we'll kill you and your fine horse!"

Percival pulled on the reins held in his right hand, and the horse stopped obediently.

"I'm not a Norseman. I was born and raised in this land, just as you."

"You lie!" another man called out. "You serve the dog Hengst."

"Your charge is false," he said in a firm but calm voice. "Now, I would have words with your leader. We have met before."

The tall archer, who'd remained quiet during the exchange, stepped forward.

"When and where have we met, rider?"

Percival fixed his eyes on the tall man in the middle of the line. "We met, Cynric of the Pendragon's archers, a decade ago, on the Aelius Bridge to the north. You received that scar on your face on that day," he noted, touching the left side of his own face with his gloved hand.

The stocky man beside the archer started to growl a response, but the tall archer raised his hand, and the man beside him fell silent. The tall archer stared at Percival, his face a mask of stone.

"I don't remember you, rider. What is your name?"

Percival reached up and slowly eased the helmet off his head, shook free his mane of black hair, and then stared across the river at Cynric. The archer's eyes widened, and as he raised his hand to block the morning sun, his hand shook slightly.

"I believe that you do remember me, Cynric the Archer," the Knight said. "I am Sir Percival of the Round Table."

There was a collective gasp among the men facing him, and the youngest of men in the line stepped forward several yards and gawked at the Knight as if he had two heads. The rest of the men lowered their bows and looked from Percival to Cynric.

The stocky man turned and yelled at the boy who'd broken ranks. "Keil, get back in that line or I'll put an arrow into you myself!"

Cynric stared at Percival for a long moment and then shook his head.

"It's been many years since that day . . . and near every man and woman in the land has heard the tale of the Aelius Bridge. It's been told and retold in every inn and tavern a thousand times. If you are Sir Percival, forgive me, but I have to make sure, and if not, I shall surely put an arrow in your chest for wrongly taking the name of that most noble of knights."

"That is a fair bargain, Archer," Percival said. "What proof would you have?"

"If you are who you say, then you will remember what I said as Morgana's wolves were near upon us, words that I have not shared with anyone since."

Percival dismounted from his horse and slowly walked to the edge of the river, stopping directly across from the man on the far bank, who was now surrounded by a band of rapt listeners. He stared at the tall man for a moment, and when he spoke, it seemed as if the forest itself stilled to hear him.

"The years between then and now have been long and hard, Archer, but I remember those words as if they were spoken yesterday. You said to me, 'You cannot hold this bridge, Knight, and I cannot make it to the castle walls. Do not waste your life dying here with me.'" Percival paused for a moment and then continued. "And I said to you, 'Whether we live or die today is in God's hands, but staying by your side is in mine, and stay I will, until I am dead, or relieved.'"

When he finished, there was a silence, and the archer and the Knight stared at one another for a long moment. At last Cynric spoke in a quiet voice.

"Aye," he nodded, "that is what you said, Sir Percival, to the very word. Forgive me."

Percival waded into the river. Cynric met him halfway, and the two men embraced.

"It has been a long time, Knight."

"Too long, Archer. It's good to be home." He turned to the men watching on the far side of the river. "Among friends and countrymen at long last."

A deep voice interrupted the scene, and Percival glanced over his shoulder to see Capussa still on the bank of the river, mounted on his destrier.

"Is it the practice in this country to allow a fine pair of greaves to rust without good cause?" he called out. "Let us pick one side of the river or the other, but not the middle."

Cynric's men stared in astonishment at the fearsome Numidian on the far bank of the river. An amused Percival gestured to his friend with one hand. "Yeoman, let me introduce you to my friend and brother-in-arms, Capussa."

Then he turned back to Cynric. "This is the second time we have met at a river crossing and faced the peril of death together. I pray that our time hereafter, however long or short it may be, is one of peace."

Cynric nodded. "I too shall pray thus, Sir Percival, but I fear there is little peace in this land to be found."

CHAPTER 7

MORGANA'S CASTLE

Morgana stood on the battlement of the castle, overlooking the cold, grey waters of the estuary and the sea beyond, and recalled a very different seascape a half a world away. Her parents' palatial estate in Constantinople afforded the family a view of the Sea of Marmara from the living quarters on the third floor. As a child, she'd spent many a day on the estate's grand balcony, watching the hundreds of merchant ships that served the needs of the great city come and go on those azure, sun-drenched waters. A cold onshore breeze whipped over the castle wall, ruffling her coal black cloak, and she drew its folds closer to her body, silently cursing the weather. In the decade she'd spent in the harsh, cold land hunting the traitor Melitas Komnenos, now reborn as Merlin the Wise, it was the lack of sun Morgana hated the most.

"I have lived among these vermin for near a decade, Melitas," Morgana said in a venomous whisper, "and that is long enough. Soon I shall find you, and I shall take your head back to the emperor in triumph. Then, the name of Igaris shall be restored to its former glory."

A warning cry from one of the sentries manning the walls encircling the castle drew Morgana's attention away from her reverie. She turned and walked to one of the crenels on the far side of the battlement and watched the column of horsemen led by Lord Aeron approach the castle from the south. Many of the two score of men had extra swords, helmets, shields, and greaves tied to the sides of their horses, undoubtedly booty scavenged from the bodies of the enemy.

She nodded in satisfaction. Lord Aeron had apparently found and destroyed the band of raiders ravaging the borders of the lands she had taken after the fall of the Pendragon. As the column drew closer, Morgana could see the victory had not been without a price. Five of the returning men were wounded, and three bodies lay in the back of a wagon drawn by a weary plow horse. Under her agreement with the Saxon war leader, Garr, she would have to pay a donative to the families of the dead men. She would also have to pay a bounty to the new men hired to replace them. These were expenses she could ill afford.

The emperor still supported her quest for vengeance against the traitor, Melitas, but he was no longer willing to pay for it. The cost of the empire's latest war with the Persians had put an end to imperial largesse. Now, she was not only expected to pay for the cost of her personal cadre of sellswords from her own coffers, she had been ordered to repay some of the imperial golds she had spent in her war against the Pendragon.

To meet the additional financial burden, Morgana had imposed a heavy tax upon the peasants within the domain she controlled, and she'd demanded more production from the slaves working in the royal silver mines—mines she had seized after the Pendragon's fall. The peasants had initially resisted her levies, but in time, resistance had melted away. The cost of her protection was a heavy burden, but it was far preferable to the slavery offered by the Norse to the south or the merciless savagery of the bands of brigands roaming the forests and roads.

As for the silver mines, increasing the pace of production had been difficult. Most of the prisoners of war she'd taken after the battle of Camlann had been worked to death in those vile pits, and the new workers, half-starved slaves from Hengst's slave market, didn't last long. Yet, despite these difficulties, Morgana had no intention of relinquishing her pursuit of Melitas Komnenos. She would meet the emperor's demands and still find the means to hunt down and kill the traitor as well, no matter the price in blood.

A soft, scuffing noise drew Morgana's attention to the archway leading off the parapet, and a moment later, Seneas, the head of her household staff, emerged, breathing heavily. She waited for the stooped old courtier to catch his breath. Seneas's family had served the house of Igaris faithfully for five generations, and she respected his counsel, although she didn't completely trust him. But then, trusting anyone was a fool's choice, particularly someone with ties to the imperial court, where power was an obsession and duplicity and intrigue were considered fine, if merciless, arts.

"Milady?"

"Yes, Seneas," Morgana answered, glancing over at him for a moment and then turning her gaze back to Lord Aeron below.

"Lord Aeron has returned. You had said—"

"Yes, I will see him in my quarters, alone."

"Yes, Milady."

When Seneas continued to stand, unmoving, Morgana turned around and faced him.

"Is there something else?"

"Yes, Milady," he said hesitantly. "In the packet of messages that came with the admiral, I received a letter from a friend, Arminius. He lives in Hydruntum, in southern Italia. Arminius is a mapmaker and scholar. He talks with travelers each day at the ports, seeking knowledge of distant lands." Seneas paused, still trying to catch his breath. Morgana waited impatiently.

"In the letter," Seneas continued, "Arminius said he talked with a traveler six months ago. The man had come on a ship from Alexandria. He said that he'd spent many years in the Holy Land and was traveling home to Albion."

"Why is this of import to me, Seneas?" Morgana interrupted curtly.

"Milady, Arminius heard this man and his Numidian companion talking. The man was Briton. His name is Percival."

When Morgana said nothing, Seneas hurried to continue. "Forgive me, Milady, but you will recall there was a Knight of the Round Table by that name. He commanded the villages on the border marches to the north during the war with the Pendragon."

Morgana nodded slowly. She didn't remember the name of the man who had commanded the forces in that remote corner of the Pendragon's kingdom. She did, however, remember putting to death the two commanders she'd sent there with orders to burn every village to the ground. Both men had not only failed in this effort, but their forces had almost been annihilated by this Sir Percival. After these defeats, she had decided the prize was not worth the cost and sent the surviving sellswords to wreak havoc in other parts of the Pendragon's kingdom.

Morgana shook her head dismissively. "This cannot be the same man. A Knight of the Table would not have traveled to the Holy Land when his land and king were under siege."

"Milady, it is said that the Pendragon sent this Sir Percival on a mission to find the Holy Grail. It may be that he is only now returning from this quest."

Morgana laughed scornfully. "Oh that is so like him, the noble fool." Her eyes strayed again to Lord Aeron. The steel-clad knight was leading his horse across the courtyard to the stables. Then she looked over at Seneas again.

"It could be him, but I think not, Seneas. No, this Sir Percival surely died with his brethren at Camlann. The Table is no more."

"You may be right, Milady, but if it is he, he brings—"

"He will bring nothing from the land of the Moor but a pox between his legs, and he is welcome to spread that among the filthy women of this sunless land. But, still, you were wise to tell me of this. You will tell me if you hear more of this man."

"Yes, Milady." Seneas bowed and quickly retreated through the archway behind him.

Morgana waited until the old man had made his way back down the steep stairs that spiraled down to the second floor of the castle, before turning to follow him. She hesitated for a moment before passing through the archway, and looked back at the grey sea visible in the distance. A lone shaft of sunlight had found an opening in the otherwise seamless grey canopy above and painted a ghostly path across the bleak estuary heading east. After a moment, the path of light vanished, and Morgana stepped downward into the darkness below.

* * *

MORGANA SCANNED THE spacious room from her place on the silk-covered divan, positioned three paces from the fire in the hearth. She had spent a small fortune converting the formerly stark and cold stone space into a room where she could greet her guests. The walls were adorned with paintings and silks imported from her homeland, the floors were covered with the finest Persian carpets, and every window and portal was fitted with glass. Although the room was still modest when compared to her former quarters in Constantinople, it was at least bearable, and that was all she could hope for in this primitive country.

The servants had followed her instructions most carefully, but then, they knew all too well the agony they would suffer if they did otherwise. The divan had been situated so the illumination from the fire and the oil lamps affixed to the columns to her right and left displayed her body in an alluring glow. She glanced across the room at the silver mirror positioned unobtrusively on a table across from her and admired the beautiful face and the cold, calculating lavender eyes staring back at her.

She reached up and positioned her long auburn tresses so they spilled over her right shoulder, past her partially exposed breasts, to her silken blue dress below. Once she was satisfied with her hair, Morgana looked down and caressed the row of sapphires in the gold chatelaine encircling her waist, each perfectly complementing the color of her dress. She was ready for her meeting with Lord Aeron.

Moments later, there was a knock at the door to her chambers, and a lean figure of medium height clad in a black hooded tunic, dark breeches, and worn leather boots walked into the room. The only armament he bore was the short sword at his waist, but the modest weapon and his common clothing did nothing to diminish the threat radiating from the silent figure. It was as if a storm of violence raged within, seeking a way out—a rage restrained only by the bands of his iron discipline. The two guards reluctantly following Lord Aeron into the room made a point of keeping their hands away from the swords at their hips, and they were visibly relieved when Morgana waved them away.

"Leave us."

For a moment, Morgana said nothing more, and the man stood as still as a statue, his face hidden within the cowl. Then she gestured to an open spot on the long divan beside her.

"Lord Aeron, come, sit, and tell me of your day." The hint of a smile touched Morgana's lips when she said his name.

The hooded figure walked over to a wooden chair positioned against a far wall and carried it to an open space two strides from Morgana. The Roman princess smiled as the knight sat down. She had known he would not sit beside her, but she found pleasure in his discomfort. No one had resisted her charms before, even those who despised her. Lord Aeron had proven to be an exception, one that she found most galling, for she knew he prized another's beauty above her own.

"May I at least see the face of the soldier who so faithfully defends my modest lands from the ravages of my enemies?" she asked.

The man hesitated a moment, and then reached up and eased back the hood of his cloak, revealing a head of golden hair cropped unnaturally short, a broad forehead, piercing blue eyes, high cheekbones, a modest but perfectly formed nose, and a strong chin with a pronounced cleft in the center. The knight's face would have been mesmerizingly handsome but for the cruel scar that ran the length of his right cheek to his jawline and the second scar marring his forehead.

A decade ago, the man sitting across from her had been known as Sir Galahad of the Round Table, and his heroic deeds, near godlike mien, and perennial roguish grin had stirred the passions of women the length and breadth of Albion. That man, Morgana knew, was no more. She had killed him as surely as if she had plunged a knife into his heart on the day that she'd captured him as he lay senseless and severely wounded outside the Pendragon's lines at Camlann.

The knight now served under her command. He'd rechristened himself Lord Aeron, after the god of battle and slaughter, worshiped by the early Britons. After bowing to her demands, he had swept away all vestiges of his past life. The gleaming armor the former Sir Galahad had once worn with pride now bore a cold blue-black hue, and his signature white stallion had been exchanged for a black destrier. Even the sword he carried into battle was new, acquired after he gave her his oath of fealty. His former blade, the one imprinted with the mark of the Table, was stored in his quarters on the far side of the castle.

Although Morgana had allowed the knight to bury his former identity and remain a stranger to all but herself, she'd assumed his desire for secrecy was motivated by vanity. She could understand how a man who had lost his near godlike beauty to the wounds of war would seek to hide his face. Later, she had realized her mistake: Galahad had not buried his former self out of pride or conceit, but to avoid bringing dishonor to the Table. Morgana found this sentiment to be as amusing as it was foolish; however, it was of no matter to her, as long as he followed her orders.

As she looked at the cold, hard face across from her, she remembered the day she first saw the knight. Galahad and another Knight of the Table had been defending a downed archer on a bridge, far to the north, against a force many times their number. The taller of the two knights had lost his helmet in the fray, and his noble visage, framed by a head of raven hair, was a mask of iron determination as he struck down attacker after attacker with controlled fury.

In contrast, Galahad's face—a face that would have put to shame the magnificent bust of Apollo outside the Hippodrome—bore a rogue's grin as the golden-haired knight waded into his enemies with reckless abandon. Where the raven-haired knight was waging a life and death struggle, Galahad seemed to be playing a game, one he was enjoying to the fullest.

As the memory faded, a small part of Morgana felt an instant of sorrow that the smiling god-come-to-earth who'd held the bridge that day with his fellow knight was now gone, leaving only the cold, hard man who served at her pleasure.

"So tell me of your victory," she finally said.

"It was less of a victory than a slaughter," Lord Aeron answered, his eyes now fixed on a point over Morgana's left shoulder. "We lured the brigands into a trap and killed them to a man, as you ordered. The body of their leader—Einarr—now adorns a tree on the border you share with Hengst the Butcher. The warning may stay further raids for a while, but only that. Hengst is behind the attacks. Einarr was just the wolf doing his bidding."

Morgana knew that Hengst, the feared Butcher of Londinium, was indeed the driving force behind the attacks on her lands. He and his brother, Ivarr the Red, had so ravaged Londinium and the surrounding area that the people there were now perpetually short of grain. Hengst had ignored the problem until hunger's bite had reached the bellies of his own reavers. Now the fool had been compelled to seek out more food and fodder or risk a revolt. Of late, Hengst's quest for sustenance had led one of his bands of pet brigands into the lands held by Morgana, more than twenty leagues to the north of his so-called kingdom.

A momentary flash of irritation crossed Morgana's brow. The emperor's gold, and some of her own, had brought Hengst and his legion of foul sellswords to this land. A dog shouldn't bite the hand that had not only fed him for years but also made him rich.

She had considered having the Norse war leader killed by one of her spies, but had decided against it. Killing Hengst would leave his brother Ivarr in control, and unlike his sibling, Ivarr was no fool. He would know that she was behind the assassination, and a costly war could follow, a war she could ill afford, and one that would play into the hands of Melitas.

Morgana set aside the conundrum for another day and turned her attention back to Lord Aeron. "And what, Lord Aeron, do you suggest?"

"I am a soldier, not a strategist."

Morgana laughed. "You have put hundreds of men to the sword and won a host of battles under my banner, Knight, and in most of those battles, your force was the lesser. I think you underrate your skills."

Lord Aeron's face froze at the mention of the word knight—a reaction Morgana had anticipated.

"I am not a knight, Milady. I am just a sellsword, like the rest."

"No, Lord Aeron, you are not like the others. Your wages are not paid in coin, but in mercy. I wonder if that coinage will lose its glitter as she loses her beauty to the ravages of age?"

The man's face showed no reaction to the wound inflicted by Morgana's verbal knife, other than an involuntary tightening of his jaw muscle, but she knew she had drawn blood.

The man's mesmerizing blue eyes found her, and he spoke in a quiet voice, as cold as ice. "Does Milady have further need of me tonight?"

Morgana held the man's gaze for a long moment and then made a small gesture of dismissal.

"No, Lord Aeron, you may leave."

The man stood, bowed respectfully, and walked to the door, easing the hood up over his head once again.

As he reached for the door, Morgana spoke again. "Lord Aeron, do you know a knight called Sir Percival?" She kept her tone casual, suggesting the matter was of no importance.

The knight froze, his hand on the door handle. Without turning, he answered in a flat, emotionless voice. "Yes. He was a Knight of the Table."

"And what became of this man?" Morgana said quietly.

"He died in the Holy Land."

"You are sure of this?" she asked, the hint of a threat in her voice.

"Quite," Lord Aeron answered and left the room.

Morgana lifted the glass of wine on the table beside her and swirled the red liquid in the silver goblet, a cruel smile easing across her face.

"I believe you are right, Lord Aeron. You are indeed the last Knight of the Table."

CHAPTER 8

ABBEY CWM HIR

uinevere gently rolled up the scroll of parchment on the desk and placed it in the basket sitting on the nearby shelf, along with a stack of other messages. After staring at the basket for a moment, she walked across her personal quarters, opened a window, and drew in the cool evening air. The sun had set two hours earlier, and the small band of guards that served under Bishop Verdino's orders—men whose wages were paid from the revenues generated from her lands— were roasting a rabbit and a small pig over a fire in the courtyard below.

As she watched one of the men turn the spit, she thought of the message she had just read. It was from the wife of a blacksmith living in Londinium. In the message, the woman said Hengst and his reavers had so ravaged the city and the surrounding area that many of the common people were surviving on rats, mice, and other vermin. The meat the guards were roasting in the courtyard would have been considered a bounteous feast by such folk.

"And I remember when it was the richest city in the kingdom," Guinevere said softly.

"Milady?"

Guinevere turned to Cadwyn. Her young handmaiden was sitting in a chair by the small hearth at the other end of the room, reading a second basket of parchments by the light of the fire.

"It's nothing. Are there any good tidings in those messages?"

"No, Milady, I'm sorry," Cadwyn said as she pored over a water-stained parchment. "But, this . . . is interesting."

"What does it say?"

Cadwyn frowned slightly. "It's from a woman in Whitstable. Her husband is a farrier, and he owns a stable. The message says that a tall man came ashore a fortnight ago with . . . with a man whose skin was as black as coal. They traveled on a galley carrying cargo from Francia. The captain of the ship, a man named Aldwyn Potter, told her husband the vessel had been attacked by Norse raiders. He said the tall man and his companion cut down the raiders like two avenging angels. He said they were invincible!" Cadwyn said, her voice rising in excitement.

"Indeed," Guinevere said, a wry smile coming to her face. "I wish we had an army of such men."

"Milady, forgive me, there is more."

"Read on, my young friend."

"The woman's husband said—"

Suddenly, Cadwyn shot to her feet and looked over at Guinevere, her eyes wide.

"Milady! The woman's husband said that the tall man was Sir Percival of the Round Table." When Cadwyn's eyes returned to the yellowed scroll, it was as if the parchment were a holy relic.

Guinevere drew in a sharp breath and, for a moment, stood motionless. Then she slowly shook her head.

"No. He must be mistaken. It has been too many years."

Cadwyn walked around the table and spread the scroll out for Guinevere to read.

"Milady, the woman says that she didn't believe her husband at first, but he insisted. He said he had seen Sir Percival in Londinium a decade earlier, and he could never forget him."

Guinevere leaned over and read the message, which had been penned in careful strokes, if common words. Then she read it through two more times. Cadwyn pointed to the name of the woman at the bottom of the missive. "Milady, do you know this woman?"

The Queen looked down at the name written on the bottom of the scroll and then slowly nodded her head.

"Yes . . . yes, I do remember her, Ada. She served Lady Evelynn . . . as a handmaiden. She is an honest woman of keen wit, but I still . . . it must be a mistake."

Guinevere read the message a fourth time and slowly sat down at the table. The words in the missive brought back a memory, something Arthur had said after he'd performed the solemn ceremony raising Sir Percival to the Table. "He's not the most handsome of the lot. Galahad takes that laurel, much to the ire of Lancelot, but this man . . . there's a power in him. He will bear watching."

"Milady?"

Guinevere slowly turned to Cadwyn, a distant look in her eyes.

"Milady, are you unwell?"

She shook her head. "No, forgive me. I am fine."

"Did you know Sir Percival? I mean . . . can you tell me of him, Milady?" Cadwyn asked softly, sitting in a chair across from her.

Guinevere nodded, smiling wistfully. "Oh yes, I knew Sir Percival. How could I not; he saved my life."

"What! Oh, please tell me of this, Milady."

"As you wish," Guinevere said, smiling at her young friend's fervor. "Sir Percival . . . he was different from the other knights. The older knights had been raised to the Table for standing with Arthur during the early years, when he was struggling to tame the land. Others, like Lancelot, were great champions, men who had achieved fame fighting other knights in individual duels. Sir Percival achieved his fame through his battles with the Norse raiders."

She paused for a moment, trying to wade through the memories unleashed by the letter, before continuing.

"In the early years, Arthur and the other members of the Table thought of the raiders as mere pirates, a nuisance the local lords and their liegemen should handle, but over time, that began to change. Traveling merchants, and then the men of the King's post, began to tell tales of fierce battles on the northeastern coast—battles where hundreds, and some said as many as a thousand men, clashed. As these tidings increased over time, it came to be known that a young knight by the name of Sir Percival was always in the thick of these battles, leading a small army against the Norse when they came ashore."

Guinevere hesitated for a moment, gently touching the parchment lying on the table in front of her.

"Milady," Cadwyn said with a frown, "why didn't the royal army march north to aid Sir Percival and his men in their fight?"

"That is a good question, my young friend," she said with a hint of regret. "Lancelot and some of the older knights insisted the threat from the Norse was overstated, and the real threat continued to be an invasion from the Saxons in the south. Those opinions changed after the attack on Eburacum."

"Eburacum? The Norse attacked Eburacum?" Cadwyn said incredulously. "I have never heard of this attack."

"Oh yes, attack they did. One summer, a fleet of more than a hundred Norse ships sailed up the Humber River and landed a force of a thousand or more raiders. Once ashore, they marched on Eburacum, intending to sack the city."

Guinevere leaned back in her chair and drew her arms across her chest, as if warding off a momentary shiver, before continuing in a quiet voice.

"I remember, as if it were yesterday, watching them come over the hill and run toward an open postern gate in the city's wall, cutting down everyone in their way—men, women, and children. I had never seen such fearsome men before, and I would not again until—"

"You were there, Milady? You were inside the city?" Cadwyn interrupted, half standing, her eyes wide.

Guinevere nodded. "Yes. I was visiting one of my cousins. She had just given birth. Very few people knew that I was there. Sir Tristan and a group of fifty men-at-arms had escorted me into the city after dark, with no fanfare."

"What happened?"

"When the attack came, Sir Tristan and his men, along with the city guard, raced to close the open gate, but some of the raiders were already within the walls. A fierce battle raged, but I could see from a window that Tristan and his force were losing the fight. As more and more of the Norsemen pushed through the gate, the breach began to widen. That's when Sir Percival arrived with his small legion."

"Legion, Milady?" Cadwyn looked confused.

"Well, yes, it was like one of the Roman legions I read about in the old Latin texts as a young girl," Guinevere said hesitantly as she recalled the scene in her mind. "The men marched in near perfect order and wheeled into line to the beat of a drum in squares. When the Norse raiders saw them, at first they were surprised, but then they charged. I thought Sir Percival's lines would break. There were so many Norse warriors, and they attacked with such ferocity."

"Did they?" Cadwyn asked anxiously. "Break, I mean?"

"No," Guinevere said, shaking her head, a distant look in her eyes. "The shield wall held. The men in that line had fought the Norse many times before, and they knew what they were about. They pressed together in a mass and stemmed the Norse charge. Then they fought side by side until one line grew tired, and then another would step into their place, all in good order.

Percival fought side by side with the men in the center, and when he wasn't in the line, he would run the length of it, calling out orders and encouragement. After two hours of hard fighting, it was over. The Norse broke off the attack and marched away. The city was saved. I was saved," Guinevere closed her eyes and said a silent prayer of thanks.

When she opened her eyes, Cadwyn was staring at her, a look of confusion on her face. "Milady, I don't understand. Why is this battle not sung of by the bards? Sir Percival won a great victory!"

"Yes, he did, and every bard in the land should indeed tell the story, but it was not to be. Arthur and the Knights of the Table did not want the people to know that the Kingdom had almost lost one of its greatest cities, along with its Queen, to Norse raiders. It would have shaken their confidence and spread fear throughout the land. So the victory was never celebrated at court nor spoken of by the royal bards thereafter."

Guinevere frowned, suddenly perplexed. A moment later, she leaned forward and read the parchment on the table again.

"Wait, something here is not right. This message couldn't have arrived so soon. It would have taken a month to come overland through the usual chain of messengers."

Cadwyn put a hand to her mouth. "You're right, Milady. I forgot to tell you."

"Tell me of what?"

"This message was brought by a sailor from a ship called the Mandragon that came ashore in Aberaeron. I didn't think anything of it, but it must be—"

"The ship those two men disembarked from," Guinevere finished with a whisper as she slowly rose to her feet. "I must see the captain of this vessel."

"Milady," Cadwyn said, rising as well. "Aberaeron is three days ride from here. Bishop Verdino would never let you go."

Guinevere smiled. "Well then, my dear Cadwyn, we can both thank the good Lord that his holiness is gone, and I have it on good authority he will not return for a week."

"It will require much—"

"Haste . . . yes," the Queen agreed. "But we shall do it."

She walked to the far end of the table, opened a drawer, and drew out a small piece of parchment, a quill, and a small pot of ink. Then she sat down and quickly wrote a message and handed it to Cadwyn.

"Find Torn. He's a skilled rider and hunter, and most loyal. Tell him to ride for Aberaeron in the morning with all haste, and to deliver this message to the captain of the ship. Potter, Aldwyn Potter, yes."

"Milady, I don't understand."

"There's a small port town at the mouth of the Ystwyth River," Guinevere explained. "The message asks the good captain to travel with Torn and meet us there, just two days ride. Torn and Potter can be there in a day and a half, so we will leave a day after Torn does."

"I see it," Cadwyn said as she ran to the door. "We meet in the middle."

After the door closed behind her young companion, Guinevere sat down in one of the chairs by the fire and walked through the memories of that fateful day. For some reason, the one she recalled most clearly was not the battle, but her meeting with Sir Percival in the mayor's quarters after it was over. A smile came to her face as she returned to that place in time.

She remembered Sir Tristan, clad in a white tabard bearing the seal of the Table, escorting the young knight into the modest room where the Lord Mayor and his councilors attended to the city's business. Guinevere was sitting in the Lord Mayor's oversized wooden chair on a small dais, with Sister Aranwen sitting in a smaller chair just beside her.

One of the councilor's chairs had been pulled to the edge of the dais for Sir Percival. There had been a slight smile on Tristan's strong, distinguished face as he walked into the room, followed by Sir Percival.

"My Queen, may I present Sir Percival."

For a moment, the tall, dark-haired man stared at her in shock and then dropped to one knee and bowed his head. She remembered trying to reconcile the young knight kneeling before her, dressed in a simple leather jerkin, brown trousers, and leather boots, with the seemingly invincible war leader racing up and down the line of battle an hour earlier. Guinevere glanced over at Sister Aranwen, who whispered quietly, "I thought he would be older."

"So did I," she whispered in return.

"Your Highness, Sister, forgive me," the Knight had said, raising his head and staring at the two women. "I . . . I thought that I was meeting with the Lord Mayor, not . . . not Your Highness."

Guinevere smiled and waved him to his feet. "Rise, Sir Percival, there is nothing to forgive. Few know that I am here, and I would keep it that way. However, Sister Aranwen and I could not leave without expressing our profound gratitude to the Knight who saved this city, and the two of us along with it."

"Thank you, Your Highness," Percival said as he stood up. "However, I am sure that Sir Tristan and his men would have held the wall and seen to your safety."

"I am grateful for your words, Sir Percival," Tristan said with a chuckle, still smiling at the look of shock on the young Knight's face, "but I fear we couldn't have held that breach much longer. You did indeed save the city and your Queen." Tristan inclined his head toward the young man. "I am in your debt, sir," he said and then turned to Guinevere.

"If I may be excused, my Queen. The Lord Mayor has—"

"You are excused, Sir Tristan," Guinevere said.

"Sir Percival, please do sit down. Sir Tristan has told me of your need to return to the coast in haste, but I would speak with you for a short while before you depart."

"Yes, Your Highness."

As the Knight took his seat in the chair across from her own, Guinevere had guessed the Knight was no older than her own twenty-one years, an estimate she later found to be correct.

"Sir Percival, I've never seen anything like what I saw today. Who trained those men to march and maneuver that way?"

"I did, my Queen," Percival answered.

"You? The perfect squares, the coordinated movements?"

"Yes, Your Highness."

"But . . . how did you come to know of this?"

The Knight hesitated for a moment and then explained, "A distant forbear was a Roman centurion in the Twentieth Legion. As a boy, I was required to read and memorize the legion's training and battle tactics, just as my father and his father were required to do before me."

"You can read the language of the Romans?" Sister Aranwen asked, surprised.

"Yes, Sister," Percival said, nodding politely.

"And so you trained those men—farmers, coopers, fishermen, and who knows what else—in the ways of the Romans?" Guinevere asked in quiet admiration.

"Yes, Your Highness, with the help of the other coastal lords."

"The other lords on the coast know Roman tactics and maneuver as well?" Guinevere asked incredulously.

Percival shook his head. "No, Your Highness, but they contributed men to the force, and they allowed me to train them in this way."

"I see. Well, I suppose, in addition to thanking you and your men, and your fellow lords, I shall have to say a word of thanks to the Romans as well," Guinevere said.

"I shall tell the men and my fellow lords of your gratitude," Percival said, inclining his head respectfully. "As for the Romans, that might be a little more difficult, Your Highness," he finished, the touch of a smile coming to his face.

"Yes, I suspect it would," Guinevere said with an answering smile. Then she stood and walked to the window overlooking the field where the battle had occurred, and watched the men and women tending to the wounded and collecting the bodies of the dead. When she returned to her seat, her face was somber.

"I have never seen these Norse raiders before. They were terrifying. Do you encounter them often?"

"Yes, Your Highness. Before the coastal force you watched in battle today was assembled and trained, the Norse would attack several times a month, during the late spring and summer. In a bad month, we would be engaged in battle with the enemy every week. Of late, their raids on our coast have lessened."

Guinevere's eyes widened, and she saw Sister Aranwen reach inside her habit for her prayer beads.

"Every . . . how many men would come ashore?"

Percival hesitated for a moment before answering. "As few as fifty and as many as five hundred in a major raid. That's why the men out there were not broken by the Norsemen's initial charge. They're used to their tactics. They know how to defeat them."

"You said the raids have lessened. Do you know why?"

"The raids on our coast have become less frequent, but then, the Norsemen have come to know we are ready for them. I have heard from sailors that the raids grow more frequent and in greater force elsewhere." The Knight leaned back in the chair as he finished, and grimaced ever so slightly as he did. Guinevere feared he had been hurt in the battle and decided not to detain him any longer.

"You must come to court and speak to the King of this. I will seek an audience for you."

"Thank you, my Queen. That would be an honor," Percival said, bowing his head slightly.

"You will be sure to bring your good wife with you when you come?"

"I have not yet wed, Your Highness."

"Betrothed?"

"My betrothed—"

"Will have to come with you to court. When is your nuptials date? I would send a gift."

Percival was silent for a moment, and then he spoke quietly.

"Thank you for your kindness, Your Highness, but there will be no wedding. Lady Ione, my betrothed, was killed in a Norse raid a year ago."

Guinevere's face turned white, and Sister Aranwen crossed herself and closed her eyes in prayer. "I . . . I am sorry to have brought up this painful matter," the Queen said with sincere regret.

A tired look came to the Knight's eyes, a look Guinevere had seen in the eyes of older men who had borne more than their share of life's sorrows and learned to endure the pain.

"Your Highness, I am told that Lady Ione was a kind and beautiful woman, but in truth, I only met her once, and that was nearly a decade ago, when we were just children. The constant battles with the Norse kept us apart. So although I shall always honor her name and memory, the greater loss was that of her family, for she was their only child."

"I pray that one day you shall find another who is worthy of you, for in the short time that we have spent together, Sir Percival, I can say that you have a true and noble soul," Guinevere said with quiet sincerity.

"Thank you, Your Highness. I pray that I shall be so blessed and that I shall live up to your kind words."

After the Knight had left, Guinevere had turned to find Sister Aranwen looking at her with a quizzical eye over her knitting. "I have never met anyone like him. It is as if . . . I . . . I just don't know."

"My mother used to say that all men are born with an angel and a devil inside them," Sister Aranwen said, "and there is a war between the two for all of their lives. From what I have seen in most men, the devil gets the upper hand, and then some." She stopped knitting and frowned. "But in that man, it's as if the war has already been won, and the angel has triumphed. I'm not sure what to think about that."

"What do you mean?" Guinevere asked, surprised and somewhat confused by the nun's comment.

Sister Aranwen folded her hands and turned to the younger woman.

"I have read the Lord's book from cover to cover many times, my Queen, and the angels of the Lord are as fearsome as they are glorious. I wouldn't want any man to have a thimbleful of that power, particularly not a man who has learned the way of war at so early an age."

When Guinevere opened her eyes, the memory had vanished, but not Sister Aranwen's last comment. She stood up, walked over to the fire, and said quietly, "You will have to forgive me, Sister, for I pray Sir Percival has returned, and I pray he carries within him the very power you feared he possessed ten years ago, for he will need every drop of that might just to cross this land in safety."

CHAPTER 9

THE HOME OF AELRED, ROYAL SENESCHAL

Merlin the Wise idly scratched his bushy grey beard as he watched Aelred, the Pendragon's former Seneschal, shamble over to the rough-hewn wooden table carrying two steaming mugs of cider. The small, thin man was dressed in an old brown monk's habit, incongruously cinched at the waist by a jewel-studded belt. Merlin recognized the belt. It was part of Aelred's former official regalia, but he had no idea why the old man was wearing the monk's habit. He had never taken holy orders or spent a single day in a monastery.

After completing his journey across the room, Aelred placed one of the mugs down on the table in front of Merlin and then slowly eased his frail body into the chair across from him.

"I'm not dead yet, old friend," Aelred said, noticing Merlin's look of concern.

Merlin nodded his head in solemn agreement. "Indeed not. You have at least another decade or two left in you."

Aelred smiled and sipped the steaming liquid. "Liar. Now, what brings the great Merlin the Wise to my humble forest abode?"

Merlin glanced around the spacious cave that had been Aelred's home since the fall of Camelot. Three separate rooms had been carved into the rock at some time in the distant past: the main room where they were sitting, Aelred's bedchamber on the left, and his beloved library on the right. Merlin glanced through the library's open door at the hundreds of dusty books, scrolls, battle flags, and other cherished remembrances neatly stacked on the rows of wooden shelves. Merlin had a similar but larger library of his own. He and Aelred were the keepers of all that remained of the great library from Camelot.

Merlin took a careful sip from the steaming cup in front of him before answering.

"You know why I have come."

"Oh, yes. I did send a message, didn't I? Well, it's nice to know that there's at least one person left who has the respect to answer the call of the Pendragon's Seneschal."

"Actually, there are least two, but I suspect you would rather avoid a visit from Morgana or one of her minions," Merlin said wryly.

"You don't think she . . ." Aelred glanced involuntarily at the door. After a moment, he leaned back in his chair, as if accepting his fate. "My life is of no moment, but the King's records, the histories, if they are lost, then the reign of the Pendragon and the Knights of the Table will truly be gone forever."

Merlin held up a hand in a calming gesture. "Her reach is long, yes, but I don't think she's uncovered my ruse yet or discovered your forest home. You are, after all, five leagues from the nearest soul."

"I pray you are right."

"Now," Merlin gently prodded, "you were speaking of—"

"Of? Oh yes, the message. Did I tell you that the message was carried by one of Cuthburt's birds? He wouldn't have used one if it wasn't a matter of great import. Getting them back to Whitstable is no easy thing. Each one must be returned by ship, and with the thrice cursed seawolves—"

"Yes, Aelred, I know the message came by pigeon. Now, may I please take a look at it?"

"Yes, yes. It's right here," Aelred said as he stood and shuffled over to a stack of dusty books lying on a stone shelf. He hesitated for a moment in front of the shelf and then shuffled over to a second shelf and drew a scroll of parchment out of a grey amphora.

"Ah, yes. Here it is."

Aelred shuffled back to the table and handed Merlin the scroll, mumbling to himself. "There's too many of those to keep track of. I need a page, or maybe two. Why, do you know that I used to have ten pages working for me in the library at Camelot?"

"You had twelve," Merlin said. He opened the scroll and read the message three times. There was a tremor in his hand when he laid it on the table.

"So what do you make of it?" Aelred asked, a skeptical look on his face. "Is it possible after all these years? Sir Percival? Cuthburt could be mistaken."

Merlin stared at the scroll in silence for a long moment, stroking his beard, and then he shook his head.

"No . . . I think not. Cuthburt's tavern is in the center of Whitstable. He keeps track of everyone who comes in and out of that port for me. If Sir Percival came ashore there, he would have seen him, and Cuthburt knows the Knight's face. Remember, he was the stablemaster at Camelot. He saw him almost every day."

"Well, why didn't he just go up to him and ask him what he was about, so we could be sure of the matter?" Aelred said irritably.

"Because," Merlin said with quiet certainty, "Morgana has a watcher there as well."

Aelred's face turned pale, and he made the sign of the cross.

Merlin closed his eyes and clasped his hands in prayer. After several moments, he whispered, "It is as Arthur said it would be."

Aelred's eyes widened, and he quickly sat down in his chair, no longer the infirm old man of a moment earlier.

"What? What did Arthur say? Tell me of this, Merlin," Aelred demanded, tapping a long, bony finger on the table. "I am in my last days, and I would know the secrets that you've been hiding all these years."

Merlin gently rested a hand on his irate friend's forearm. "And so you shall, my friend, and so you shall. However," he said with a smile, "the price will be a mug or two of that fine mead of yours."

Aelred leaned back in his chair and frowned. "And how would you know of that?"

Merlin just looked up at the ceiling, steepling his fingers together.

"Cuthburt!" Aelred said scornfully. "I should have known he couldn't keep a secret. Well, if that's the price I have to pay for your tale, so be it."

The Seneschal leaned over and lovingly drew a pewter tankard out of a nearby cupboard and filled both empty mugs with a golden mead. Merlin noted that Aelred's cup was noticeably fuller than his own.

"There's your payment," Aelred said grudgingly. "I'm sure you shall find it to your liking. The pot of honey that yielded this batch was quite wonderful."

Merlin took a sip and nodded his approval. "It is truly a fine mead. This reminds me of the map room in Camelot's old west tower. Why, we enjoyed many a fine cup of mead there. Yes, we would argue about one matter or another long into the night. Do you remember the night that Arthur came by, and we spoke until near dawn of what the future would bring?"

"Yes, I do remember," Aelred said quietly.

"He was the rarest of men—a just King. I miss him," Merlin said, the memories bringing a new depth of sadness to his voice.

"To Arthur Pendragon," Aelred said solemnly, lifting his mug.

"To Arthur," Merlin repeated, and the two men drank a long draught.

"Now," Aelred said, lowering his voice and leaning forward, "tell me your secret, Merlin."

Merlin put his mug back down on the table and clasped his hands together.

"It happened two or maybe three years before the fall. Arthur had a dream. At first, he ignored it, but when the same dream returned a second and a third time, he told me of it." Merlin stopped for a moment, took a drink from his mug, and nodded in appreciation.

"Well, go on," Aelred said impatiently.

Merlin held up a hand. "Patience. In the dream, Arthur was standing in a verdant glade, deep in the forest. In the center of the glade stood a magnificent oak. Its mighty plume was alit by the golden rays of the morning sun. As Arthur watched, a black vine burst from the ground and wove its way up the tree's mighty trunk, spreading its tendrils to even the smallest of branches. In time, the vine deprived the oak of the sustenance of the sun, slowly killing the forest titan. Arthur's soul was laid low by the death of the beautiful tree, for he knew it was an omen of things to come, and he grieved for his people. But all was not lost. Just before the light of the sun yielded to night, a beautiful woman emerged from the trunk of the dying oak."

Merlin paused for a moment and took another long draught from his mug. Then he examined the finely crafted sigil on the side of the cup, as if seeing it for the first time. Aelred stared at Merlin, his eyes narrowing.

"That is fine mead," Merlin said, "but let me continue . . . the forest—"

"No, we are past the forest, the vine and tree. We are watching the woman," Aelred said in quiet exasperation.

"So we are," Merlin said, nodding. "The woman crossed the glade and stared into Arthur's grief-stricken face for a moment, and then she handed him a sprig from the oak and said, 'Send the Knight who forges the many into an army of one from the shores of Albion. Upon his return, he will replant the oak.'"

"A foretelling," Aelred whispered. "Why didn't you speak of this?"

"It was Arthur's wish that I remain silent."

"But why choose Percival? Why not Tristan, or one of the others?" Aelred asked.

"Arthur . . . we both struggled with that. We had to be sure of our reading of the dream, or all was lost. In the end, we knew. You will remember what Percival did with the men of the border marches."

"Oh yes, I read the reports . . . I still have many of them in my library. My God, that was masterful," Aelred said, striking the table softly with his gnarled fist. "Forging a motley group of dirty, poor, illiterate peasants into an army that marched and fought with Roman precision. That little army thrashed Morgana's raiders so soundly they stopped attacking on that front. I remember what that arrogant fool Lancelot called them—"

"'Percival's band of vermin,'" Merlin interrupted, shaking his head in regret. "He was wrong. We were all wrong not to see that Morgana's foul host was too mighty to be defeated without the help of the common people. I'm not a soldier, Aelred, but even I could see that Arthur and Lancelot placed too much faith in the power of mounted knights. Yet," Merlin said in a heartfelt voice, "for all his arrogance, Lance was magnificent at Camlann."

Aelred nodded. "That he was. He led the charge with Arthur that broke their lines, and he died from his wounds, moments after Arthur."

Aelred took a long draught of mead and gestured sadly to his small library. "And all we have left is the memory of what once was."

Merlin leaned forward and spoke with an intensity that drew a look of surprise from his friend. "I do not believe that. I know it has been years, Aelred, but Arthur's foretelling . . . he believed in it. I believed in it. That's why we sent Percival away on the Grail quest."

"The quest!" Aelred scoffed. "That wasn't a quest, Merlin, it was madness. Sending a Christian knight into the land of the Moors, alone, in search of a cup that disappeared over five centuries ago. What was Arthur thinking?"

"Contrary to what you believe, my friend, the King and I, his humble councilor, possessed at least a thimble's worth of wisdom when we made that decision," Merlin said.

Aelred harrumphed, "Humble, indeed. Well then, enlighten me, if you will. I suspect that's quite a tale as well."

Merlin smiled and leaned back in his chair. "It surely is, but alas, my old throat is dry and my spirit is flagging. Another day perhaps." Aelred's face took on a reddish hue, but Merlin interrupted him before the explosion came. "Perhaps," he said, raising an eyebrow, "another cup of that glorious mead might give me the strength to go on."

"Oh, very well!" Aelred growled. "I suppose I could drink in worse company, although I cannot imagine who that would be."

Merlin smiled as Aelred grudgingly poured him another cup of mead. He took a long drink. After putting his mug down, he silently stared at the scroll on the table. The burden of the decisions he had made so long ago had grown heavier with each year the Knight had remained absent from the land, but now it seemed at long last his prayers had been answered.

"It was," Merlin began hesitantly, "a complicated matter. Arthur knew that Percival wouldn't leave the country without good cause, in the face of Morgana's growing strength, and telling him of the dream was deemed unwise."

"Why? He . . . had . . . a . . . right . . . to . . . know," Aelred said, rapping his knuckles on the table in time with each word.

Merlin raised his hands in frustration. "Know what? That his liege had experienced a mysterious vision, one that foretold the breaking of the Table? Once he heard that, Percival would most certainly have refused to depart. Or worse—the knowledge of what was to come could have led him to follow a different path, undoing the skein that fate had spun for him." He shook his head. "Sadly, the truth is not always the best course in matters of state."

"The skein of fate? That's no way for a Christian to talk. So let me guess," Aelred said, folding his arms across his chest, "you lied to him."

Merlin frowned and waved off the accusation. "That's a rather harsh way of putting it. Let's just say that I devised a plan—a plan Arthur embraced and one that threaded the needle presented. Unfortunately, fate, or Divine Providence, if you will, intervened, as it is wont to do."

"I see," Aelred said in a voice laced with skepticism.

"We . . . Arthur . . . told Percival that the Archbishop of Aquileia, Maximus, was embarking on a quest to find the Holy Grail, and the assistance of a Knight of the Table was requested. Arthur told Percival he had been chosen to serve as one Maximus's guards. Arthur wouldn't countenance the scheme unless Percival had the right to decline the honor, which unfortunately he did. He insisted that he, the least of his knightly brethren, should not be accorded this great honor. Although Arthur tried to persuade him, he was adamant, insisting that his place was at home, fighting Morgana's legions, but—"

"You managed to change his mind on the matter," Aelred said with more than a hint of condemnation.

Merlin nodded reluctantly. "Yes. That I did."

"And what ruse did you employ in that endeavor?"

Merlin looked up at the curved ceiling of the cave, unwilling to bear

Aelred's accusatory stare. "A rather base one, I fear. I told him that he was right. That he was, alas, the least of his brethren, and none of the others could be spared for this quest. I told him that the whole matter could be just a fool's errand, but I also told him there was some evidence that the whereabouts of the cup had been discovered. Still, he was unpersuaded."

"And?"

"Well, I took him aside and told him . . . that Arthur was dying and that—"

"Only a drink from the Grail could save him." Aelred finished, his voice full of scorn. "Merlin, that was indeed a most base deception."

"And, what pray tell, would you have done?" Merlin said, glaring at the other man. "The loathsome deed had to be done, and I, my sophistic friend, was assigned that burden, so I bore it."

"Did Arthur know of this?"

"No, of course not," Merlin said, recovering his composure. "He would never have consented, and it wasn't as much of an untruth as you charge. Arthur was dying."

"What? How can you say that?" Aelred said incredulously.

"You forget, Aelred, I was the first physician to the Roman Emperor in Constantinople, before my exile. It was an ague that I had seen before. The pain started in the King's stomach and grew over time. He hid the affliction well, but by the last battle, he only had months left to live."

"That does not excuse what you did," Aelred said.

"I do not offer excuses," Merlin said, feeling suddenly weary. "Nor do I seek forgiveness. It had to be done."

"Because of a dream that haunted a dying king?"

Merlin stared at his friend in silence for a moment, and then lowered his voice. "Not just the King, Aelred."

"What do you mean?" the man asked.

Merlin remembered waking up bathed in sweat, with the dream burned into his memory. When he opened his eyes, Aelred was staring at him, his brows furrowed. Merlin waved off his concern.

"To quote a friend, 'I am not dead yet.'"

"Thank the Lord. For a moment there, I thought you would die before you finished your tale," Aelred said with a chuckle.

"Such a thoughtful fellow," Merlin said dryly. "To continue . . . after Percival's first refusal, a week passed as I contemplated how to make him accept the 'honor.' During that week, I had the same dream—but in my dream, the oak was already dead, and the surrounding forest was dead as well. In my dream, no one came to offer the promise of life. It was just death. When I awoke, it was just before dawn. I remember looking out upon the forest to the west of the castle and listening to it come to life with the morning light. Then I went to see Sir Percival, and I did what had to be done."

"You are the wisest man I have ever known, Merlin, but sometimes I think you take too much upon yourself."

"You may be right, Aelred the Seneschal, but if I have come to know anything in this life, it is that evil cannot always be defeated through the good and noble, and I would have you know my deed was not as foul, nor the quest as foolhardy as you suppose; at least it was not intended to be. A courier traveled to Aquileia months before Sir Percival's arrival with a message to the Archbishop, Maximus, a man I had met and befriended in my travels. In the message, I told Maximus that Percival was coming and that a Grail quest was to be arranged, in and around Rome only, to satisfy his knightly ardor."

"Another ruse," Aelred said with a scowl.

"You are quite insufferable at times, old man," Merlin said.

"That would make two of us then," the Seneschal retorted.

Merlin made a dismissive gesture with his hand and continued with the tale. "I told Maximus that I would send word when Percival was to be released from his service. Alas, Maximus died when Percival was aship, and his successor, Severus, quite the fool, embraced Percival's quest and sent him to the Holy Land. When I learned of this, I sent a second messenger, but Percival had already left, and the messenger's ship, which followed in pursuit, was lost in a storm."

Aelred's stern glance softened, as did his voice. "And so, for the past ten years, Percival has been scouring the lands of the Moor, looking for the Grail."

"I sought information from every source," Merlin said, staring down at the table, "anyone who might know of his whereabouts, but little came of it. In truth, I do not want to dwell on the travails Sir Percival may have borne in the past decade, for I fear I would be unable to bear the burden of this guilt. All I can do is rejoice at his return."

Aelred's face had grown solemn. "Alas, my friend, the last line of the message suggests otherwise."

"What do you mean?"

He pulled the piece of parchment from his pocket and read the last sentence. "The man who stepped off that ship was Sir Percival, of that I am sure, but he is not the man who left a decade ago.'"

Merlin stared at Aelred for a moment and then looked at the flag hanging from a wall in the library. It was the flag that had been carried in the last charge at Camlann.

"We cannot know what Sir Percival has endured, Aelred," Merlin said, "or how he may have changed during the past decade, but I can tell you this: Once he learns that Arthur is dead, he will seek out his only remaining sovereign."

"Queen Guinevere? How can you be sure?"

Merlin leaned back in his chair. His cup was empty. "I know this," he said, "as surely as I know the sun will rise in the east tomorrow."

CHAPTER 10

THE CAMP OF CYNRIC THE ARCHER

Cynric emerged from the primitive wood and stone shelter, one of the twenty or so structures encircling the small clearing, and looked around at his motley band of followers. Most of the men had escaped with him from Londinium after the city fell to Hengst the Butcher, although a few had joined the band from the local villages. They had never intended to stay there for any length of time.

The plan had been to assemble a force and retake the city, with the help of the people still living within Londinium's walls. Alas, this hope had never come to fruition. Hengst and his brother Ivarr had quickly broken the will of the people in the city and ravaged the surrounding land so thoroughly there were few left to aid their cause.

With Londinium denied to him, Cynric had focused his efforts on barring Hengst from expanding his territory. His men attacked every Norse patrol that strayed too far south and also protected the local villages from Hengst's raiders. It was a hard life. When they were not attacking the Norse, Cynric's small band of men were scratching out a living trapping and hunting, and smuggling the farmers' excess food into Londinium. Still, the archer knew their lot was better than the slavery and starvation being endured by those who had remained in the once proud city.

Cynric's eyes were drawn to the trail at the southern end of the camp by a flash of movement. A moment later, Keil raced into the camp and ran toward him. The archer instinctively grabbed the bow and quiver just inside the door of the shelter and checked the long knife at his hip before turning back to the younger man.

"Sir," Keil gasped, pulling up short five yards away, "it's not an attack, but Tylan said you should come. He said you have to see this."

Cynric hesitated for a moment and then gestured in the direction that Keil had come from. "Lead on." He knew Tylan wouldn't ask him to make haste without a good reason.

Keil started out at a fast jog, and Cynric followed. The sight of Cynric loping through the camp, armed with his long bow, drew the attention of the half-dozen men who had risen with the sun, and by the time Keil had reached the trail, half of the men in camp were in tow.

The trail ran along the edge of the meadow and wound its way up to the top of a hill where a guard was posted at all times. As they neared the crest, Cynric could see Tylan, his short, muscular second-in-command, crouching there with six or seven other men. A row of bushes and thick ferns hid the men from whatever they were staring at on the far side of the bluff.

When Cynric and Keil were thirty paces distant, Tylan turned and raised a finger to his lips, calling for silence, and made a sign directing the approaching men to crouch down like the rest of the watchers. Cynric dropped into a crouch and made his way to his friend's side, followed by the other men. Tylan pointed downward and Cynric stared through a gap in the bushes at two men on the bank of the river below. They were fighting.

For a moment, Cynric was so mesmerized by the combatants' blinding speed and the ferocity of their attacks, he didn't recognize them. Then he realized the combatants were Sir Percival and Capussa. They were naked to the waist, except for the gauntlets covering their hands and forearms, and bathed in sweat, despite the chill in the air. Muscles like ropes of steel writhed in their arms and torsos as they moved back and forth across the sand in a deadly dance, giving life to the web of scars that marred each man's chest, back, and arms.

From the waist down, the men were clad in black cloth breeches cut short just above the knees, and their feet were shod with heavy sandals laced to the calf. Each man wielded a practice sword, a wooden weapon precisely leaded to have the weight and feel of a steel sword. As

Cynric watched, the Numidian attacked Percival and called out a series of commands in a language the archer had never heard before. With each command, Percival would execute a counterattack or defensive maneuver. Although Cynric had been a soldier for two decades, most of the attacks and defenses were unknown to him, and he had never seen two foes move with such speed and precision.

As the battle raged on without respite, Cynric expected one or both men to collapse from exhaustion, but neither man slowed nor yielded ground to the other for more than an instant. The only concession they afforded themselves was a guttural grunt of pain after a rare blow was landed. Finally, Capussa called out a command, and both men stepped back, sheathed their swords, and bowed to one another.

Percival turned, took off his sword belt, laid it on a nearby rock, and walked into the river, exposing his back to the men on the ridge. Cynric heard Keil's intake of breath and glanced over at the younger man. He was making the sign of the cross.

The archer tapped Tylan on the shoulder and gestured for the men on the bluff to follow him back down the hill. Tylan passed the signal down the line, and the men quietly eased their way down the slope. When they reached the bottom of the hill, Keil ran up alongside Cynric.

"Sir," Keil said in a hoarse voice, "did you see his back? I've never seen . . . what could have done that?"

Cynric walked in silence for a moment toward the camp, and then he looked over at the visibly shaken younger man. "He was flogged with something . . . something terrible, many times," he said, an undercurrent of anger in his voice.

Tylan nodded, his face grim. "The scars on their chests and arms, those I recognize as the work of a sword and a spear, but that set of three marks on Percival's chest and on the African's right arm, I've never—"

"A trident," Cynric said quietly.

Tylan eyes widened. "Heard of those, but I've never seen one."

Keil slowed and walked behind the two other men, apparently lost in his own thoughts. As they neared a bend in the trail, he ran forward and caught up with Cynric.

"Sir, is that how they fought? Is that how the Knights of the Round Table fought?" he asked.

Cynric stopped and looked back up the hill for a moment before turning to the younger man, his face grim. "No, Keil, they didn't fight like that. I've never seen anyone fight like that in my life." After a final glance back up the hill, Cynric turned and started back toward the camp. Tylan kept pace with him.

"Before they started in with the swords," Tylan said, "the two of them ran up and down that hill, over and over again. Then they spent nearly an hour doing all sorts of other things—lifting heavy rocks from the stream, pushing up off the ground with their arms. Each one squatted up and down with the other one on his back more times than I could count! It's like . . . well this is what they do all the time." Tylan was silent for a moment.

"Who does that?"

"Someone who fights for a living," Cynric answered curtly.

Tylan slowly shook his head, a frown on this face.

"Cynric, I'm a blacksmith, not a soldier, but I have made shields, swords, axes, and knives for knights and other men of the sword for two decades. When you work such a trade . . . over time, you get to know what they want and how they live and train. Well, I can tell you, I have never seen anyone train like that."

Cynric glanced over his shoulder at Keil. The young man had veered off the trail to stalk a rabbit that had crossed their path a moment earlier.

Tylan's frown deepened. "I suppose," he said hesitantly, "what I'm trying to find out is how well do you know Sir Percival? Is he going to join us or fight for someone else? I just would like to know," Tylan said, looking back toward the bluff.

"So would I," Cynric said.

"And so?"

Cynric smiled at his friend's persistence.

"And so," Tylan went on, "maybe we can have a word with them once they are done trying to kill each other."

"We?" Cynric questioned, raising an eyebrow.

"Well," Tylan said with a rare smile, "you do know him."

"No, Tylan," Cynric said quietly, glancing over at his friend. "I do not know this man. I don't think anyone alive truly knows him other than Capussa. But we shall have a talk when he returns to camp."

* * *

AN HOUR LATER, Cynric watched Percival and Capussa lead their horses into the camp. Cynric stood, walked over to the two men, and nodded respectfully.

"Sir Percival, Capussa, may I offer you food and drink?"

"Thank you, Cynric," Percival answered, "but we have already broken our fast. We would not burden you with our needs, but, if you have a moment, my companion and I would have a word with you."

Cynric nodded and gestured to a giant stump someone had hewn into a primitive table. Two long benches were drawn up on either side of the table.

"Please, you are welcome at my table. It is not much, but it serves my needs."

"Why, it is a table fit for a king, friend," Capussa said with smile. "Lead on."

Cynric hesitated. "Would it be acceptable if Tylan joins us? He's the master-of-arms for our little band."

"We would welcome his company," Percival said.

Cynric gestured to Tylan, waiting a short distance away, and the four men sat down at the crude table. Tylan nodded to the two men as he sat down.

Percival looked across the table at Cynric. "Cynric the Archer, I have one last duty that I must honor before my service to the Pendragon is at an end. I must find the Queen and tell her of my quest. If you can tell me of her whereabouts and the safest road to this place, I would be in your debt."

Cynric was silent. He had feared this moment would come. The moment when he would be forced to tell the last surviving Knight of the Round Table that all he had known and loved was gone, washed away by a tide of violence, misery, and death.

"That road, Sir Percival," Cynric said hesitantly, "will be a most treacherous one."

Percival nodded. "That may be, but it is one I must travel."

"Sir, the Pendragon is long dead and the Table is gone. The land . . . is broken," Cynric said, his eyes fixed on the table in front of him.

"I know of the King's death, Cynric," the Knight said patiently. "That is why I must give my report to the Queen."

There was a long silence.

Percival leaned forward, his hands clasped in front of him. "Please. Tell me she yet lives," he said.

Cynric looked up and nodded. "Yes, the Queen is still alive, thank the Almighty, but the Kingdom, you must understand . . . all that we . . . all that you knew, it is gone."

"Now," Cynric said with a mixture of anger, despair, and guilt, "Albion is a place where death waits behind every tree and around every bend in the road."

"Cynric," Percival said in a voice filled with regret, "I was a Knight of the Table. If anyone should bear a measure of guilt for the Pendragon's fall, it is I, not you. I was not here in the King's hour of need."

There was a long silence as Cynric remembered what once had been and what had been lost. From the look on the Knight's face, he too was remembering a time that was now gone.

"My friends, let me show you something," Capussa said gently as he drew three small coins from a pocket in his jerkin. He placed the coins on the table and pointed to a small coin with a reddish hue.

"The home of my people lies outside the ruins of a great city by the sea that separates my land from the land of the Romans. This coin was forged by the kings of the great empire that first seized that ground from my people and built the great city."

Then the Numidian's finger lightly touched a second, larger coin. "This one was forged by those who conquered this great empire and took the city for themselves. This last coin," Capussa said, his finger moving to the largest and brightest of the coins, "is the work of the Romans. In their time of power, they razed the great city to the ground, and now, the City of Rome labors under the heel of its own conqueror. You see, great kingdoms rise and fall; that is the way of it. All that we—" Capussa said, gesturing to the men and women in the camp, "—can do is bear our burdens each day with honor and thank the gods for what little we have."

Tylan nodded and said gruffly, "I think you have the right of it. We did what we could."

Cynric nodded to Capussa. "Your words are kind, my friend." Then he turned to Percival. "I will tell what I can, Sir Percival. It is little enough."

The archer stood and walked over to a stick lying next to a patch of dirt by the table and quickly drew a crude map. When he finished, he pointed to a small circle at the top of the map.

"This is to the northwest. It's Queen Guinevere's ancestral land. An old monk, a friend, told me she took refuge there after the fall, in an abbey."

Cynric then moved the point of the stick to a second line. "This is the road between Caer Ceint and Londinium. Our camp is here, about three or four day's travel south of Londinium," he said, resting the point on a circle.

Percival interrupted, his brow furrowed, "Why will it take so long? I can recall covering the entire distance between the port and Londinium in four days, and Capussa and I have already been on the road for two."

"The road isn't safe now," Tylan said, shaking his head. "You should count yourself lucky that you didn't meet Korth and his foul band of brigands on the way here."

Capussa looked over at Tylan and drew a line with his finger from his right temple to his jawline. "Would this Korth have a scar that runs thus?"

"Aye, that's Korth," Tylan said.

"We did 'meet' this man, as you say," Capussa said with a small smile. "He will not trouble anyone ever again."

A slow smile came to Tylan's face. "That was a good day's work."

Capussa nodded. "Indeed it was."

Cynric glanced over at the Numidian, remembering the ferocity of the battle by the river an hour earlier. He suspected Korth was not the only brigand lying dead on the road to Caer Ceint.

Cynric turned back to the map and pointed to the circle designating Londinium.

"Londinium and its surroundings are controlled by Hengst, a Norse chieftain, and his foul raiders. Most travelers making their way past the city stay off the road. They use the forest paths to get around it. There are guides that make a living helping people stay clear of the raiders; some are honest, some not. There are two forest paths. We will use this path," he said, pointing to an arc on the south side of the Tamesis River. "It is a longer journey, but it is usually safer."

Percival frowned. "I would not burden you or any of your people with this journey."

"You won't make it without a guide," Cynric said, shaking his head, "and Tylan and I have business there. We live off the forest, but we get help from the local farmers. In return for food, we smuggle their grain and vegetables into Londinium and barter for the goods they need in return. Since food is short in the city, the people pay well for what we bring."

"I'm in your debt, Archer."

"No, sir, I am in yours," Cynric said quietly, remembering for an instant the battle on the Aelius Bridge in what seemed like a different lifetime.

"When would you leave on this journey?" Tylan asked.

"As soon as you are able," Percival said as he stood up.

Cynric turned to Tylan. "What say you?"

Tylan shrugged. "The grain hut is near full. So, tomorrow is as good a day as any."

The archer nodded. "Then tomorrow it is. We should leave by first light."

CHAPTER 11

MORGANA'S DOMAIN

organa idly caressed the haft of the bejeweled knife resting on the table in front of her before spinning it again with a tap of her finger. When the knife came to rest, the tip of the blade was pointing at the chair across from her—the chair awaiting Ivarr the Red. She smiled and then lifted the hem of her ankle-length white tunic and restored the blade to the sheath on her leg. The hidden knife violated the rules of the parley, but she was untroubled by the risk. Her transgression would only be discovered if it became necessary to slit Ivarr's throat, and if it came to that, the knife could mean the difference between life and death.

She scanned the broad, open field encircling the table in satisfaction. Lord Aeron had chosen a strategically good site for the parley with the Norsemen. The ground offered both parties a clear view of the other's approach, making any attempted ambush a difficult and bloody choice.

A movement on left side of the field drew her attention, and a moment later, Lord Aeron and six other riders emerged from the forest line, returning from their second patrol of the morning. As she watched the knight cross the field toward her, clad in his blackened armor and helmet, she once again found herself mystified by the knight's honesty. The noble fool despised her, and yet, he dutifully honored every promise she had extracted from him, even his promise to keep her safe.

"One day, I will ask your beloved Guinevere what magic she used to ensorcell you. Then I will take it for myself, along with her life," Morgana whispered.

When the riders were within fifty paces of the table, Lord Aeron gestured for the rest of the soldiers to join the line of mounted men waiting fifty paces behind her. Then he continued forward alone, bringing his horse to a halt five paces from the table.

"He comes," the knight said, gesturing to the forest wall to the south.

"And how many men does he bring with him?" Morgana asked, raising an eyebrow.

"Fifty men accompany him, as agreed, but there is a second column with at least twice that many men following not far behind."

Morgana smiled at the anger in Lord Aeron's voice. "But of course. You didn't expect Ivarr to honor the rules of this parley, did you, Lord Aeron?"

Lord Aeron rode his horse a step closer to the table. "You will not find it amusing if the Norseman attacks with that many—"

"He won't," Morgana interrupted, waving his retort away with a flick of her hand. "Ivarr is not Hengst. Yes, his thirst for gold and power is equally insatiable, but Ivarr is a clever man, a man who seeks power in his own right. He will wait to hear what I have to offer before he reaches for his sword."

"And what if your words are not to his liking?" Lord Aeron asked coldly.

"Why then, I have you to protect me," Morgana said, a quiet threat in her voice. The sound of a horse pounding across the field stilled Lord Aeron's reply. He wheeled his horse to face the rider and, after a moment's hesitation, galloped to meet him. Morgana recognized the man as one of the scouts.

Seneas walked over to Morgana and refilled the silver goblet in front of her with more wine. Morgana glanced up at the old man's face and said coldly, "Do you have something to say, Seneas?"

The old man hesitated and then spoke in a low voice. "Princess, is it wise to goad him so? If we are attacked, your life is in his hands. Surely, he must see that your death will—"

"Release him from his bondage?" Morgana interrupted with a cruel laugh. "It might, but at a price he will never pay. You see, Lord Aeron knows that his precious Queen will be killed by one of my spies within the abbey upon my passing."

Morgana was quiet for a moment as she watched the knight talking with the scout. Then she shook her head and spoke in a tone laced in scorn and a touch of regret.

"In the end . . . that's not why he will protect me from the Norse dogs. You see, Seneas, his precious honor wouldn't let him do anything else. Alas, if I had a thousand such fools to manipulate, I would wear the purple in Constantinople."

Before Seneas could reply, Lord Aeron wheeled his horse and rode toward the table at a full gallop, pulling up short a few feet away. As if sensing Lord Aeron's tension, his giant black steed strained at the firm hand holding the reins.

"The Norseman approaches with fifty riders, but the second column waits just behind the tree line. We cannot withstand an attack from that many men," Lord Aeron said urgently.

Morgana stared at the knight for a moment, swirling the wine in her silver goblet, and then said with a smile, "Be at ease, Lord Aeron. Cinioch and his band of Picts await just behind that hillock over there. They will join your line if we are attacked."

The muscles in Lord Aeron's jaw visibly tightened. Morgana had expected the reaction. The Pict and his band had raided a farmstead within the borders of her domain, killing the farmer and selling the remainder of his family into slavery. In the midst of Lord Aeron's preparation for a retributive attack on the Pict war leader, Morgana had secretly negotiated a pact with the raider. In return for a monthly stipend of silver, the Pict and his band had agreed to plunder the lands claimed by Hengst, instead of those within her control.

"I know you think I should have let you put the Pict and his band of reavers to the sword," Morgana said, brushing off the rebuke in his eyes, "but had I done so, they would not be here to meet your needs today. Using one group of barbarians to counter another is a very old and wise Roman tradition, Lord Aeron. Their blood is cheap. Now, stop scowling at me and arrange your men so that we can provide a proper welcome for our guest."

The knight turned to the man in the center of the line of mounted men behind him and gave a terse order. "Finn, half of the men to the right, there, half to the left, there."

The line of horsemen divided and flanked either side of the table. When the movement was complete, Lord Aeron turned to Morgana and said in a quiet voice that only she could hear, "I know of your knife, Morgana. Ivarr the Red will know of it as well. If this matter does not go well, do not engage him. Throw yourself to the ground. I will take the Norseman with a throw of my lance."

Then he turned his horse without another word and rode to a position thirty paces in front of the table and waited for the approaching Norseman.

Moments later, a column of fifty mounted Norse warriors emerged from the forest and advanced across the open field. Morgana watched their approach with interest, but her eyes were drawn to the tree line, where the larger force of warriors was hiding. Her gaze came to rest upon the knight standing between her and the men approaching. Seneas had been right, if an attack was made, her life would be in the hands of Lord Aeron.

The Norseman riding the lead horse was a tall, rangy man with sunken cheeks and a long nose that looked as if it had been broken several times, giving him a hard, cruel look. Unlike the men riding behind him, whose hair fell to their shoulders, the lead warrior's reddish-brown hair was cropped short, and he wasn't wearing a helmet. His red woolen shirt was sleeveless, revealing arms with iron-hard muscles that were marred by a patchwork of scars.

The Norseman stopped at the white flag that stood a hundred paces from the table, his eyes moving from Lord Aeron to the soldiers lined up on either side of the table and finally to Morgana. She returned the Norseman's stare for a moment and then called to Lord Aeron.

"Have your men fall back to the flag."

"Finn!" Lord Aeron called out, without taking his eyes off the line of Norsemen in front of him. "Move the line in groups of ten from the outside in."

Ten men on the end of each line wheeled and rode back to the white flag, one hundred paces behind the table, and formed a new line. When the entire line of horsemen had moved to the new position, Ivarr dismounted, along with a second Norseman. The other man was as tall as Ivarr but broader in the shoulders and neck, and his long, black hair was streaked with grey. The older Norseman scanned the soldiers behind the table and the surrounding forest for a moment and then said something to Ivarr. The Norse leader nodded, and the two men walked toward the table, their eyes wary.

Lord Aeron waited until the two had covered half the distance to the table before he rode his horse around behind it, dismounted, and took up a position behind Morgana's chair.

Ivarr the Red stopped just behind the chair on his side of the table and nodded to Morgana.

"May I join your table, Roman?" he said, his voice a deep rasp.

"Sit. My table is yours this day," Morgana answered solemnly.

Ivarr eased into the chair across from her, his eyes moving from Morgana to Lord Aeron.

"The road from Londinium is a long one. May I have Seneas pour us some mead?" Morgana said, gesturing to the old Greek servant.

Although the expression on the Norseman's face didn't change, Morgana had anticipated his suspicion. He was well aware that she was not only skilled in the use of poisons, but had used the noxious weapon to kill at least two of the Knights of the Table.

The ghost of a smile crossed Morgana's face, and she turned to Seneas.

"Seneas, bring two cups of mead, and place them in front of me."

Seneas filled two silver mugs and placed them in front of Morgana. She took an ample drink from each cup and then pushed the two mugs into the center of the table.

"We fought side by side against the Pendragon, Ivarr the Red. You have nothing to fear at my table."

The Norseman's reaction was quick and laced with a threat.

"I fear nothing, Roman."

Morgana leaned forward, picked up one of the cups, and drank deeply, her eyes locked on those of the Norseman. Then she took a long drink from the second cup.

"Of course you don't, Ivarr," Morgana said as she set down the second cup and pushed it across the table to him.

"Now, let us discuss the matter of our borders."

The Norseman grasped the cup with a scarred hand and took a long draught. After lowering the cup, he nodded appreciatively.

"A good mead. Talk."

"We will, but we shall talk alone," Morgana answered and turned to Lord Aeron and Seneas.

"You will step back fifteen full paces."

The two men hesitated, and then both moved backward.

Ivarr stared at Morgana for a moment and then, without turning, spoke in his own language to the man behind him. The warrior nodded and also took fifteen paces back.

Morgana leaned forward and spoke in a quiet voice as cold and hard as steel.

"I will speak plainly, Norseman. Your brother's ravages have driven the farmers and the shepherds and their flocks from the lands around Londinium, so the people are starving. I know Hengst could care less if the people die—he may even enjoy it—but now hunger's bite has begun to reach his soldiers, and that is not something they will abide. So, in desperation, the fool seeks to take from my—"

"You go too far, Roman," Ivarr growled, his eyes blazing.

Morgana leaned back in her chair and stared at the Norseman in silence for a moment and then leaned forward again and spoke in a voice devoid of emotion. "Do I? You know the truth of what I say. Having turned his own holdings into a wasteland, he seeks to feed his wolves from the fruit of my lands."

Ivarr put his forearms on the table and leaned forward, putting his face within two feet of Morgana's.

"And what of it? If Hengst wants your land, he—"

"Could take nothing," Morgana finished coldly, unmoved by the Norseman's attempt to intimidate her. "I know of your plight, Norseman. In the last year, Hengst has lost more than half of his men, and those who remain are living on half rations. Many have not been paid for months. Such men are for sale, and I, Ivarr, have the money to buy them."

Morgana hesitated for a moment and leisurely took a drink of mead. For a moment, she feared she had overplayed her hand, but the rage in the Norseman's eyes remained under control.

When she continued, her tone was softer, and her words were laced with flattery.

"Unlike your brother, you are a wise man. You know that it's just a matter of time before Hengst loses all that you both have bled to gain. But . . . there is an alternative, one that offers Ivarr the Red the power and wealth he has been so unjustly denied."

The rage in Ivarr's eyes ebbed as she spoke. When she finished, the Norseman leaned back in his chair for a moment and looked at her impassively, weighing what she had said. "I listen, Roman," he said with a scowl.

As Morgana watched the seed of avarice grow within the Norseman, she knew the game was hers. Her people had been bribing and manipulating barbarians for over six centuries, and the outcome was always the same—greed always triumphed over loyalty and, in this case, familial bonds. Ivarr could be bought. All that remained was the price.

"Your men are hungry, including the hundred or so that you have hidden in the forest."

Ivarr's jaw muscle tightened, but his expression didn't change.

Morgana leaned forward and spoke in a quiet, conspiratorial tone.

"There is a meadow at the foot of that hill to the southeast. I left enough food and fodder there to feed your men for a week. There is a compartment built into the bottom of the third wagon. You cannot see it unless you crawl beneath it. There, you will find a bag of silver coins."

"Silver?" the Norseman questioned, his voice lowering as well.

"Silver," Morgana answered firmly. "A wise man would dole that money out to his most loyal men and not disclose its existence to . . . others. A week hence, or thereabouts, Hengst will go to sleep, and he will not awake. None will know the cause, and most will celebrate his death. You, Ivarr the Red, will then be the Lord of Londinium. Once you are in control, you must do what is necessary to restore the wealth of the land. You must—"

"I know what must be done, Roman," the Norseman interrupted, waving off her advice. "But I will need time. It will take a season or two. In the meantime—"

"In the meantime, you will receive the grain and silver you need to pay your men."

The Norseman stared at Morgana for a moment and then leaned forward again, suspicion in his eyes. "And what does the empire of the East Romans want in return?"

Morgana smiled. "Why, peace and friendship, what we have always sought."

Ivarr's eyes widened, and then he threw his head back and roared with laughter. Morgana's smile widened.

"Peace! Yes, you have brought so much of that to this island, Roman, I dare say Odin himself is laughing this morning," the Norseman said scornfully.

"Peace, Ivarr the Red, is a child of the sword," Morgana said coolly, her smile vanishing.

For a moment, the Norseman stared at her and then clasped his calloused and scarred hands together, inches from her own. "Tell me, Roman Princess, what you truly seek from Ivarr the Red, in return for your . . . gifts?"

Morgana lifted her cup of mead and took a sip, savoring it for a moment, before answering. "I want the raids to cease."

"Agreed. What else?"

"I am looking for a man," Morgana said, in a tone suggesting the matter was of little importance. "A man of the empire. He is about my height and nearing his sixtieth year, a man of learning. If you find such a man, I will pay you well if he is brought to me alive."

The Norseman made a dismissive gesture with his hand. "There are few enough of your kind in this land. If one is found . . . you will be told."

Morgana did not react to the man's answer, but she knew what he was saying. She would have to pay for Melitas if they found him. The price was a matter for another day.

She set her cup down on the table and nodded to the Norseman.

"Then we are agreed. It would seem, Ivarr the Red, that our meeting is at an end."

Ivarr stood up and nodded solemnly. "So it is."

As the Norseman turned to leave, Morgana said in a veiled tone, "There is one more matter . . . a small thing. I have heard that a Knight of the Table, Sir Percival, may be returning to this land from the east. He may already be here. Have you heard any tidings of this?"

"The Knights of Pendragon's Table," Ivarr said with a cruel smile, "are all dead. The last was fool enough to challenge Hengst to battle. His rotting body hangs on the east wall of the tournament field. I will introduce you to this great man when you come for a visit." Ivarr chuckled at his own joke, and then he turned and strode away.

As Morgana watched the Norseman mount his horse and ride south with his men, she leaned her chin upon her palms, wondering if she should order the spy within his camp to poison both Hengst and Ivarr. After a moment, she rejected the thought. She could control Ivarr as long as he needed her coin.

CHAPTER 12

THE ROAD TO LONDINIUM

apussa leaned back against the wall of the cave, enjoying the warmth of the fire burning two steps away. The cavern was located in the hills above a small village, a day's ride south of Londinium. Thankfully, the cave's expansive interior was large enough to shelter all fourteen men in the party, as well as their horses, from the intermittent rain that had fallen during much of the day.

Cynric and Percival had left to climb a nearby hill to look for campfires indicating the nearby presence of brigands or a Norse patrol, leaving Capussa alone with Tylan, Keil, and the other nine from Cynric's band. The Numidian was tired from the day's ride, but he sensed the men on the other side of the fire wanted to ask him something. He watched with a smile as a short whispered argument ensued between the men, and the group reached a decision. A moment later, a rotund fellow wearing an oversize traveling cloak, with more than its share of rips and holes, stood up and walked toward him.

The Numidian had never spoken to the man, but they had traveled together for the past two days, and he knew his name was Bray. He also knew the man was affable, drank liberally from a wineskin throughout the day, and was inclined to hoard more than his share of the company's mead. Earlier in the day, Cynric had sent Bray into the local village to trade a bag of wool for a sack of hard bread and smoked venison, supplying the company with the evening's meal. Although Bray had turned over most his bounty, he had attempted, unsuccessfully, to keep a large jug of mead to himself.

After reinforcing his courage with another draught from his wineskin,

Bray stopped a respectful distance of away and said, "Sir, might I sit down and ask after a matter or two?"

"Sit, my friend, and ask what you will," Capussa said, gesturing to a nearby log.

Bray sat down on the log and, after a moment's hesitation, said, "I'd . . . well, we'd all would know some things. We watched you and Sir Percival practicing by the river the other morning, and we'd like to know where you learned to fight like that. We've never seen the like. And, the two of you have enough scars for ten men . . . and those scars on Sir Percival's back . . . how, I mean, what—"

"That was the work of a scourge," Capussa said in a quiet voice. When he spoke, the men on the other side leaned forward to hear his words. He waved them over.

"Come, friends, draw near. I will tell you a tale, one that is true, mind you. This is a story you will tell your children, and one that they will tell theirs as well."

He waited until the men walked over and joined Bray on the log, or found a comfortable rock to sit on. Keil sat on the rock closest to the Numidian, drawing a frown from Tylan.

When the men were seated, Capussa stared into the fire for a moment, as if returning to a distant place, and then began to speak.

"Sir Percival and I were the prisoners of a powerful Moorish lord in the ancient City of Syene, in the land of Egypt. It is a cruel place—a sea of sand, where the days are like fire and the nights are like ice. But, Syene is also a place of great wealth, for the nearby mines yield beautiful gems, and traders from the southern peoples come there to sell their wares to the Moors.

"There is an evil emir in Syene called Khalid El-Hashem, who found a way, a terrible way, to extract some of the great wealth that flowed through Syene for himself. He restored an old Roman arena outside the city, and there . . . there he holds the most celebrated gladiatorial games in all the land. People would come from near and far to see men fight to the death, to see them die in agony." Capussa paused, remembering for a fleeting instant the acrid taste of blood and dust in his mouth, the screams of agony, and the hated roar of the crowd. Then he continued.

"At first, Khalid grew rich from this slaughter, but over time, interest began to wane. So Khalid, like the Romans before him, had to bring new and different blood to the games in order to draw the crowds. That, my friends, is why he paid a small fortune to enslave Sir Percival, who was serving a one-year sentence of imprisonment."

"Sir Percival? Why was he a prisoner, if I may ask, sir?" Keil burst out in a rush.

"That is a story for another night, my young friend, but I will tell you this: Sir Percival did no wrong. A one-year jail term was unjustly imposed upon the son of Jacob the Healer, a man from the City of Alexandria. Jacob had saved Sir Percival's life, and so when this injustice was imposed upon Jacob's only son, Sir Percival served the prison term in his place."

"Jacob saved the Knight's life?" Bray interjected.

Capussa nodded. "Sir Percival was traveling across a great desert with a caravan on the way to the City of Alexandria, in Egypt. He had been told there were men of wisdom and learning there . . . men who might know the whereabouts of the Holy Grail."

The eyes of the men watching widened, and Keil whispered, "The Grail!"

"When the caravan was attacked," Capussa continued, as if there had been no interruption, "most of the men guarding the travelers fled, leaving Sir Percival and several other men to fight off the brigands. The caravan was saved, but Sir Percival had been sorely wounded in the fight. When the caravan arrived in Alexandria, the Knight was brought to Jacob, a man with great skill in the healing arts. This man saved his life, and in time, he and Sir Percival became friends. When Jacob's son was falsely accused and convicted of stealing, by a Moor of wealth and power in the city, the Knight volunteered to serve in his place. And so it was that my friend came to fight as a gladiator, in the arena of Khalid El-Hashem."

"And you, sir, why were you there?" Keil asked.

Capussa forestalled Tylan's growl of irritation with a smile, and turned to Keil. "I, my inquisitive friend, fought on the losing side of a border war to the south of Syene and lacked the gold to ransom my freedom from the victor. Khalid offered to buy my freedom if I served as a gladiator in his arena for a year. Since the alternative was a decade of slave labor in the mines, I accepted. As fate would have it, I was tasked with fighting alongside a Christian knight from a faraway land called Albion."

Bray took a long draught from his wineskin and offered a drink to Capussa, who declined. After a nudge from Tylan, Bray reluctantly passed the skin around to the rest of the men.

"Sir, the wounds on Sir Percival's back—why . . . why was he scourged?" Keil asked.

Tylan leaned forward and glared at Keil. "He might get to that, Keil, if ye'd stop badgering him."

"Aye, sir," Keil said sheepishly.

Capussa hid a smile and then continued. "Now, Khalid paid a handsome sum for Percival in the belief that people would come in droves to see a Christian Knight from a distant land fight in his arena, but it was not to be. The Knight had agreed to serve a prison term. He had not agreed to draw his sword and kill for the pleasure of others, and so, he refused to fight. This enraged Khalid, and he had Percival scourged and tortured in an attempt to force him to yield to his will, but he would not."

When Capussa hesitated for a moment, Keil sprang up and burst out, "So what happened?"

Tylan started to stand up, "Why, if I have to knock—"

Capussa smiled and raised a conciliating hand before turning to Keil. "One night, my anxious young friend, Khalid was having dinner with a clever Venetian trader. He told the Venetian of his troubles with the unyielding Christian Knight, who served the Round Table. The trader told Khalid he had heard of these Knights, and for them, honor was everything. Such a man would not fight for the pleasure of others, but he would, the trader suggested, fight with all his heart to protect an innocent. And so it came to pass that Khalid was given a weapon more potent than pain to use against the Knight."

Capussa hesitated for a moment, drew out the silver flask from his cloak, took a measured sip, and then closed his eyes in appreciation as the fiery liquid coursed down his throat.

"Yes, now where were we?"

"Sir Percival, he, he—" Keil said quickly.

"Ah, yes," Capussa said, smiling at the younger man. "And so it came to pass that one day, Sir Percival found himself in the arena with his sword at his feet, standing in front of a young woman chained to a post anchored deep within the earth. As the Knight stood listening to the howling crowd, a boy ran over and dropped a parchment at his feet from Khalid El-Hashem. The message on the parchment said, 'If you keep her alive for three days, I will set her free. Otherwise, they shall have her.' A moment later, two brigands entered the far end of the arena, one carrying a sword, the second a spear, and they attacked the Knight.

"The brigands were killed, as were those who drew their swords against Sir Percival on the next two days. At the end of the third day, a day where the Knight was forced to fight two separate battles, Khalid honored his word and set the woman free in a grand ceremony. The crowd, which had grown with each passing day, roared their approval. Khalid was well pleased, for he could all but taste the gold he would make from Percival's sweat and blood.

"The very next day, the Moor ordered Batukhan, a fierce warrior from the other side of the world, and myself, to hone the Knight's fighting skills. He wanted Sir Percival to be as invincible as a man can be, for the Moor did not want to lose his prize gladiator to an errant sword stroke. And so we taught the Knight fighting skills unknown to him, and we practiced those skills over and over again, until he had mastered them."

"Did you fight in the arena, sir?" Keil asked when Capussa hesitated just long enough to take another drink from his flask.

"Indeed. Whenever the Knight faced a pair of challengers, either I or Batukhan would fight beside him, and after Batukhan was killed, I was the only one Khalid would trust by the Knight's side."

The Numidian was silent for a moment, and then he stood up and nodded to the enraptured group of men. "And that, my friends, is the end of tonight's tale. Good night to all."

As Capussa laid down on his bedroll, Percival and Cynric walked into the cavern. The men in the camp stood up as one and stared at Sir Percival, as if seeing him for the first time.

Cynric glanced over at Keil and said, "What is it, lad? You look as though you've seen a ghost."

Capussa smiled as he rolled over and closed his eyes.

CHAPTER 13

PEN DINAS, WALES

uinevere walked down the narrow path leading from the stone tower at the top of the hill to the low stone wall encircling the crest. The old Roman fort had been used as a watchtower and a royal way station during Arthur's reign, and she had stayed there for a week during the summer before her wedding.

She stopped at the wall for a moment and looked out at the grey sea crashing against the rocks far below. The cold wind whipped her golden locks and lifted the hem of her dark blue cloak, bringing back a wave of memories that now seemed so distant as to be mere fairy tales.

The cry of a gull winging its way over the hill drew the Queen back to the present, and she continued walking down the overgrown stone path that ran alongside the wall. She stopped when she was aligned with a large, flat rock farther up the hill. In another life, a wooden bench carved from a single oak tree had graced the slope in front of the rock, allowing a couple to sit and watch the sun set over the ocean beyond.

The bench was no longer there. She glanced at the slightly discolored stone in the middle of the nearby wall and said a prayer of thanks to the younger woman who had used the rock on the hill as the marker for the ring of gold hidden in the wall, instead of the wooden bench.

Guinevere took one last look at the hiding place and walked up to the peak of the hill. From there, she could see the horse trail that led from the fortress to the small but once thriving town by the sea, a half league to the north. For a moment, she could almost see the small mounted party of yesteryear: her younger self, a carefree young woman with flowing golden tresses and a ready smile, accompanied by a younger, but still dour, Sister Aranwen, and four of Arthur's most trusted retainers.

When the vision faded, she was left standing on the overgrown trail, staring at the ruins of a town that had long since been burned to the ground by the seawolves. Guinevere closed her eyes and spoke in the softest whisper.

"Had the crown been placed on the head of another woman, one who was stronger and wiser, would the realm have survived? God forgive me if that is so."

"Milady?"

Guinevere quickly wiped away the tear rolling down her cheek and turned to look up the slope at her younger companion. She was standing on the rock that marked the location of her hidden keepsake in the wall behind the Queen.

"Yes, Cadwyn?"

"It's Captain Potter. He's waiting in the sacristy of the old chapel. Torn and his men cleaned it up as best they could, but it's not—"

"We shall make do."

"Milady, I know it is presumptuous, but may I join you?"

"Of course, Cadwyn. I know you are as interested in this mystery as I, and so is Sister Aranwen, although she tries to hide it. So have her join us as well. I will be with you in a moment."

"Thank you, Milady. I shall fetch her right away."

Guinevere took one last look at the sea and started up the hill to the small stone chapel behind the circular stone tower. She noted that Torn, and the eight men who'd accompanied her on the two-day ride from the abbey, were patrolling the perimeter of the hilltop. Although Torn had expressed concern about the risk posed by local brigands or by a Norse raid, Guinevere was confident the huntsman and his bowmen could protect them.

After removing her cloak, Guinevere walked into the sacristy, followed by Cadwyn and Sister Aranwen. Like the chapel, the modest stone room was old and musty, having been abandoned years earlier. However, the subdued fire burning in the hearth lessened its dreary appearance. A small, wiry man with a full head of silver hair was sitting in a rough-hewn chair on one side of the small wooden table that Torn and his men had placed next to the hearth. Three other chairs were arranged on the other side.

When the man at the table realized he was no longer alone, he quickly stood and then dropped to one knee.

"Forgive me, Your Highness. I didn't see you. The light is dim and my eyes are not—"

"Rise, good Captain," Guinevere said with a smile as she approached the kneeling man. "You have no reason to apologize. It is I who owe you a debt of gratitude for making such a long journey in dangerous times."

"I would have come many times that distance, Your Highness, had you desired thus," Potter said, his head bowed.

"You are too kind. Now please, rise and meet Lady Cadwyn and Sister Aranwen, my retainers and dearest friends."

Potter rose to his feet, hesitated a moment, and then bowed to the two women. "I am honored, gentle ladies."

Cadwyn and Sister Aranwen nodded politely, and Guinevere gestured to the table.

"Please, Captain Potter, sit, and let us talk of your recent voyage."

Potter bowed again and backed up to his chair, only sitting after the three women were seated. For a moment, Potter was silent and then with a nod, began.

"Yes, yes, the voyage. The Mandragon is my ship, Your Highness, and a good ship she is. The crew and I have been sailing between the lands of the Franks and the Saxons and our own blessed island for near on a decade, carrying just about anything that pays the fare. Alas, of late, the voyages have become more and more dangerous. The sea-wolves . . . they are always about. I have managed to stay clear of them, but only just."

Guinevere glanced at the fading light outside and gently interrupted Potter.

"You were telling us about your last voyage, Captain Potter?"

Potter nodded. "Oh . . . yes. We were making our run from the land of Franks, around the tip of Amorica, to Albion. We left at dawn, and for a while, it seemed as if our voyage would be an uneventful one, but then our luck ran out. We nearly ran into a dragonship coming from the north, and the seawolves were aboard the Mandragon before we knew it. My lads and I tried to throw them back into the sea, but the boarders were a savage lot, and their leader, he was a giant of a man. I . . . I thought we were lost, but then the two of them came out of the hold, ready for battle. Why, Your Highness, I've never seen the like, and I can tell you I have seen my fair share of fighting. Aye, I've never seen the like."

For a moment, Potter just nodded his head slowly, his eyes staring in the distance.

"Who came up from the hold? What happened?" Cadwyn burst out, drawing a disapproving look from Sister Aranwen.

Potter looked over at Cadwyn and Sister Aranwen, and finally, his eyes returned to Guinevere.

"There were two men . . . passengers. They came from below deck armed with swords. The first was tall, near four hands taller than I, with hair as dark as the night. The second was shorter, but he was as strong as an anvil and just as black. The two of them were like scythes, the seawolves the wheat. The giant Norseman came for the tall man, and I was sure that he was done for, but I was wrong. That man moved like the wind itself on a stormy night. Aye, he struck the giant down with a mighty blow, and the rest of the seawolves fled."

"Yes!" Cadwyn whispered, striking her small fist into the table, drawing a shocked gasp and rebuke from Sister Aranwen.

"Cadwyn! Have you lost your senses? We do not celebrate the death of our fellow men!"

Guinevere laughed, but quickly recovered. "Of course we don't, Sister Aranwen." Then she turned her attention back to Captain Potter. "Did you speak to these two passengers? Did they tell you their names, where they were from, or where they were bound?"

Potter ran his hand over his bearded face.

"Why, yes, we did speak after the battle. Let me see . . . hmm, yes, the black man . . . his name was Capussa, an odd name. Never heard the like, but then I've never seen a man like that before. Now, the tall one, he told me the black man's name, but he didn't tell me his own, and I didn't ask. That was not right, Your Highness. Forgive me. I should know the name of two men who saved my life, at least that. Now, you asked me if I knew where they were bound, and I can't say I do, but I know they made landfall at Whitstable."

Guinevere leaned forward to emphasize her words. "Captain, the tall man may be someone of great import to the realm, what little there is left of it, so I need you to tell me everything he said to you. Can you do that?"

"Why, why, of course, Your Highness," Potter stammered and then took a deep breath.

"He asked if we were landing at Londinium, and I told him that no one ports in Londinium, not with Hengst and his wolves there. But he didn't know of Hengst. He said that he'd left ten years ago."

"He said ten years?" Guinevere questioned with quiet intensity.

"Yes, Your Highness. He knew that the King, forgive me, Your Highness, had died and that the Table was broken, but no more than that. He asked me if any of the Knights of the Table were still alive . . . he asked about Galahad in particular."

Potter froze when Guinevere raised a hand to her mouth and closed her eyes.

"Your Highness, have I offended you? Are you ill?"

The Queen opened her eyes and lowered her hand to the table. "No, Captain, all . . . is well. Please continue."

"Your Highness, I am sorry, but that is all I can remember."

"Captain," Guinevere said, leaning forward, "can you tell me more about what the tall man looked like? Whatever you can remember."

"Yes, Your Highness," Potter answered, nodding slowly. "That I can. As I said before, he was tall, four hands taller than I, and he and the African, well they had sinews of steel in their shoulders, arms, and legs, like those of a blacksmith. The tall man's hair was as black as night, and it ran near to his shoulders. His eyes are blue, his mien is a hard one,

Your Highness, but also a handsome and noble one." He paused and frowned. "There was something odd . . ." He shook his head. "Well, it's a thing of no moment."

"Please, Captain," Guinevere quietly prompted. "What was odd?"

"When I took the tall man's hand in greeting, his forearm . . . well, there was nary a part that didn't bear a scar. I'd never seen the like. The black man was the same way, but his face also bore the mark of the blade. The tall man's face was unmarred . . . and it was the face of a man in the early years of his third decade. But his eyes, Your Highness, they were those of a man who'd traveled the road of life for a much longer time and who'd paid dearly for every league—"

A knock on the door to the sacristy interrupted Potter's narrative. Guinevere glanced over at the door, and a moment later, a man in his middle years dressed in a worn woolen cloak, sheepskin leggings, and leather boots stepped into the room and bowed quickly.

"Your Highness, forgive me, but we must go. Two dragonships have ported at Aber, and there's a scouting party on the road coming this way. It's the smoke from the fire. They've seen it."

Guinevere nodded. "Thank you, Torn. We shall be there in a moment." She turned back to Captain Potter. "You have been so kind, Captain. Would you travel with us, or can you make it on your own?"

Potter smiled. "Your Highness, God has blessed me with the honor of meeting the Queen of the Britons, and for that, I am eternally grateful. As for the seawolves, I grew up a league to the south. There's nary a trail through yonder forest that I don't know. I shall be safe."

"Then let this be our parting, good Captain," Guinevere said, inclining her head toward him. "I shall pray for your safe return to your family and hearth."

"Thank you, Your Highness," Potter said and bowed deeply before following Torn out the door.

After Potter left, Guinevere, Cadwyn, and Sister Aranwen rose, and the Queen stood there in silence for a moment. Cadwyn looked over at her and whispered, "Milady, is it he?"

Guinevere shook her head.

"I . . . I must think on the matter," she said quietly. "Now, let us make haste."

Royal Post Station

Guinevere leaned back in her chair, quill in hand, listening to the light rain showering the plume of the elm tree just outside the room's single window. Her eyes strayed to the water bucket beside the modest bed in the corner and from there to the room's wooden ceiling. Thankfully, there was no sign of the leak the miller had apologetically prophesied might appear if the light rain became a downpour.

Her room was one of three on the third floor of the conical stone tower. Cadwyn and Sister Aranwen were quartered in the other two. The tower was a former royal post station, a four-hour ride inland from Pen Dinas. The miller and his wife, Mary, lived on the ground floor with their two young children.

Mary, one of Guinevere's loyal sparrows, had been told to expect the small party on their return trip to the abbey, and the three guestrooms had been ready upon their arrival. Although the rooms were plain and somewhat drafty, they were a godsend, for there were no other inns or lodging on this lonely stretch of the road.

Guinevere turned her attention back to the parchment in front of her and finished the last paragraph. She wanted the women receiving the message to be ready to aid Sir Percival if he passed through their villages on his way to the abbey. At the same time, she wanted the women to keep the tidings of his return secret, since there were many who would see him dead if they knew of his arrival.

After finishing the note, Guinevere handed it to Cadwyn.

"My friend, I will need this message written in cypher, on three separate parchments. As soon as we return to the abbey, three of Torn's best men must ride with these like the wind to the sparrows who live outside Londinium."

Cadwyn read the message and slowly raised her eyes to the Queen.

"So it is he, Sir Percival?" she said in prayerful whisper. "He has returned?"

Guinevere hesitated, putting the quill down upon the table. "It could be him. I cannot be sure, but if it is, then he will need someone to guide him safely to the abbey. No one who left this land before the fall of the Table could know how dangerous it has become."

"Milady, how can you doubt that it is Sir Percival after what Captain Potter said?"

"Perhaps . . ." she paused, remembering how many dreams had faded and fallen by the wayside in the long years since Camlann, "I fear that an early tide of hope will only lead to a later sea of despair if I am mistaken. I . . . I have much to ponder, but it will have to wait until the morning." She rose from her chair with a tired smile. "It has been a long day, my young friend, and we should rest."

"Of course, Milady. I shall see you in the morning."

Although she was tired and sore from the last three days of riding, Guinevere could not find the respite of sleep. The meeting with Captain Potter had opened a Pandora's Box of memories and feelings, and raised troubling questions about the man who'd disembarked from the Mandragon. An hour after lying down to rest, she rose and walked over to the tall, narrow window on other side of the room and stared down at the somnolent forest three floors below. The light from the full moon cast the tower's long shadow deep into the forest, like a giant sword warding off all who might approach.

The scene below drew Guinevere's thoughts back in time to the great stables at Camelot and the rides she used to take through the forests, towns, and villages surrounding the castle, in the first hour after dawn. Although there was little danger in the years before the war began, Arthur had insisted that one of the Knights of the Table, along with six guards, accompany her on each outing. Since most of the Knights had been reluctant to rise at such an early hour, more often than not, this duty had been imposed upon the two youngest Knights, Percival and Galahad.

Both of the young Knights had seemed to enjoy the outings, but

Galahad's nocturnal trysts frequently left him in a poor state at such an early hour, forcing his friend, Percival, to serve in his stead on many occasions. Guinevere smiled as she remembered Percival's discomfiture when she had raised the matter with him on one of their morning rides.

The small party had dismounted by a stream to allow the horses to drink, and she and Percival had walked over to a nearby bluff, where they had a view of Camelot in the distance.

"Sir Percival, I was told that Sir Galahad would be accompanying me on today's ride. Is he unwell again?" Guinevere said, feigning concern.

"Alas, yes, my Queen, otherwise he would surely have come," Percival answered, avoiding Guinevere's eyes.

"Is it a serious matter? If so, I can ask Merlin to attend him," Guinevere said, raising an eyebrow.

Percival nodded, still avoiding Guinevere's inquisitive gaze. "Your kindness is much appreciated, my Queen, but I suspect only time will cure what ails him."

"I see," Guinevere said, nodding thoughtfully before continuing. "Do you remember the alehouse we passed earlier, the one with the wooden rooster above the door?"

Percival stiffened. "Uh . . . yes, my Queen."

"When we stopped outside to tighten my saddle strap, I heard one of the stable boys telling another that Galahad was still dancing with the miller's daughter at this . . . reputable establishment—on the tables, mind you—three hours before the cock crowed. Would his ailment have anything to do with this nocturnal outing?" Guinevere said with a small smile.

"Not being a healer, my Queen," Percival said hesitantly, "I cannot say. But I would concede that Galahad has taken at least two of the admonitions in Ecclesiastes to heart."

"And those would be?"

"There's a time to dance, and there's a time to laugh."

"Oh, he is quite the rogue, is he not?" Guinevere said with a laugh.

"He is that, my Queen," Percival conceded, a smile touching his lips for a moment. Then it disappeared, and he turned to face her. "He is also a true and loyal friend, and the bravest knight that I have ever known."

Guinevere and Percival's eyes met for a long moment, and then she looked out upon the vista before them.

"Do you know, Sir Percival," Guinevere said quietly, "that you and Galahad share something unique?"

"My Queen?"

"You both saved my life."

Percival shook his head. "My Queen, the battle at Eburacum—"

"Saved the city and all within it, including your Queen," Guinevere said quietly and then continued. "The year the plague came to Albion, I was sent to live with my uncle. His manor lies to the north, near a lake, far from any of the cities or ports where the illness struck. The lands held by Galahad's family adjoined those of my uncle, and sometimes we would ride together."

Percival looked over at the Queen, a look of surprise on his face.

"I was seventeen, he eighteen. One day, our party—I, three of my handmaidens, and Galahad and two of his friends—were having a picnic in the forest, when a wild boar charged out of the woods straight toward me.

"Galahad distracted the creature and it charged him instead. He leaped in the air when it was just a few feet away, and it ran right under him. Then he dodged behind a tree and teased the creature until it charged him again and again. Each time, he would dodge behind the tree and circle to the other side, just barely evading its deadly tusks. To this day, I remember the expression on his face," Guinevere said, shaking her head in wonder. "He loved every minute of it. He was actually upset when one of the men in his company killed the boar with an arrow."

"Galahad enjoys the dance with death too much," Percival said quietly, his eyes fixed on the distant towers of Camelot. "I don't know whether it is that he doesn't fully understand the price of a misstep, or whether he doesn't care. In either case, I have sworn to do my best to keep him safe, for the world would be a darker place without him."

Guinevere looked over at the Knight. "Yes, Sir Percival, it would indeed."

The memory faded and Guinevere was surprised to find she had walked to the other side of the room. She walked back to the window, drew in a heavy breath, and allowed the memories pressing in on her to return again and have their way.

Over the next six months, Percival had ridden along with her, two and sometimes three days a week. Over time, she had begun to hope that he would be the Knight assigned to accompany her each morning. One day, after a ride, she remembered sitting down, alone in her royal quarters, trying to understand why she was so drawn to him.

He was disciplined and honorable to a fault, but many of the other Knights were as well. He was also handsome, but not so much so as Galahad, Lancelot, or Tristan, and although she'd heard rumors that Percival was a most formidable swordsman, martial prominence and glory had never meant much to her. She'd never enjoyed the tournaments she was called upon to attend with Arthur several times a year, with all their pomp, ceremony, and, too often, blood.

Then she had come to the realization that Percival had two traits that most of the other knights lacked. The first was the depth and breadth of his knowledge. Unlike most of the other Knights and nobles, Percival could read and write, like herself, in the languages of the Greeks and Romans, and he had read many of the books she had read. Many times, she found their morning talks so interesting that a ride of an hour or two seemed to pass in minutes, leaving her wishing the trail had been a league or two longer.

The second trait she treasured was the way Percival treated the common people. Whenever they stopped at a town or village, he would speak to one or two of them as if they were equals, and he made a point of helping them whenever he could. Guinevere remembered a time when they'd stopped to water the horses in a town, two leagues to the south of Camelot, and Percival had helped a woman carry a bucket full of water from the town well to her house.

Percival had spoken to the woman at some length outside her

modest home. After the woman went inside, Percival had walked across the street to the tavern and spent several minutes inside. From there, he'd walked over to the blacksmith's shop. She remembered the square, middle-aged smith turning a shade of white during their short conversation, and then quickly nodding his head in assent to whatever Percival had said.

As they were riding out of town, Guinevere glanced over her shoulder and saw a thin, balding man of middle years emerge from the tavern and run over to the smith. The two men had then hurriedly walked over to the woman's house and knocked respectfully on her door.

Unable to resist, Guinevere had turned to her escort. "I must confess, Sir Percival, I am most intrigued by yon happenstance. What business did you have with the woman at the well, and with the tavern keeper and blacksmith?"

After a moment of hesitation, the Knight had answered, keeping his eyes fixed on the road ahead. "I noticed the woman had been crying, and I asked what vexed her. She was reluctant to say, but I insisted. Her husband recently died, and she'd obtained work at the tavern to help pay for her needs and those of her son, a boy of ten. The lad was apprenticed to the smith. When she'd declined the tavern keeper's advances, he took away her job and persuaded the smith to end her son's apprenticeship."

"And so, Sir Percival, what did you do?" Guinevere said quietly.

"I told the tavern keeper that the woman was a relative of mine, and I considered his treatment of her a personal affront. I made it clear I would be compelled to seek satisfaction if she wasn't rehired and treated with the utmost respect. I conveyed the same message to the smith about the boy's apprenticeship."

"That . . . was most noble, Sir Percival."

"Thank you, my Queen."

"And are you related to the woman?" she asked with a small smile.

Percival's brow furrowed for a moment, and then the hint of a smile touched his lips. "Well, in some sense, yes, my Queen. If you go back far enough, we're all related."

A soft knock at the door of her room drew Guinevere back to the present. When she opened the door, she was surprised to see Cadwyn and Sister Aranwen standing there, looking anxious. At first, Guinevere assumed there must be a threat to the tower.

"Is something wrong?"

"No, Milady," Sister Aranwen said. "We just heard you . . . walking back and forth, and we were concerned."

"I . . . I didn't realize that. I'm sorry to have awakened you."

"Is something wrong, Milady?" Cadwyn asked softly.

Guinevere smiled, realizing that both women were curious as to her thoughts and desired to talk. "I am troubled by today's talk with Captain Potter, but I will not burden you with my thoughts at this late hour. You should sleep."

Cadwyn spoke almost before she finished. "It would be no burden at all, Milady. We would very much like to listen." Sister Aranwen nodded in rare agreement.

The Queen nodded and gestured for them to come in. "Very well then, come in, and let us sit at the table. Cadwyn, can you put another log on the fire?"

"Yes, Milady."

After placing a small log on the fire in the hearth, the young woman joined Guinevere and Sister Aranwen at the modest wooden table. A narrow stream of moonlight from the window flowed across the table and merged with the light from the hearth, bathing the three women in a gentle light. Guinevere ran one of her hands through the ghostly stream, as though trying to catch its substance in her palm, and then leaned back in her chair.

"It's Galahad. That's how I knew it had to be Percival."

"Galahad, Milady?" Cadwyn said.

"Yes."

Guinevere was quiet for a moment, as if gathering her thoughts, and then she continued.

"Percival and Galahad were raised to the Table in the same year, they went through the training together, and, being the most junior Knights, they often shared the least desirable duty assignments. The two of them also made the mistake of crossing Lancelot, who was one of the most senior Knights, and the one that had Arthur's ear."

"What did they do?" Cadwyn asked.

"In the case of Galahad, he drew much of Lancelot's ire upon himself and deserved many of the hard duties and punishments assigned to him. That man," Guinevere said, shaking her head in amusement, "loved to break the rules, he loved playing tricks, and he wasn't one to miss a party. It was rumored that Percival had to get up at four bells and scour the taverns for his fellow knight on the mornings when they were assigned to a dawn patrol."

"I suspect Lancelot's ire had another cause as well," Sister Aranwen said wryly, glancing up from her prayer beads.

"True," Guinevere said with a nod. "Before Galahad came, Lancelot was reputed to be the most handsome knight at court, and more often than not, he had a trail of women following him."

"That he did," Sister Aranwen said with disapproval. "It was rather unseemly, if you ask me. He should have shooed them away, like bothersome flies."

Cadwyn glanced over at the usually reserved nun, surprised at the interruption.

A smile touched Guinevere's lips, but she continued without commenting.

"Well, after Galahad was raised to the Table, Lancelot was relegated to second place with the women of the court. Even Arthur used to chuckle about how vexed Lancelot was about that."

"Why did Lancelot dislike Percival?" Cadwyn asked. "Did the women follow him as well?"

"Oh, many of them wanted to, but he was rarely at Court, so it was more difficult. No, the dispute between Lancelot and Percival arose from a very different cause."

Guinevere idly ran one of her hands through the stream of light flowing across the table as she continued. "Most of the Knights, and in particular, Lancelot, believed that the expanding war with Morgana and her forces would be won by the Knights, supported by the King's archers. Percival disagreed. He believed a trained infantry, an infantry of peasants to be exact, had to be the centerpiece of the King's force. He made this known to Arthur, directly, in a meeting of the Knights. This enraged Lancelot, both the idea and the fact that Percival had the temerity to make the argument directly to the King."

"Why?" Cadwyn questioned, confusion in her voice. "Why not have more men in the ranks? A bigger army might have saved the Kingdom."

Guinevere looked across the table at the young woman and said in a voice tinged with regret, "Oh, my dear Cadwyn, I wish . . . others had seen the matter as clearly as you do, but it was not to be."

There was a long silence, and Sister Aranwen looked up from her prayers for a moment and exchanged glances with Guinevere. The Queen nodded her assent as if acknowledging the futility of walking down a painful path that led nowhere.

"In the end," Guinevere said, turning to Cadwyn, "Lancelot retaliated by assigning Galahad and Percival to the hardest and most unpleasant postings."

"So that's how they became friends?" Cadwyn asked.

"Yes, but it was at the battle of the Aelius Bridge where they became brothers."

"Please, Milady, tell us of that day! It must have been glorious!"

Guinevere smiled at Cadwyn's enthusiasm, but her smile faded when she spoke.

"The bards who have told and retold the story a thousand times have truly made it so, and . . . I am glad of that. In these dark times, the people need . . . we all need . . . heroes, to give us hope. But I will tell you this, my friends, as I watched events unfold that day, it was as terrible a thing as it was magnificent."

Guinevere hesitated and drew in a breath, as if summoning the will to tell the tale.

"In early spring, three years before the fall, spies in the northern part of the kingdom sent word that Morgana was amassing a force to attack a town on the River Tyne, near the Aelius Bridge. Reports of this kind had become more and more frequent in the last years, and Arthur and the Knights never knew whether a threat was real or a ruse, or worse, a trap."

"Was it a trap, Milady?" Cadwyn asked, her eyes wide and anxious.

"Listen and you shall learn, Cadwyn," Sister Aranwen said quietly, not looking up from her prayer beads.

"Yes, Sister Aranwen," Cadwyn said with a sigh.

Guinevere reached over and patted Cadwyn's hand before continuing. "Lancelot had discounted the threat as a mere rumor, but a raid on the town of Caer Luel, twenty leagues to the west, a month earlier had nearly overrun the town's defenses. Sir Owain and over three hundred royal soldiers were lost."

Sister Aranwen made the sign of the cross when Guinevere mentioned the deaths, and Cadwyn did so as well without thinking.

Guinevere closed her eyes as she recalled the dark day the messenger had brought the ill tidings to court. After a moment of silence, she continued.

"The disaster at Caer Luel enraged Arthur. When he heard the report, he made ready to march north with a force of Knights, hoping to exact retribution against Morgana's forces. He also ordered Sir Percival, who was still farther north in the Marches, to come south and meet him at the Tyne.

"At this point in the war, there were so many threats of assassination that Camelot had become a velvet prison for me, so I asked Arthur if Sister Aranwen and I could accompany him, and he agreed."

Sister Aranwen nodded her head, but the look on her face suggested she had been less than happy about the King's decision.

"When we arrived at the castle on the north side of Tyne, three days later, Arthur discovered that the earl in charge of the post had not received word of our coming from the royal messengers, and he was unaware of the threat from Morgana. This vexed Arthur greatly, since he knew Morgana could be planning an attack on the town and castle, and that time would be needed to prepare.

"Scouting parties were sent out in all directions to find out if Morgana's forces were in the area. One of these parties crossed the Aelius

Bridge and spotted an enemy camp with over three hundred armed men, many on horseback. Although the scouts—six royal archers—tried to return to the castle with the tidings, they were discovered by the enemy. Two of the archers were killed in the forest, and a third was killed in the race to get back across the bridge to safety."

Guinevere stood up and walked over to the window. The sky had cleared and was alit with a cascade of stars. Her gaze traveled from the sky to the forest below, and when she spoke, it was almost as if she were watching the terrible scene happening all over again.

"I was walking on the battlement of the southern tower with the Earl's wife when I heard the shouts below. I could see . . . everything. The swiftest of the two archers reached the Aelius Bridge and crossed safely to give the alarm, but the other two were cut off in an open field by four horsemen. Sir Percival, on the north side of the bridge, charged across and drove the enemy back, but his horse was killed in the fight."

Guinevere placed a hand against her chest and rested the other on the stone sill in front of her.

"Percival and the two remaining archers retreated to the bridge, but more and more of the enemy were pouring out of the forest. They had to fight their way back, step-by-step. By the time they reached the middle of the bridge, one of the two archers had been killed, and the second had been wounded so badly he could barely walk. Percival wouldn't leave the archer. He made a stand at the midpoint of the bridge, where the passage had been narrowed by the remains of an old toll gate."

Cadwyn, hanging on every word, interrupted, "Forgive me, Milady, but why didn't they send help?"

Guinevere turned and walked back to the table and sat down before continuing.

"Arthur didn't know what was happening until later. He was in the north tower of the castle trying to prepare a defense. Some of the men on the southern wall ran to open the main gate to mount a rescue, but Lancelot ordered them back to their posts."

Cadwyn's eyes widened, and Guinevere raised a hand, forestalling the girl's explosion of outrage.

"The order was not cowardly, Cadwyn. Lancelot was many things, but he wasn't a coward. His first duty was to save the castle, and everyone in it. Since he didn't know the size of the enemy force that was attacking, he couldn't risk opening the gates. If he'd done so and the castle had been lost, I would not be here today to tell you this tale."

"I understand, Milady," Cadwyn said softly.

"I sent a messenger racing to find Arthur, but I feared it would be too late. Over a hundred of Morgana's men were on the bridge, and although only a few could reach Sir Percival at one time through the narrow gap, I knew he couldn't stand against so many for long. And that," Guinevere said with a smile, "was when Sir Galahad threw a rope over the wall of the castle, climbed down, and raced out to join the fight."

"Yes!" Cadwyn said triumphantly, striking her small fist into the table.

"Jesus, Mary, and Joseph, child, are you trying to wake the dead?" Sister Aranwen whispered in exasperation.

Guinevere couldn't help but laugh. "Oh, it was a wonderful thing. I could see the smile on Galahad's face as he raced toward that bloody melee; and when Lancelot bellowed over the wall for him to come back, he laughed and ran faster. What a magnificent rogue he was," she finished.

"And so the two of them, Percival and Galahad, fought together, side by side, on that bridge. At first, they just held the narrow position in the center, but then they began to drive the enemy back. It was . . . truly a wondrous thing.

"When Arthur arrived on the battlement, he raced to the wall and watched the fight for a moment, mesmerized, and then turned to Lancelot, who had followed him. He ordered Lancelot to assemble a force of six knights and a score of archers in the bailey. He told him that he intended to drive the attackers from the bridge.

"When Lancelot told him it could be a trap and they could lose the entire castle, I remember his words as if they were spoken yesterday. He said, 'Lance, if we don't ride out, we will lose far more than that.'"

The room was quiet as a tomb for a moment, and then Guinevere reached a hand into the vanishing stream of moonlight, closed her fist, and said, "And he did as he promised. He drove Morgana's force from the bridge. By nightfall, they'd retreated into the forest."

Guinevere closed her eyes for a long moment, remembering the two young knights covered in blood, walking back across the bridge together after the battle. Galahad had cuffed Percival on the shoulder as they walked and said something. Percival had stopped and looked at him incredulously, and then a moment later, the two men had broken into a fit of laughter. She smiled, remembering how much she had wanted to know what Galahad had said. "So you see, when Captain Potter said the man on the ship had asked after Galahad, I knew it was Sir Percival."

"I knew it had to be him," Cadwyn said, clasping her hands together.

Sister Aranwen, whose expression was more reserved, leaned forward. "Milady, there's something that vexes you . . . perhaps something the captain said?"

Guinevere hesitated for a moment. "There is. Sir Percival and I were born in the same year. So he would be in his thirtieth or thirty-first year, but the captain said his face was that of a man in his early twenties. It is . . . odd."

"Milady," Cadwyn said, "the captain only met him for a moment, and who knows what potions they may have in the faraway places Sir Percival has visited? Why, Sir Percival may have found the fountain of youth!"

Sister Aranwen scoffed. "The fountain of youth! How ridiculous. You are surely in need of rest if that is—"

"I'm fine, thank you, Sister," Cadwyn responded tartly.

Guinevere reached across the table and rested a hand on the arm of each woman.

"It's late, my loyal friends, and we have a hard day's ride in the morn. So we should get what sleep we can before then."

CHAPTER 14

MORGANA'S DOMAIN

Morgana tied the reins of her horse to a yew tree just below the crest of a hill and continued her ascent to the top on foot. She scanned the thick, virgin forest surrounding the narrow trail with a measure of unease. The Pict warrior hidden in the woods at the top of the hill was a merciless killer, and this was his domain. He lived in the forest, like any other animal—eating, sleeping, and hunting for his daily fare.

Although she detested the man, Morgana had used the Pict's services before. He was a useful tool. He was also a very dangerous one. Unlike other men, the Pict had little interest in silver or gold and even less interest in power. He followed his own set of rules, and if you transgressed them, death was immediate.

Morgana paused just below the crest and nocked an arrow in her bow before walking up to the clearing above. She knew her guards would never get there in time if the meeting did not go as planned. She stood at the edge of the small clearing and waited in silence. She could feel the Pict's eyes on her, but she could not see him. Suddenly, a wiry man of middle height, dressed in animal skins, emerged from the forest wall thirty yards away, as if emerging from an unseen door. Brown, black, and green markings adorned almost every patch of the Pict's exposed skin, including his bald head.

Two knives were sheathed in the leather belt at his waist. The Pict used the long knife for killing and the shorter knife for skinning his kills, both animal and human. Morgana had seen his handiwork. The hunter's bow gripped in the warrior's right hand was painted black, as was the arrow nocked loosely in its bowstring. The fletching at the end of each of the Pict's arrows was dyed a bright blue.

The warrior hesitated a step outside the forest wall, sniffing the air like an animal and extending his tongue, as if he could taste the presence of an enemy, before walking across the space that separated them. He stopped five paces from Morgana, his coal black eyes sweeping every inch of her body. After finishing his inspection, the Pict nodded and spoke in a quiet, heavily accented voice, "You have need of me, Roman?"

"Yes."

"Are you prepared to pay my price?"

"And what is that?"

"The same as before, two wagons of grain for my people, and . . . a life, for sacrifice."

Morgana could care less about the blood price demanded by the Pict, but she decided to resist the demand. An animal had no right to bargain for human blood.

"You can have the grain, and then some, but not the life."

The Pict smiled, exposing teeth that had been dyed black and filed to points.

"Then our time is at an end," he said and began to back away, his eyes never leaving Morgana's.

"Why, Pict," Morgana said coldly, irritated by the man's temerity, "do you need a human sacrifice?"

The Pict smiled again. "Why do you care, Roman? You have sent many souls into the darkness. What is one more?"

Morgana's eyes narrowed, and the two stared at each other in silence. Then the Pict's smile vanished, and he spoke in a quiet voice laced with anger.

"When your legions first invaded our lands, the rivers ran red with the blood of my people. Their spirits will haunt me if I perform a service for you. Only the sacrifice of a man or woman will suffice to atone for my wrong."

Morgana stared at the man, wondering idly if she could draw and release the arrow nocked in her bow and kill him before he reached her. For some reason, she suspected the Pict would win the contest, and his eyes told her that he knew this as well.

"The price will be paid, Talorc."

A flash of rage rippled across the Pict's face, and he spoke in a hiss, "Do not say my name, Roman. My ancestors will hear you, and they will curse me for not killing you. The blood price for lifting that curse would be far higher than even you can bear."

"Threaten me again," Morgana said slowly and softly, emphasizing each word, "and I will see that you join those precious ancestors of yours before the sun sets."

For a moment, the Roman princess thought the Pict would attack her, and she tightened her grip on her nocked bow, but then he smiled without humor.

"I will join them soon enough. Now, tell me what you would have me do. I have far to travel before the sun sets."

*   *   *

LORD AERON HAD learned of Morgana's secret meeting in the usual way. Whenever his master intended to secretly leave the castle before dawn, Leofric, Morgana's Saxon guard, would order old Tom to wake him when he rose to milk the cows. Once Lord Aeron had discovered this practice, he'd offered Tom a silver coin if he would leave his staff outside his hut on the night before, instead of taking it inside.

Lord Aeron had left the castle four hours before dawn, through a passage unknown to Morgana, a passage he'd learned of more than a decade earlier from the lord of the castle's daughter. After emerging from the passageway on the far side of the wall, clothed in the simple attire of a woodsman, he'd traveled on foot to a nearby farmhouse, where a horse was waiting for him.

From there, the knight rode to the crest of a hill, half a league distant, and waited. He knew Morgana had a practice of meeting with her spies in one of two locations. One was visible from the north side of the hill, the other from the south. He would not know which slope to ascend until she passed this spot.

After dismounting from his horse, the knight took a seat on a rock that gave him a view of the trail below. As he watched the stars descend in the clear night sky, the memory of a distant summer night drifted through the iron bars he'd forged around the past, like a cool morning fog.

It was the summer Guinevere had come to stay in her uncle's manor, a half league away from his family's ancestral home. He remembered being surprised at her beauty when they were first introduced at the formal welcoming dinner, but he had kept his distance. Like everyone else in the kingdom, he knew she was betrothed to the King, and he had known many beautiful women, some more beautiful than Guinevere. They had always been at his beck and call. Being denied this one woman had seemed a matter of no moment at the time.

Over the next three months, his feelings had changed. A flame had begun to grow inside him with each outing and social gathering, one he had never felt before—one that shook him to the core of his being. In an effort to extinguish the growing maelstrom within, he had thrown himself into his training, caroused with his friends until dawn, and spent many a night abed with other women. It had all been for naught. His days and nights were haunted by her enchanting laugh, mesmerizing smile, and noble soul.

On the night before her parting, he remembered sitting on a hill like this one, hidden in the shadows, watching her stroll alone through her uncle's walled gardens in the moonlight. He could hear the soft notes from an old melody being played within the manor as they drifted over the wall and into the forest, carried on the warm breeze.

When the golden-haired Queen-to-be reached a marble circle hidden from the sight of those within the manor by a fountain, she paused to listen to the music. After swaying back and forth for a moment, she turned, bowed to an imaginary partner, a sad smile on her face, and began to dance. He remembered standing, as if in a trance, and matching her graceful steps and pirouettes on the worn forest path in front of him, as if he were her partner in the dance below.

When the song ended, Guinevere bowed in his direction, unaware of his presence, less than a stone's throw distant, but an eternity away. He had made the answering bow and watched her walk back into the manor, knowing it would be the last time he would see her before the royal wedding. The flame within had begged him to scale the wall and to take her to some faraway place, where they could be together, but in the end, he had done nothing. There was nothing to be done. Fate had already chosen Guinevere's path, and he was powerless to change it.

An hour before dawn, the pounding of hooves drew the knight's mind back to the present, and he watched Morgana, accompanied by Leofric and five other men, veer northward. He took a final look at the sky before leading his horse down the trail toward the north slope of the hill.

An hour later, Lord Aeron saw Morgana proceeding to the meeting place alone. As he watched from his vantage point atop the hill, a Pict warrior emerged from the far side of the clearing wearing a patchwork of animal skins. The knight noticed that both Morgana and the Pict were carrying bows, and arrows had been nocked in both weapons. The two talked for a quarter of an hour, and then the Pict left. As the painted warrior walked back into the forest, Lord Aeron noticed that the fletching on the arrows in the quiver on his back were a bright blue.

The Road to Londinium

Percival checked his saddle one last time and turned back to the campsite. Cynric was talking to four of his men on the other side of the clearing. In the hour after sunrise, the archer and some of his men had met with a group of merchants in the forest south of Londinium and sold the bags of flour and beans they had carried with them on their trip. Now that the trade was done, Percival expected Cynric and his men to return to their camp to the south with the goods they had acquired from Londinium's tradesmen.

As Percival watched, four of Cynric's men mounted and headed south down the forest trail. The rest walked their horses over toward the Knight, with Cynric in the lead. Percival frowned and walked over to Capussa. The Numidian was sitting on a nearby rock sharpening his sword.

"What is this?" he asked, gesturing to the four horsemen leaving the camp. "Cynric and the rest of the men should be leaving as well. This is our agreed place of parting."

Capussa smiled but didn't look up.

A moment later, Cynric and seven of his men stopped a pace away.

"Why aren't you returning home with your other men?" Percival asked.

Cynric glanced at the departing men and then looked back at Percival. "We will return home, but later. We travel with you to find the Queen."

Percival shook his head. "Archer, I cannot burden you and your men with the perils and hardships of this journey."

Cynric nodded, his face set. "I know that, Sir Knight, but each of us has made our decision. We will travel with you."

Capussa sheathed his sharpened sword, walked over to Percival, and gripped him by the shoulder.

"Well, then, we are a party of ten. A good number, I think."

Percival looked over at the Numidian skeptically. "And you, of course, knew nothing of this?"

Capussa shrugged, barely restraining a smile, then he turned to the archer, ending further argument. "So, my friend, shall we get started on our quest to find Queen Guinevere?"

Cynric and Capussa exchanged amused looks, and the archer turned to Percival.

"Is that acceptable to you, sir?"

Percival looked at each of the men who'd volunteered to share the perils of such a journey and then answered, "I would be proud to travel in such company."

Cynric turned to Tylan. The other man stepped forward.

"We had planned to take the road just ahead, on the south side of the

Tamesis past the city, but the men from Londinium we bartered with this morn said two bands of Hengst's reavers are spread out along the road collecting taxes. So we must cross the Tamesis and take the road and trails on the north side of the city. We'll pass within sight of the north wall."

"Is it wise to travel so close to the city?" Percival questioned.

"Today is tournament day," Tylan said, glancing at Cynric. "We should be able to pass by without being noticed."

"Tournament day?"

"It's something that Hengst holds in the old tournament stadium every month," Cynric answered, his face tight. "He forces the people of the city to attend. The distraction will help us." Then he nodded for Tylan to continue.

"There is a boatman awaiting us. He will take us to the north side of the river. The fog is heavy this morning, so we should be able to get across without being seen. Once we're north of Londinium, we'll stay off the main roads until we reach Corinium. We should be able to avoid the bands of brigands that serve as Hengst's tax collectors in that area. From there, we can take the Roman roads most of the way to the abbey."

Percival gave Tylan a solemn nod and said, "Then let us pray for a safe passage and begin our journey."

FOREST ROAD EAST OF LONDINIUM

Percival eased his horse down the forest trail, following Cynric and Tylan. Capussa and the rest of Cynric's men followed behind. The winding trail was so narrow they had to ride in single file, and on one long stretch they had been forced to dismount and lead their horses to avoid the thick canopy of branches and foliage overhanging the path.

Four hours after dawn, Tylan led the party of men to a small clearing hidden from the trail and dismounted. He walked over to the other men and pointed to the north. "Ten or so of Hengst's men are on the road about a furlong up ahead. The trail is visible from the road there. We can wait and hope they move on, or we can try to climb over that hill."

Percival looked over at the hill on their right. The slope was steep and thickly wooded at the bottom, but the tree line ended sixty or more paces from the crest. The Knight shook his head. "Let's wait and see if they move along."

Cynric and Capussa nodded in agreement. After the party had dismounted and tied their horses to a nearby tree, Tylan glanced around the clearing and growled, "Where is that boy? I swear—"

His tirade was cut off by the sight of one of Cynric's men sprinting up the trail toward the clearing, fear etched across his face. Capussa and Cynric reached for their bows at the same time, and Percival grasped the hilt of his sword. The man stumbled to a stop a pace away from Tylan, gasping for breath.

"The Norsemen have taken Keil! He . . . went after a rabbit . . . they saw him . . . ran him down with the horses. He's alive . . . but I heard them talking . . . they're taking him to the tournament."

A wave of emotions crossed Tylan's face from rage, to fear, and finally to anguish.

Cynric stared at his friend for a long moment and then looked off into the forest when he spoke. "Tylan, I know the boy is your brother's son, but—"

Tylan lowered his head and nodded, his face ashen.

Percival stepped over to the two men. "What is this 'tournament' of which you speak?"

Cynric gestured toward a small rise on the far side of the clearing, his face grim. "Come, you can see the tournament field from up there."

Percival followed the tall archer to a dense copse of trees on the top of the rise, with Capussa and Tylan trailing behind him. Looking down, Percival was surprised to see how close they were to Londinium's northern wall. The city was laid out before them. He stared at the rows of wooden houses, churches, shops, and winding streets—streets that had once been teeming with shopkeepers, farmers, merchants, women, and children. Now they were all but deserted, and most of the larger royal buildings and churches had been burned to the ground. Many other buildings were in disrepair. Londinium was a city in the midst of its death throes.

Cynric pointed to a line of men with ropes around their necks, jogging single file behind a man on a horse. They were heading toward a gate in the city's northern wall. The captives were followed by a line of fifteen horsemen wearing a motley array of animal skins, clothes, weapons, and helmets. Percival recognized them. He had killed six similarly dressed men on the Mandragon.

Tylan pointed to the last captive in the line of men.

"It's Keil. God save the boy," Tylan gasped, his voice wracked with pain.

"Where are they taking him?" Percival demanded.

Cynric pointed to the wide, oval-shaped dirt field encircled by a dilapidated wooden wall. Wooden and stone viewing stands lined both sides of the field. "There," he said.

Percival recognized the place. The site had originally been a Roman amphitheater. It had been used to host jousting tournaments during the Pendragon's reign. When he was nine years old, he had watched a tournament there with his father. The great Sir Lancelot had unhorsed five challengers that day before retiring from the field as the tourney champion.

Percival looked at Cynric. "Why are they taking him to the jousting field?"

Cynric hesitated and then answered in a voice imbued with long-restrained anger. "It's what they call tournament day."

The archer pointed toward the tournament field. "Look, in the center of the field. Do you see that wooden post? On tournament day, once a month, Hengst invites challengers to come and fight him for lordship of the city. At first, some accepted his challenge, but he killed them, one and all. When challengers stopped coming, Hengst upped the ante. His men seize a local woman, a farmer's wife or daughter usually, and he ties her to that post. If no one comes to defend her, he either kills her or gives her to his men. Husbands, sons, relatives . . . well, they used to come to try to save their women." He shook his head, as if remembering each futile death. "It was a slaughter. Hengst . . . he is as close to invincible as they come. So now, no one comes to take up the challenge, and that . . . that's not acceptable—"

"So he forces people to fight him," Percival said in a cold, hard voice, remembering another arena on the other side of the world.

Cynric nodded. "Yes. Hengst can't live without the fear, the blood. And this is his way of keeping the people down. The mayor, the guildsmen . . . the people, they have to attend and watch, unless they can find a safe place to hide."

Percival stared at the field, and a storm of memories raged through his mind. He remembered being escorted to the center of the stadium by ten of Khalid's soldiers, where his sword awaited him at the foot of the bound captives. Sometimes, the daily fare offered for slaughter would be a woman, sometimes a child, sometimes both. More often than not they were young slaves, but sometimes they were just poor travelers taken by force. Before each battle, he would kneel and pray before taking up his sword. Then he would turn, and the challengers would come, yet again.

"When does it begin?" the Knight asked quietly.

"Noon," Cynric answered.

"Then," Percival said in a voice as cold and hard as the sword by his side, "I have an hour or so to present myself as a challenger."

Cynric stared at him, confused, and then his eyes widened.

Capussa stepped over to Percival, as if to block his way. "This is not your fight," he said with quiet intensity. "You bore more than your share of pain and suffering in the arena. Surely this God in which you place so much faith did not bring you home so that you could once again take up the sword of the gladiator."

Percival looked off in the distance for a long moment, and then his eyes met those of his friend. "And what, Capussa of Numidia, if all the pain that I have suffered and all the terrible skills that I have learned were intended to prepare me for this day . . . to give me the courage, the strength, and the means to defeat this Hengst the Butcher and save the people he would slaughter on this day? And if that were true, what would I be, if I just rode on?"

Capussa stared at the Knight in silence for a moment, and then he shook his head, the anger and frustration in his eyes fading. "You are either a fool, my brother, and you will die a useless death today, or . . . this is a day that shall be long remembered."

And then he smiled.

"So let us go together and face the steel of our enemies, as we have so many times before."

"Capussa, you have no—"

"Of course I do. You have just said that your God may have forged you into a weapon—one to be wielded today against this dog, Hengst. Could he not have chosen Capussa as his sword as well? What would my ancestors think of me, if I, as you say, just rode on? No, I too must seek my fate in this tournament."

Percival stared at his friend for a long moment. "I would argue, but you're as stubborn as a rock."

"Indeed, and as strong as one too," Capussa said with a smile.

"You're both mad!" Cynric said. "Hengst and his brother Ivarr have near a thousand men in that town. Even if you kill the Butcher, you will die minutes later, as will Keil and the rest of those rounded up for today's slaughter."

"Cynric," Tylan said, "the men we traded with before dawn said that Ivarr and about two hundred men traveled north three days ago. Also, a shipment of mead came in yesterday, and most of Hengst's remaining men will be sleeping off a long night of drinking."

"None of that matters," Cynric said, cutting him off. "There will still be enough men on that field today to kill all of us."

"Not," Percival said with quiet conviction, "if the people rise and join us."

"Rise?" Cynric said incredulously. "Sir Percival, the Londinium that you once knew is no more. Hengst and his reavers have had their boot on the neck of every man, woman, and child in that godforsaken place for near five years. This bloody tournament he puts on is his way of daring them to rise against his power. They've had many chances—it's just not in them anymore."

Percival walked over to Cynric and gripped his shoulder. "If they have hope, then they may rise up and cast down their oppressor. With God's favor, I can give them that. Now, I would ask a boon of you. I would ask that you take a message to the Queen—"

"We will take it to her together, or not at all," Cynric interrupted, an unyielding look on his face. "I am going to that field with you, come what will, and with all due respect, Sir Percival, do not try to dissuade me. I have chosen my path."

"And I as well," Tylan said in a low growl.

"We . . . we will be coming along as well, Sir Percival," said a voice from behind him.

Percival turned to face the man who'd spoken. It was Bray and the other five men. The Knight stared at the hardy woodsmen. For a moment, he wanted to rage at their foolhardiness, to demand they think long and hard on the fate they were embracing, and then he realized they already had. In the end, all he could do was nod and pray he was not leading them to a wasted death.

Capussa walked over to Percival, slapped him on the back, and then spoke, a broad smile on his face. "Well, now that you've decided to start a war, do you mind overly much if I propose a plan to win it?"

CHAPTER 15

THE TOURNAMENT FIELD IN LONDINIUM

ynric sat on the north side of the tournament arena in one of the upper rows of tiered stone seats. The surrounding crowd of nearly a thousand strong was quiet, submissive, and clearly afraid of the ten armed men standing along the wall that separated the stands from the tournament field below. Most of the people around the archer were men, but there were some women and even a few children.

The guards, who ranged from Norse warriors to common brigands, were armed with an array of poorly maintained swords, axes, and clubs. Four of them were sharing a large skin of mead, and the other six looked as if they'd been dragged out of bed after a hard night of drinking. Only one of the guards seemed interested in the crowd. His eyes were fixed on a young woman whose long, blond tresses had accidentally strayed from beneath the hood of her brown cloak, drawing the man's attention.

Cynric glanced quickly over at Tylan and his other men. They'd taken up positions throughout the stands that would enable them to quickly kill the guards near the wall and then provide protective cover for Sir Percival. His gaze returned to the tournament field just as two of Hengst's men walked through a gate, half dragging a young woman of perhaps sixteen years. Their entrance was met with a roar from the boisterous crowd of Norse warriors and local brigands seated in the rows of stone seats encircling the south side of the field. The woman in the brown cloak seated below Cynric started to rise when the captive was brought into the arena, but the larger cloaked figure sitting beside her quickly pulled her back down.

The two men led the captive young woman to the tall wooden post in the center of the field and bound her hands to an iron ring embedded in the wood. After she was secured, the smaller of her two captors tried to embrace her, but she kicked him with surprising strength, and he dropped to his knees in pain. This drew a howl of laughter from the men in the reviewing stand on the other side of the field. When the man recovered, he stood up and raised a hand to strike the woman, but his larger companion yanked him away from the woman and pushed him toward the gate they had entered moments earlier.

A murmur went through the crowd in front of him, and for a moment, Cynric couldn't see what they were looking at. Then he saw Keil. He and two other bound men were being roughly herded onto the field by two guards whose dress and crude weaponry marked them as common brigands. The captive to Keil's right was a tall, thin man on the edge of middle age. Cynric suspected he was a farmer, with a wife and a brood of children at home. The second captive, on Keil's left, was short, square, and balding, and although he looked as though he might be able to defend himself, the ample belly overhanging his worn leather belt made it clear he would have no chance against Hengst.

When Keil glanced back at the people in the stands, the guard behind him shoved him, and he stumbled and fell. The brigand kicked him as he scrambled back to his feet, drawing a gasp of pain from the young man. Cynric gripped the long wooden bow hidden inside his cloak in quiet rage and promised himself that the man would be one of the first to die.

One of the brigands called out a guttural command, and the three captives stopped a step outside the ring of stones. Keil glanced over at the bound young woman, drawing another blow from the man behind him.

"Don't look over there, dog. You'll be spitted on Hengst's sword long before your grubby—"

The man's bellow was cut short by a cacophony of horns, followed by the opening of the main gate to the tournament field.

Cynric was surprised when Hengst walked through the gate without any ceremonial entourage, but then he decided the Norseman didn't need one. A man who'd once seen the Norse warrior up close had told Cynric that Hengst's face was his most terrifying feature, and now Cynric understood why. The Norseman's mane of reddish-blond hair framed a bulging forehead, a broad face, and a massive jaw. An outsized bony ridge formed a roof over two blazing grey-blue eyes, a broad, flat nose, and a cruel, thin mouth. A red scar ran from the Norseman's missing right ear across his cheek to the cleft of his jaw. The wound had taken a part of the giant's upper lip and red mustache, giving his face a permanent snarl.

The Norseman stood over twenty-one hands tall, weighed more than twenty stone, and despite the tales told of his legendary bouts of drinking, eating, and wenching, he had lost none of his physical might. The bulging muscles in the warlord's massive arms and legs rippled under his pale skin as he strode across the field.

The giant wore black leather boots, fine woolen breeches, and a heavy leather jerkin, but no chest armor. His forearms were protected by black gauntlets, but his upper arms, which were heavily scarred, were bare to the shoulder. A blackened steel shield was slung across his right shoulder, held in place by a leather strap. In his right hand, the Norseman held a long steel sword, the blade of which was resting on his right shoulder. In his left hand, he held a massive two-bladed axe, the neck of which rested on his left shoulder.

Cynric's gaze returned to Keil and the other prisoners and the woman tied to the post. He could almost feel their terror across the dirt expanse separating them. Keil and the other three men tried to step back as the giant approached, but the brigands behind shoved them into the ring of stones encircling the center of the field.

When the Norseman reached the post in the center of the ring, he stopped a mere foot from the visibly trembling young woman and towered over her in silence. Then he let out a roar and buried the two-bladed axe in the wooden post just above her head. She screamed as if her arms were being torn from her body and then collapsed, sobbing hysterically.

As soon as the axe struck the wood, the crowd of Norsemen in the southern stands bellowed their approval. Cynric stared at the unruly mass of men. He knew they would pour onto the field seeking vengeance if Percival vanquished the monster now parading around the stone circle, with his shield and sword raised in triumph above his head. The archer quickly assessed his targets.

There were nearly two hundred men, and an equal or greater number of women. Less than half of the men were Norse warriors, and many of them were either drunk or working toward that goal. The rest were a motley collection of outlaws and brigands, men who served as Hengst's tax collectors in return for a share of the scraps from his table. Cynric had told his men to focus their fire upon the Norse warriors. If they were killed or broken, the others would flee.

After three trips around the circle, the Norse giant stopped in the center and bellowed out his challenge.

"People of Londinium, I am Hengst the Butcher, Lord of Londinium and Southern Albion. Anyone who would challenge my rule, step forward, and try to take my beautiful head."

The crowd in the far stands howled at the joke and then fell silent as Hengst continued.

"If you can defeat me, this woman shall be your slave, and you may have my kingdom—if you have the might to hold it against my kin."

Hengst finished by pointing to the men and women in the far stands who thundered, "Never!"

Then the Norseman turned and faced Cynric and the people of Londinium sitting around him. His eyes roved over the silent crowd with scorn.

"And who among you would challenge me today? Who?" the giant bellowed.

Cold fury raged through the Archer, but he sat unmoving. When no response was made, the crowd in the far stand screamed insults and taunts as their champion stood awaiting. Then the boisterous cacophony suddenly subsided, and the tournament field grew quiet.

Hengst stood for a moment, appearing confused by the sudden stillness, and then turned around. His eyes widened.

Cynric followed the Butcher's gaze. A man had entered the field from another gate. He was walking toward the stone ring.

It was Sir Percival.

*　*　*

PERCIVAL SILENTLY WATCHED the Norseman's arrogant display from an archway on the west side of the tournament field, unseen in the shadows, and gauged the reaction of the crowds on both sides of the arena. He had heard raucous cheers and taunts like those of the Norsemen many times before in another arena on the other side of the world, just as he had watched many a gladiator revel in this adulation, only to die moments later. This was of no moment to him. What mattered on this day was not the clamor on the south side of the arena, but the silence on the north.

His gaze touched on the faces of the people of Londinium, staring at the cruel spectacle unfolding before them. Over the centuries, they had endured plagues, fires, and invasions, and yet each time, they had retaken and rebuilt what was theirs. Unlike Cynric, Percival did not believe their silence bespoke despair, but instead cloaked a terrible rage—a rage he intended to unleash.

Percival waited until the Norse giant had bellowed out his challenge before he emerged from the archway and started across the arena. The hood of Bray's tattered traveling cloak hid his helmet. The rest of the garment covered his gauntleted forearms, the polished steel shield affixed to his left forearm, and the coat of arms emblazoned on the white tabard he wore underneath. The only evidence of a weapon was the pommel of the sword, just visible through a hole in the cloth near his waist.

He stopped ten paces from the ring of stones, shrugged off the wineskin draped across his right shoulder, and turned to the stands filled with Hengst's supporters.

"I challenge," he called out in a loud, clear voice.

Then he turned to the stands where the people of Londinium were watching him, with a mixture of incredulity and hope, and spoke in a loud and defiant voice.

"I challenge on behalf of the good people of Londinium. I stand in their stead, every man, woman, and child."

When he finished, Percival turned to face Hengst, his visage only partially visible under the hood, and called out in a voice that carried no hint of fear, "Do you accept my challenge?"

The Norseman stared at Percival for a moment and then threw back his head and let out a roar of laughter, drawing a round of laughs and screams for blood from the crowd in the stands across the field. The people on the north side of the field were deathly silent. After enjoying the moment, the Norseman's amusement turned to disdain.

"Step forward, you drunken beggar, that I may take your head, and then," he turned to Keil and the other two men, "I shall spit the three of you, making it a foursome."

Percival looked at the Norseman for a long moment, and then he made the sign of the cross. Hengst sneered, "Your prayers will not help you now, dog. Your life was mine the moment you entered this arena."

"My prayer was not for me, Norseman, but for you," Percival said quietly as he stepped into the ring of stones and drew his sword.

As he began to circle the larger man, he remembered Capussa's words of advice: "You cannot kill this man too quickly. The crowd will see it as mere chance. You must defeat him in a way that destroys what he stands for." Percival knew his Numidian friend was right. Survival alone would not bring victory. He had to rip away Hengst the Butcher's cloak of invincibility, cast it into the dust, and trample it underfoot. Only this would spark the uprising he needed.

The Norseman made a show of leisurely taking the blade of his sword off his shoulder and lowering his shield. Then he exploded across the circle, bellowing a battle cry. His upraised sword sliced downward in a strike that would have cleaved Percival's body from shoulder to waist had it landed.

The Knight sprang forward and to the right the instant the Norse warrior began his rush. As the giant raced past him, Percival smashed his buckler shield into the side of his head with bone-crushing force. The blow rocked the Norseman, and he stumbled and dropped to one knee. When he regained his balance and turned to face his opponent, blood flowed down the side of his face and one knee was covered in dust and blood. Percival waited in the middle of the circle for the Norseman to recover. He wheeled his sword in a circle, in a single fluid movement, inviting the giant to attack him again.

"Who are you?" the enraged Norseman roared as he warily circled his opponent in a fighting crouch.

Percival drew off his hood and unhooked the clasp at his neck. Bray's cloak fell to the ground, revealing a white tabard emblazoned with a black circle, anchored with a white cross. A ring of swords encircled the cross. The largest and brightest of the swords bore the word *Excalibur*.

A murmur surged through the crowd on the north side of the arena, and people began to stand up and push forward. An old man in front yelled out, "It's the mark of the Table!"

"I," Percival answered in a voice that could be heard by every ear, "am Sir Percival of the Round Table, and I call upon you, Hengst, to account for your foul deeds. Yield and face the King's justice, and you may be spared."

The giant stared at Percival, the surprise on his face turning to a black rage. He spat in the dirt and pointed to the wall on his left.

"Do you see that sack of rags and bones hanging from the wall? Sir Dinadan he called himself . . . said he was a Knight of your precious Table, he did. I killed him, slowly. He died begging for his life, just like you will."

Percival glanced over the Norseman's shoulder at the remains of the body hanging from a crude hook in the far wall. The ravages of weather, and the teeth and claws of carrion, had rendered the body unrecognizable, but he could still make out the faint symbol of the Table on the now tattered and frayed tabard.

A picture of Dinadan, the dead and now defiled Knight, flashed through Percival's mind. His brother Knight had been a square powerful man, always smiling and laughing when attending the many celebratory dinners held at court. Percival remembered the man's petite and quiet wife, a Lady from Londinium. Dinadan must have been wounded at Camlann and then come to the aid of his adopted city once he had recovered.

Rage surged through Percival, but he mastered its power as quickly as it swept over him. Anger was a two-edged sword—one side of its blade made a warrior quicker and stronger, but the other made him precipitate and predictable. Hundreds of brutal training sessions with Capussa and the Mongol, Batukhan, had given him the ability to harness its power, while avoiding its weakness.

Percival forced a smile to his face and spread his arms wide as he circled the giant and spoke scornfully, his voice carrying across the field.

"Then come, Hengst, the butcher of farmers, tradesmen, women, and children; come and kill me. Or has Hengst the thief, rapist, and murderer grown fat killing the weak and innocent? Could it be that your arms have become as frail as your face is ugly? No? Then come and prove otherwise to the rabble over there that licks your boots!" Percival pointed his sword at Hengst's supporters as he finished, drawing howls of rage.

Fury swept over the Norseman's face, and he moved toward Percival, striking his sword against his shield. As he approached, Percival circled to the left and then to the right and then quickly back to the left again, forcing the giant to change his stance each time he moved. Hengst's movements and his prior attack had disclosed a weakness. The Norseman was explosively quick in a linear attack, but he lacked the skill to adapt to rapid lateral movements.

Hengst closed to within four yards of Percival and once again rushed him, but this time he was more cautious, swinging his sword in a more controlled horizontal strike at Percival's chest. Percival moved away from the blow, but he was forced to use both his shield and sword to stop the Norseman's blade from cutting him down.

The impact of the clash momentarily numbed his shield arm and sent a lancing pain through his left shoulder. He bought a moment's respite by stabbing his sword at the Norseman's face, forcing him to step backward. After the exchange, Percival knew he couldn't continue to trade blows with Hengst and wear him down. His blade was half the weight of the Norseman's, and the power behind the giant's strokes was so great any single blow could disable him, even if he was able to parry it. He would have to defeat the Norseman quickly using a high-risk maneuver the giant would not suspect.

As Percival circled to Hengst's right, he watched the giant's feet, knowing from the last two rushes that the Norseman would partially rise from his crouch a second before he lunged, and lead with his left leg. The second his opponent committed himself to a third charge, Percival threw himself forward in a dive that flowed into a roll. Hengst struggled to alter his own direction and, at the same time, change the path of his sword to strike his foe, but neither effort succeeded. Percival blocked the sword stroke with the shield on his left forearm and slashed the giant's left thigh as he passed, drawing a scream of rage and pain.

As the Knight completed his roll and came to his feet behind him, the Norseman pivoted on his wounded left leg and wheeled around, swinging a crushing stroke at Percival's head. Percival knew he was too close to escape the sweep of Hengst's sword, so he wheeled inward, bringing himself within a foot of the giant, dropped to one knee, and plunged his sword in a reverse stroke into the giant's chest with all of his strength. Hengst's face contorted in shock, and his sword fell to the ground.

Percival stood and ripped his sword from the giant's chest. For a moment, the Norseman stood facing him, his face a mixture of rage and disbelief, then he dropped to his knees and fell face-first into the dirt. A silence fell over the tournament field, and then cries of rage exploded from the Norse in the southern stands. Percival stepped over the body of Hengst the Butcher and walked toward the two brigands standing behind Keil. The Knight wheeled his sword in a circle with practiced ease as he approached. The two men hesitated and then ran for the main gate. Percival cut the captive men's bonds, nodded to Keil, and then pointed to the woman tied to the post.

"Keil, free the girl, quickly."

As Keil ran toward the woman, men armed with swords warily entered the tournament field through the main gate—Hengst's men.

Percival knew his rescue was about to become a desperate battle of retreat, unless the people in the north stands joined him. He strode toward them and then stopped and pointed to the armed Norsemen walking through the gate.

"People of Londinium," he shouted to the shocked and exultant faces staring at him in awe, "Albion is your land, and this city is your home! I call upon you to join me and take it back from these wolves. I, Sir Percival of the Table, call upon you to rise and take back what is yours! Rise!" Percival thundered.

Cynric, Tylan, and the rest of the men bellowed their approval and leaped out of their seats, running toward the guards waiting in the first row with swords drawn. Cynric shouted to the men and women around him. "There's a thousand of us and less than two hundred of them! Rise and crush them!"

One of the guards started toward Cynric, sword drawn, but he stopped midstep as an arrow from Tylan's bow struck his chest, knocking him over the wall onto the tourney field below. There was a moment of hesitation, and then it was as if a dam broke. The people of Londinium surged forward, threw the remaining guards over the wall, and jumped down to the tournament field.

The closest of Hengst's men raced toward Percival with swords drawn, and the Knight turned to meet them. The first two men fell to the ground in rapid succession, pinioned by arrows from Capussa's bow. Seconds later, Cynric and all of his men rhythmically sent arrow after arrow into the throng of shocked Norsemen. The more hardened warriors continued to run forward, but most of the men, who were common brigands, slowed, and some retreated as the men from the Londinium stands surged toward them, screaming for blood.

Two of the Norse warriors reached Percival; he dodged a blow from one and cut down the second. As he whirled to meet a second attack, he saw the man was already falling to the ground, cut down by Capussa's blade. He and the Numidian then turned to face the rest of the Norse, but the attack had been broken.

The exultant crowd chased the survivors out of the main gate and into the streets beyond. As word of Hengst's death spread, the crowd swelled and surged through the streets, killing or subduing the remainder of Hengst's men.

Capussa walked over to Percival and pointed his sword at the slain giant.

"You have grown soft, Knight. For a moment there, I thought he had you."

"For a moment there, I thought he did too," Percival said, a small smile coming to his face. "Thank God I remembered Batukhan's reverse stroke."

"Bah! Your life was saved by the footwork and positioning that I taught you. That and relentless training!"

Percival laughed and rested a hand on his friend's shoulder.

"Whether it was both or neither, I am glad to be alive. Now, let us see if the good people of Londinium need any help with the rest of Hengst's brood, and then," Percival said, his smile fading as he turned to look at the remains of Sir Dinadan, "I have to bury one of my brothers."

CHAPTER 16

ABBEY CWM HIR

ister Aranwen moved from one chair in the sitting room outside Guinevere's personal quarters to a second chair beside the window where the light was better, and once again tried to thread a string of yarn through the eye of an old wooden needle. Her vision was still as sharp as ever, but her fingers were no longer as dexterous as they used to be, making the task a daily struggle. At the moment when success seemed certain, the outer door to the room burst open, and Cadwyn ran in, whereupon she whirled about, pantomiming a sword fight.

Sister Aranwen was so shocked she dropped both her knitting needles and ball of yarn on the floor. For an instant, she watched the younger woman whirl about the room and then erupted.

"Cadwyn Hydwell! I swear by all the saints you will be the death of me! What is it you are doing?"

Cadwyn ignored the demand and continued to strike to the left and the right with her invisible sword, punctuating each blow with the cry, "He is invincible!"

Sister Aranwen put her hands on her hips and opened her mouth to reprimand the young woman. Before she could say a word, Guinevere, drawn by the commotion, opened the door to the library and walked into the room. The nun quickly curtsied and then pointed to the whirling Cadwyn, who was still unaware of the Queen's presence.

"I fear she has finally lost her mind, Milady, but then, I'm not surprised."

Cadwyn stopped suddenly in the midst of another whirl, her face flushed as she curtsied to the Queen. "Milady! Forgive me . . . I . . . I ran all the way from the stables. It's wonderful!"

Guinevere gestured to the pitcher of water and goblets resting on the nearby table.

"Please, Cadwyn, have a drink of water."

"Yes, please do," Sister Aranwen said wryly. "Maybe that will bring you back to your senses."

Cadwyn ignored the water and spoke in a torrent. "Milady, Sir Percival . . . it is he! He, he challenged Hengst the Butcher in Londinium on tournament day. He demanded that the Norseman yield to the King's justice or face his sword."

The bemused smile on Guinevere's face faded, and she raised a hand to her lips.

"No. That cannot be. He—"

Cadwyn, seeing her distress, rushed on. "Milady, Sir Percival slew the Butcher before all the people of Londinium . . . and then he called upon them to rise up . . . and . . . and, Milady, the people . . . they heeded his call! Londinium is free!"

Sister Aranwen's eyes widened, and she looked over at Guinevere.

The Queen was staring at her young friend, a look of confusion on her face. "Free? I don't understand."

Cadwyn rushed over to Guinevere, an exultant smile on her face. "Milady, the people rose up and took over the city! Hengst's men . . . they're either dead or captured, or they just ran away. Londinium is free! It is free!"

Trembling, Guinevere slowly sat down in one of the chairs beside the table. Sister Aranwen hurried to sit next to her, laying one hand upon the Queen's arm.

"Cadwyn, who . . . who told you of this?" Guinevere asked, the disbelief evident in her voice.

"Harri told me."

Guinevere shook her head. "Harri?"

Cadwyn rushed on. "Milady, you told me to send three messengers to seek out Sir Percival. Harri—he's one of Torn's men—was one of the three. He stopped in Isca to stay the night, and the town was aflame with the good tidings. So he raced back here to tell us."

Guinevere stared at the young woman, her face frozen, and then she slowly slid to her knees beside the chair and clasped her hands together in prayer.

"Thank God, thank God! Please, let us give thanks."

Sister Aranwen gazed upward to heaven, not knowing if she was more grateful for the news or for the shining look on Guinevere's face. Both were beautiful. She bowed her head then and felt Cadwyn kneel beside her.

After several minutes, Cadwyn whispered loudly, "Milady, there is more."

Sister Aranwen scowled at the interruption and continued to pray, but when Guinevere made the sign of the cross and resumed her place at the table, the nun quickly stood and resumed her seat as well. For the first time in many a year, she felt a flicker of hope, but she kept any hint of the inner feeling from her face.

Cadwyn jumped up and took the seat across from the two women.

"Please," Guinevere said calmly, placing both hands on the table in front of her, "tell me everything."

The young woman opened her mouth to continue her story, but instead, struck her petite fists down on the arms of the chair and said, "Milady, he is invinc—"

"Cadwyn Hydwell, we have heard that!" Sister Aranwen interrupted. "Now please, tell us the rest of the bloody story."

Guinevere's eyes widened, and she restrained a smile. "Yes, please go on, my dear."

"Yes, Milady," she said, chastened for a moment, and then continued in a rush.

"Harri said that Hengst holds a tournament in the city every month. He forces the people in the city to come to it. He always ties a woman to a post in the middle of the tournament field and threatens to give the woman to his men unless someone comes to defend her. This time, Sir Percival walked out on the field and took up the challenge. They say he wore a knight's tabard with the sign of the Table!"

Cadwyn stopped to draw in breath and then continued. "There was a terrible battle, and Sir Percival struck down the Butcher with a mighty blow. Then . . . then he turned to the people of Londinium in the stands, and he ordered them to rise up against their oppressors, and they did. Harri said there were bowmen in the stands—they were Sir Percival's men. The bowmen and the rest of the crowd leaped onto the tournament field and killed Hengst's men. Then the whole city rose up!"

Sister Aranwen sat on the edge of her chair, for once mesmerized by the younger woman. Guinevere was staring at her handmaiden, rapt with attention.

"And then what?" the nun prodded.

After a moment of hesitation, Cadwyn leaned over and said conspiratorially, "He is coming."

Guinevere frowned. "Who is coming?"

"Sir Percival, Milady!" Cadwyn jumped out of her chair, her eyes exultant. "He comes here. The messenger said he is coming north at great speed. He travels with the man from Africa that Captain Potter spoke of, and others have joined him along the way. The people in Isca told Harri that his ranks grow with every league he rides."

"Who are these people?" Guinevere asked.

"Harri said they're just common folk. They come from the forests, the towns, and the villages. He does not call for them, but they come anyway."

Guinevere stood and walked to the window and then spoke in a quiet voice. "Arthur said that Percival would return. He left me a note before he took the field at Camlann. I didn't find it until months later. It was in a box of personal things I kept hidden. I . . . I didn't think he knew about it. At first, I hoped and prayed what he prophesied would come true, but . . . as the years passed, I no longer believed." She turned and faced Sister Aranwen and Cadwyn, a radiant smile on her face. "I should have had faith. God be praised. It has come to pass, just as he said it would."

"God be praised," Sister Aranwen echoed.

Guinevere moved back to the table and took her seat, a smile on her face, her eyes alight with joy. "We, my dear friends, have much to do before the good Knight pays us a visit," Guinevere said. "So let us prepare."

North of Londinium

Ivarr the Red sat in an oversized wooden chair, salvaged from one of the burning houses in the village behind him, holding a pitcher of mead. The chair sat astride a path that led to a circular stone tower, thirty yards distant. During the Pendragon's reign, the tower had been the quarters of a royal sheriff. It was about to become a funeral pyre for the men, women, and children of the village barricaded within.

The Norseman watched in satisfaction as his men piled logs, branches, and hay around the base of the tower. The village had nothing of value other than the villagers themselves. Those who surrendered when the fire and smoke made their refuge unbearable would be taken to Londinium and sold into slavery. The others would die in the flames.

Ivarr knew the village's half-starved peasants would not sell for much, but then he hadn't laid waste to the village for coin. He was sending a message. The village was located just across the river, marking the border between Morgana's lands and those claimed by Hengst. He wanted Morgana to know he could ravage her lands as well, any time he desired.

"Ivarr!"

The Norse warlord took another leisurely drink from the pitcher of mead before turning to the tall, blond warrior walking toward him— Ulf. Ivarr disliked the man, but he had made him second-in-command. His fellow countryman was both a doughty fighter and a shrewd tactician. Smart men, Ivarr knew, were dangerous men. Keeping the other man close made it easier to keep an eye on him, and to kill him if it became necessary.

"Speak," he ordered.

"A messenger has come from Londinium. He killed two horses getting here. He says . . . he says . . ." The man's voice trailed off.

"Speak, or I shall have your tongue!" Ivarr growled.

The man swallowed heavily and continued, "He says Hengst is dead, and Londinium has fallen, my lord."

Ivarr exploded out of his seat and faced the scarred warrior, his face a mask of incredulity and rage. "What! Bring this man to me!" he roared.

Ulf pointed toward the center of the village. "He cannot walk. We must go to him."

Ivarr brushed the other man aside and walked toward the circle of men gathered around the village well. The crowd parted as the Norseman approached.

A small, filthy man was sitting on the ground gasping for breath. His face was battered and swollen and covered in a heavy patina of dust mixed with blood. Ivarr recognized the man. He was one of the brigands his brother used to collect taxes. He strode over to the man and kicked the ladle of water he held from his hands.

"Speak, dog! What is this about my brother?"

"He's dead . . . slain by a Knight of the Table," the man said in hoarse gasps.

Ivarr kicked the man viciously in the side. "You lie, dog. The Knights are all dead."

The man groaned and held up his hands in fear. "Please, Lord Ivarr . . . I speak the truth. One lives. I saw him. He challenged Hengst on tournament day . . . and killed him. Then he called upon the people of the city to rise."

"Rise? What do you mean, *rise*?" Ivarr demanded.

"To rise up against us, and they did. It happened so fast . . . there were too many of them—we were slaughtered."

Ivarr stared at the man, struggling to contain his rage. "What say you? The city is taken? Who is this knight? How many men did he have?"

"They say he is Sir Percival. They say he returned from the Holy Land. I have never seen a man fight like that. I—"

Ivarr ripped his sword from its sheath and pressed it against the man's throat.

"I asked you, how many men did he have?"

The brigand's eyes widened as he gasped out his reply. "T-ten, m-maybe twenty, mostly bowmen."

"When? How many days have passed since the town was taken?"

The man hesitated and Ivarr pressed the tip of the sword into his flesh, drawing blood. The man frantically tried to move away from the pointed sword as he answered in a raspy whisper. "T-two days ago, maybe t-three. Been riding for so l-long, I—"

Ivarr's boot smashed into the side of the man's head, and he slumped to the ground. The Norseman turned to Ulf, his face a mask of rage. "Every man with a horse will ride with me to Londinium, now. The men afoot will follow at a forced march."

"But it is late in the day and the fortress—"

"We ride and march, now!" Ivarr shouted, putting the point of his sword against Ulf's chest.

"So it shall be," Ulf answered, a mixture of fear and anger in his eyes.

Ivarr turned to the men watching the tense confrontation and roared, "Abandon the siege! We ride and march for Londinium, now! Riders, mount your horses! All others prepare to march. You will leave your booty."

Howls of protest followed the order.

Ivarr stepped past Ulf and jumped up on the stone wall encircling the well, so all of his men could see and hear him.

"Heed my words well, you fools! Hengst is dead! Londinium has been retaken by the Britons!"

The rumblings from the men ceased, and for the first time in hours, the small village was deathly quiet.

"You want your booty? Slaves to sell? Where will you sell them? Londinium is the slavers' port, Londinium is where you spend your coin, and Londinium is where you sleep. Without that city you have no home, unless you would return to your cold, hard villages in the north, like a pack of cowardly beggars."

The men were silent for a moment, and then a man in the front roared, "Never!" Others in the back took up the cry.

"Then we take back Londinium, and we shall show no mercy! Any man who stands against us shall be put to the sword, and his wife and children shall be sold as slaves!"

The Norsemen roared their approval.

"Now, mount! We ride for Londinium!"

CHAPTER 17

LONDINIUM

ir Percival watched the raucous celebration in the town square from a block away, on the second floor of a three-story stone tower. In the middle of the square, four men were playing a lively tune on an assortment of pipes, flutes, and stringed instruments, and several hundred men and women were dancing a simple step to the rhythm. Hundreds more were outside the circle clapping and keeping time, while drinking what Percival suspected was beer or mead.

Two pigs were being roasted over fires that had been built at each end of the square. The people of Londinium had apparently decided to put the ample stores stolen from them by Hengst and his men to good use.

Percival's gaze traveled from the square to the piles of burned and rotted timbers at the base of the tower—the remains of what had once been Londinium's great cathedral. The Knight remembered attending a mass in the church on a Sunday morning in another world, in another time.

Arthur, Guinevere, Londinium's Lord Mayor, and their retainers had been seated in the first pew on the right side of the church, and the Knights of the Table had occupied the pews behind them, in order of seniority. Percival and Galahad, as the Table's youngest knights, had been seated in the last pew. The lesser knights were seated behind them. The pews on the left side of the church were occupied by the bishops and the great lords and ladies of the land.

Throughout the mass, Galahad's blue eyes had roamed over the adoring women in the pews to the left, drawing smiles and twitters of laughter. Percival remembered surreptitiously striking his elbow into Galahad's side during the reading of the gospel, after the young knight winked at a particularly attractive and attentive young noblewoman. Galahad's grunt of pain had drawn an amused look from Sir Dinadan, the Knight of the Table killed by Hengst and left to rot in the stadium. He had been sitting in the pew ahead of them. Percival had buried the knight's remains in the church cemetery just an hour earlier.

The bittersweet remembrances were chased away by a respectful knock on the old oak door separating the room from the corridor beyond. Percival walked to the door and opened it, revealing Capussa, Cynric, and a smaller man, whose face was all but hidden in the cowl of his cloak.

Capussa stood behind the man, and Percival noted his friend had his right hand resting on his belt, an inch from the haft of his dagger. Cynric stood to Capussa's right, his eyes also wary. The archer nodded to Percival and spoke in a tone tinged with suspicion.

"Sir Percival, this man says that you know him. He says—"

"It is imperative that I see you," the man in the cowl finished.

Percival's face froze at the sound of the man's voice, and then he stepped to one side and waved the men into the chamber.

"Please, come in and close the door."

Capussa, his eyes still on the man in the cloak, followed him into the room along with Cynric. The archer closed the door behind them.

Percival turned to Capussa and Cynric and gestured to the man in the cloak. "Capussa, Cynric, meet Merlin the Wise, or should I say, Melitas Komnenos."

There was an audible intake of breath from Cynric as the man in the cloak reached up and lowered the cowl from his head, revealing a full head of grey hair and a face that was all but obscured by a bushy grey beard and mustache.

Merlin turned to Capussa, his intelligent grey eyes scanning the man's features with interest. "Numidian?" he asked.

Capussa raised an eyebrow and nodded. Merlin inclined his head and turned to Cynric.

"Cynric the Archer . . . you were in the Royal Fifth as I recall."

"Yes, I was," Cynric said, surprise in his voice.

"An exceptional outfit. You won the silver archer's cup at the royal fair one year. A fine shot that was."

"Thank you, sir," Cynric replied, his eyes widening.

The grey-haired man turned to Percival. "As for the name, Sir Percival, if you don't mind, just Merlin will do. It . . . reminds this old man of a happier time."

Percival stared in silence at Merlin for a moment and then nodded respectfully. "Then Merlin it is."

Merlin raised a quizzical eyebrow. "How did you know it was me? Even the Queen doesn't recognize me with all this wretched hair."

"In truth, I wouldn't have recognized you but for your voice. You were clean-shaven and your hair was black, not grey, when I left." Percival hesitated and glanced out the window at the crowd dancing in the street. "I only knew one Roman from the City of Constantine before I left. I met quite a few more on my . . . recent travels. Although you hide it well, you share the accent of your countrymen."

Merlin looked at Percival for a long moment in silence.

"I fear you have every reason to bear me ill will, Knight, but there were reasons for the path we chose," Merlin said in a voice laden with a thousand burdens.

Percival reached over and rested his hand on the older man's shoulder.

"I am sure there were, Merlin, and I would like to know them one day. As for ill will, I bear you none. I followed the orders of my King. What befell me on my travels was the will of God."

A sad smile came to Merlin's face. "I so wish I had your faith, Sir Percival. As for what I would tell you of yesteryear, it must wait. Today, we face imminent peril."

Percival gestured to a small table in the corner of the room that was surrounded by four chairs. "Please. Let us sit."

As soon as they were seated, Merlin pulled a scroll of parchment from beneath the folds of his cloak and unrolled it on the table. It was a detailed map of Londinium and the surrounding area for forty leagues.

He tapped the map with one finger, indicating a square drawn beside the river Tamesis.

"You and your men, and the people of Londinium, achieved a great victory today, but it will all be for naught if you do not prepare for what is to come. Ivarr the Red, Hengst's brother, is two, maybe three days' march to the north. He returns from a parley with Morgana."

The room was silent. It was as if the name had poisoned the air, and no one was willing to take the first breath.

"Morgana," Percival said quietly. "What was the purpose of this parley?"

"A border dispute," Merlin answered with a dismissive wave of his hand, "a matter of no moment. The threat we face today is from Ivarr the Red. He has two hundred men, all hardened Norse warriors. Possibly seventy-five are mounted and the rest are afoot. As soon as he learns of—"

"The death of his brother, he will seek vengeance," Capussa finished.

"Mm . . . not quite," Merlin said, leaning back in his chair. "I suspect Ivarr will welcome the passing of his brother. My spies tell me that he hated him as much as everyone else. No, what Ivarr cannot accept is the fall of Londinium. He and his fellow Norsemen have turned Londinium's port into a slaver's paradise. Every month, they round up and sell hundreds of souls into bondage and collect enough coin, along with the local taxes that they levy, to keep their coffers full of silver. Without Londinium, they have nothing."

"We can fortify the town and hold him off," Cynric said with conviction. "The people here will fight."

"And what say you, my friend?" Percival asked Capussa, who was studying the map intently. The Numidian shook his head.

"If we had a month to prepare, I would agree with the Archer, but we have what, a day, maybe two? The walls that I have seen have not been maintained, and I fear the Norse still have friends in this town—friends who will open one of the city's many gates while we sleep."

"And so what do you propose to do?" Merlin asked, stroking his long beard.

Capussa turned to Cynric. "How will they come?"

Cynric traced his finger along a line on the map that began north of Londinium and ran south to the city. "Here. Ivarr will come down the Roman road. It is the quickest way."

"Who controls these lands?" Percival asked, pointing to the lands alongside the road running north from the city.

"Local brigands and outlaws. They swore fealty to Hengst. He used them as tax collectors and sheriffs. The people in the area hate them, and but for the Norse, they would have put them to the sword long ago."

"Ivarr," Merlin corrected, "not Hengst, controls the men along this stretch of road, and they will surely join his force as he moves south."

Capussa nodded and traced his finger along the Roman road to a place where it crossed a shaded area. "Archer, tell me of this ground, if you know it."

"I know it," Cynric said. "The road here crosses the Wid River. The surrounding area is a fen."

"Fen?" Capussa questioned.

"A lowland area where the land is flooded. Passage on horseback is difficult and in some places, impossible." The archer tapped a spot on the map. "There is a bridge here. Ivarr will have to cross the river there on his way to the city."

"Many of the rivers we have passed have been shrouded in fog in the early morning," the Numidian said thoughtfully. "Would this river be thus as well?"

Cynric nodded. "Yes, but it burns off by late morning."

Capussa turned to Percival. "If you await this Ivarr, he will pick the time and place of battle, and his strength will grow as he nears the city. He is weakest now, and he will not expect you to attack him."

Percival looked over at his friend, and their eyes met. Then he slowly stood up. "I agree. We must march north, in all haste, and take them unawares."

"Do we march in the morning?" Merlin asked.

Percival looked out at the celebratory crowd and shook his head. "No, today, within the hour, if it can be done. I will speak to the people of Londinium. They must take the field with us in strength, or, as Merlin has said, all will be lost."

"That," Merlin said with a smile, "will just give me enough time to shave, which is something I've been waiting to do for a long, long time."

MORGANA'S CASTLE

The persistent knocking on the outer door to her chambers drew Morgana out of a deep sleep. After glancing at the angle of the light flowing through the window, she climbed out of bed, pulled on a luxuriant white silk robe, and slid the bejeweled knife on her night table into one of the robe's pockets. When she opened the outer door, Seneas was standing there, breathing heavily, a look of trepidation on his face.

"I trust you have a good reason for waking me?" Morgana said coldly.

Sencas nodded submissively. "Forgive my intrusion, Milady, but yes. It is a matter of urgency."

Morgana stared at him, glanced past him into the hall, and then curtly waved him into her chambers.

"Come in."

She walked across the anteroom, followed by Seneas, and sat down on a divan in the center of the room. She gestured to a chair across from her.

"Sit. Tell me what is so important that I must be awakened at this ungodly hour."

Seneas bowed his head and quickly sat down. "Yes, Milady. One of your spies just brought word from Londinium. The man rode for almost two days without—"

"The message, Seneas," Morgana said curtly.

"Hengst is dead, and Londinium has been retaken by the people."

Morgana's eyes widened. "What? Tell me of this—no, bring this man to me, now," she said as she stood up.

"Milady, he is in need of—"

"I don't care about his needs! I will have him tortured if he cannot rouse himself."

"Yes, yes, Milady, a moment only, please," Seneas said as he stood, bowed, and walked hurriedly to the door.

Minutes later, two guards came into her chambers, half carrying, half dragging a small man whose boots and woolens were caked in mud from his feet to his waist. Morgana looked at him in disgust. The man reeked of sweat and horse dung, and although she suspected he was barely twenty years of age, his drawn and pale face made him look ten years older. One of the guards started to shove the man to his knees, but he froze when Morgana spoke, her voice as sharp as a knife.

"Stop, fool! Have him sit on that wooden bench. I will not have him befoul my silken rug. Seneas, get him a drink of that wine there. Use the wooden cup."

Morgana waited until the man was seated and had taken a long drink of the wine before she spoke. "Your name?"

"Ulric, Milady," the man croaked in a hoarse voice.

"Take another drink of the wine," Morgana ordered, reluctantly moving closer to the foul-smelling man. "You will tell me, Ulric," she said in a tone laced with threat, "all that you know of recent events in Londinium. If you can do this, you will be well paid for your loyal service. If not, you will die this day. Do you understand?"

"Yes, yes, Milady," the man answered in a rush.

"Then speak!"

"Hengst the Butcher . . . each month he has a tournament where—"

"I know of this," Morgana interrupted. "Go on."

"Yes, Milady. Tournament day was two, no, three days ago. Hengst came to the tournament field and called for challengers. None . . . none have taken up the challenge in years, so men are seized and forced to fight. A woman is tied—"

"As I said, I know of this tournament day," Morgana said in a tone that made it clear he would get no more warnings. "Tell me what happened!"

"Yes, yes. Forgive me, Milady. But on this day, a man came and accepted Hengst's challenge. He walked right onto the bloody tournament field, he did. At first, he was dressed in a ragged old cloak, but when the fight started, he took it off, and . . . and he was wearing the mark of a Knight of the Table! He said he was Sir Percival, and he called upon Hengst to yield or die. Hengst attacked him . . . there was a fight like none I've ever seen before, Milady, and this Sir Percival, he killed Hengst. Struck him dead, he did. Then he freed the prisoners and the girl, and . . . and then he turned to the crowd. He called upon them to rise up against the Norse."

"And?"

"And? Oh yes, well Milady, the people in the stands, they rose up! There were bowmen among them. They knew what they were about, and there was a man with them, a man as black as coal—a warrior friend of Sir Percival's. The crowd raged through the streets, killing Hengst's men. Why, Milady, it was something to see! I've never seen a Knight of—"

Morgana turned a cold eye upon him and the man fell silent, a look of terror in his eyes.

"F-forgive me, Milady. That is all I know. Sir Percival and the people of Londinium, they hold the town now. There's not a Norseman within miles, I suspect."

Morgana picked up the dagger on the table beside her and approached the man. He pressed backward against the wall behind him, and his hands began to shake.

"Please, Milady. I've told you everything. I am a loyal—"

"Hush," Morgana whispered. "Answer this next question very carefully, my loyal servant. Did you or anyone else see a man with Sir Percival—an old man, with slightly darker skin than one of your land. He would be a hand shorter than I, and he would speak your language like a man from a foreign land, as I do."

Ulric looked to the left and right at his guards and then back at Morgana, terror growing on his face. He started to shake his head, but then froze.

"Wait. I did see this man—I mean, what I saw was a man of that height, but I couldn't see his face or hair. He kept himself hidden. The hood of his cloak was always up, but this man, he, he did go to see Sir Percival. I watched the man with the coal skin and the man known as Cynric the Archer take him to Sir Percival."

"And then?" Morgana demanded. "What else did you see?"

"That . . . that is all, Milady. I took to the road after that. I . . . I'm sorry, please . . ."

Morgana straightened up and smiled. She turned to Seneas. "Pay this man well. See that he gets a bath, food, and a night's rest. Then he is to return to Londinium on a new horse."

"Yes, Milady."

She looked down at her spy. "You have done well, but you will do much more, and you will be paid well for your service . . . very well. You are to return to Londinium and follow Sir Percival wherever he goes. You will join his men, if you can do so without suspicion. Once every ten days, marked from this day, I will send a messenger to you. He will tell you that he knows your brother. That is how you will know him. Tell him all that you have learned of the man in the hooded cloak. You will also learn as much as you can about this Sir Percival's plans. Do you understand this?"

The man nodded. "Yes, Milady. I will do as you say."

"Good. Now go; bathe, eat, and rest. Then ride like the wind back to Londinium."

"Yes, Milady."

Morgana nodded to the guards as they followed the man out of the room. Seneas moved to follow them, but she raised a hand, and the old man stopped and turned to face her.

"Seneas, after I have bathed and eaten, I would speak to Lord Aeron of this."

"Is this wise, Milady? He was once—"

"I will decide what it is wise, Seneas," Morgana said sharply. "If Lord Aeron knew of this Sir Percival in his former life as a Knight of the Table, then all the more reason to question him on the matter. And if, as you have implied, his loyalty may be at risk, then I would know it now. But, in truth, I have no worries in that regard. Lord Aeron is a prisoner of his honor and his love for his precious Queen. He will not break his vow."

"Yes, Milady, forgive me."

* * *

LORD AERON KNOCKED on the door to Morgana's chambers. A servant girl opened the door and gestured for him to enter, and then left the room without a word.

"Come in, Lord Aeron, and seat yourself."

Lord Aeron ignored the plush chair closest to Morgana's divan and instead sat on a wood bench that he knew was placed there for the servants. A look of irritation crossed Morgana's face, but it vanished a moment later.

"And how do you fare this morning, Lord Aeron?"

"I am well, but I suspect you didn't ask me here to inquire after my health."

A cold smile came to Morgana's face. "No, I did not. I have every confidence that you will live at least as long as she does."

The muscles in Lord Aeron's face tightened, but he didn't otherwise react to Morgana's verbal jab. After a tense silence, Morgana spoke, her tone once again pleasant.

"Your fellow Knight, Sir Percival, is apparently not dead."

Lord Aeron stared at Morgana, unmoved. He knew that words were just another weapon for her, and lies were her sharpest and most oft-used blades. Yet, he sensed a measure of unease behind the facade that was her cold, beautiful face, and a flicker of hope rose from the ashes within.

Morgana leaned forward, her eyes fixed on his, like those of a raptor a moment before its talons closed on its prey. "To the contrary, it appears that he walked into Londinium and killed the invincible Hengst the Butcher in a duel, on the tournament field, no less."

There was a long silence, and every sinew in Lord Aeron's body wanted to rejoice at the tidings, but he suppressed the feeling, knowing Morgana would see any reaction as a threat.

"Do you have a question for me, Milady?" Lord Aeron asked in a flat, emotionless voice.

Anger flared in Morgana's eyes for an instant, and the knight watched as she regained her iron control. She leaned back against the cushions behind her and continued.

"Yes, quite the hero this Percival, and apparently, quite the leader as well. Why, after his victory over Londinium's oppressor, this man demanded that the people of Londinium rise and throw off the yoke of the Norse rule, and they did just that."

Lord Aeron's eyes widened, and the flicker of hope within flared into a small flame.

"I don't understand," Lord Aeron said.

"Londinium has been retaken by its people. Hengst's Norsemen are either dead or they have fled. Now do you understand?" Morgana said harshly.

"Yes," Lord Aeron answered, not reacting to her ire.

Morgana stood up and walked to the window that overlooked the estuary and the sea beyond. A moment later, she turned around to face him, her face white with anger.

"Yes? Is that all you have to say, Lord Aeron, or should I call you Sir Galahad, now that your brother Knight has returned? Is this the first step in a scheme to resurrect that foolish Table that I sundered a decade past? Remember, your precious Guinevere's life is mine to take at any moment, so if there is some grand plot afoot—"

Lord Aeron stood up and stared down at Morgana, struggling to control his rage. He had never known hatred until he met this woman, and despite his prayers, he feared a day would come when he would yield to its cries for vengeance and strike her down. At this instant, the screams for blood within him were deafening, but he ignored them, as he had done so many times before.

"Sir Percival," he said in a voice of stone, "was sent on that fool's quest a decade ago—a quest that I knew nothing about until after he'd left port. I have neither spoken nor heard from him since the day of departure, and I can assure you that neither he, nor I, envisioned, even in our vilest nightmares, the unholy havoc that you have wrought on this land. So no, Morgana, I have no knowledge of any plot, and as for the life of the Queen, we struck a bargain, and I have honored, and continue to honor, my promise. I expect you to honor yours. Good day."

As Lord Aeron strode from the room and across the castle to the stables, a flood of emotions raged through him. A part of him wanted to ride like the wind to Londinium to see his long-lost friend, and another part prayed death would take him before Percival learned he served their common enemy under the nom de guerre, Lord Aeron.

As he saddled his black destrier, he heard a young woman's voice outside the stable. He turned and looked out the open window at the nearby well, knowing he was invisible in the stable's semidarkness. An older woman dressed in a worn woolen dress was struggling to lift a bucket full of water over the top of the well. Another woman, younger, but dressed in similar attire, ran over and helped her lower the bucket to the ground. The younger woman whispered something, and the old woman scoffed.

"What! I don't believe it for a moment! It can't be."

The younger woman put her hands on her hips and said in an indignant voice, "It's the truth, Maud! Alf, the stable boy, heard the messenger speak to the old Greek when he arrived. Sir Percival, a Knight of the Table, has killed Hengst the Butcher and retaken Londinium!"

The older woman shook her head. "One man! Even a Knight of the Table—and I tell you, Marian, they're all dead—couldn't take back Londinium from Hengst and his Norse reavers. No, it's just idle gossip."

Lord Aeron tightened his grip on his saddle's girth strap and grew very still. As the women chattered on, he could see the gate to the castle wall being raised through the window. A moment later, two men on horseback galloped through the opening and down the road to the south.

"And I suppose," Marian sneered, pointing toward the two men racing through the castle's front gate, "those men are racing south at the break of dawn for nothing?"

Maud grabbed the younger woman's arm in a tight grip, drawing a look of anger.

"Shush, Marian! I pray you're right, but if you would keep that pretty head on your shoulders, I wouldn't talk of the Table and the Pendragon whilst you work in this castle. Remember who rules here!"

Lord Aeron turned back to the horse and spoke quietly to his mount. "Londinium. Do you remember, brother, the last time we were there?" For a moment, Lord Aeron allowed himself to remember a time when he had another name, when life was not a place of pain and darkness.

It was the day of the annual parade. The Knights of the Table had ridden in procession behind the Pendragon and Guinevere through the center of the city. People had lined both sides of the street, waving and calling out greetings. In accordance with the rules of decorum insisted upon by Lancelot, the other knights did not acknowledge the cheers. They rode in silence, their faces carved in stone—the very picture of stalwart power. Much to Lancelot's ire, the two knights in the rear of the procession, Galahad and Percival, often flouted this order. Worse, they did so with impunity, since Lancelot could not turn around and catch them in the act without violating the rule himself.

As the column had passed by one of the houses that overlooked the street, five or six young women standing on the second-floor balcony had cheered hysterically when Galahad and Percival came abreast of them and called out to the golden-haired knight.

Lord Aeron rested a hand on the saddle in front of him as he remembered the words they had spoken that day.

"Why, Sir Galahad," Percival had said, glancing over at him, the hint of a smile on his face, "could it be those women have made your acquaintance?"

"Indeed, they have," Galahad had said, unable to hide a smile.

"Hmm, I seem to remember that his high and mightiness ordered all knights to remain in camp last night."

Galahad's smile widened. "Well, let's just say that Lancelot has his rules, and I have mine. You really must come along on one of these nocturnal romps. Life was meant to be lived."

Then he turned to the women and bowed his golden head in their direction, drawing screams of pleasure.

"Percival," Galahad said quietly, "since neither you nor I can have the woman of our dreams, why not drown our sorrows in the arms of those we can have?"

As the memory faded, Lord Aeron whispered, "It has come full circle. Where once you held back the enemy alone, and I came to your aid, now you have come to mine, and none too soon, brother, for I have grown weary of carrying this burden alone."

* * *

MORGANA WALKED TO the window overlooking the estuary below, pondering Lord Aeron's reaction to the return of his brother Knight. She sensed his nonchalance was feigned, but she did not believe he would try to join this Sir Percival and risk Guinevere's assassination, at least not yet. Still, the risk was there, and killing him would end the matter.

In the end, she decided to keep the knight alive. His end would come soon enough, as would Guinevere's. Morgana smiled as she remembered the particularly fine wine she had set aside to celebrate the death of the Pendragon's Queen.

Morgana's pleasant reverie was interrupted by a soft knock on the partially open door to her chambers. "Come."

Seneas walked into the room and bowed. "Milady, may I ask what Lord Aeron—"

Morgana made a dismissive gesture with her hand. "No, you may not. Now tell me of Ivarr and his force. When will they reach Londinium and put an end to this foolish uprising?"

"Milady, they would already have arrived but for . . . a diversion," Seneas said carefully.

"What are you talking about?" Morgana demanded.

"A second messenger has arrived, Milady. Ivarr and his men strayed from the road and attacked a town on the edge of your lands—on the border itself."

"Tell me of this attack," she said, with restrained anger.

"The town, or more of a village, is at a crossroads, a day and a half ride south. The herdsmen and farmers meet to trade—"

"What happened, Seneas?" she demanded.

"Ivarr and his men killed near half the people in the village and burned their homes. The rest took refuge in a stone guard. It seems they were about to burn them out, when they received word of the fall of Londinium. Ivarr left for the city at once, with his mounted soldiers. Those afoot were ordered to follow as fast as possible."

A cruel smile crossed her face for an instant. She recognized the primitive message Ivarr had been sending by attacking the village. *Such a fool*, she thought. *You will never see my knife, Norseman. You will only feel its blade.*

Morgana glanced over at Seneas. "How many men does the Norseman have?"

"Near seventy-five mounted and over a hundred afoot."

She nodded. "Others will join him as he approaches Londinium— outlaws and brigands looking to join in the loot and pillage when the town is retaken. The people of Londinium will soon regret their moment of impudence. And as for this Sir Percival," Morgana said in a voice laced with scorn, "I should so like to see the pain in his eyes as his moment of glory turns to ashes.

"Yet, I would not have him die too soon. No, I need him to live long enough for me to lay my hands on his would-be mentor and guide, Melitas Komnenos. And then, Seneas, the devil himself shall gasp at the agonies that I shall inflict upon my teacher."

Morgana punctuated her last sentence by driving the blade of her bejeweled dagger into the table beside the divan. Its flawless point found near a half inch of purchase before coming to rest.

Seneas took a step back. "Of—of course, Milady," he whispered. "What—what would you have me do?"

"Send two more spies to follow this Sir Percival wherever he goes. Melitas will be where he is. I am to receive reports from each spy, every week, and they are not to know of one another. Arrange for riders to meet with them so this can be done. Go now. I will not allow the traitor to slip through my hands a second time."

CHAPTER 18

THE WID RIVER

As Ivarr rode alongside the line of horsemen on his way back to the head of the column, the road ahead disappeared in the drifting fog. A moment later, the grey cloud moved on, into the fens on the other side of the road. The Norse warlord had ridden to the rear to tell the stragglers to keep pace or die. They were still a long day's ride from Londinium, and he intended to mount an attack on the city the next morning at dawn.

As he rode by Ulf, the other Norseman pulled his horse out of the line and caught up with him, matching his gait.

"Speak, if you have something to say."

"The horses tire, and the men would break their fast. They would know—"

"We ride," Ivarr growled, "until I say otherwise."

"That will not go well with—"

"I do not—" Ivarr's shout died in his throat. A horse on the narrow wooden bridge ahead reared up, and his rider fell heavily to the wooden deck below. The other riders crossing the bridge slowed and began to mill about in confusion.

"I told you!" Ulf snarled. "The horses are tired. We must—"

Ivarr turned to the other Norseman, his mailed fist raised to strike him down, but Ulf was already falling from his horse, an arrow buried deep in his chest. Ivarr stared down in confusion at the man lying on the ground. When he looked up, the bridge ahead had become a seething mass of frantic horses and men. Two more men fell from their horses as he watched, one screaming in agony.

Ivarr drove his heels into his horse and galloped forward, roaring, "We are attacked! Get off the bridge! Move!"

As he pressed forward, trampling over fallen men and horses, the Norseman saw ghostly bowmen in the fog, sending arrow after arrow into the massed warriors, killing men and animals alike. For a moment, it seemed as if the bowmen were standing on the river itself, but then he realized they were shooting from small islets.

Ahead of him, at the crest of the bridge, Ivarr saw mud-covered chains beneath the horses' hooves. Rage welled up inside of him. Once the column of horses had been evenly split between one side of the river and the other, men hiding beneath the bridge must have snapped the chains tight, tripping the horses and now barring passage across. This was a well-planned ambush.

Ivarr wheeled his horse, smashing into the rider to his right, and roared out a command.

"Move! Go back! It's a trap!"

The warriors on his right and left struggled to turn their mounts, cursing and screaming at each other and their horses. The panicked animals attacked each other in the desperate frenzy. An arrow slammed into Ivarr's breastplate, and a second scored a furrow across the upper part of his right arm. Another arrow pierced the thigh of the man behind him, drawing a scream of rage and pain.

Realizing he couldn't force a passage through the melee of men and horses to either the front or rear, Ivarr forced his mount to gallop directly at the wooden rails on the right side of bridge. Although the horse tried to slow its momentum as it approached the obstacle, the Norseman forced the animal to smash through the barrier and jump into the flowing water four feet below.

As soon as the horse splashed into the chest-high water, Ivarr wheeled the animal toward the shore, where he could see the rest of his column still riding toward the bridge. He drove his booted feet into the horse's sides, and it leaped forward, but the mud on the bottom of the river slowed its progress.

The men on the islet closest to him focused their fire on him, and

Ivarr felt two arrows glance off his breastplate and a third score a fur-row across his left thigh, drawing a growl of rage. A moment later, his horse found firmer ground and galloped up the river bank to the safety of a row of trees.

Other men followed Ivarr's lead and leaped through the gap in the side of the bridge and plunged into the river below, but not all were as fortunate as their leader. The archers on the islet in the middle of the river were now ready. Many of the riders didn't make it to the far shore, and others who did were either wounded or dying.

* * *

AN HOUR BEFORE noon, Ivarr stood on a bluff, looking down at the growing force of men camped in a clearing on the far side of the bridge. The sight filled him with wrath. The approach of a man with a heavy step drew the Norse leader's attention, and he glanced coldly back at Geir, the old warrior who'd accompanied him to the parley with Morgana.

Geir had sailed with the Norse warlord's father on a longship in the early days. It was said they had raided as far south as the sea of the Romans. The warrior had joined Hengst and Ivarr's band five years ear-lier, after losing his own ship in a dicing match. The Norseman walked over to Ivarr, and the two men stood in silence for a moment, staring at the enemy camp on the far side of the river. When Ivarr finally spoke, his words were dripping with scorn.

"A week ago, this rabble cringed in fear at the sight of Ivarr the Red and his men. They cried and mewled like kittens as we took their wealth and women, and now they would be warriors. I shall kill them all, and their women and children shall labor under the slaver's lash all of their days."

Geir waited a moment, until the Norseman's anger subsided, then pointed to the enemy camp in the distance. "Do you see the holes that those men over there are digging?"

Ivarr nodded.

"Those are for dung and urine. Do you see those men cutting wood?"
Ivarr grunted an acknowledgement.

"Those are for barrier walls. And those men, lined up there with their bows at the ready, they provide cover in case of attack. And—"

"What are you saying, Geir?" Ivarr said, with a mixture of impatience and anger.

"War leader, these men are not the sheep of yesterday. They now have leaders who know what they are about."

"Bah! Sheep are sheep, and so what if they have found a farmer who was once a soldier to lead them."

"War leader, whoever leads these men is not a farmer. Look at the white markings on the bridge, there, there, and there."

Ivarr leaned forward and for the first time noticed the white chalk markings that divided the bridge into sections. Each section was marked with either a "I," "II," or "III."

"Now," Geir continued, "look at where their leader positioned his archers. I have seen this before. Each group of archers is told to fire only on the men within one section. This allows men to shoot from both sides of the bridge without hitting one another. Do you remember a voice calling out commands from the far shore during the battle?"

Ivarr hesitated and then nodded grudgingly.

"Their leader was commanding the archers in one location to target the men in a different section of the bridge as we tried to escape."

"Why do you tell me this, Geir?" Ivarr said, his voice cold and hard.

"The men who set this trap and commanded this battle are truly skilled in the way of war. We must be wary—"

"Do not tell me what we must do, Geir!" Ivarr roared, his eyes blazing. "I know what we must do! We must slaughter these men and their leaders. This will happen on the morrow. Have Keld ride back up the road until he finds Ragnar and the men afoot. Tell him that if he is not here by the morn, I will have the skin flayed from his body!"

Abbey Cwm Hir

Guinevere reviewed the ciphered message a third time and then stood up from her desk. She carefully rolled up the parchment and slid it into a small leather pouch. Then she placed a metal sheath over the candle on the desk to hide its light, and walked to the window overlooking the darkest part of the courtyard. Torn was barely visible there, sitting on a wooden bench in the dark, sharpening his knife. She opened the shutter and dropped the leather pouch to the ground. A moment later, Torn sheathed his knife and started across the courtyard, stopping to tie his bootlace beside the leather pouch. When he stood up, the pouch was gone.

The message was one of many Guinevere had sent out in the past week to the sparrows who lived along the roads she expected Percival to travel on as he made his way to the abbey. She knew every village and town he approached would assume the worst and prepare for a fight. A single errant arrow could take the Knight's life, bringing his long quest to a tragic end. In each message, she advised the women of his approach and told them to take whatever precautions they could to protect him.

Guinevere walked back to her desk, lifted the sheath from the flickering candle, and returned the book of cypher codes to the iron strongbox on the table. The light from the candle illuminated two golden rings. They must have fallen out of the white, silken bag, where she kept them, when she placed the strongbox on the table. She stared at the rings for a moment, and then she picked them up and slowly sat down.

One of the rings was made from the finest gold in the land, and it bore the seal of the house of Pendragon—a dragon. The second ring was smaller, and the gold of a lesser grade. The only visible marking on the smaller ring was a single word etched on the inside, where it would touch the skin of the wearer. The word was *Forever*.

As she stared at the rings, the memory of her wedding day returned. The ring that Arthur had placed on her finger that day was the larger of the two rings—the ring that the Royal Council had ordered the royal forge to make for the occasion. Although it was magnificent, her wedding ring was not the cherished family heirloom she had chosen for the occasion—the ring worn by her deceased mother and grandmother on the day of their nuptials. That ring waited under a stone at Pen Dinas, for a day that would never come.

When she'd asked Arthur for the right to choose her own wedding ring, he had made light of it, saying, "Guinevere, rings are a thing of no moment. Let the Royal Council have its way on the day of the wedding and wear another thereafter. For my part, I am no ring wearer, so I shall surely set aside whatever trinket they would have you give me on that day."

A sad smile came to Guinevere's face as the scene faded from memory, for the truth, as she later discovered, was that Arthur did faithfully wear a ring. He wore it on a chain close to his heart, every day without fail.

Guinevere didn't realize Cadwyn had knocked on the door, or that she'd told her handmaiden to come in, until she was standing in front of her.

"Milady? Are you unwell?"

"Oh, Cadwyn, yes. I mean no, I'm fine. Why do you ask?"

"Your face," Cadwyn said, "you look so sad."

There was a moment of silence, and then Cadwyn asked in a soft voice, "Milady, those rings, I have never seen them before. If they make you so sad, why not hide them away?"

Guinevere glanced down at the bands of gold resting in her palm.

"I could do that, but the memories would still remain, and, in truth, I pray that those remembrances stay with me until my dying day. They have within them equal shares of joy and sadness, and I need to remember both, for although the first brings happiness, often the second brings wisdom."

"Would . . . you speak of this, Milady . . . the story of the rings?" Cadwyn said in a near whisper.

"You would know all my deep, dark secrets, Cadwyn Hydwell," Guinevere said with a laugh.

"I'm sorry, Milady, it's just that you have lived such a life! I could only dream of the things you have done . . . the people you have met, and, Milady, now that Sir Percival comes, why, who knows what the future will bring?"

Guinevere smiled. "Who knows, indeed? Very well, sit, and I will tell you of a girl who was much like you so many years ago."

Cadwyn sat in the chair across from the Queen, her eyes glowing and face rapt with attention. Guinevere leaned back in her chair, a pensive look on her face.

"Where to begin? My father promised my hand to Arthur when I was still a child. At that time, Arthur was not yet King. He was one of a number of powerful and ambitious warlords seeking the throne left vacant by the death of Uther Pendragon. He needed the support of my father—an old and respected lord of great wealth—to achieve that end. So they met to discuss the matter. After meeting with Arthur and his councilor, Merlin the Wise, my father decided to support Arthur's claim to the throne."

Cadwyn leaned forward in her chair, looking confused. "But, Milady, Arthur was Uther Pendragon's son, was he not? So he was the rightful king."

Guinevere placed the two rings on the table and clasped her hands together on her lap.

"That, my dear, is the tale that has been told, and there is some truth to it. You see, the wiser Roman emperors had a practice, as they neared the time of their death, of adopting as their son another Roman who was wise and strong enough to rule the empire. It is said that King Uther, who didn't have any male heirs, followed that practice when he chose Arthur to be his successor."

Cadwyn's eyes widened.

Guinevere nodded. "Yes, that is the truth of it, my dear. Alas, the matter did not end there. Uther's brother denied Arthur's claim after Uther's death and insisted that the crown was his by right. Others, who claimed lineage through King Aurelius, and even distant King Vortigern, also laid claim to the crown. So, a war of succession followed. It was a fearful time."

A distant look came to Guinevere's face, and she was quiet for a moment as she remembered the look of fear on her mother's face every time her father rode off with his liegemen in those years. Then she continued.

"When Arthur sought my father's aid in this war, he agreed to support Arthur's claim. In return, Arthur agreed to take me for his Queen, when I came of age."

"Milady, did your father ask you if . . ."

Guinevere smiled a sad and knowing smile.

"No, Cadwyn. That is not the way of things. The daughter of a powerful lord is a coin in the game of power, a thing to be bartered away for gain. It has been thus for centuries."

Cadwyn sat up in her chair, a look of defiance on her face. "I will choose the man that I marry."

Guinevere laughed. "I suspect you will, Cadwyn, and he will be a very lucky man."

"I shouldn't interrupt, Milady. Sister Aranwen says that it is a bad habit. Please—"

"It may be that," the Queen said with a laugh, "but life would be so much less interesting without that bad habit of yours. So I must ask you to keep it. Now, where was I?" She tapped one finger against her chin. "Why, I am becoming quite the old woman, forgetting myself every other moment."

"You are not, Milady. Why, you are as young and beautiful as a spring rose."

"I'll settle for a late-summer bloom," Guinevere said with a smile. "Oh yes, I remember now. Arthur spent a year fighting to secure the throne and another two years subduing the endless revolts that seemed to arise in one part of the land or another. In time, he came to reign as the undisputed king of the land, and when I was eighteen, he sent for me, and a grand wedding was arranged.

"This," Guinevere said, touching the larger of the two golden rings on the table, "is my wedding ring. It was designed by a famed court artisan, forged by the court smith, and then approved by the Royal Council as fitting for the occasion."

Cadwyn stared at the magnificent ring and spoke in a whisper.

"It is a magnificent ring, Milady."

"Indeed, it is, and most would choose it over the other. I suspect that I would have as well, had I been given the choice as a young woman. But," Guinevere said in a voice tinged with regret, "the more modest ring is the one I would choose today, or even a ring of the crudest wood, if it was given by my beloved with all his heart, as Arthur gave this one."

"Milady, Arthur gave you the smaller ring as well?" Cadwyn asked, confusion in her voice.

A sad smile came to Guinevere's face. "No, Cadwyn, Arthur did not give me this ring."

"But you said—"

"I did. You see, I was not Arthur's first wife."

Cadwyn's eye widened, and she lifted a hand to her mouth.

Guinevere looked over at the flickering candle and spoke as though she were describing the life of another woman.

"When I married Arthur Pendragon, he was the unchallenged King of the Britons and the first knight of the invincible Knights of the Round Table. He was also late in his fourth decade of life. Although few know of it, long before he reached those powerful heights, the young Arthur—a man who was just one of many lords fighting to defend his family's ancestral fiefs like many other—fell in love. His beloved was the daughter of a lesser noble, and his family frowned upon the union, but Arthur rejected their advice. He chose love over power, and I'm told that she loved him as dearly as he loved her."

"Milady," Cadwyn said, her voice hesitant, "if you will, how did you learn of this?"

Guinevere gently took the smaller of the two rings and rested it in her palm. "This ring . . . it was brought to me by a messenger after Arthur's death at Camlann. They assumed it was mine. For a year after Arthur's death, I kept it locked away, not wanting to know the truth of the matter, but one morning, I decided otherwise and asked the abbess what she knew of it. She had known Arthur in the early days and had attended his wedding to . . . Alona, his first wife.

"She died in childbirth," Guinevere said, her eyes on the ring, "in the second year of their marriage. The child died as well. The abbess said Arthur was a broken man for a very long while. Over time, he recovered, but the abbess said he was different—colder, more distant. That was the man who became King."

Guinevere fell silent and gently returned the two rings to the silken bag and then placed it back in the strongbox. "I have kept both my ring and Alona's to honor him, for he was a great and wonderful man in so many ways, and Alona must have been . . . most wonderful as well, for him to love her so dearly. But sometimes, in my weaker, more selfish moments, I envy her, for she and Arthur married for love, whereas we . . . our union . . . was one of duty."

"Milady, one day you will marry for love!" Cadwyn burst out.

Guinevere looked over at her young friend in surprise and smiled.

"Oh, Cadwyn, you are precious, but alas . . . those days are gone."

CHAPTER 19

CAMP ON THE RIVER WID

Percival stood on the edge of a stand of trees bordering a broad, open field on the south side of the River Wid—a field that was quickly becoming a fortified camp. As he watched the lines of men digging a ditch and building a palisade across the exposed part of the field, he remembered doing this same work side by side with the men of town near his home, under the watchful eyes of his father and grandfather.

Capussa walked over to stand beside Percival and nodded toward the rows of stakes protruding from the ground forming a palisade along the ditch dug on the perimeter of the camp. "You have done this before, Knight. I would not have thought a man of noble blood would know of these things."

Percival smiled, remembering his protestations as a younger man at the effort he considered wasteful, and his grandfather's stern reply: "Percival, a wise commander prepares for both victory and defeat. If you are driven from the field, this ditch and palisade will mean the difference between life and death for you and your army."

He glanced over at Capussa and smiled ruefully. "When I was ten years old, I was forced to dig a ditch and build a palisade like this one in the hot sun. I was quite sure the work was beneath me. My grandfather thought otherwise. When I threw down my shovel and tried to climb out of the ditch, he knocked me back into the mud and told me to keep at it."

"I think I would have liked this man," Capussa said with an approving nod.

"Because he was right, or because he knocked me back into the ditch?" Percival asked, raising an eyebrow.

"Both," Capussa said.

The Knight smiled. "I thought as much."

Percival turned at the sound of approaching horses and saw Cynric, Tylan, and a clean-shaven Merlin riding toward him. The three men dismounted, and Percival walked over to meet them, with Capussa at his side. Capussa nodded to Cynric. "Does the enemy make preparation for battle?" he asked.

Cynric shook his head. "Not yet, but the Norse will attack again, once their foot soldiers arrive. The scouts say that may be tonight, but certainly by morning."

"Aye, he will come," Tylan concurred with a nod.

"Will the attack come tonight or at dawn?" Capussa asked.

"Ivarr would attack tonight, if he could," Cynric said. "But the scouts say his men have been coming at a forced march for near a day and a half. They'll want to eat and rest before battle. I wager he will come in the morning."

Merlin nodded his agreement. "That would be the wiser choice."

"How many men do we have?" Percival said.

Cynric looked over at Tylan.

"Near three hundred and more come by the hour," Tylan said, looking across the field at a group of men carrying axes and logs toward the palisade.

"And what kind of men are they?" Percival asked quietly.

"They're brave enough," Cynric answered, "but most of them have never been in a fight before, and they're not well-armed. Most of them only have axes, knives, and staffs. I can't say how they will hold—"

"They will hold, my friend," Capussa interrupted. "Thanks to the endless sea of trees in this land, and the two hundred axes at work out there, we will be able to put two hundred pikemen into the field by dawn."

"A phalanx of pikemen may stop the cavalry, my Numidian friend, but they will only delay hardened warriors afoot," Merlin said. "Once the Norse get among them, they will break our line, and it will become a slaughter. Ivarr will know this."

"Then," Percival said, "we must choose our ground well, so this does not come to pass."

Capussa gestured toward a large, flat rock they had used as a make-shift desk earlier in the day. "Let us look at that map of yours, Merlin the Wise."

The five men walked over to the rock, and Merlin rolled out a parchment, revealing a map. "I drew this after talking to the scouts and a local farmer."

Percival pointed to the line on the map designating the River Wid. "Where will he seek to make his crossing?"

Cynric leaned forward and stared at the parchment for a long moment. "If he crosses to the south," he said, "his men will have to ride through a foul marsh to reach this camp. A crossing to the north would be easier. There's a path on this side. It runs alongside the river."

"What is this ground like?" Capussa said, tracing the south bank of the river to the north of the camp.

"It's flat until you reach this stretch," Cynric said, tapping a spot on the map. "There's a wooded hill there on this side of the river. The path runs along its base."

"So the path there is bordered on one side by the river and on the other by a slope?" Capussa questioned.

"Yes?"

"Can a line of men take a position on this slope?"

Cynric stared at the Numidian for a moment and then answered, a tinge of excitement in his voice, "Yes, yes. I believe they could."

"I would see this place," Capussa said quietly and turned to Merlin. "A man named Hannibal led my people, and other barbarians, as you Romans used to call us, to a great victory. There was a fog that morning, and the enemy was drawn down a narrow road bordered on one side by a hill and—"

"On the other by a lake—Trasimene," Merlin finished.

"Indeed," Capussa said, a smile coming to his face.

* * *

CAPUSSA LOOKED ACROSS the darkened field at the ordered and fortified camp, alit in the light from the full moon. Three sides of the perimeter were protected by a ditch and a palisade of wooden stakes, and the fourth by a natural barrier of rocks. Sentries were posted at regular intervals along the barriers. Some of the roughly four hundred men enclosed within the camp perimeter were sleeping on the ground, wrapped in simple cloaks or blankets; others were talking quietly in circles around a score of cooking fires. Wooden pikes were stacked next to each fire, ready for use in the morning. Capussa nodded in satisfaction and took a drink from the silver flask he was holding before returning it to a pocket in his black cloak.

After a final look at the perimeter, the Numidian walked back to a long, flat rock where his sword lay. A fire burned in a shallow pit two paces away. Merlin sat on another rock to his right, and Cynric, Tylan, Bray, Keil, and a number of other newly arrived men were sitting on logs and rocks to his left, talking quietly. As he took a seat on the flat stone, Capussa looked over at Cynric and asked, "The Knight?"

"There is a spring just outside the wall. He bathes and then—"

"He will pray," Capussa finished.

"Eight bowmen watch over him, at a distance," Cynric said.

Capussa nodded his unspoken thanks and looked over at the fire.

Several minutes after Capussa sat down, Keil rose and walked hesitantly toward him. He sat down on a smaller rock a pace away, and Capussa glanced over at the younger man. "You would ask a question of me, my young friend?"

"Ah, yes, yes sir. The other night, you said, well, you said that you might—"

"Continue my tale of the time Sir Percival and I spent in the land of the Moors? Indeed, I did. Well, the night before a battle is as good a time for a story as any."

As soon as he finished speaking, Bray and the rest of Cynric's men moved closer.

"Now, where were we? . . . Oh yes, our time as prisoners of Khalid El-Hashem—our time in the arena."

Capussa stared at the fire for a moment in silence and then spoke in a musing tone.

"I have been a soldier for more than two decades, and I have closed with the enemy and traded blows in the heat of battle many a time, but . . . it is a different thing to rise each day as a gladiator. When you awake and watch the sun rise, you know that you will be dead by sundown, unless you can defeat another man in mortal combat; and when you go to bed each night, you know that the next day will be same."

Five other men walked over from the other side of the fire and sat down quietly.

Capussa nodded at them and continued. "I found, as did other men, that once I survived a month in the arena, the burden of fear receded. You become more comfortable with death. It's as if he is a neighbor who you see at the village well each day. You greet each other and talk of things, and then part. With each parting, you breathe a sigh of relief, but," Capussa paused, his eyes roving over the growing crowd of listeners, "you know that there will come a day when you will not leave the well. You know one day he will take you."

Capussa was quiet for a moment, and his eyes grew distant.

"Some men couldn't bear the waiting, and they would choose the day of their death, embracing a blow they knew would take them quickly. But this . . . this changes as the end of your time of imprisonment nears. Then you begin to hope again. You begin to think of a life where you will not have to meet death every day, and that is a dangerous thing."

Merlin nodded in understanding.

"As fate would have it, Khalid was bound to release both Sir Percival and me in the same week, and as our last month approached, we pledged to remain vigilant that we might survive and live out our days in this—" Capussa smiled and made a gesture that took in the armed camp "peaceful land."

After the chorus of laughter ended, Capussa returned to his tale. "Then fate cast us a boon, or so it seemed. In that last month, the plague came to the City of Syene, and the ruling Vizier forbid public gatherings. Although Khalid was enraged at being denied the gold that he might otherwise have earned from the Knight's blood, his rage was tempered by his new obsession—Sumayya."

"Sumayya?" Keil interjected.

Capussa paused for a moment and stared into the night sky as the circle of listeners, which had grown to over forty men and boys, waited in silence for him to continue.

"Yes, my young friend, Sumayya. She was a Moorish princess. She was, it was said, the most beautiful woman in all of Egypt, and some claimed, in all the lands of the Moor."

"Did you see her?" Keil said in a whisper.

"Keil, would you like to be the next log on that fire?" Tylan growled.

"No sir."

"Then be silent."

Capussa smiled. "I did indeed, but only her face, and as for that I will say this: I have never seen nor dreamed of such beauty, and I, my friends, have traveled through many a land and seen many a woman. Why, I could tell you stories . . ." Capussa said, shaking his head. "Ah, but that is for another day."

A look of disappointment crossed Bray's face, and he took a long draught of wine.

"As is the way of it," Capussa continued, "every man of wealth and power in the land sought Sumayya's hand, and although her father, a wealthy Emir, could have traded his daughter to the wealthiest and most powerful suitor, he would not. He let it be known that Sumayya would choose her own husband. This meant that all of Khalid's gold would avail him nothing in his quest for this woman's hand, for you see," Capussa leaned forward, as if to tell a secret, "Khalid looked rather like a cross between a vulture and a rat."

The description drew a howl of laughter from the crowd.

"Yet, Khalid would not be denied this prize. He believed that he had within his hands the means to make this beauteous young woman accept his hand in marriage, for he had Sir Percival."

"Sir Percival?" Keil said, confused.

"Sir Percival," Capussa answered with a solemn nod. "You see, Sumayya's father would often come to the games in the arena and wager on the fights, and although she hated the bloodshed, as a dutiful daughter, she came as well. Over time, the princess came to admire Sir Percival for the honor, courage, and mercy he displayed in the arena, and it is said she even prayed for his life before each battle. Now Khalid, being a clever man, saw an opportunity in this. He asked Sumayya if she would like to meet Sir Percival, and indeed, the princess did. And so it came to pass that Sumayya spent many an afternoon with Sir Percival."

Merlin's eyes widened ever so slightly when he heard this, and Capussa smiled inwardly, knowing even the old Roman was mesmerized by the story. As he drew out his silver flask to take a drink, the Numidian remembered listening to the stories his father had told around the village fire when he returned from his long sea voyages. The man was a master, weaving a spell over his listeners that left them begging for more when the tale came to an end.

After taking a drink from his flask, the Numidian continued with his tale.

"The princess was always veiled when she met the Knight, and the meetings took place in the presence of her father, Khalid, and many guards. However, what Sumayya and Sir Percival spoke of was not known to Sumayya's father and Khalid, for Sumayya was as learned as she was beautiful. She, like the Knight, spoke the language of the Romans, a language the Emir and Khalid did not understand. So the two of them were able to keep their words secret."

Keil opened his mouth to say something, but Merlin spoke first.

"Do you know, my Numidian friend, what it is they spoke of during these . . . meetings?"

Capussa started to shake his head, and Keil's face fell, but then the Numidian slowly raised his right hand, as if he had just recovered a long forgotten memory.

"The Knight is a man of few words and keeps his own counsel, but over time, I did learn something of what was said between the two. The princess wanted to learn about the Knight and his land and its people. So Sir Percival told Sumayya of your King Arthur, Queen Guinevere, and the Knights of the Table; and no matter how long he would speak of these things, Sumayya wanted to know more, for she'd never heard of such a noble and wonderful thing. And the Knight, for his part, desired to know of the princess and her life, thoughts, and desires as well.

"So it came to be, over time, that Sumayya came to care greatly for the Knight, and I suspect, he for her. Now Khalid, being a cunning man, could see that these feelings offered him the means to achieve his evil ends. But then, that is often the way of it—a thing of innocent goodness between two noble souls becomes the bait for the foulest of traps."

Capussa hesitated for a moment, and the crowd of men around him waited in silence for him to continue. Tylan's brow, he noted, was now as furrowed as Keil's.

"It happened the day before our release. I suspect Khalid used Sumayya's feelings for Sir Percival to induce her father to visit on that day, possibly by offering Sumayya one last meeting with the Knight before he became a free man. Sometime after dusk, three of Khalid's guards came to our quarters and ordered us to gather our armor and to follow them to the armory. We were told that our time of release was near, and we would no longer have need of it."

Capussa stood up and walked over to the fire, warmed his hands for a moment, and then turned around and faced his waiting audience.

"We were led out of the walled area where the gladiators were confined, and from there, through a series of beautiful courtyards. As we passed through the last courtyard, we could see Sumayya and her attendants sitting at a table at the far end. A moment later, the wooden gate that separated the courtyard from the desert outside burst open, and men on horseback rode in and thundered toward the women. The men guarding Sumayya threw down their swords and ran, leaving the women to face their attackers alone."

Capussa raised a hand and pointed into the distance and spoke more rapidly. "The Knight, who was walking ahead of me, ran toward the women. I followed, seizing one of the swords dropped by the fleeing guards as I ran. By the time we reached the women, the horsemen had left through another gate, leaving the women untouched. A moment later, Khalid, surrounded by guards, ran into the square and confronted us. Sumayya told Khalid that we had come to her rescue, and although Khalid thanked us for our noble effort, he said that he, nonetheless, had no choice but to enforce the law."

"The law?" Tylan said, his eyes wide.

Capussa nodded his head in regret as he returned to his seat on the rock, and then spoke in a solemn voice. "Any prisoner bearing arms outside the arena was to be put to death. That was the law of their land. And, I, alas, was bearing arms."

"No!" Keil exploded. "It was a trap! You were saving the princess!"

Capussa held his hands out, palms up, as if in surrender.

"Indeed, it was a trap, and a clever one. Khalid had known that the Knight and I would go to Sumayya's aid, and he had assumed we both would seize the swords left by the guards—the guards he'd paid to drop their swords and run away. Had the scheme worked as Khalid had planned, both Sir Percival and I would have been condemned to death . . . unless—"

"Sumayya agreed to marry Khalid, in which case Khalid would show mercy. Yes, it was quite a clever scheme. I will give him that," Merlin finished.

"But Sir Percival wasn't carrying a sword!" Keil cried, standing up in outrage. "How could Khalid force her to marry him?"

"Patience, my friend," Capussa said with a calming gesture.

"When Khalid realized his trap had only ensnared me, but not Sir Percival, his wrath was great, for he assumed Sir Percival would depart, leaving me to my fate, and he with no hold over Sumayya. Worse, Sumayya, being a clever girl, saw through Khalid's ruse, and this made it certain she would not only never be his bride, but would be a dangerous enemy in the future."

Capussa stood up and stretched, looking over the crowd of men waiting intently for him to continue. "There is more to this story, but I would not keep you up on the—"

"No, you must go on!" a chorus of voices pleaded from the crowd.

Capussa nodded in acceptance and sat back down. He was silent for a moment and then shook his head slowly in disbelief.

"It was at this point that Sir Percival did something most noble, a thing that to this day brings tears to my eyes. He met secretly with Khalid and struck a bargain. It was agreed that the Knight would return to the City of Alexandria with a parchment confirming he'd served the one-year sentence imposed upon the son of Jacob the Healer, and he would then return . . . and trade his life for mine."

Capussa was staring at the ground when he finished, but he could see the shock on the faces of his enraptured audience.

"Now, Khalid didn't believe the Knight would return, and his ire was such that he was reluctant to delay my death. He only agreed to delay my execution until noon on the day of the second full moon. This only gave Sir Percival sixty days to travel near three hundred leagues up and down the River Nile. Although it could be done, it left him no time to spare."

Capussa raised his balled fists in front of him and slowly stood.

"When I learned of this bargain, my grief and rage could not be restrained. I told the Knight not to return, and that if he insisted on doing so, I would die by my own hand before I allowed him to yield his life for mine. But this was to no avail. The Knight told me that he had pledged to return, and return he would, whether I was dead or alive. So taking my own life would only ensure that the loss of his was an empty sacrifice.

"And so it came to pass that the Knight left in the morning and undertook the long journey to Alexandria, and as he promised, he returned before the rising of a second full moon, prepared to die in my place."

"But . . . you live, you both still live," Bray said, shaking his head in confusion.

Capussa smiled and nodded. "Indeed we do, my friend. You see, Sumayya saved both of our lives. On the day of the second full moon, I was brought into the arena, where I was to be beheaded. As always, a great crowd was there to witness the spectacle, for Khalid had told many of his bargain with the Knight, and many had agreed to pay to see what would happen that day.

"An hour before the sun reached the midpoint in the sky, Sir Percival raced into the arena on the finest of horses and then rode slowly over to the executioner's block, in the center of the arena. There he dismounted and cut my bonds with the sword that he still carries today. Then he turned to Khalid and said, 'Honor your bargain.'"

Capussa hesitated and drew in a breath, lifting his eyes to focus upon a distant star in the sky.

"Khalid turned to Sumayya, sitting beside her father, as if waiting for her to speak, and when she refused to look his way, his face turned black with rage. He turned back to Sir Percival and said, 'Honor it, I shall. Executioner, take the head of the Christian Knight.'"

An angry murmur swept through the crowd of listeners, but they fell silent when Capussa stepped forward, his hand outstretched as if to seize something.

"I moved to seize the Knight's sword, intending to strike down as many of Khalid's foul henchmen as I could, but at the instant, a force of horseman, near thirty in all, rode through the gate of the arena. A Moorish prince was mounted on the lead horse, a man Khalid recognized, for I could see the fear and respect in his eyes.

"This man, I later learned, was both a man of power and a man of the sword, and when he rode his horse to a place in front of Khalid, I was gratified to see that foul spawn bow deeply to this man. Then this prince spoke in a voice that all could hear. He said, 'I am Abdul-Aziz ibn Musa, the governor of this land, and my betrothed has asked that I spare this man's life.'"

Capussa lifted a finger and whispered, "Do you hear that?"

The men surrounding him froze in place, listening for a sound that was not there.

"Silence," he said, "and on that fateful day, my friends, it was more silent still."

Capussa leaned forward as he continued, his eyes roving over his audience. "Khalid stared at the man in confusion for a long moment, and then he slowly turned to Sumayya, who stared back at him with eyes as cold and hard as the finest steel. And then the man at the head of the horseman looked at Khalid and said, 'And so, it shall be.'"

Capussa looked around solemnly, and then he smiled. "And so it was."

For a moment, the crowd was silent, and then there was an explosive round of applause. Capussa bowed and then held up one hand and said in a quiet voice, "Tomorrow, my fellow soldiers, we, like the Knight, on that distant day and place, must do great things. So let us rest in preparation."

Later, as Capussa was spreading his blanket on the ground, Merlin walked over to him and said quietly, "That was a magnificent tale."

"It is that, and one that I would not have believed myself, had I not lived it. You Christians would call it a miracle," Capussa said with a laugh, but then a thoughtful look came to his face. "But, in truth, that was not the real miracle."

"No?"

"No. The real miracle, Merlin the Wise, came to pass when the Knight was racing back to the arena to save me, on the return trip from Alexandria. A miracle that you can see today, when you look at his face."

"His face?" Merlin said.

"Yes. Do you see the scars on my face, and yet the Knight's face bears none?"

Merlin nodded.

"It was not always thus, Merlin the Wise. Percival . . . his face was once a tapestry of pain. You see, he was scourged many times, in the early days, when he refused to fight in the arena. Those who wielded that cursed implement—may my sword one day find their entrails— were careless with their strokes, and there were blows that struck his face and neck. And he, like I, suffered wounds to his face in the arena as well. Yet, when he returned from Alexandria, his face was unmarked. It was—" Capussa said, a measure of astonishment in his voice. "It was as if the gods had not only healed every mark, but given him back some of the years that had been taken from him."

Merlin stepped closer and put his hand on Capussa's shoulder before speaking in a near whisper. "Did he speak of this?"

"Yes . . . yes he did," Capussa answered. "He said that he became lost in the desert when he was returning from Alexandria, and he was dying of thirst. In his last moments of life, he came upon a spring and drank deeply from it and then bathed his face and neck with its cool waters. He said that as soon as the water touched his lips, face, and neck, it was as if a great weight was lifted from him. When he leaned down to drink a second time, he said that he could see, from his reflection in the water . . . the scars . . . they were gone." When he finished, Capussa looked up at the older man and said with quiet conviction, "Now that, Merlin the Wise, was a miracle."

CHAPTER 20

THE BATTLE OF THE RIVER WID

apussa stood overlooking the three lines of men on the slope thirty paces below him and nodded approvingly—the men waited patiently and remained as silent as a grave, just as ordered. The first two lines of men carried long wooden pikes with sharp points. The third was made up of men with swords, clubs, and an occasional spear.

The billowing morning fog rendered the path at the base of the slope, one hundred paces distant, invisible. That would change with the coming of the morning sun. If fate favored them, the fog would fade enough to make the Norsemen visible as they marched by, but not so much as to reveal the men waiting to attack on the slope above.

Capussa looked over at Percival, a pace to his right. Although the Knight's face did not reveal his inner turmoil, he could sense his friend's unease.

"You fear they cannot do this thing?" Capussa asked.

"I fear many things this morning, my friend," Percival replied. "I fear I have unwittingly started a war that will bring more misery to a people who have already borne far too much pain and suffering. I fear many of these men will die today, leaving no one to provide for their women and children, and yes, I fear that men without training, who only yesterday were tilling fields, herding sheep, and milling corn, may falter when faced with hardened warriors like the Norse."

"You worry too much, Knight. When this day is over, either victory shall be ours or we shall be dead," Capussa said.

"That is reassuring," Percival said dryly. "Yet, you are right. It shall be as God wills." Then he walked to his waiting horse, mounted, and rode into the fog.

Capussa smiled and looked down at the ghostly lines of men below him.

"You have your faith, my friend, and I have my sword. Together, we shall crush them."

* * *

IVARR THE RED watched in satisfaction as the last of the Norse warriors waded across the Wid River and joined the rear of the column marching south. The crossing was a league north of the bridge where they'd been ambushed the day before. Dawn was less than an hour away, and he intended to attack the enemy camp just after the sun rose. He smiled as he thought of the coming slaughter.

He turned to the old warrior mounted on a horse a few paces away. "You see, Geir," he said with a scornful laugh, "your fears are those of an old man. When we return to Londinium, I shall send you back home with a ship full of slaves to sell. You can eat, drink, and get fat there with your share of the spoils."

Ivarr smiled scornfully at the rage in the old warrior's eyes and pointed to the line of men marching south. "Stay in the rear of the column, old man, and sweep for stragglers. You will be safe there."

Then he turned and galloped after the column of men marching along the riverbank. The other mounted Norse warriors waiting on the riverbank roared with laughter at the insult and galloped after Ivarr, leaving the seething Geir behind.

When he reached the head of the column, Ivarr turned in his saddle and looked back at the line of men behind him and nodded in satisfaction. He had given two orders to his subcommanders when they gathered an hour earlier. The first was to summarily kill any straggler. The tired men marching behind him had taken the threat to heart. There were no gaps in the line. If anything, the fear of death had caused the men to march too closely together.

As the compact column marched through a defile formed by the slope of a hill on the right and the river on the left, the Norse warrior smiled as he recalled the second order of the day—no survivors. A moment later, the hill on his right erupted in screams, and a line of men bearing pikes drove into the men behind him. The Norse warlord began to wheel his horse around to face the enemy, but froze in mid movement at the sight of a fully armed knight on a giant black horse racing toward him at full gallop, followed by fifty other mounted men.

MORGANA'S CASTLE

Morgana stood on the battlement watching the line of thirty men marching toward the castle from the south with Ivarr the Red in the lead, riding a horse with a pronounced limp. Half of the men were wounded. Although she'd learned of the outcome of the battle a day earlier from one of her spies, the sight of the battered remnants of the Norse column was still a shock. The Norseman's force of nearly two hundred strong had been all but annihilated by Sir Percival and his men.

She glanced over her shoulder at Lord Aeron, standing a respectful distance behind her. The knight wore a simple black tabard, woolen breeches, and leather boots. His eyes were fixed on the sorry column of men approaching the castle.

"In less than a fortnight, this Sir Percival has killed Hengst, retaken Londinium, and nearly annihilated Ivarr the Red's force. Should I expect to see him at my gates in the morning?" Morgana said.

"He has neither the men nor the means to conduct a siege," the knight answered in a voice devoid of emotion.

"No? I am told that he now has almost a thousand men."

"I do not believe he desires to start a war."

Morgana wheeled around, anger flaring in her eyes. "He's already started one. Ivarr will not let this stand. He will seek to raise another force and retake the city."

"And to wreak a terrible vengeance on the people of Londinium," Lord Aeron said coldly.

"That he will. But then, that is often the fate of those who rise up against their masters," Morgana said, a less than subtle threat in her tone.

"And is it your intent to aid him in this noble cause?" Lord Aeron said, his voice laced with contempt.

Morgana's eyes narrowed.

"Remember your place, Lord Aeron. And as for what I will do, or not do, that is for me to decide. You will escort Ivarr the Red to the main hall when he reaches the gate, accompanied by two guards. The rest of his men are to stay outside the walls."

"As you wish," he answered and walked to the stairs leading off the battlement to the castle below, his face carved in stone. Morgana watched him leave and then returned to the battlement, fuming, and hissed, "Be assured, Sir Galahad, your brother Knight will not resurrect what I have buried."

Two guards escorted Ivarr the Red into the castle's main hall, without his sword. Morgana sat on the far side of a massive wooden table in a chair grand enough to be called a throne. There were no other chairs in the room. The guards escorted Ivarr to the table and stepped back a pace. The Norse war leader ignored the intended slight, but Morgana could sense the anger behind his calm facade.

She took in the Norseman's filthy appearance, the wound to his left arm, and the dried blood on his leather jerkin. For a moment, she reveled at the Norseman's humbled state, remembering his arrogance at their meeting just days earlier. Morgana nodded to the Norseman and spoke with a hint of amusement in her voice.

"It seems that your gods have abandoned you as well as your brother, Ivarr the Red."

"We shall retake Londinium," Ivarr snarled, "and those who rose up against us will wish they'd never been born."

"And you will do all of this with, what . . . ?" She gestured one hand toward the window looking out on the courtyard. "The score of men outside my gates?"

The muscles in Ivarr's jaw visibly tightened. "I will bring more warriors to this land."

"As I recall, it was Roman gold that brought Norse swords to this island, not Ivarr the Red, or Hengst the Butcher."

Rage flared in the Norseman's eyes, and the guards at his sides stiffened. For a long moment, the Norseman stood motionless, his eyes locked on hers, and then he spoke in a cold rasp. "Do not be too sure of yourself, Roman. There are near a thousand men two days' march south, and the man who leads them is a Knight of the Round Table. He will surely seek vengeance against the woman who pulled down his precious Pendragon and broke the Table. This reckoning may be tomorrow, or two months from now, but it will come, and I am the only one who can raise a force of Norse warriors in time to aid you in that fight."

Morgana stared at the man in front of her, clad in dirty furs and skins, and weighed his words. Before the Norseman had walked into the room, she had decided to kill him once he told her all that he knew of this Sir Percival, but his words had shaken her. A thousand men led by a Knight of the Table and guided by the wiles of Melitas Komnenos was indeed a deadly threat. They might not be able to take her castle, but they could seize the silver mines, and such a loss would not be taken lightly by the emperor.

"Where will you find these new warriors, and how quickly can you bring them to these shores?" Morgana said, her voice revealing nothing of her inner tumult.

"There is a settlement of my people in Hibernia. I will raise a host there. Others will follow from my homeland."

"You have no gold or silver, Ivarr the Red. How will you pay them?"

"I will offer them the sack of Londinium and the right to sell half its people into slavery."

Morgana stood and walked to the window and looked across the courtyard. Lord Aeron was just outside the gate, talking to one of the wounded Norsemen. She turned around and said curtly, "What do you seek from me?"

"I need a ship with enough food and water for a three-day journey."

"And what am I promised in return?"

"I will return with enough warriors to crush this Sir Percival . . . and I will give you the old man, a Roman, who now rides with him."

Morgana's face froze for a moment. Although she quickly recovered, she knew the Norseman had seen her reaction.

"Yes," the Norseman said with quiet confidence, "the Roman you seek is with him. My spies tell me that this man and the man with skin like the night rarely leave the side of this Knight of the Table. You cannot take him without my help. Give me that ship and I will return with the forces needed to do this."

Morgana stared at the Norseman for a moment before answering. "And why should I believe you will honor your word, Ivarr the Red?"

The Norseman drew a knife from beneath his jerkin, and the guards behind him started forward, but stopped when Morgana raised a hand. Ivarr held the knife in front of him and spoke in solemn voice. "This knife, Roman, was given to me by my father's father. I give you my blood oath that I shall honor my promise, or die trying."

As he finished speaking, Ivarr drew the knife across his palm, drawing blood. Then he closed his fist, and crimson drops fell from his hand to the floor.

Morgana watched the display with a smile. She believed the Norseman would honor his promise, if it was within his means, but not on account of his blood oath. His word, like her own, was not worth a farthing. No, Ivarr the Red would return for another reason—to regain the jewel that was Londinium.

"You shall have your ship, but my price is one slave for every two that you take or sell after the sack of Londinium, and I want the old Roman."

THE RIVER WID

Percival looked back at the fifty men standing patiently beside their horses waiting for him to mount his black destrier. Shaking his head, he turned to Cynric.

"I am honored by their vow to serve as my retinue, but I neither deserve nor need an armed column to accompany me."

"Sir, I told them that, but they're free men, and they have made it clear that they intend to follow you, whether you like it or not."

"What is it they seek?" Percival asked, confused.

Cynric scratched his head and looked over the line of men. "Sir Percival, things have been so bad, for so long, that what we were a part of—the Pendragon, Queen Guinevere, the Table—it is almost like a myth to them . . . a time of magic. And then suddenly, that myth has become real. Now they have hope. They believe you will resurrect what was, and they want to help . . . to be a part of that. And then there's the baker's wife . . ."

"The baker's wife?" Percival repeated in confusion.

"Aye. She came with wagons of bread and told the men Morgana would try to kill you. She said it was their sacred duty to protect you, and—" he shrugged "—they intend to do that."

Cynric moved a little closer and lowered his voice. "The truth is, Sir, we had to argue half the night to keep a lot more of these men from following you, and they may change their minds if you—"

"Delay any longer?" Capussa interrupted, clapping Percival on the shoulder. "Well said, Archer. I suggest we leave, Knight, before your retinue stretches from here to Londinium," the Numidian finished, trying to hide a smile.

"Since I suspect your nightly tales may have contributed to this, maybe you can tell me how we will feed these men?" Percival said with a measure of exasperation.

Merlin, who was listening to the exchange with amusement, walked over to Percival and raised a mollifying hand. "Your concerns are well considered, Sir Percival, but I can assure you that we shall find ample food along the way. This day has been long in coming and preparations have been made."

Percival looked at Merlin, a question in his eyes, but he nodded in acceptance. "So be it."

As he turned back to his horse, the Knight looked out on the field below him, where a small army of men were loading wagons, packing up horses, and preparing for the march back to Londinium. He walked to the edge of the road, dropped to one knee, closed his eyes, and whispered, "May God keep them safe."

After making the sign of the cross, the Knight rose to see hundreds of men staring at him in silence. He raised his right hand in a sign of parting and mounted his horse. As he rode off at the front of the column, the sound of hundreds of voices followed him.

"Sir Percival! Sir Percival! Sir Percival!"

After the column had ridden north for a league, Merlin rode up beside Percival and pointed to a square stone house by the side of the road.

"That's an old Roman post house. The Roman road north is ahead. We should reach the town of Cestreforda by nightfall. The town escaped most of the ravages that occurred after the fall. We will find friends there."

"I am grateful for your guidance . . . it has been many years since I traveled this way, but I sense that you would speak of something other than the road, Merlin."

Merlin looked over at the Knight and then returned his gaze to the road.

"You must have many questions for this old man."

"Many, indeed. Although, I fear I shall not like the answers," Percival said quietly.

Merlin nodded but said nothing.

Percival was silent for a moment. Then he turned to Merlin.

"First, I would know of the Queen's welfare and the state of the kingdom, but before you speak of these matters, I would ask that Capussa join us. He has agreed to complete my mission if I cannot, and hence, he must be prepared for what is ahead. Is that acceptable to you?"

"It is. He is a true and . . ." Merlin smiled, "a most formidable companion."

Percival motioned to Capussa, who was riding to the right with two mounted bowmen at the head of the column. The Numidian slowed his pace and eased his horse into place on the other side of Merlin.

"My friend, I have asked Merlin to speak of the state of the kingdom. I would ask that you listen as well."

Capussa smiled. "Why, it is a peaceful land where men of noble birth while away the hours drinking mead and catching fish. What else is there to know of it?"

A wry smile came to Percival's face. Merlin raised a questioning eyebrow and then cleared his throat before beginning his narrative.

"The Queen is well. She lives at the Abbey Cwm Hir to the northwest, with her handmaiden, Lady Cadwyn, and Sister Aranwen."

"I remember the Sister, but not Cadwyn. There was another . . ."

"Enid," Merlin said. "She died of a fever. Cadwyn is younger . . . barely eighteen years but quite a tigress. She's the Queen's fiercest protector."

Percival frowned. "You mean other than her knights and men-at-arms?" When Merlin was silent for a moment, the Knight's brow furrowed. "Merlin, please tell me the Queen of the Britons does have men-at-arms protecting her?"

Merlin made a mollifying gesture as he answered, "There are men at the abbey who . . . have some skill in arms, and there are many hunters and bowmen in the nearby town that would come to her aid if—"

"So there are none?" Percival interrupted, shaking his head in disbelief. "How can that be? There were over three hundred knights when I left, other than those of the Table, and the King's army was thousands strong. Were there none left who would defend their Queen?"

"Percival," Merlin answered reassuringly, "she is not undefended. My spies track everyone who comes within a day's ride of the abbey, and when threats have arisen, they . . . have been dealt with. Plans have also been made to defend the Queen, or to take her to a place of safety, if there was an attack in force."

Percival looked over at the older man. "Forgive me. I thank you for your service to the Queen, but I still would know why she does not have a strong standing force guarding her at all times."

Merlin sighed and looked at the winding road ahead. "You don't know what it was like after the death of the Pendragon . . . the land descended into chaos. There was no King and no Table. As for the army and the knights . . . the army that fought at Camlann carried the field that day, but it died gaining that victory.

"After the battle, Morgana stopped paying the Norse, Pict, and Saxon sellswords that had followed her banner. With nothing to hold them together, they broke into roving bands and began to ravage the land. When the remaining foot soldiers, archers, pikemen, and knights that served the King—the few who survived—realized there was no one to lead them, and no one left to protect their women and children from being slaughtered, they did what they had to—they returned to their homes."

"And you and the other members of the court . . . you could not hire a force of men to protect the Queen?" Percival asked with a measure of anger and frustration.

"Percival, we could and we did, but we had to do it in a way that would not draw Morgana's interest. In the year after Camlann, she still controlled enough sellswords, brigands, and Norse warriors to mount an attack on the Queen—an attack that could have succeeded. We forestalled that possibility by convincing Morgana's spies that the Queen was nothing more than a helpless, distraught widow cowering in a remote abbey."

Percival's ire abated, and he looked over at the old man.

"Forgive me. I . . . spoke in ignorance. The Queen has been well-served by your wisdom."

"No forgiveness is necessary, and I suspect," Merlin said with a chuckle, "that the Queen, and in particular Cadwyn, may have a different view on that matter."

The trio rode on in silence for a while as Percival struggled to reconcile the kingdom of the present with the one he had left in the past. It was as if a cruel sea had swept over the land and left behind just a ravaged shell of what had once been.

After a time, Merlin turned to the Knight. "Percival, I have a question for you as well. Capussa has told me of your near death in the desert, and of the miracle that saved you. Can you tell me of this?"

Percival hesitated for a moment and then gestured to Capussa. "If

Capussa has spoken of this, then you know all there is to tell. I was lost in the desert, on the brink of death, when I came upon a spring. It must have been blessed by the Almighty, for when I filled my cup and drank of it, my strength was restored, and my face and neck were cleansed of the many scars that I bore from . . . my time in the arena. Afterward, I rode on, for time was short. I had hoped to return to that holy place another day, but it was not to be."

"A cup you say?" Merlin asked with a frown.

"Yes."

"Tell me of this cup, if you will?"

"Merlin, it was not the Grail."

"How do you know this to be true?" Merlin said.

Percival shook his head, and a sad smile came to his face. "Merlin, for six years I searched for the Grail. I can draw you a map of nearly every street in Galilee and Jerusalem from memory. I can tell you the names of the many priests, rabbis, and men of learning from Edessa to Damascus and from Jerusalem to Alexandria that I spoke to in my search. Some relinquished their knowledge willingly, others were bribed, and God forgive me, others spoke at the point of my sword. In the end, I failed. The Holy Grail remains lost."

"Percival, forgive me," Merlin said in a quiet voice. "I would not have you relive the pain of those times again. You need not speak of this."

Percival turned and looked at Merlin, and then spoke with quiet conviction.

"My friend, that pain was lifted from me on that day in the desert, so I do not fear these memories. As for the cup I drank from, I will gladly tell you all that I know. It is little enough. When I arrived in Alexandria, I rode to the home of Jacob the Healer, only to find he had passed away a month earlier. I gave the writ of release from Khalid to Joshua, his son, so that all would know his sentence had been served. It was then that Joshua gave me the cup, along with my sword, and a long note from Jacob.

"Joshua told me that his father had left a deposit of gold in my name with a trusted Venetian merchant, and he conveyed his profound thanks, and Jacob's thanks, for my sacrifice. As for the cup, Joshua told me that his father had died in the throes of a fever, and when he spoke of the cup, much of what he said made little sense, but some of it was clear."

Percival looked over at Merlin, amused at the older man's earnest attention to every detail of the story.

"Jacob said the cup was not the Grail, Merlin. That was the only clear part of Jacob's fever-ridden ramblings. As for the note that he left me, it's written in a language that I am unable to read. Joshua said it could be an ancient Aramaic tongue. You're welcome to try your hand at deciphering it, and you can see the cup as well, but I would ask that you return them to me when you are done. Jacob the Healer saved my life, and these gifts are all I have to remember him by."

"Percival," Merlin said quietly, "if you would, please tell me the exact words Jacob is said to have spoken about the cup."

Percival hesitated for a moment, remembering his parting words with Jacob's son. "He told Joshua, 'This is not the cup that the Knight seeks, but it is one that has served.' As I said, Jacob was old and dying of a fever at the time. Do you still desire to see the cup and the note?"

"Yes, I would, if that is acceptable to you."

The Knight glanced over at the old man and shook his head, a wry smile on his face.

"Then see them you shall, Merlin the Wise."

CHAPTER 21

TOWN OF CESTREFORDA

ercival looked up at the late afternoon sun and then turned to Merlin, riding alongside on his right.

"The horses tire, and we have about an hour of daylight left. Do you know how far we are from the town you spoke of this morning?"

A look of uncertainty crossed Merlin's face when he answered. "I have not traveled this road in many a year, but it should be less than a league distant. The scouts should—" Merlin hesitated at the sight of two riders galloping toward them and then finished his thought "—have spotted Cestreforda."

Percival raised a hand, halting the column, and he and Capussa rode forward to meet the two riders. They were Cynric's men. The younger of the two men, Keil, his face flush with excitement, spoke in a rush.

"Sirs, the road ahead—"

"Keil, isn't it?" Capussa interrupted, raising a calming hand. "Don't tell me that you've managed to pick a fight with another one of those blond giants."

The hint of a smile crossed Percival's face.

The younger man's eyes widened, and he smiled self-consciously.

"No, no sir. It's Cestreforda . . . it's a half league up this road, but the townsfolk, they've blocked the road with a wagon. They've prepared for a fight, sir."

Merlin rode up alongside Percival and Capussa. "Every town is a fortified camp of necessity. We need to convince them we mean no harm."

Percival nodded and turned to Capussa.

"We'll ride forward and halt the column just out of bowshot, and I will go forward alone."

Capussa shook his head. "Alone? I think not."

"Very well," Percival said, "young Keil will come with me."

Capussa raised an eyebrow.

Percival gestured up the road. "My friend, those aren't brigands or Norse warriors up ahead. They're decent, honest folk trying to protect their homes from raiders. The less threatening we are, the better."

"Honest folk or not, it only takes one arrow to kill a man, Knight," Capussa said dourly.

Percival nodded. "Agreed, I will wear chain mail under my tabard."

Merlin eased his horse forward and leaned over so only Percival and Capussa could hear his whisper. "We must do all within our power to enter this place peaceably, my Numidian friend. I have friends in this town. They have been entrusted with a great store of royal supplies—supplies we will need for our journey. If I can get a message to these men, we will be welcomed."

Capussa stared at the old Roman for a long moment and nodded reluctantly.

"So be it."

Percival dismounted from his horse, took off his cloak, and pulled a mail shirt over his undergarment. Then he donned the white tabard with the seal of the Table on the front.

The mounted column rode forward, after Percival remounted his horse, and came to a halt a furlong and a half from the village. The wagon barring the entrance into the village was plainly visible ahead of them. Ten or twelve men armed with bows, swords, and wooden pikes were standing behind it. Percival slowly rode forward with Merlin and Keil beside him. When they were still a good distance away, he motioned for the other two men to halt.

"Wait here. I will ride ahead alone and speak with them."

"I would ride with you," Merlin said.

"And I, sir," Keil added quickly.

"I am sure you would," Percival said, "but I am wearing chain mail forged of the finest steel beneath my tabard. I will survive a bowshot. You two, on the other hand, would be severely wounded or killed. I cannot allow that. I will proceed and see if we can parley."

"So be it," Merlin said, nodding reluctantly. "Ask to speak with Lestinius. He is the man that I know. If he's dead, ask to speak to his son, Luccus."

Percival nodded and nudged the destrier forward into a slow walk toward the barrier in the road.

When the Knight had closed half the distance to the wagon, a balding man of middle age, with the well-padded middle of an inn or tavern keeper, stood on a small barrel and called out, "Come no further, or the archers will kill you."

The trees lining the sides of the road left part of the road in shadow and part bathed in streams of light. Percival eased his horse to a stop on the edge of a shadowed patch, dismounted, and stepped in front of the destrier.

"May I ask the name of the man with whom I speak," Percival called out respectfully.

There was a hesitation, and then the man on the barrel answered, "I'm the mayor of this town. My name is Gethin."

"We would speak with Lestinius, if he is among you," Percival called out.

The men behind the wagon spoke among themselves, and the mayor turned back to Percival.

"And who would speak with him?"

Percival gestured back toward Merlin, but kept his gaze on the man in front of him. "Merlin the Wise." An audible murmur ran through the crowd behind the wagon.

The mayor stared at Percival for a moment, straining to see him in the shadow. "And who would you be?"

"I am Sir Percival of the Round Table."

The reaction was immediate. The men hiding behind the wagon pressed forward to peer over the top of the barrier, while others behind them crowded forward, straining to see the figure standing in the shadows. Gethin almost lost his balance as he, too, leaned forward to get a better look.

After he steadied himself, the mayor turned to the men behind him, and an argument ensued. A few minutes later, a woman dressed in a brown dress and an apron pushed forward and spoke sharply to the mayor. Although Percival couldn't hear what she said, her words had an effect upon him. When Gethin spoke again, his tone was more respectful.

"Sir, we have been told that all of the Knights are dead. I . . ."

Percival stepped forward into the patch of light a pace away, his arms opened wide. The last rays of the evening sun illuminated the coat of arms on his chest as he spoke in a voice that reached every man and woman on the road ahead. "In the name of Arthur Pendragon, I tell you that I am Sir Percival of the Round Table."

The crowd behind the wagon fell silent, and then a swell of voices rose as more people tried to press forward. Percival could hear the mayor insisting, "I tell you, it cannot be! It cannot be!" Then the people quieted, and Gethin turned to someone behind him and more argument ensued.

At last, a tall, thin man with white hair, wearing a simple brown cloak, squeezed past the stone wall on one side of the wagon and walked with some difficulty toward the waiting Knight. Head bowed, he walked toward Percival, planting his staff firmly, before he took each step. He stopped a pace from the Knight.

The old man hesitated for a moment, his eyes scouring Percival's face. Then he spoke in a querulous, if respectful, voice. "I am Lestinius, the man you seek. You say that you are Sir Percival . . . hmm . . . well, it's been a long time, but you do have the look of him. I saw you ride through Londinium a decade ago . . . on a cloudy day, a morning, I think. You were riding a white horse . . . yes, beside Sir Geraint . . . Sir Lionel, he was in front of you, with Sir Galahad."

Percival smiled. "Good Sir, I suspect your memory is far better than mine on most days, but as to this, I must respectfully disagree. I remember the day well. We rode through Londinium in the afternoon, not the morning, and the spring sun shone in a near-cloudless blue sky. And it was Galahad who rode by my side. Geraint rode beside Sir Lionel, two rows ahead of us. As for my horse, his name was Rowan, so named by my mother, for his reddish color."

The old man raised his free hand slowly to the sky and bowed his head. "God be praised, God be praised. It is true. A Knight of the Table lives. Forgive me if I do not kneel, my old bones are—"

"You have no cause to kneel to me, good sir."

His eyes brightened as he gazed at Percival. "And is it true, what we have heard, that you have slain the Butcher and Londinium is free?"

"It is true."

"God be praised. And is that old scoundrel, Merlin, really with you? Why he owes me a coin or two from our last game of dice," the old man said with a raspy chuckle.

"He lives. May I call him forward?"

"Yes, oh yes."

Percival waved to Merlin and Keil to come forward as the old man turned to the crowd behind the wagon, now swelled to over fifty men, women, and children.

"It is he!" he called out. "It is Sir Percival of the Round Table! You need not fear!"

Before he finished speaking, people were climbing over and under the wagon and running toward the Knight.

* * *

THE NEXT MORNING, an hour after dawn, Percival and Capussa stood in a field outside the town, bathed in sweat and gasping for breath. Capussa laid his training sword on his cloak and nodded to the throng of people hiding in the nearby woods.

"It seems that half the village has come to watch today . . . and it seems as though Keil has persuaded some of those fetching lasses who were following him about last night to bring you water for bathing."

Four young women walked to the edge of the field carrying buckets of water, with Keil walking behind, his hand resting on the pommel of a sword he'd taken from the body of a Norse warrior the day before. The young women set their buckets down, curtsied shyly, and walked back to the edge of the wood with Keil between them.

Percival nodded his thanks, and Capussa waved a hand toward the retreating Keil. "It seems you have a would-be apprentice, Sir Percival."

The Knight shook his head. "He's a good lad, if a foolhardy one, but my days of fighting are at an end. I intend—"

"To live in peace," Capussa finished. "I can clearly see that you are on that path. Why, we haven't had a battle in what, a whole day?" the Numidian finished with a chuckle.

Percival stood and started toward the buckets of water. "Have faith. We shall find the peaceful life I promised."

Capussa casually glanced into the depths of the forest, where he knew a small man with a thin, hard face was watching them from behind an oak tree—a man who'd been stealthily following them for the last three days. Then he looked over at his friend kneeling beside a bucket, running a cloth soaked in water over his face and neck. Capussa sighed and spoke in a whisper Percival couldn't hear.

"I fear that peace will only come with death, my friend, but with a little bit of luck, we shall avoid both for a while to come."

Two hours later, the column of men rode out of Cestreforda, with Percival and Capussa at the head. As the column reached the open road, Percival glanced backward.

"How is it that we had fifty men yesterday, but today, we ride out with near a hundred?"

Capussa smiled as he answered, "It seems another forty or so men from the army of Londinium rounded up some of the horses left by the dead Norsemen and decided to join you. There are also some local lads who have decided to march under your standard."

Percival raised a hand in exasperation. "I have no standard. In truth, I have little more than the clothes on my back, so I cannot possibly provide for this retinue. They need to return to their homes and farms."

Merlin eased his horse up alongside the two men, the trace of a smile on his face. "You did say, my good Knight, that the Queen needed a proper guard. Well, here it is," he said, gesturing toward the men riding behind them.

"Well said," Capussa agreed.

The two men looked at one another and then burst into laughter. Percival scowled as he watched two more young men on country nags join the mounted column.

"At this rate, half of Albion will be marching with us by the time we reach the Queen."

CHAPTER 22

ABBEY CWM HIR

Talorc squatted behind a stand of bushes on a hill outside the abbey's walls, watching the stone tower at the northern end. As the receding sun touched the hills in the distance, a flaxen-haired woman wearing a pale blue dress opened the tall, porticoed window on the third floor. She watched in silence as the light yielded to darkness, and then gently closed the window and disappeared within.

The Pict found himself intrigued by the beautiful Queen. He did not sense guile or evil in the face of the woman, and surely, she posed no threat to Morgana in this faraway place. Yet, when he had met with the Roman witch, he sensed she hated the golden-haired queen with a cold and terrible passion.

Talorc shook his head and whispered, "You are almost too beautiful to kill, Guinevere, Queen of the Britons. But, honor my oath I will, when the order is given."

As Talorc rose out of his crouch, the end of his bow jostled the bush in front of him. The movement, although small, was enough to draw the attention of the rangy man sitting on a bench in the courtyard below the Queen's window. Talorc froze. The rangy man in the courtyard stared at the bush without moving. After several minutes, the rangy man picked up the bow and quiver resting on the bench beside him and sauntered into the shadow near the abbey's outer wall.

The Pict sensed the man was not just a guard. He was also a hunter, like Talorc. Talorc could feel the man waiting patiently in the shadows—waiting for a target. Wary, he remained frozen for almost an hour and then made his way to the far side of the hill with extreme care, staying well below the line of the underbrush.

Talorc didn't fear the hunter, but he knew the man would unleash his dogs and hunt him if he sensed a threat. Although he knew he could evade the dogs, once they found his scent, the hunter and the other guards within the abbey would know an enemy stalked their Queen, and precautions would be taken. In the end, he would still kill his prey. It would just be a more dangerous task. He would be more careful the next time he returned to the abbey.

*　*　*

IN THE FOURTH hour after dawn the next morning, Cadwyn walked to the window on the east side of the sitting room and scanned the length of the road that ran from the front gate of the abbey to the village a half-league distant, and from there, to the hills beyond. It was empty. She stamped her foot in frustration.

"Where are they?"

"A watched pot never boils, Cadwyn Hydwell," Sister Aranwen said from the chair in the corner, where she was knitting a sweater.

"What? That doesn't make a whit of sense, and don't think you're fooling me, Sister. I know you're just as impatient as I am."

"That's ridiculous. I've seen many a knight in my day. We may need them, but they're a rather troublesome lot, if you ask me."

"Really. Then how do you explain the rat's nest you've woven in the past hour?" Cadwyn said, pointing to the tangled strands of yarn woven into the bottom of the sweater on the other woman's lap.

Sister Aranwen glanced down at the sweater and raised a hand to her mouth. She glared at Cadwyn as she stood up and angrily dropped her knitting into the basket beside the chair.

"Well, if you hadn't been jumping up and down like a spring robin, I—"

Sister Aranwen froze in midsentence as Guinevere opened the door to her quarters and walked into the room. The Queen was wearing a dark lavender dress that was as beautiful as it was regal. The jewel-encrusted silver tiara atop her head was encircled by a braid that flowed down her back with the rest of her locks, like a golden waterfall. Cadwyn and Sister Aranwen stared at the Queen for a moment, struck by her radiance, and then quickly curtsied.

Guinevere smiled at the two women and nodded to the open window.

"They are almost here."

Cadwyn's eyes widened, and she ran to the window. A long column of mounted men, riding in pairs, was coming over the rise a half league distant, followed by hundreds of people from the village. She leaned out the window and stared at the two men leading the column, but they were too far away for her to make out their features.

"Come, my friends," Guinevere said. "We are all that remains of the royal court, and I would make as good a showing as conditions will allow when we meet the good Knight and his companions."

"Forgive us, Milady," Sister Aranwen said as she pulled Cadwyn away from the window and ushered her toward the door. Guinevere glanced back at the column of men in the distance and whispered softly, "God be praised," and then followed the other two women out the door.

As they walked across the green, to the rear of the Great Hall at the far end of the abbey's grounds, Guinevere looked up at the once-grand stone edifice. The building had been built at royal expense to serve as the centerpiece of a place of great learning. The mountain of stone and marble set aside for the rest of the buildings lay outside an abandoned quarry a league to the south, covered in grass.

A month after the hall had been dedicated in a grand ceremony, the war with Morgana had begun, and work on the project had ceased. Now the old and worn building was a monument, like so many others, to what could have been, and a reminder of what had been lost.

The three women entered the hall through the rear door, where they were greeted by the abbess and the prioress, both dressed in their finest habits. Although the two nuns were in their seventh decade of life, there was a restrained excitement in their eyes and a spring in their step. They bowed to the Queen, and the abbess gestured toward the door leading to the dais.

"All is ready, my Queen."

Guinevere smiled and nodded. "Thank you, Abbess. Let us take our places."

As she walked through the door and ascended to the ornate wooden chair in the center, Guinevere remembered what the building had looked like on the day of its dedication. Grand tapestries and flags had hung from the marble walls, the magnificent murals on the ceiling were freshly painted, and rivers of light had flowed through the building's many windows, illuminating the hundreds of nobles and knights who'd come to the ceremony.

Sadly, years of neglect had left the hall worn, dirty, and in disrepair, despite the recent restoration efforts undertaken by the abbess and the sisters with the help of many of the men and women from the village. Although they had tried to banish the aura of gloom pervading the structure by lighting the few candles still remaining in the wall sconces, the morning clouds blocked the sun, largely thwarting their efforts.

For a moment, the contrast between the past and the present almost brought tears to Guinevere's eyes, but then the moment of weakness passed as she looked out on the hundreds of faces filling the gallery below. From the mayor of the local village, to the sisters, to the tradesmen and farmers, all of whom were dressed in their finest clothes, there was a common expression of excitement and hope she had not seen in a very long time.

Guinevere took her seat in the center of the dais and gestured for the crowd to sit as well. As they did so, she glanced over at Cadwyn and Sister Aranwen. They too shared the same look of expectation as the crowd below. Guinevere silently prayed their hopes and expectations would not be dashed by whatever came in the days ahead.

Moments later, the two massive doors at the far end of the Great Hall were pushed open, bringing in a flood of light from the now-visible midday sun. Six men walked in pairs down the broad marble aisle, led by a seventh man. The six men in the rear halted halfway down the aisle, and the man in the lead, wearing a white tabard bearing the crest of the Table, continued toward Guinevere.

As the tall figure emerged from the sun's glare, the Queen struggled to reconcile the features of the man walking toward her with her memory of the young Knight of yesteryear. Though he bore the same face as the man she remembered, his features were leaner, harder, and strikingly bronzed, and they were framed by a fuller mane of black hair.

Like the younger Sir Percival, he was tall, but the physical resemblance ended there. Where the younger Knight had been lean and strong, the man in front of her was the most physically formidable man she'd ever seen in her life. The muscles in his neck were like ropes of steel, his shoulders, chest, and arms were those of a blacksmith compelled to forge the most unforgiving steel without respite, and his thighs were like the boughs of a mighty oak.

The Knight stopped at the edge of the dais, dropped to one knee, and lowered his head. As Guinevere stared down at him, she found her heart was racing. It was more than the Knight's intimidating physical presence. She sensed an inner power within him and a capacity for terrible violence, one reinforced by the scarred hand resting on the pommel of his sword.

Without turning her head, Guinevere glanced over at Cadwyn and Sister Aranwen and then at the abbess and prioress. They were frozen in place, staring at the kneeling figure with awe and a measure of unease. She sensed the same feeling from Torn and the other guards standing at attention on both sides of the platform, steps from the Knight. It was as if they knew it was beyond their means to stand against this man if he drew his sword and unleashed the terrible power within.

"We bid you rise and declare yourself," Guinevere said in a loud voice that echoed across the silent hall.

The tall Knight stood and looked into her eyes, and the unease she had felt a moment earlier disappeared. The blue eyes that met her own were imbued with the same honesty and loyalty as those of the younger Knight she remembered, but at the same time, they were different. The iron within had become steel, knowledge had become wisdom, and pain had yielded to an implacable endurance.

"Your Highness, I am Sir Percival of the Round Table, and I am at your command," the Knight said in a calm and respectful voice, his eyes never leaving hers.

For a long moment, the hall was as silent as a grave in the depths of the forest, with every breath held in abeyance. Then Guinevere took a step forward, a radiant smile on her face.

"Your Queen and Kingdom welcome you, Sir Percival, and rejoice in your long-prayed-for return." She lifted her arms, and the crowd in the Great Hall broke into thunderous applause. When the applause fell silent, Guinevere walked across the dais and stopped a pace from Sir Percival. "And who are your companions, Sir Percival?"

"They are friends who guided me to this place, and more."

"Then we would meet them and thank them for their service."

"Yes, Your Highness," Percival answered. He turned and gestured to the men to come forward. They approached in a line. The man in the lead, whose skin was as black as coal, halted a step away from the Knight.

"Your Highness," Percival said, "this is Capussa, my friend and brother-in-arms. We endured many trials together in the land of the Moors, and he has saved my life more times than I can count. His sword was at the forefront of the battle that set Londinium free, and he was the general in charge of the forces that defeated those of Ivarr the Red on the River Wid."

As the black soldier took a step forward and dropped to one knee, Guinevere was struck by how alike the two men were, despite their physical differences. Like the Knight, the man kneeling before her seemed to be forged from steel itself, and he carried within him the same restrained but terrible capacity for violence she sensed in Sir Percival. Yet, she also sensed within him the same wisdom and goodness she had discerned within the Knight.

"Rise, Capussa," Guinevere said with a smile, "and accept our sincerest gratitude for all you have done to bring Sir Percival home and to free the oppressed people of this Kingdom."

Capussa stood, bowed his head, and stepped to the left.

Percival then gestured to Cynric, Tylan, Bray, and Keil, who stepped forward together and knelt.

"This is Cynric, one of your finest archers, my Queen, and these are his men, Tylan, Bray, and Keil. Cynric and these men, and many others, fought to free Londinium. They provided noble service in the defeat of Ivarr the Red and guided me safely to this place. I am in their debt."

Guinevere inclined her head and smiled. "Rise, noble yeomen, and accept our gratitude for your service. The Kingdom is in your debt."

She noted the hint of a smile on Percival's face when one of the older men had to usher the awestruck young man named Keil to the left.

"And last, but surely not least, Your Highness, is a man whom you know, Merlin the Wise. He has graced me with the benefit of his wisdom since the retaking of Londinium, and I am in his debt as well."

Guinevere's eyes widened for a moment, as Merlin walked forward and knelt.

The sight of Merlin unleashed a river of memories, both good and bad. During Arthur's reign, a part of her had resented the special relationship he had shared with the King and their endless secret meetings. And yet another part of her had recognized that Arthur had desperately needed every ounce of Merlin's wisdom and guidance—treasures that she had sorely missed when the old Roman disappeared shortly after the fall of Camelot.

"Rise, Merlin the Wise. I thank you for your service to the crown, both past and present. It has been a long time since our last meeting. We have much to discuss."

Then Guinevere turned back to Percival. "Are there any others, Sir Percival, whom we should acknowledge?"

Percival hesitated for a moment, and then he nodded. "Yes, Your Highness. A . . . few more, if you would be so gracious."

"It would be our pleasure. Where are they?"

"They're waiting outside, and it might be . . . preferable, if it is acceptable to Your Highness, for me to introduce them on the steps of the Great Hall."

"Very well. Lead the way," Guinevere said, and then turned to the other women on the dais.

"Come, ladies. We shall all go."

Guinevere, the abbess, the prioress, Sister Aranwen, and Cadwyn followed Percival down the corridor, through the crowd, and out through the open doors at the rear of the Great Hall.

As they emerged into the sunlight, Guinevere's breath caught in her throat. There were more than a thousand men gathered on the green in front of her.

"Mother of God," the abbess said, "there's an army at my door."

MORGANA'S CASTLE

Morgana was poring over a large and detailed map of Albion, with Seneas at her side, when the door to the room crashed open. One of her Saxon guards backed slowly into the room, followed by Lord Aeron. The point of the knight's sword was pressed against the Saxon's chest.

Morgana took in the dust and blood splattered across much of his usually spotless armor and the simmering anger in the sky-blue eyes, just visible through the opening in his steel helmet.

"Am I to surmise," Morgana said, "that you have successfully put down the slave revolt in my silver mines?"

Rage flared in Lord Aeron's eyes, and for a moment, Morgana was sure he would run the Saxon guard through with his sword and seek vengeance upon her. Then the moment passed, and the iron control that had made him her most trusted tool of violence and oppression reasserted itself, and he sheathed his sword.

"Yes, Morgana. The revolt by the peasants, whom you have enslaved, is over. Many are dead, but the work in that hell will go on," the knight answered, in a voice filled with anger and pain.

Morgana made a disdainful gesture with her hand. "Men taken in battle are slaves, as are those bought in the slave markets. Their deaths are a thing of no moment. Now leave, and wash off their foul blood before it stains my floors."

Lord Aeron stared at her and spoke in a quiet tone, as cold as the grave, "And will I wash the stain from my soul as easily?" Then he wheeled around and walked out the door, the sound of his steel-clad feet echoing through the stone corridor.

Morgana looked over at the Saxon guard. "Go, and close the door."

When the door closed, Seneas spoke in a cautious tone, "He is a useful tool, Milady, but he is also a dangerous one."

Morgana turned her attention back to the map. "I have a tight hold on his leash, Seneas. Do not worry yourself."

"Yes, Milady, but he has changed since the other knight returned. I fear that he remembers what he once was and loathes what he has been forced to—"

She spun toward the older man and spoke in a hiss, "Enough! Lord Aeron will heed my commands, as he has in the past, for I hold the life of the woman he loves in the palm of my hand. As for the future, I only have need of his sword in one more battle, then . . . then the man who was Sir Galahad will die, but not before he knows that I have killed his precious Queen and brother Knight."

"Yes, Milady," Seneas said, nodding submissively.

Morgana turned back to the map in front of her and traced a line across the middle of Albion from her castle on the island's east coast to a circle on the southwestern coast.

"Ivarr has sent word. He joined forces with Sveinn the Reaver, another Norse warlord. Between the two of them, they have more than one hundred dragonships and can field a thousand fighting men. They will land near the old Roman city of Noviomagus Reginorum, southwest of Londinium. I will meet them there with near a thousand Saxon sellswords. The Pict, Cinioch, has promised to meet us there with three hundred warriors, who will also be under my command."

Morgana's finger traced a second line, from the southwestern port to a circle on the Tamesis River. "Our combined force will then march toward Londinium, ravaging everything in our path. This havoc," she said with a smile, "will draw that noble fool, Sir Percival, south, with his army of farmers, and with him will come Melitas."

"Milady," Seneas said hesitantly, glancing over at Morgana, "we only have a hundred and fifty men under arms in and around the castle, and some of those men will have to remain here as a defense force. Where will you find the additional men?"

Morgana brushed off his question. "Sellswords are always available, Seneas, if you have the coin to pay them. I sent a messenger to the land of the Saxons seeking more warriors. They will come. I will also hire some of the brigands that grew fat eating the scraps off Hengst's table. They're desperate now that their patron is dead."

"Yes, Milady."

Morgana took one final look at the map and then turned to the older man. "Now go, and, Seneas, say nothing to anyone else and assign a spy to watch Lord Aeron. I would not have him discover my plans until it is too late."

* * *

AFTER LEAVING MORGANA'S map room, Lord Aeron walked across the bailey toward his quarters in the westernmost corner of the castle. The memory of the day's slaughter weighed heavily on his mind. When the half-starved slaves laboring each day in the black hell of the silver mines heard of Sir Percival's return and the fall of Londinium, they rose up and killed their guards.

He and Morgana's cadre of sellswords had caught up with the sorry column of men, women, and children the next day as they were walking toward Londinium seeking safety. After a sharp, bloody, but sadly futile fight, the survivors had been herded back to their lives of misery and death.

As he rode past the bodies of the slaughtered miners after the battle, the knight had come upon a group of ten men. They had fought to the death, side by side, rather than yield and return to slavery. The body of the leader of the uprising was among the ten. He wore a ragged brown jerkin with a patch on the right shoulder—a patch bearing a red dragon with a pike underneath it.

At the sight of the insignia, the knight had dismounted and dropped to his knees, tears flowing down his face. This man—and possibly the others lying there beside him—had been a pikeman in the Pendragon's army, one of his brothers-in-arms. These men could well have fought by his side at Camlann.

As he walked by the open door of the storehouse at the far end of the bailey, Lord Aeron stopped and drew off his helmet. A motion in the storehouse caused him to wheel and reach for his sword. He froze when his eyes came to rest on the terrifying figure staring back at him from a full-length silver mirror resting against the far wall. The mirror had been scored and dented by Morgana's Saxon sellswords when they first seized the castle, but he could still recognize the visage.

It was a face that had once been adjudged by many to be the most handsome in the realm. The knight recognized the scars that had deprived him of that laurel, but what he didn't recognize were the empty blue eyes staring back at him—the eyes of a man who was already dead.

As he turned to leave, Lord Aeron's gaze drifted to the right side of the cracked mirror, and for a moment, another figure appeared—a knight with a mane of gold riding on a magnificent white steed through the streets of Londinium in a long parade, surrounded on both sides by cheering crowds. As he watched the strikingly handsome man ride past, with a roguish smile on his face, the laughter in the knight's sparkling blue eyes wounded Lord Aeron to the core.

In that instant, a hundred memories raced through his mind: the parties at court, the victories on the tournament fields, the battle at the Aelius Bridge, and finally . . . Guinevere's face. And then they were gone.

Lord Aeron stumbled away from the storehouse, through the arched stone door that led to the bleak corner tower where he'd lived for what seemed an eternity. He stopped just inside the door and sat down heavily on a cold stone bench and lowered his face into his hands.

CHAPTER 23

ABBEY CWM HIR

ne of two new guards now posted outside of Guinevere's quarters walked into the sitting room where she was waiting, along with Cadwyn and Sister Aranwen. Guinevere sat in a chair in the center of the room, while Cadwyn and Sister Aranwen were seated at a small table to her left. Each woman had a stack of parchment, several quill pens, and an inkpot in front of her. A third chair faced Guinevere, a few feet away.

Much argument had ensued over the seating arrangements, with Cadwyn wanting Sir Percival's chair to be closer to the Queen, and Sister Aranwen insisting it had to be against the far wall to be proper. Guinevere had chosen a compromise location that would allow the Knight to tell his tale without having to raise his voice every time he spoke.

"Your Highness, Sir Percival is here for his audience," the guard said formally as he bowed.

"Very well. It would be our pleasure to see him now," Guinevere said with a small smile.

"Yes, Your Highness."

A moment later, Sir Percival entered the room. He wore a clean, full-length white tabard bearing the crest of the Table, a fine black leather belt, and worn leather boots. The Knight bowed to Guinevere.

"My Queen," he said. Then he turned to Cadwyn and Sister Aranwen and made a slightly less formal bow. "Ladies of the Court."

Guinevere smiled, amused at the expression of pleasure on Cadwyn's face. She gestured to the chair across from her.

"Sir Percival, please sit. We have much to talk about. And, as you can see, we are not at court. That . . . is no more, and I . . . am Queen in name only. So I would ask that you address me, Sister Aranwen, and Cadwyn less formally and that you speak today as freely as you would with, say . . . your friend, Capussa."

Percival's eyes met hers, and he spoke with quiet sincerity.

"For me, you are the Queen of all the Britons, and you shall always be thus, and your wish for less . . . formality in our conversation is my command. However," Percival said hesitantly, "I would ask that you relieve me of the burden of speaking with you as freely as I would with my Numidian friend. That might be a bit . . . awkward."

"I see," Guinevere said with a small smile. "Then you are so relieved. Now, if you would be so kind, I, and my good friends, would hear of your travels, both the good and ill. Sister Aranwen and Cadwyn shall endeavor to keep an accurate record of everything that you say."

Percival nodded, his eyes meeting hers for a moment. "Yes, my Queen."

* * *

MERLIN AND AELRED sat at a table in a small stone room on the third floor of the abbey's southernmost tower. Merlin glanced down at the plate of cheese, sausage, and dark brown loaf of bread on the table and decided to wait until their guest came before eating. He stood and walked over to a window on the north side of the room and looked across the green to the tower where he knew Guinevere was meeting with Sir Percival. After listening to Capussa's telling of only a part of the Knight's saga, he suspected the Queen was about to hear a story like no other.

Aelred looked across at the crackling fire warming the room, and then turned to Merlin. "You trust this Numidian?"

Merlin shook his head in mild exasperation. "You have asked me that before, Aelred, and the answer is the same—yes."

"I am just being—"

"Certain, I know, and I also know that if I am in error, it may well cost all of our lives, but I am certain. This man has laid down his life for

Sir Percival many times, and he has traveled across half the world with him. He can be trusted, and he is a man, like us."

Aelred harrumphed, "You mean like you, a man of secrets and a consummate schemer."

"You have done your share of scheming, my friend," Merlin said with a smile.

Aelred nodded his head in reluctant assent. "Yet, but of necessity, not choice. That's the difference between us."

Merlin shrugged. "If you wish. The Numidian is like us in that he sees the world as it is—a cruel and merciless place, where evil will thrive and the weak will be persecuted unless men of goodwill are prepared to do what is necessary to defeat it."

"To be equally cruel and merciless, you mean," Aelred said dryly.

Merlin nodded. "Sometimes, yes, but, to quote a wise man, the difference is we do it of 'necessity, not choice,'" Merlin finished with a smile.

"Bah, I don't know why I put up—"

A knock on the door interrupted what Merlin suspected was going to be another of Aelred's frequent tirades.

"Come in," Merlin called.

Capussa opened the door and walked into the room, his right hand resting on the pommel of the sword by his side. He gave a slight bow. "Noble sirs, to what do I owe the honor of this invitation?"

Merlin stood up and returned his bow. "The honor, my friend, is ours. May I introduce Aelred, the Pendragon's Seneschal."

Aelred stood up slowly and spoke in his usual irascible tone. "The Pendragon, bless his noble soul, has long passed, so I'm not Seneschal of very much, but I'm honored to meet Sir Percival's comrade in arms, and, I am told, the man who planned the battle that laid low the barbarian, Ivarr the Red."

Capussa nodded to Aelred. "And I am honored to meet the Seneschal of such a mighty king."

"Please, sit," Merlin said, gesturing to the available chair at the table, "and have a mug of Aelred's mead. It is the finest in all the land."

Capussa sat down, poured himself a mug of mead, and after taking a draught, turned to Aelred. "I tasted a thousand cups of mead, in a hundred cities and towns, and this is surely one of the finest, sir."

A rare smile came to Aelred's face. Merlin waited for Capussa to enjoy another drink before rolling a map out on the table.

"Good Sir, you and Sir Percival have managed to retake Londinium and to defeat the forces of Ivarr the Red, but that will not be the end of it."

"Are you suggesting that more battles loom on the horizon?"

"Sadly, yes," Merlin said.

"Well then, we have something to celebrate. For a while there, I thought I was going to be condemned to live the life of a country squire," Capussa said with a smile.

Aelred struck the table with his fist. "That's the spirit! This time we will crush Morgana and lay waste to—"

"Patience, Aelred," Merlin interrupted. "Let us first find a way to survive until the next full moon. Now, here is what my spies tell me is afoot." He pointed to a spot on the map. "After his defeat, Ivarr marched north to Morgana's castle, where the two of them—"

Merlin paused when Capussa politely gestured for him to stop.

"Merlin the Wise, I do not know of this Morgana, and all I know of the Norse warrior, Ivarr the Red, is that Sir Percival unhorsed him on the bank of the River Wid. To defeat these enemies, I must know more of who they are and what they seek."

Merlin nodded. "You are wise, my friend. Very well, let me tell you of the people we fight. Ivarr . . . his story is a simple one. He is a Norse warlord. He came here seeking power and wealth, and he will put to the sword anyone—man, woman, or child—who stands between him and those desires. That is not to say he will be a foe of no moment in the contest to come. To the contrary, Ivarr is a savage and cunning enemy in his own way, but his desires, they are simple."

Merlin hesitated long enough to take a drink of mead, and then he continued.

Morgana, however, is the most formidable enemy I have ever faced. She is learned, ruthless, disciplined, patient, and merciless."

"It seems," Capussa mused, "you know this woman well."

"Indeed, I do. She was the second most gifted student that I ever taught."

Aelred choked on the mead he was swallowing. When he recovered, he pointed an accusing finger at Merlin. "You taught that foul witch? Now I know why she is such a human scourge!"

Capussa smiled and gestured for Merlin to continue.

"Yes, I bear much of the blame for this 'scourge,' as you say, but hear the whole story before you condemn me, old friend. In another life, I was a healer in the City of Constantine, and I also taught the healing arts to the students of the wealthy and powerful. One night, the imperial guards came to my door, and I was rushed to the bedside of the emperor. His body was wracked with a fever, and his physician—a fool—had nearly bled him white in an effort to save him. I was told that if I saved the emperor's life, I would be accorded great power and status, but if he died, I would die a moment later."

"Seems rather unfair," Aelred said. "Why you, and not his own physician?"

"He'd already been killed, so they couldn't kill him twice," Merlin replied, "and yes, it was unfair, but the emperor . . . well, he was the emperor. Thanks be to almighty God, the fever afflicting him was one I had treated before with some success. So, I was able to cure him. From that day on, I was made the court physician, and I was also assigned to teach the emperor's heir, Alexios, and the other children of the city's most powerful nobles. It was in this role," Merlin said with regret, "that I met Megaera Igaris—the woman you know as Morgana. She is a distant relative of the emperor, and her father served as the head of the palace guard.

"Alexios and Morgana were the most gifted students that I ever taught, but they were also very different. Alexios was a kind and honest young man. He loved learning for its own sake, and he truly aspired to be a man of wisdom. For Morgana, knowledge was just a means to an end—power."

"Sounds like a typical Roman, always seeking power," Aelred said in a slurred growl.

"Alas, good Seneschal, all men seek it in some measure or another, that is, excepting myself," Capussa said and then drained his cup of mead.

"Indeed?" Aelred said skeptically. "And what do you seek?"

"Another cup of mead," Capussa said, drawing laughs from the other two men.

Aelred refilled all of their cups, and the Numidian nodded toward Merlin. "Please, continue with your tale. I would know more of this woman."

Merlin nodded. "Intrigue and the pursuit of power are obsessions at the imperial court, and Morgana not only loved the game, she played it with consummate skill, despite her youth."

Merlin hesitated as a vivid picture of Morgana walking through the palace grounds with one of the emperor's courtiers flashed through his mind. He remembered her courteous nod as they passed on that day. In that instant, he knew she was arranging his death. It was a just a matter of when. The old Roman took a draught of mead before he continued, trying to wash down the fear the memory had resurrected.

"When the emperor took a new wife, Eudokia, upon the death of Alexios's mother, Morgana managed to become one of her closest friends and confidantes. A year later, Eudokia gave birth to a son, Leo, and Eudokia, at Morgana's urging, attempted to persuade the emperor to name Leo as his successor instead of Alexios. The emperor declined to do so. Several months later, the emperor suddenly died. The day after his death, his brother, an ambitious and dissolute man, seized the imperial throne. A month later, he married Eudokia and named Leo as his heir."

Capussa raised an eyebrow but said nothing.

Merlin sighed. "The scheme was Morgana's, and like all of her schemes, it was well planned and executed. All that remained was Alexios's claim to the throne. That had to be eliminated, and so it was. The day after the wedding, Alexios was seized and blinded—that was the accepted, if barbaric, way of rendering an heir to the throne ineligible without killing him. Alas, the blinding was crudely done and the boy died three days later, in agony."

There was a long silence.

"Since I knew that I was next on Eudokia and Morgana's list, I planned my escape, but," Merlin said, shaking his head with regret, "foolishly, I felt compelled to take revenge for the wrong done to the boy. I laced Eudokia's and the new emperor's meal with a potion that should have killed them both after a night of suffering, but I was only partly successful. Eudokia died, but the emperor did not. He'd drunk heavily before he supped and only ate a bite or two, so the effect of the poison was diluted. Still, he didn't escape unharmed. His left arm and the left side of his face were paralyzed by the effect of the poison."

"Well, some vengeance is better than none," Aelred said with a sniff, "but I do wish you could have piped the three of them into hell for their heinous deed."

Capussa laughed. "I am thankful we fight under the same banner, Seneschal. Were it otherwise, I suspect I would be denied both the pleasure of this fine mead and my life."

Aelred joined in the Numidian's laughter, but Merlin only smiled.

"I have now come to regret what I did," Merlin said when the two other men fell silent, "for as is the way of things, it has begat far more pain and suffering than I could ever have imagined."

"Bah. It was a good thing, I say," Aelred scoffed.

"And so I thought at the time," Merlin replied, "but as I say, much ill came of it. You see, the new emperor lashed out at those around him. He ordered Morgana, and many others, put to death for failing to protect Eudokia. Morgana evaded the death sentence by persuading the emperor that her father, the head of the palace guard, was my coconspirator in the killing. And so, he was put to death in her stead."

"A noble wench, this Morgana," Capussa said dryly.

"Well, the apple didn't fall far from the tree. Her father was a vicious man of no scruples. I suspect his dying regret was that he'd failed to cast suspicion upon her, before she did upon him. Be that as it may, Morgana offered to hunt me down for the emperor and to bring him back my head." He took a deep drink of his mead and then shook his head. "For the past decade, she has sought to make good on that promise."

"This Morgana must be a woman of great wealth to pay for so many sellswords, for so long," Capussa said.

Merlin nodded. "Her family was not without means, but most of the gold used to hire the Norsemen, Picts, and others during the war against the Pendragon was provided by the empire. The small cadre of sellswords that protect her castle are now paid from the silver she extracts from the royal mines—she seized them after the fall—although, I am told that most of their yield is now shipped to the emperor."

Capussa stared at Merlin for a long moment before speaking, "So we face a woman who has sworn a blood oath to kill you and who will not be denied. This is not something you should spread about, my friend. There are those who would kill you and end the matter."

A tired look came upon Merlin's face. "If that would have saved Arthur, then I would have drunk a cup of poison many years ago and spared this land the maelstrom of violence that has descended upon it. But my death would not suffice. Once the emperor came to know of this country's great mineral wealth, he would not let it go. He is once again at war with the king of Persia, and he needs every coin he can find to pay his armies."

Capussa nodded and then tapped the map in front of him. "Now that I know something of who our enemies are, tell me what you know of their forces and what they mean to do with them. For I can tell you this, my friends—Sir Percival and I have not crossed half the world to die by the sword of a Norse pillager or by the knife of a Roman assassin."

CHAPTER 24

ABBEY CWM HIR

Guinevere stood at the window, looking out upon the emerald green hills to the west, but their beauty was lost on her. All she could see were the images Percival described in his enthralling narrative: the sea battles with pirates on the long voyage from Venice to Joppa, fighting off the raids by thieves and slavers on the overland journey from Joppa to Jerusalem, and his relentless but fruitless search for the Grail—a search that had taken him to nearly every city from Constantinople in the east to Alexandria in the west. Guinevere marveled at his perseverance.

During the course of his tale, Guinevere had sensed when Percival had been reluctant to speak of the more painful hardships, bloody battles, and the near-death escapes, and she had gently insisted he tell the entire story. Although the Knight had honored her request, in many instances, she almost wished that he had not. Many of the incidents were either heartbreaking or horrific.

After the Knight had left, the three women had retired to their separate quarters and taken their midday repasts alone. It was as if each woman had needed a measure of solitude to recover from the captivating but heart-wrenching story.

As she turned away from the window, Guinevere glanced at the untouched plate of grapes, cheese, and bread sitting on the small table in her room but ignored it and walked to the door. She would eat later. A meeting with Merlin the Wise could wait no longer.

When Guinevere walked into the sitting room, she found Sister Aranwen knitting quietly in the corner and Cadwyn writing in the parchment book where Sir Percival's story was being recorded. She could tell Cadwyn had been crying. The two women stood up and curtsied as she entered.

"Cadwyn, please have one of the guards find Merlin," the Queen said. "I would have words with him about many a matter."

"Yes, Milady," the young woman said and began to gather up her writing utensils. Guinevere turned to Sister Aranwen.

"Sister, please ask the abbess if we may convene with her after morning mass. I would know what has happened to the ever-meddlesome Bishop Verdino."

"I suspect the coward is in hiding," Cadwyn scoffed as she rolled up a parchment. "He's probably worried Sir Percival will learn of his thieving ways and take off his head."

"Cadwyn Hydwell, he is a man of God; you cannot say such terrible things!" Sister Aranwen sputtered.

Guinevere raised a calming hand, gently cutting short Sister Aranwen's coming tirade.

"Sister, Cadwyn, we cannot squabble among ourselves. Sir Percival is right. I am the Queen, and you are my court, and we must serve the needs of the kingdom, however small it might be. So please, see to your duties."

"Yes, my Queen," the two women said in unison and hurried out the door.

MORGANA'S CASTLE

Morgana stared down from one of the windows in her quarters at the Saxon war galley docked below, at the far end of the stone pier. Over seventy more warriors had arrived on the ship, bringing her growing army to over six hundred men. Although Garr, the leader of the largest Saxon war band, had been displeased with the order, she had insisted the men camp outside the castle walls under the watchful eye of the castle guard. She had learned early in life that trust was the gift of a fool.

Morgana weighed her agreement with Ivarr the Red and his new ally, Sveinn the Reaver, calculating each opportunity for treachery with extreme care. She turned at the sound of Seneas's light tread, and he handed her a glass of wine.

"Milady, I sense you are not at ease with the . . . pact you have reached with Ivarr the Red," Seneas said respectfully.

Morgana took a sip of wine and walked over to the map of Albion pinned on the wall before answering.

"We are about to play a very dangerous game, Seneas. Ivarr is the snake, I the mongoose. Each of us would kill the other without mercy, given the chance. The pact between us merely defers our enmity until we have killed a third common enemy—Sir Percival and his forces."

Seneas followed Morgana over to the map. "You suspect the Norseman will betray you before the battle?"

Morgana laughed. "I do not suspect. I know he will, if it is to his advantage, and not just before but during the battle as well. And most certainly after it is over, as I would him. Yes, the days ahead will be most dangerous ones, indeed."

"When will the forces of Ivarr and this Sveinn land?"

"Forty days hence."

Seneas drew closer to the map and pointed to the circle on the southeastern coast. "May I ask why the Norse land at Noviomagus, instead of sailing up the Tamesis and landing south of Londinium? You could meet them there. That would save you—"

"No, it would not," Morgana interrupted.

She took another sip of wine and stared at the circle denoting Londinium. "Remember, the objective is to force Sir Percival to race to the aid of Londinium, and then to defeat his tired and unprepared army at a place of our choosing. If the Norse sail up the Tamesis and land on Londinium's doorstep, we could well take the city before he knows that it's under attack. Once the city is taken, many of the Norse will leave with their human booty. Ivarr and I will then be forced to fight Sir Percival's army alone, at the time and place of his choosing."

Seneas nodded respectfully. "You are wise, Milady. May I ask how you persuaded Sveinn the Reaver to accept this plan? Surely he would have demanded a direct attack up the Tamesis River?"

Morgana smiled. "He did, indeed, but I played on his fears. You see, Sveinn and his raiders sailed into the Roman Sea two years ago, intending to raid the empire's cities throughout Italy. His force was almost annihilated by a much smaller fleet of imperial ships armed with clay pots—pots filled with Greek fire. Knowing Sveinn and his men fear this weapon, I told them the Roman named Merlin the Wise had armed hundreds of ballistae within the City of Londinium with this terrible fire, and this fire would rain down on his ships as they approached. The fool accepted the story."

"What will happen when he discovers the ruse?" Seneas said with unease.

Morgana made a dismissive gesture with her free hand. "It will be too late. We will meet Sir Percival's forces in battle somewhere between Noviomagus and Londinium. Sveinn's forces will be in the van. They will suffer the most losses. After Sir Percival's force is crushed, Sveinn will die by poison. If his followers refuse to submit, they will be killed by my forces and those of Ivarr's acting together. We will then march on Londinium unopposed."

"And the city, Milady, what of that?"

Morgana stepped closer to the map and drew a circle around Londinium with one finger. "It will be sacked. I will be allotted one of every three survivors as slaves. This will replenish my losses in the mines. The rest will be sold. I almost pity the people there."

"Milady, you will surely be leaving Lord Aeron behind when you march upon Londinium?"

"No, he will come. He has a part to play in this drama. It will not be one to his liking, but play it, he will," Morgana said with a cunning smile.

* * *

IN A SECLUDED courtyard on the far side of the castle, Lord Aeron laid his sword and belt down on a wooden bench with the rest of his armor and pulled the coarse wool shirt he wore over his head, revealing a sweat-soaked chest and abdomen striated with cords of muscle. He trained alone each day for several hours, practicing over and over again the drills and moves he'd been taught over a decade ago by the finest knights in the land. The regimen was grueling and exhausting, but he savored every moment of it, for the physical challenge and pain gave him a respite from the mental torment that was his constant companion.

As Lord Aeron reached for the pitcher of water on the bench, the last rays of the sun struck the four crude training dummies tied to wooden stakes in the center of the courtyard, and for a moment, their slashed and battered bodies were real. The gruesome scene conjured up the memory of the battle at Camlann. Although the bloody scenes had haunted his dreams for years, the pain of the remembrance had not waned with time.

Arthur had anchored the center of his line with the Knights of the Table and his stoutest foot soldiers, intending to break Morgana's force with a charge when the two armies engaged. Morgana had anticipated the tactic. She knew her army of sellswords, although twice as large as Arthur's force, could not withstand a charge led by the Table, so she'd positioned almost a thousand pikemen across from the Knights. This wall of steel had rendered an early charge futile, and it had also allowed Morgana the time to use her greater numbers to wear down Arthur's weaker flanks.

As the greater weight of Morgana's numbers began to take its toll, Arthur had been forced to dispatch contingents of knights to shore up the weaknesses in his army's flanks, dispersing their combined striking power. Over time, the battle turned into a bloody contest of endurance.

Although Morgana had undoubtedly assumed her larger force would eventually grind down and overwhelm Arthur's forces, as the day grew longer and bloodier, the ardor of the sellswords within her ranks began to fade. The price being paid for the promised spoils had become too high. When Arthur, whose forces were nearly spent, sensed this change, he'd assembled what was left of the Knights of the Table and prepared to charge a weakened area in Morgana's right flank.

As the man who had been known as Sir Galahad rode forward to join the line of riders preparing for the charge, Lancelot had raced over to him on his black charger, yanked up the face plate of his helmet, and seized Galahad's arm. Blood was flowing freely down the older knight's face from a wound in his scalp, and small rivers of blood flowed down the back of the hand that gripped Galahad's arm.

"Morgana has sent a force around our left. We have no one to stand against it. Go to the tent with the wounded and take every man who can mount a horse or bear a sword and hold them off."

"But the charge—"

"Galahad," Lancelot interrupted, his voice hoarse and laced desperation, "there is no one left but you and the wounded! If they break through the line, we are lost, and the charge will yield us nothing. You must be our left flank. Do you understand? You must hold that line."

As Galahad nodded grimly and began to wheel his horse away, Lancelot called out to him, "Brother, forgive me, and . . . if Percival returns, ask that of him for me, as well."

Then the Table's first Knight wheeled his own horse and raced to join the battered line of Knights gathering around Arthur for a final charge. Until that moment, Galahad's faith in the invincibility of the King and the Table had been so complete that the possibility of defeat and annihilation had never crossed his mind. In that instant, his world changed forever. He suddenly realized Arthur's army was dying, and unless it was saved, all that he knew and loved would pass into the night.

As the young knight raced around the camp, gathering the wounded men still capable of wielding a sword, a terrible wrath had overtaken him. Who were these foul creatures to think that they could pull down the mighty Arthur Pendragon and the Table? The men who followed Galahad seemed to sense this rage, and they drew strength from it, as they approached the boiling melee ahead.

When the knight saw the line of Picts and Norsemen pouring through a gap in the line, he had bellowed out his defiance and galloped into their midst, striking men down to his left and right with each crushing downstroke of his sword. In what seemed the blink of an eye, but what was in reality an hour of savage fighting, the enemy had broken and fled.

The knight's fury had been so all consuming that he'd pursued the fleeing men down the hill and into a wooded ravine beyond, a place well outside his own army's lines. As he wheeled about, seeking other opponents to strike down, Galahad suddenly realized his own peril and turned to gallop back to safety. In that instant, a Pict archer hiding in the wood released his arrow, and it flew across the intervening space, striking the young knight in the face with the force of a mace. As the knight slipped off his horse and slid into blackness, he could see the last rays of the sun slipping behind the hills in the distance. The battle of Camlann was over, for good or ill.

As the memory faded, Lord Aeron found himself standing alone in the empty courtyard, in the cold darkness.

He'd been in captivity since that terrible day, the prisoner of an oath he'd given to Morgana of his own free will, but a prisoner nonetheless. Although he'd prayed every day to be relieved of the burden he had undertaken, his prayers had not been answered, until now. He sensed, with the coming of his brother Knight, his time of bondage was nearing an end.

CHAPTER 25

ABBEY CWM HIR

erlin the Wise sat in the same chair Sir Percival had vacated two hours earlier, facing the Queen, Cadwyn, and Sister Aranwen. As Guinevere stared at the diminutive man who had been her husband's closest advisor for over two decades, she recalled the anger she had felt toward him, particularly in the last years of Arthur's reign. Arthur had taken the Roman into his confidence and relied upon his advice throughout the war, but he had declined to tell her the true state of affairs.

Although she knew Arthur had not wanted her to bear any of the burdens imposed by the war, in the end, this had made matters worse. After his death at Camlann, all of those burdens had come to rest upon her shoulders alone. Her ignorance had only made them more difficult to carry.

Now, however, the old antipathy she had felt toward this man in the past was gone. She couldn't change what had been, but she could learn from it, and that she intended to do. The man in front of her knew more about Morgana than anyone in Albion, and she suspected he also had stores of knowledge about many other things that could bring relief to the people. She intended to make use of every scrap of that knowledge.

"We have much to talk about, Merlin, and in another time and place, I would, in accord with court etiquette, exchange niceties with you for a while before addressing the most pressing matters, but I do not have that leisure. I must know certain things today, so that what is left of this Kingdom will survive the morrow."

"My Queen, I am, and I always have been, your loyal servant," Merlin said, bowing his head. "Please ask me what you will."

"That I will surely do, but I would ask more of you. I would have you tell me what I need to know—the whole truth of the matter—even if you believe I am not wise enough to see the gravity of the matter, even if you feel that I would not like to hear of it. Do you fully understand this?" Guinevere said with quiet intensity.

Merlin's eyebrows rose and he nodded his assent. "Yes. You have my word, my Queen."

"Very well then, the first thing that I need to know is how I am going to feed, clothe, and outfit that army outside the abbey's wall—an army that seems to grow with each passing day."

"Those men will be provided for, my Queen," Merlin said confidently.

Guinevere stared at Merlin, somewhat vexed by his nonchalance. "Provided for? Merlin, contrary to the gossip of the common folk, you are not a sorcerer who can conjure fodder, bread, cheese, meat, and arms for over a thousand men from thin air. These things must be bought or taken by force, and we don't have the gold to do the former, and I will not countenance the latter."

Merlin nodded apologetically. "Forgive me, my Queen, I do not want you to think I am taking this grave matter lightly. It is just . . . well, there are secret storehouses filled with grain, cheese, salted fish, and meat—also with the arms needed to outfit an army."

Guinevere looked at Merlin in disbelief. "Merlin, how . . . where did this wealth come from? Where are these storehouses?"

Merlin eased himself back in the chair and closed his eyes for a moment before answering. "Forgive me, my Queen. There is much that you don't know . . . much that you should have been told, but were not. The Pendragon began to plan for this day, years before the fall."

Guinevere shook her head in confusion. "This day? How could he know? How could he—"

"He had a foretelling, my Queen. He knew . . . what was to come."

Cadwyn's eyes widened, and Sister Aranwen made the sign of the cross. Guinevere just stared at Merlin in silence. A hundred disparate memories from every corner of her mind came together into a single whole, and she knew what Merlin said was true. It took her a moment to repress the feelings of grief, frustration, and anger that threatened to overwhelm her, and then she spoke in a quiet but firm voice. "Tell me."

The old Roman drew in a breath, like a man preparing to unshackle a great load from his back after a long and difficult journey.

"Two years before the fall," Merlin began, "Arthur came to me and told me of a dream that had come to him more than once. In the dream, he was sitting in the forest near an ancient oak tree, a tree as old as the land itself. As he watched, a black vine wove its way up the trunk of the tree, and over time, starved the tree of light, killing it. Upon the death of the oak, a ghostly woman emerged from the tree. She told Arthur that if he sent 'the Knight who forges the many into an army of one' from the shores of Albion, then upon the Knight's return, this man would replant the oak, and a mighty tree would grow again."

Merlin was quiet for a moment, his eyes distant, and then he continued the story.

"I told Arthur that dreams were a thing of no moment, and he should ignore it, but it came to him a second time, and he said that he knew what it meant. The oak was his Kingdom and the Table, and both would fall, and—"

"That Sir Percival had to be sent away, so he might later return and resurrect what was lost," Guinevere finished in a whisper.

Merlin nodded, a look of surprise on this face. "Yes, my Queen. May I ask how you knew—"

"That it was Sir Percival? It could be no one else," Guinevere said softly.

Both of Cadwyn's hands were now covering her mouth, and her eyes were nearly bulging out of her head. Sister Aranwen was quietly praying with her eyes closed.

There was a long silence, and then Guinevere's eyes met Merlin's. "So he prepared for this day . . . storing away the arms and the gold that would be needed to restore what he knew would be lost."

"Yes, my Queen. Armor, shields, swords, spears, pikes, wagons, and yes, gold and silver to buy supplies."

"Where?"

"In secret caves, my Queen. There is one in the south, not far from Londinium, one in the far north, near the Roman wall, and a third not more than twenty leagues south of here. As we speak, my Queen, a line of wagons carrying supplies for the men outside the gates, from that very cave, is on its way here. If you will allow me the use of a hundred more men, then I can assure you that those making up this new army will soon be both well fed and well armed."

As Guinevere pondered his words, she realized he was not telling her the entire story. "And should I assume, Merlin the Wise, that you have taken the liberty of distributing the crown's stores in the south to the man who now defends Londinium—Cynric the Archer?"

Merlin shifted uncomfortably in his chair.

"Why, yes, my Queen, that I have. It . . . it seemed the prudent thing to do."

"Might it also have been prudent to tell me of these things before they were done?" Guinevere said in a tone that was both understanding and chiding at the same time.

"Yes, my Queen, forgive me. We . . . could not know when Sir Percival would return, and there were those who'd lost hope that the day would ever come. Once we came to know of his landfall, matters transpired so quickly that we had to make decisions in haste."

Guinevere was silent for a moment, torn by two emotions—resentment and gratitude. She was angry at Arthur and Merlin for failing to share the burdens they bore and for failing to give her the opportunity to try to stave off the fall, or at least to prepare for its aftermath. At the same time, she was humbled by their sacrifice. They had chosen not to rip the veil of happiness from her eyes, but instead to bear the burden of what was to come on their own.

When she opened her eyes and stared at the man in front of her, Guinevere suddenly realized Merlin was a tired old man. Yes, he was brilliant, learned, and cunning, but none of those gifts could have lightened the load he had been compelled to carry in these last years. In the end, he, like herself, had made decisions, good and bad, and borne the consequence of both.

Guinevere leaned forward and said with quiet force. "Merlin, you have my gratitude for all that you have done for the Kingdom. However, from this day forward, you will seek my consent on all matters of importance."

"Yes, my Queen."

Guinevere nodded her approval and continued. "Now, I am still confused by the matter of these storehouses."

Merlin nodded, but Guinevere sensed his unease when she continued. "Arthur could have stored arms, wagons, and gold, and things of that nature, but grain, meat, and cheese, these would have rotted over such a long time. If stores of food exist, then someone would have had to gather and store much of that food in the past months and years."

"Yes, someone would have had to do that, and . . . that person would also have had to keep a watch over your person, as well, my Queen, but in a . . . let us say, surreptitious way . . . one that would not arouse the interests or suspicions of Morgana and her allies," Merlin said as he shifted uncomfortably in his chair.

"Indeed," Guinevere said, her eyes narrowing, "and who might that have been?"

Merlin clasped his hands together before answering. "That would be . . . Bishop Verdino, or more precisely . . . myself, playing the role of Bishop Verdino."

The instant Merlin finished, Cadwyn exploded out of her chair and shouted, "I knew you looked familiar!"

Cadwyn's outburst so shocked Sister Aranwen that she let out a shriek and dropped her knitting to the floor. A moment later, the two guards outside the Queen's quarters burst into the room, swords drawn, and stared at Guinevere in confusion as her peals of laughter filled the room.

After a semblance of order had been restored, and the bewildered guards had left to return to their posts outside, Merlin cleared his throat and asked hesitantly, "My Queen, might I provide some explanation for my . . . ruse, shall we say?"

"Yes, I think you should, Merlin. Some people might think your actions were in the nature of high treason," Guinevere said in a cool reprimand.

"Like me," Cadwyn said, her eyes filled with righteous anger.

"Well then, let me try to persuade you otherwise, Lady Cadwyn," Merlin said with a tired sigh.

"As you know, my Queen, I was with the King at Camlann. I am not a warrior, but as a healer, I knew my place was there, doing what I could. For most who came to my table, it was little enough, for the slaughter was great on both sides and little quarter was given. Before the last charge that drove Morgana from the field, the one where . . . Arthur met his end, we spoke for a moment. He gave me a sacred charge on that day, one that I pledged to carry out until my dying day."

"To keep me safe," Guinevere said softly.

"Yes . . . that was his last order to me, in his last minutes of life. And although it is a charge that I willingly undertook, until Percival and that small army surrounded this abbey, it has been one that has taxed me to the limit of my resources."

"Was I truly that difficult, Merlin the Wise?" Guinevere said with a small smile.

"Yes . . . I mean no, my Queen. It is just that you did not know the perils that you faced."

"What perils?" Cadwyn interrupted in a voice full of scorn. "We have seen neither hide nor hair of an assassin or a Norse raider."

Merlin was a silent for a long moment, and then he drew a small book from his cloak.

"Lady Cadwyn, I kept a diary of every attempt on the Queen's life in the past seven years in this book. I wrote down the date that we caught or killed each assassin and what we learned from them. In the first year after she came to the abbey, fifteen men and three women came through yonder forest to kill the Queen. All of them were sent by Morgana. If you do not believe my words, I will gladly bring you to their graves, and to the graves of the forty-two men who either died discovering these plots or killing the assassins. They were all good men."

"I didn't know," Cadwyn said, taken aback by Merlin's quiet but intense words.

"I did not know, either, Merlin, but then you, or Bishop Verdino, if you will, did not tell me of these matters," Guinevere said in quiet reproach.

"I did not," Merlin said, with another apologetic nod. "And maybe I should have, but to do that I would have had to disclose my own existence, and that would surely have drawn a full-scale attack by Morgana, for she covets my death more than your own. We could not have held off such an attack. I could have sent a secret message through Torn or another trusted retainer, but how could you know it was me? None in this abbey except yourself, Sister Aranwen, and the abbess have ever seen me before, and . . . Morgana had eyes and ears within the abbey."

"Spies? Here? And you let them be?" Cadwyn whispered incredulously, glancing at the door and window.

"Yes, there are at least three. The cook's assistant, Bowen, Sister Ann, and Eldor, the man who brings firewood to the abbey. Bowen's sister and Sister Ann's brother were enslaved by Morgana. They work in the silver mines she seized after the fall. Morgana keeps them alive in return for information. Eldor brings their messages in and out. He does it for the coin. As for letting them be, Cadwyn, better the spy you know than the one you do not. If they were to . . . disappear, Morgana would just send others."

"God save us from that woman," Sister Aranwen said quietly as she made the sign of the cross.

"Why did you take on the guise of Bishop Verdino, Merlin?" Guinevere asked.

"During the first year, there were so many attempts on your life that I had to find a way to keep you inside the abbey's walls but, at the same time, not alert Morgana to my presence. Verdino's persona enabled me to do that. The more you hated me, and the more it was rumored that I stole from your lands, the less likely it was that Morgana would suspect

Verdino was Merlin the Wise. My Queen, the guise enabled me to keep my promise to my King. Unfortunately," Merlin said with regret, "it was at the price of keeping the truth from my Queen."

"Merlin, twice you have mentioned that the assassins came in the first year. Did something change after that?" Guinevere asked.

"Yes. I . . . I am not sure why, but for some reason, Morgana stopped sending assassins. There were other threats, but not from her."

"Other threats?" Cadwyn interjected.

"Oh yes," Merlin leaned back in his chair, "there were a number of others. A year after he seized Londinium, Hengst sent a force of men to kidnap you. The fool thought that if he forced you to marry him, it would somehow make him the king of Albion. Another time a band of brigands from the south started this way with designs of their own, and other Norse leaders have made noises about raiding the abbey from time to time."

"And you . . . and your minions stopped them all," Guinevere said, assessing the quiet, serene man across from her.

"Hengst's raiders were served a pitcher of poisoned mead, the brigands were killed while they slept . . . and so on," Merlin said, spreading his hands in an apologetic gesture.

Sister Aranwen made the sign of the cross again, her eyes widening.

Guinevere stood up, walked to the window, and looked out upon the growing army training just outside the walls, and the guards diligently patrolling the abbey perimeter with regular precision. For the first time in many years, she was truly safe. Although a part of her was angry at Merlin's manipulative and deceitful tactics, the truth was they had kept her alive so she could see this day—so she could see Sir Percival again. She turned and walked back to her chair and sat down, her eyes fixed on Merlin's.

"You have honored your promise to Arthur," she said gravely, "in the fullest measure, Merlin the Wise, and although I cannot say that I . . . approve of your methods, I am in your debt. Why, I think even Cadwyn would agree that you can be quite the useful scoundrel, when the need arises," Guinevere finished, smiling at the younger woman.

"Well . . . there is that," Cadwyn said grudgingly, and then she smiled as well.

* * *

PERCIVAL STOOD ON a rise, two hours after sunrise, just outside the walls of the abbey. In the broad, open field below him, a nascent army was preparing for war. One group of men practiced swordcraft, another group was learning to maneuver in formation, while still others were struggling to master the long bow, spear, and pike. He glanced down at Capussa, approaching from the field below with an amused look on his face.

"Do not look so dour, Knight. All will be well."

Percival nodded toward the men below. "I did not come home to start a war, Capussa."

Capussa nodded agreeably. "And you have not done so. You merely invited the people of Londinium to take back what was theirs, and they did. Who could fault you for that?"

"The wives and children of the men who died in that taking and in the battle by the Wid River," Percival answered.

The look of amusement on Capussa's face faded, and he turned to face his friend.

"Let us speak of things as they are, Knight. This land is dying. Brigands control many of the roads, and every town and village is a fortress. The men, women, and children within those fortresses live in desperate fear that the morrow will bring enslavement or death. When you cut down Hengst the Butcher and Londinium rose, you gave those people hope, and that, my friend, the forces of evil in this land cannot abide. So yes, there shall be war. There are only two things that now lie in the balance: whether you will bring the war to them or they to you, and who will be the victor."

Percival gave Capussa a skeptical look. "You've been talking with Merlin."

Capussa's smile returned. "We did share a cup of mead while you were with the Queen."

The Knight raised an eyebrow. "More than one, I suspect."

"Well, it was a fine mead."

"And what," Percival said dryly, "does Merlin the Wise counsel?"

Capussa looked out upon the field below and spoke in a solemn tone. "His spies say that Ivarr the Red has formed an alliance with Morgana, and it's only a matter of time before they take the field against us."

Percival stared into the distance, remembering how the men and woman on the northern coast would become restless and fearful as the spring thaw presaged the onset of the Norse raiding season. The lull before the first attack was always the hardest to bear.

"How much time do we have?"

"Merlin cannot say for sure. Ivarr must raise another army from his people, and Morgana must buy one. So we must do everything within our power to prepare this small army for war as quickly as possible."

"That's not an army, Capussa. Those are farmers, hunters, shepherds, and who knows what else."

Capussa looked over at his friend, an eyebrow raised. "Merlin told me you forged quite a formidable army from men very much like these. Moreover, he said your army of peasants soundly defeated Morgana's raiders in the north in many a battle. You did that alone, Knight. Together, we shall build an even more formidable army."

"Capussa, the men of the Marches were a hard breed, and I lived and trained with those men for almost a year," Percival said quietly.

"There are more than farmers down there, my friend. Do you see those men over there?" Capussa pointed toward a group of men standing together on the far side of the field.

Some of the men were wearing uniforms Percival recognized. He nodded.

"They are soldiers," Capussa said with satisfaction. "They served in the army of your dead King, and most of them have brought their arms with them. Yes, there are only a hundred or so, but more come every day. I have met these men, Knight. They know what they're about, and they have a score to settle. They will be the backbone of this army."

Although Percival felt reassured by the sight, he knew there were hundreds of other men who needed arms.

"What we need," Percival said with quiet intensity, "are swords and shields for the rest of the men. If we could arm them . . . and train them in the use of those arms, then we would have a chance. Alas, we would need a town full of blacksmiths working day and night to forge the steel we need."

Capussa walked over to the Knight and slapped him on the shoulder, a broad smile on this face. "Your prayers have been answered."

The Knight looked at Capussa skeptically.

"I speak the truth. Merlin borrowed a hundred men and rode south at dawn with nearly every wagon and cart available, along with over two hundred horses. He promised to return in three days with enough arms to outfit an army of two thousand and to bring enough supplies to feed that army for a month."

"And you believed him?" Percival said, incredulous.

Capussa shrugged. "I had no choice. I received orders from the Queen."

"The Queen," Percival said in confusion.

Capussa nodded, an amused look in his eyes. "Yes. Merlin bore a message with two royal commands. The first ordered me to give Merlin the men, wagons, and horses that he requested."

"And the second?"

"Oh, yes. That was for you. You are to attend the Queen this morning to continue your report."

Percival stared at Capussa in surprise.

Capussa laughed and pointed imperiously toward the abbey. "Don't just stand there, soldier! Attend your Queen."

CHAPTER 26

The Queen's Sitting Room, Abbey Cwm Hir

When Percival entered Queen Guinevere's sitting room, the Queen, Cadwyn, and Sister Aranwen were seated in the same places the three women had occupied during their last meeting.

"Forgive me, my Queen, I did not receive your message until moments ago," Percival said as he bowed.

"Please, sit, Sir Percival. The fault is mine. Your story of yesterday was so enthralling that I neglected to tell you when to return. Now, please continue your account of your time in the Holy Land."

"Yes, my Queen," Percival answered as he eased himself into the chair across from her. Percival was quiet for a moment as his thoughts returned to a modest house in the City of Alexandria.

"I . . . I spent many months recovering from my wounds under the care of Jacob the Healer. When my strength returned, Jacob guided me to the houses of men of learning in Alexandria who might have knowledge of the Holy Grail. Although these men were at first suspicious, over time, I earned their trust. I was allowed access to the secret libraries they maintained—libraries that contained many of the scrolls that survived the destruction of the great library of Ptolemy. Although many of these writings spoke of Christ and his disciples, and there were some that even spoke of the Grail, none told me of its whereabouts. The journal that I kept will attest to this."

"You kept a written journal of your search for the Grail?" Guinevere asked in surprise.

"Yes, my Queen. At the end of each day, when it was possible, I would write down what I had discovered."

"Sir Percival," Guinevere said, leaning forward in her chair, "such a writing is a treasure in itself. Do you still have this journal?"

Percival hesitated before answering. "Yes, my Queen. I do have it."

"I would speak with you about its safekeeping another time. Please continue with your story."

"Yes, my Queen. One afternoon, as I returned to Jacob's home, he was sitting at his table surrounded by his friends, overcome with grief. When I asked what was wrong, he told me that an ambitious nephew of the Emir of Alexandria had demanded that his son, Joshua, reveal the contents of a message he had translated for another man of power in the city. When Joshua refused to break his oath of secrecy, the man slipped a jewel into Joshua's cloak without his knowledge. He was then seized by the palace guards as he left the grounds and charged with theft. Although the Emir held his nephew in low regard and would have dismissed the charge, he was away on a pilgrimage to Mecca, and so Joshua was tried as a thief."

"What would be his punishment?" Cadwyn asked in a hushed whisper.

"He was offered a choice: the loss of his right hand, or a year in a Moorish prison . . . a prison from which a man such as Joshua, a small, kind man of books and learning, would never return."

Sister Aranwen's hand went to her mouth.

After a short pause, Percival continued.

"After the trial, which lasted a mere hour, Joshua was convicted. This was not something that I could allow to stand. I owed my life to his father, so . . . I took Joshua's place."

Guinevere looked at Percival in confusion.

"His place? Sir Percival, how could that be?"

For a moment, Guinevere's eyes met Percival's, and the Knight hesitated for a moment before continuing. As Guinevere watched him gather his thoughts, it was as if a part of him was returning to that far-away place.

"In my search for the Grail, I came to know a Moorish scholar, a man named Rashid. Like Jacob, he assisted me in my search by giving me access to his library and also securing access to the libraries of other men of learning. When I learned of Joshua's fate, I asked Rashid to intercede, for he was a man of high station in Alexandria. Alas, the matter was beyond his realm of influence. There was, he explained, only one way of saving Joshua's life. There was a law that would allow one man to bear the burden of another's punishment."

Guinevere's eyes once again met Percival's, and she said in a soft voice, "You offered to serve his prison term."

"I did."

"Did Jacob the Healer or his son ask you to do this?" Cadwyn asked.

Percival looked over at Cadwyn. "No, Lady Cadwyn. Neither Jacob nor Joshua knew of my intentions in this regard. Had they known, they would have refused to allow me to make this offer. I appeared before the court with Rashid, without their knowledge, and asked to serve Joshua's prison term in his stead. At first, the judge declined my offer, when the Emir's nephew opposed, but then a man approached him, a man who I would later come to know was Khalid El-Hashem, and had words with him. After this conversation, my plea was granted."

Percival eyes grew distant when he continued, and he spoke in a faraway voice.

"I later came to know why Khalid El-Hashem intervened in the matter. You see, the Emir of Alexandria, and the Moors who controlled all the surrounding cities, allowed Khalid to take the prisoners of his choosing to a prison where men were fed well, where they slept in clean beds, and where they were trained daily by men skilled in the use of the sword, spear, and every other implement of war."

"I don't understand," Guinevere said.

Percival looked down at the scars crisscrossing his hands for a moment, and then he looked up, his eyes meeting Guinevere's. "You see, my Queen, Khalid ran the finest gladiatorial games in all of Egypt. Thousands would come to see men fight and die in Khalid's arena, and they paid dearly for this privilege. Since men would not volunteer to die in his games, Khalid needed men to serve as the wheat for his golden scythe, and so prisoners such as I were brought to this place of slaughter."

"Mother of God," Sister Aranwen whispered.

Guinevere's breath caught in her throat, and she could see Cadwyn rising in the seat to her left, her small fists balled in fury. She raised her right hand slightly to forestall the coming explosion of verbal outrage, and Cadwyn sat back down again.

Percival spent the next hour describing his life in Khalid El-Hashem's prison and as a gladiator in the arena. As the Knight told the tale, Guinevere realized he was only telling a foreshortened narrative to spare his audience the pain of hearing the truth. As in the prior session, she gently tried to persuade him to tell the entirety of the story, but in this instance, her remonstrances failed. The Knight would not yield the memories she could sense he held within, and with each polite evasion, Guinevere's trepidation grew. It was as if Percival knew the women could not bear the nightmare waiting behind the door she was seeking to open. In the end, it was all she could do to hold back the flow of tears—tears that were freely rolling down Cadwyn and Sister Aranwen's cheeks as well.

When Percival finished his tale of his life in the arena, Guinevere found she was fascinated by the role the woman called Sumayya had played in Percival and Capussa's drama. She felt at once deeply indebted to the woman for saving Percival's life, while at the same time, a part of her was uneasy and even jealous of the Knight's relationship with the Moorish princess.

"Sir Percival, tell me of this woman Sumayya. How did she come to know you, for surely, she would not have made so great a sacrifice without cause?"

Percival hesitated for a long moment, avoiding her eyes, before answering.

"We . . . we were allowed to talk under the watchful eyes of her father and Khalid from time to time. She knew the language of the Greeks and Romans, as well as the language of the Moors, so we could speak without the aid of others, and . . . we could speak without the others knowing what we said."

"And what did you speak of?" Guinevere said quietly.

Percival closed his eyes for a moment to gather his thoughts. When he opened his eyes, all three women were staring at him, rapt with attention.

"Sumayya wanted to know of our land, the people, our customs, and to know of all the lands that I journeyed through. When I told her of the King, and of you, my Queen, and the Table, she was consumed with a desire to know more. If it had been within her power, she would have traveled here. I . . . I believe she would have found favor with you, my Queen, had you known her."

"She has my favor, Sir Percival," Guinevere said with a depth of feeling, "in the fullest measure, for it was her sacrifice that allowed you to come home."

Percival and Guinevere's eyes met, and it was as if they were all alone in the room. Then he nodded, breaking the spell. "Thank you, my Queen."

For a moment, the room was silent, and then Guinevere stood and walked to the window that overlooked the range of hills to the west. She looked at the sun and was surprised to see the day had slipped well into the afternoon.

"It is later than I realized, Sir Percival, and I know there is much that you have to do. I would ask that you return tomorrow, after you break your fast."

Percival stood and spoke as he bowed. "Yes, my Queen."

As he started for the door, Guinevere called after him. "Sir Percival, wait, please. Cadwyn and Sister Aranwen, would you wait in the library for a moment? I would speak to Sir Percival alone."

Sister Aranwen and Cadwyn stood up, curtsied, and walked through the open door to the smaller room beyond. After they had left, Guinevere walked across the room and stopped a pace away from the Knight, her hands clasped in front of her. She was quiet for a moment, and then she spoke in a voice full of regret. "You . . . you have every right, Sir Percival to . . . bear ill will toward Arthur, and myself as well, for . . . for the terrible wrongs you have suffered, and . . . and for the years that you have lost. I ask, more, I pray for your forgiveness. I know Arthur would also seek your forgiveness if he were here himself, but he cannot. If you knew . . . knew why . . ."

Tears welled up in Guinevere's eyes, and she closed them for a moment as she struggled to find the words to continue. When she opened her eyes, Percival had taken a step closer to her.

"My Queen," Percival said, "I bear no ill will toward the King, and I bear nothing toward you but . . . devotion and my steadfast fidelity as a Knight of the Table. I know that the decision to send me on the quest was against your wishes."

Guinevere's eyes widened. "You . . . you knew of my objection?"

"Yes," Percival said quietly, "and . . . I also knew that there were two women who watched me leave for the Holy Land . . . so long ago. One was my mother, who was on the dock. The second watched from the hills above Londinium."

Guinevere and Percival looked into each other's eyes, now a mere step away from each other, and then the Knight stepped back and bowed.

"My Queen, if I may take my leave?"

She nodded and spoke in a near whisper. "Yes . . . Sir Percival. I will see you on the morrow."

When the door closed, Guinevere stood there, a hand resting on her chest, as she recalled her tears of grief on that distant hill a decade earlier. He had seen her . . . he knew of her feelings.

*   *   *

IN THE LIBRARY next door to the sitting room, Cadwyn had quietly stood up on a wooden bench in order to peer through a hole in the wall that allowed her to see Guinevere and Percival. As Cadwyn climbed down from the bench, her shoe made a scuffing noise, drawing the attention of Sister Aranwen, kneeling on the other side of the room, praying with her eyes closed.

"Cadwyn, what are you doing!" the nun said in exasperation.

The younger woman turned quickly, an innocent look on her face, and stepped down from the bench.

"I thought I saw a . . . a wasp, but it was nothing."

"And you thought to swat it with your hand! Have you no sense at all?"

THE COAST OF HIBERNIA

Ivarr the Red and Ragnar looked down on the ruins of the town that Sveinn's warriors had sacked and burned to the ground a day earlier. The townsfolk who hadn't been fast enough to escape into the hills had been killed, every last one.

"The fools," Ivarr growled as he scanned the hundreds of sleeping men lying in the field just outside the smoldering town, wrapped in an array of foul-smelling animal skins. "We could have slept the night in that town, warm and dry, with women to serve us mutton and mead. Instead, we have spent the night in the cold, wet grass."

"They are vargars," Ragnar said. "Only blood and death satiate them. If we let them take Londinium, there will be nothing—"

"Sveinn and his pack of wolves will never set foot in Londinium," Ivarr said in a harsh whisper as he glanced over at the giant man wrapped in a black bearskin, sleeping near the campfire in the center of the hill.

"As soon as we have put this Sir Percival and his army of peasants to the sword, we will kill Sveinn and his men."

Ragnar glanced down at the well-ordered camp that had been set up by the force under Ivarr's command and then looked back at the disparate confusion that was Sveinn's camp.

"War leader—Sveinn's reavers, they outnumber us."

"They do," Ivarr said with a cunning smile, "but when the battle with the Knight of the Table is done, it will not be so."

MORGANA'S CASTLE

Morgana looked down at the courtyard from the turret of the castle where Lord Aeron and one hundred men waited beside their restive mounts. Some of the men were the Saxon warriors who'd served as her castle guard for years. The rest were newly recruited sellswords from the north and from Hibernia. Morgana turned to Seneas, who was waiting a step behind.

"When will the rest of the Saxons sail?"

"They should depart within the week, Milady."

"How many?"

"Four hundred, maybe five."

"And the local rabble that you hired, what of them?"

"We had enough silver to hire one hundred or so. They used to serve as tax collectors for Hengst. They will meet you a league to the south, at the crossroads. Milady, I . . . I do not trust them."

Morgana made a dismissive gesture.

"They will be placed in the front line when the battle is joined, Seneas. The Saxons will be behind them. They will either die on the swords of the enemy, or on those of the Saxons if they try to run. The few who survive will be no threat."

"Yes, Milady. Would . . . would it not be wiser to wait for your entire force to be assembled before you ride?"

Morgana ignored him. "The rest of the Saxons will land at Noviomagus well before Ivarr and Sveinn arrive. So my entire force will be there when the two Norse leaders come ashore."

"Milady, does Lord Aeron know that you march against his brother Knight?"

"No. He only knows that we ride to meet with Ivarr. He will not know that we march to destroy Sir Percival until the time is right."

"Yes, Milady."

The Hills above Abbey Cwm Hir

Guinevere watched the sun rise in silence from the crest of a hill, a league north of the abbey. Torn, Keil, and four other members of the newly formed and outfitted Queen's Guard waited a respectful distance behind them with their horses. As the morning's first light illuminated the stone ruins encircling the small party and the surrounding forest, Cadwyn, who was sitting beside her on an ancient stone bench, whispered, "Milady, what is this place?"

"No one really knows. Some say it was a Druid temple, others a Roman lookout post," Guinevere answered.

After several minutes of solitude, the Queen reluctantly stood and relinquished the sense of peace she felt in this place. "Alas, my friend, we cannot dally any longer. We have much to do today."

"Yes, Milady."

Guinevere glanced down the side of the hill as she walked over to her waiting palfrey, and saw two men on the banks of the river far below. She slowed and then stopped. The two men looked familiar.

Cadwyn walked over to where Guinevere was standing, discretely followed by Keil, and looked down the hill as well. "Milady, is that Sir Percival and General Capussa?"

"I . . . I can't tell from here," she said as she stared down the hill.

"If—if I may—Your Highness," Keil said hesitantly, "it is the Knight and General Capussa. They train every morning for near two hours. We were told not to follow them into the forest, but some do anyway. I saw them go hard at it in the forest outside Londinium. Why, it's a sight like no other!"

Cadwyn turned to Guinevere, a flush of excitement on her face. "Milady, can we go watch, just for a short while?"

"I would not want to disturb them," the Queen said, but she too was curious.

"I could show you a spot where you could watch without being seen," Keil said enthusiastically.

"And how," Guinevere said, raising a questioning eyebrow, "Guardsman Keil, would you know of this spot?"

Keil's face turned red. "Ah, well . . . I do love to wander about in these woods, Your Highness," he stammered.

"I see. Well then, I guess Lady Cadwyn and I should be thankful for your wanderings, for I would see this, as you say, 'sight like no other,' Guardsman Keil."

"Yes, Your Highness. Please follow me," Keil said, a smile on this face.

The party mounted their horses and followed Keil to a clearing at the bottom of the hill, where the guardsman pointed to a line of bushes.

"Your Highness, the river is on the other side of that line of bushes.

Sir Percival and the general are on the far bank. We need to be quiet and stay out of sight, or they'll see us."

Guinevere, Cadwyn, and Torn dismounted, and Keil led them to the top of a rise that bordered the river they had seen from the hills above.

As Guinevere stared through an opening in the foliage, at first, all she could see was the morning fog. Then a cool breeze parted the billowy clouds, revealing two men stripped to the waist, bearing wooden practice swords and buckler shields. As she watched, the two men clashed furiously, disengaged, and then clashed again, their hands and feet a blur of movement. As the battle raged back and forth, wisps of fog would obscure the men for a moment, and then they would reappear, like two titans fighting a duel in the clouds.

Guinevere found herself both shocked and mesmerized by the terrible ferocity of the ongoing battle. She had never seen two men display such a mastery of violence, nor seen or heard tell of the exotic panoply of attacks they employed in their struggle. At last, the two men stepped back and bowed to each other, and Sir Percival walked toward the river.

Another wafting cloud of fog swept by, hiding the two men for several moments. When it drifted away, Guinevere could see Percival standing in the river up to his waist with his back to her. For a moment, she frowned at the sight of the red lines crisscrossing the Knight's back and then realized they were scars. Cadwyn gasped and covered her mouth with her hand, taking an involuntary step back.

Guinevere closed her eyes for a moment, struggling to understand how the Knight could have borne so much pain and why he would have been the object of such cruelty. When she opened her eyes, Cadwyn stood at the bottom of the rise, staring into the distance. Guinevere walked down the hill and guided the silent young woman back to the horses.

As the small party rode back to the abbey in silence, Guinevere glanced over at Keil, whose face was crestfallen.

"Guardsman Keil, please ride by my side," Guinevere said.

"Yes, Your Highness," Keil answered, easing his horse between those of the two women.

"You have no cause for regret, Guardsman Keil," Guinevere said quietly. "That was, indeed, a sight to behold. Lady Cadwyn and I thank you."

Keil bowed his head respectfully. "You're welcome, Your Highness."

Guinevere hesitated and then asked the question she feared would yield an answer she could not bear. "Do you know how Sir Percival received those scars on his back?"

"Yes, Your Highness. General Capussa spoke of this."

"I would know what the general said."

"Yes, Your Highness. The Knight . . . he was forced to fight as a gladiator."

"Yes, Keil, I know of this," Guinevere said quietly.

The guardsman swallowed heavily and continued. "Well, at first, he refused to fight. He said that it was wrong. So, so they flogged him—the general called it scourge—to try to make him fight, but it didn't work. So they had to do it a different way. They tied women and children to a stake in the arena . . . that's what they called the place, and told him that if he didn't defend the women, they would be killed by their attackers, and if he defended them . . . and won, they would be set free."

As the young guardsman relayed the story, Guinevere's chest tightened, making it difficult to breathe, and for several moments, she struggled in silence, trying to force air into her lungs. When she recovered, a part of her wanted to scream in rage and seek vengeance against those who had done this terrible thing and another to shed an ocean of tears. In the end, she said a prayer of thanks to the Almighty for the Knight's deliverance and a second prayer for a woman on the other side of the world named Sumayya.

CHAPTER 27

ABBEY CWM HIR

s Capussa and Percival rode across the field outside the abbey's walls, the Numidian nodded in satisfaction. The lines of men maneuvering to the sound of the horn blasts were beginning to move and look like an army, and almost all of them were now armed with swords and shields. Although he and the Knight had labored tirelessly in the past month to forge the disparate group of men into a lethal weapon of war, the tide had been turned by the older soldiers who had once fought in the Pendragon's army. These men, acting as company commanders, had instilled discipline and provided leadership in the lower ranks, turning chaos into order.

As they approached the large command tent at the end of the field, a gust of wind ruffled the array of flags affixed to the tent's broad triangular roof. The older soldiers had brought the flags with them. Each bore the sigil of a former royal regiment.

Merlin emerged from the tent as Capussa and Percival dismounted. The expression on his face was grim. The old Roman gestured to the open tent flap. "Please, come in. We must speak."

The two men followed Merlin into the tent. After closing the tent flap, he turned to face them. "I have fell tidings, my friends. The Norse intend to land in force on the south coast within a fortnight. From there, they will march on Londinium."

Capussa glanced over at Percival. A look of consternation crossed the Knight's face, but it passed as quickly as it came.

"So be it," Percival said with a grim nod.

"You bear these tidings well," Merlin said in muted surprise. The Knight reached out and put a hand on the Roman's shoulder.

"You forget, Merlin the Wise, I have been fighting the Norse since I was thirteen years old. There was a never a time when we were attacked at the time of our choosing, or when our ranks had already been formed. Yet, we still managed to drive them back into the sea. We can do it again."

Capussa nodded in approval. "Well said. Now let us make our preparations."

Percival turned to Capussa. "I must first tell the Queen, my friend. Then if it is her will, we can meet forthwith."

"Percival, I have a map room in my quarters," Merlin said as he stroked his chin. "We will need to see the roads, the ports, and the lay of the land to plan for the defense. Would you ask the Queen if we might convene there?"

Percival nodded. "Yes. If she agrees, I will meet you there within the hour."

"So be it," Merlin said. "Let us make haste."

Percival strode out the door. Capussa turned to Merlin after he heard the sound of Percival's horse pounding away from the tent. "I somehow think Sir Percival will have no trouble persuading the Queen to come."

"Of that," Merlin said, "I am sure."

"He doesn't see it, does he?" Capussa said with amusement.

Merlin hesitated for a moment, and then shook his head. "His sense of honor blinds him."

"Well then, you will have to do something about that," the Numidian said with mock gravity.

"I?" Merlin said, raising an eyebrow. "Why not you? You are his most trusted companion."

Capussa rested a hand on Merlin's shoulder. "Alas, I am but a soldier, a simple man who prudently contents himself with the company of simple women. I surely am not the one to offer advice on such a delicate matter. Merlin the Wise, on the other hand, could most assuredly do so."

Merlin laughed. "You are a clever scoundrel, Numidian. I suspect Morgana would hire far more sellswords if she knew of your talents."

"Oh, she will know of them soon enough, my friend," Capussa said quietly. "Now, let us go. We don't want to keep the Queen waiting."

South Tower, Abbey Cwm Hir

In the past, Guinevere had made a point of avoiding the stone tower located in the southwest corner of the abbey's grounds, knowing that this was where the odious personage of Bishop Verdino was quartered. Although she now knew the bishop had been Merlin in disguise, she still felt an involuntary measure of unease as she climbed the stairs to his quarters, followed by Cadwyn and Sir Percival. She smiled inwardly. Merlin the Wise had played his role all too well.

When the Queen reached the fourth-floor landing, Merlin was waiting there. He bowed respectfully and gestured for her to enter the open door to his right.

"This way, Milady, if you will."

Guinevere nodded and followed Merlin into the room. She was surprised at the size of the chamber. The stone room barely accommodated the small bed, writing desk, and the rickety wooden chair in the corner. The only decoration in the room was a long tapestry that hung on one wall, depicting the castle at Camelot as it had been at the height of the Pendragon's power.

As she stared at the magnificent work, her breath caught in her throat. The view of the castle captured in the weave was from a small hill to the east of the castle. She remembered bringing her horse to rest alongside Sir Percival's steed on that very hill, on many a morning ride, in another life. Guinevere glanced over her shoulder at Percival, and his eyes left the tapestry and met hers. He remembered as well.

Merlin walked over to the tapestry and pulled a silken rope. The movement lifted the tapestry upward, revealing an open door in the wall behind it. Merlin tied the rope to a hook in the wall and gestured for the Queen to precede him into the next room. Intrigued, Guinevere walked through the door, followed by Cadwyn and Sir Percival. She could hear Merlin closing the outer door to his chambers and then the inner door behind them.

The room she entered was many times larger than the small bedroom, and the distance from floor to ceiling was nearly sixty hands. The walls were covered with bookshelves, and each shelf was filled with old dusty tomes, scrolls, and wooden boxes. When the Queen's eyes came to rest on the ceiling above, she froze. Two flags hung from the four wooden rafters that supported the roof: the battle flag of the Pendragon and the flag of the Table. The last time she had seen these flags, they had been hanging in the great hall of the castle at Camelot, behind the ceremonial thrones, where she and Arthur had sat on occasions of state.

Merlin walked over to her side and gestured to a long table at the far end of the room, where Capussa was waiting. Guinevere turned to the old Roman, struggling to contain a hundred emotions, and said with gratitude, "You were able to save a part of the library."

"Some of it, my Queen. There was little time and few wagons available, but Aelred and I did what we could."

Guinevere smiled. "It is a treasure worth more than its weight in gold. Another day, I would speak with you about this."

"Yes, my Queen."

Guinevere walked over to the table, and Capussa stood and bowed. "Queen Guinevere."

As the Queen looked into the Numidian's eyes, she sensed he had watched the storm of war approach before and had weathered its harshest winds. She wished Arthur could have had this man's counsel during the war with Morgana.

"General Capussa, I am thankful that you are here to aid this kingdom in its hour of need," she said with feeling.

"It is my honor to serve in such noble company, Your Highness," the Numidian said with a smile.

Merlin looked back across the room at Cadwyn. The young woman stood gazing up at the books lining the walls.

"Lady Cadwyn," Merlin said with smile, "may I ask you to join us?"

"Join . . . yes, yes . . . ," she said, awestruck. "I have never seen so many books."

After everyone was seated, Merlin walked over to a map that covered almost half the wall directly across from the table and reached for a long, narrow stick. The map, which displayed the entirety of Albion and Hibernia, had a mark for every city and town of any size, and it was crisscrossed with lines and other markings reflecting roads, rivers, and mountains.

"My Queen, I have come to know that Ivarr the Red and another Norse war leader, Sveinn the Reaver, sail toward our land in strength. Their combined fleet could have as many as thousand or more warriors. Once they make landfall, Morgana will meet them with an army of Saxons, Picts, and brigands of equal might. Together, this force will march on Londinium."

Guinevere was silent for a moment, and then she asked, "When and where will they land?"

"A fortnight. As for where—the Norse warrior captured by my spies only knew the landing would be on the south coast." Merlin tapped two of the port towns on the map. "But we can be assured they will come ashore at either Noviomagus Reginorum or Dubris."

"Why there?" Capussa said.

"The Roman roads to Londinium run from both places," Percival said quietly. "With an army of that size, they will need to travel on one of those roads."

Guinevere's gaze was fixed on the map, her eyes tracing the length of the Roman roads from Noviomagus and Dubris to Londinium. She had traveled on both roads and knew there were small villages and towns along both. The Norse would surely ravage those villages as they passed by, inflicting another wave of pain and suffering on her people.

"Merlin, how did you come to know of this?" Guinevere said in a quiet voice, trying to hide her distress.

The older man hesitated for a moment and then nodded toward the island of Hibernia on the map. "The man who warned me of the approach of the Norse lives in Hibernia. He sent a pigeon with a message to another friend four days ride south of here. The message said Sveinn's raiders sacked and burned a town on the coast there." Merlin paused, looking down at the floor. "No one was left alive, my Queen. One of Sveinn's men was captured and made to talk before he died.

"As for my knowledge of Morgana, the castle she seized for herself after the fall was the home of an old friend of mine. He was killed during the war, but some of his retainers still work at the castle, and they remain loyal. They report to me what they see and hear."

Capussa walked over to the map and pointed to the narrow sea separating the coast of Hibernia from the coast of Albion, just west of the abbey. "I would think they would land on this coast and march on the abbey. If they seek battle with the Queen's Army, this would be the most direct approach."

"Morgana would surely have preferred that," Merlin said, "but Ivarr and Sveinn would never agree. Londinium is their target."

"Then why not sail up the Tamesis and land north or south of Londinium? That would save them a three-day march," Percival said.

Merlin nodded. "It would. That is Morgana's doing. I am told she has convinced Sveinn that a river attack is expected, and plans were made to burn the raiders' ships with Greek fire as they came ashore."

"And why," Guinevere said in a guarded voice, "would she do that?"

Merlin moved back to the map. "My Queen, Morgana wants to make sure the battle happens before the sack of Londinium, not after, and at the time and place of her choosing. An attack on the city from the Tamesis could well be over before Sir Percival arrived. Sveinn would then leave with his loot, and Morgana would be forced to fight alone, or possibly with Ivarr the Red. It is a clever scheme."

"So it's a trap," Guinevere said, her voice barely above a whisper.

"It is indeed," Capussa said with a nod as he stood and walked over to the map. "But, it is also an opportunity. As she waits for us to fall into her snare, we shall lay a trap of our own. At the end of the day, we shall see who is the predator and who is the prey."

Guinevere glanced over at Sir Percival. Memories of the survivors of Camlann straggling back toward Camelot, accompanied by wagons full of the dead and dying, flooded through her mind. She remembered one wagon in particular, covered by the flag of the Pendragon, the wagon that carried Arthur's body. She closed her eyes briefly, banishing the images, and then opened her eyes and stood.

"Sir Percival and General Capussa," she said, "I am not skilled in the way of war, but I surmise you propose to march against a greater force with a lesser one—one that is not fully trained or blooded in a fight. I cannot agree to this. You must wait and build your strength and numbers."

The three men exchanged glances, and Percival slowly stood. "If we wait, my Queen," he said, "Londinium will fall, and Ivarr and his men will exact a terrible retribution on its people."

She turned to him, struggling to control the anger and fear in her voice. "If you are dead, Sir Percival, and your army is destroyed, Morgana and the Norse will take Londinium anyway. Your army is too small to defeat both of them."

"My Queen, I assure you, the army will grow as we march, and I have sent a rider north, to the Marches. There is a legion there. I have asked—"

"A legion?" Guinevere said in an incredulous voice. "Sir Percival, the Romans left this island over two centuries ago. What are you talking about?"

"Milady, do you remember when I was sent north to aid the men of the Marches against raiders—raiders who later turned out to be Morgana's mercenaries?"

"I remember. You volunteered for the assignment," Guinevere said, the barest hint of censure in her voice.

Percival did not react to the subtle rebuke, and Guinevere regretted it the instant it was said.

The Knight nodded. "In the year that I was there, I formed and trained a force of men. It was not a full legion . . . but it was at least two thousand strong, maybe as large as three thousand at the end of my time there. I have sent a rider to the north seeking the aid of those men. I believe a part of that force will come south to—"

"You believe, Sir Percival?" Guinevere interrupted, her voice rising. "You would have me gamble all on a mere belief?"

"My Queen," Percival said with certainty, "no man can know what the morrow will bring, but I know those men. If they get the message, they will come in force."

Guinevere turned and walked across the room, her gaze coming to rest upon the Pendragon's battle flag for a moment. When she turned, her eyes, full of trepidation, met Sir Percival's. "And if they come, in force, a day late," she said quietly, "it will not matter."

Before Percival could respond, Capussa intervened. "May I speak on this matter for a moment, Queen of the Britons?"

Guinevere turned to the Numidian and nodded. "Yes, of course."

Capussa walked slowly around the table, his hands clasped behind his back, a contemplative look on this face.

"The army—your army—is not well trained, nor are its numbers equal to that of the enemy yet, but the training will continue on the march, and our numbers grow by the day. If we march south at speed, we can link up with the forces of Londinium and choose the ground where the battle will be joined. If we wait, Londinium and its forces will be destroyed, the enemy's ranks will grow with that triumph, and that greater force, flush with victory, will seek us out. Morgana will then choose the time and place of battle."

The Numidian paused two paces away from Guinevere and hesitated. He looked around the room, and his eyes met those of Merlin, Cadwyn, and Percival, and then came to rest on Guinevere.

"Yes, on the day of the next battle, our force will have grown and it will be better trained, but the men in that army will also know we let their countrymen die, when we could have marched to their aid. Those men, Queen Guinevere, will know we feared Morgana and her forces, and they will carry that fear into battle."

Capussa's eyes fixed on Guinevere, and he spoke in a voice that carried no doubt.

"You are the Queen of this land, and the decision is yours, but I will tell you this: I have fought in four wars and in more battles than I can count, and I believe we must join forces with the might of Londinium and attack—now."

Guinevere stared at Capussa in silence, and then she closed her eyes, struggling to weigh what had been said. The fate of thousands of men rested upon her shoulders—as well as the fate of the kingdom. The ghosts of Camlann that haunted her dreams begged her to retreat from the abyss, and they almost carried the day. In the end, what tipped the balance was her belief in Percival and his Numidian companion. They had prevailed against countless men in gladiatorial battles, killed Hengst the Butcher, freed Londinium, and crushed Ivarr the Red in the battle of the River Wid. If they believed they could conquer yet one more enemy, she must have faith in their judgment.

After a long moment, she opened her eyes. "Very well," she said, "we march south—but I would know every part of your plan down to the smallest detail."

"We, my Queen?" Percival said. "I'm not sure I—"

Guinevere turned to Percival. "Yes, we, Sir Percival. I am riding south with you, along with Cadwyn and Sister Aranwen, if they so desire."

"Yes!" Cadwyn said, striking her small fist on the table, drawing a look of surprise from everyone in the room except Guinevere, who restrained a smile.

"It is too—" Percival started.

"Dangerous? According to General Capussa, the greater danger lies in staying here, and in any event, I will not allow one extra man to stay behind to guard my person when that man could hold a sword and shield in the line."

Percival's brow darkened, and Guinevere knew he was about to object again, when Merlin intervened. "Sir Percival, there are royal waystations along the road that can provide safe accommodations for the Queen and her small court. The army will be camped outside the walls of those waystations. You can be assured the Queen will be safe."

Guinevere turned to Merlin and gave him a regal nod. "Then so it shall be, Merlin the Wise."

Capussa slapped an unhappy Percival on the shoulder and said with a smile, "Then the matter is settled, Knight. The Queen and her army will march south. Let us make our preparations."

CHAPTER 28

THE MARCHES

Aeddan the Broad carefully examined the wooden doll he'd been carving for his three-year-old granddaughter for the past hour. Although the delicate work was becoming increasingly difficult for the old blacksmith's rough and gnarled hands, he knew the near-lifelike figurine would find favor with the child. As he reached for the carving knife resting on the stump beside him, he heard the sound of hooves pounding up the road toward the village. His hand moved from the carving knife to the sheathed sword leaning against the far side of the stump.

A moment later, a single rider galloped into view. Aeddan strained to see whether the man's saddle bore a white strip of cloth, a marker the outer sentries would have tied there to signal the rider posed no threat.

"I can see the white, Aeddan," his son-in-law, Connor, called from the base of the hill below.

"I have eyes, lad," Aeddan growled in response, and then smiled at the peal of laughter that followed from his russet-haired daughter, Wynne. She was busy washing clothes in a wooden bucket, steps away from where her husband was chopping wood. The blacksmith returned to his carving, finishing the last strokes necessary to put the outline of an apron on the little doll's dress. As he returned his carving knife to its place in his belt and stood, Connor called up to him again.

"Aeddan! The rider has a message for you. Says he's on the Queen's business, he does," Connor finished, amusement in his voice.

Aeddan scoffed as he strapped on his sword belt and started down the hill. One of the heads of the other villages must have sent the message and told the lad carrying the missive to make a jest at his expense. When he reached the bottom of the hill, the blacksmith looked over at his son-in-law. The younger man was a hand taller than he was and almost as broad in the chest. His full head of brown hair framed a plain face with friendly brown eyes.

The blacksmith nodded to the five piles of wood Connor had stacked up against the rear wall of the four-room wood and stone structure.

"Preparing for a cold winter, are ye?"

"Well, you never can have too much firewood," Connor said defensively.

"Now where have I heard that before?" Wynne said as she walked around the corner of the house, wearing a worn brown dress. Somehow, the simple garment seemed beautiful when she wore it. Aeddan pretended to scowl when he saw the impish smile on his daughter's face.

"Bah! Where's this messenger?" he said in a gruff voice. "I need to be about the Queen's business."

Wynne and Connor laughed together, and she pointed toward the front of the house. "He's waiting by the gate."

Aeddan chuckled to himself as he entered the home he shared with his daughter and son-in-law. He washed his face and hands in a wooden wash bowl, straightened his worn leather jerkin, and then walked through the house to the front door. He laid one hand on the pommel of his sword before opening the door and walked into the yard.

The man standing outside the gate in the stone wall that surrounded the house was about the same height as Aeddan, seventeen hands, but where Aeddan was broad in the chest and had heavily muscled arms and shoulders, the man at the gate was lean and rangy. Aeddan was surprised to see that the messenger, like himself, looked to be in his fourth decade of life. Most of the messengers from the other villagers were younger men, or even lads.

As Aeddan approached the stone wall, his attention was drawn to the sigil woven into the right shoulder of the messenger's brown jerkin: a red dragon with an arrow beneath it. It was the mark worn by the Pendragon's core of archers. A full quiver of arrows was just visible above the man's left shoulder. The blacksmith glanced over at the rider's horse and saw both a long and a short bow attached to the saddle.

Aeddan stared at the man, unaware of Connor and Wynne's presence in the yard behind him.

"Aeddan, is all well?" Connor said, unease in his voice.

He ignored the younger man and walked toward the man at the gate. The man stared back at him with cool grey eyes.

"I haven't seen that uniform in a long time," Aeddan said in a guarded voice.

"Aye, and I thought that I would never have cause to wear it again," the man answered.

"And what cause, Archer, changed your mind?"

"I was asked to do so, by a Knight of the Table."

Aeddan stared at the man, taking his measure, and then said gruffly, "That cannot be. They be gone, all of them."

"All, except one—Sir Percival."

Anger stirred inside of the blacksmith. "You would be wise not to jest about that particular Knight in the Marches. We hold him in high regard."

The man reached into his jerkin and pulled out a scroll that was sealed with a red wax stamp. "I do not jest, Aeddan the Broad. I have had the honor to meet Sir Percival. He said you would know how to decipher this."

Aeddan stared at the archer, unmoving, and then strode forward and took the scroll of parchment, broke the seal, and opened it. He stared at the writing for a moment and then turned and walked back into the house without a word. Wynne followed him inside. The blacksmith walked into the small room that served as his personal chambers and sat down at a rough-hewn oak desk. The desk was bare except for a candle, a worn Bible, a pot of ink, and a quill.

"Father, who is this man? Can what he says be true?" Wynne said in a hushed voice.

"I . . . I don't know, lass. It's . . . it's been so long."

Wynne watched as her father lit the candle and opened the Bible to a particular page. Then he took a small roll of parchment from the drawer in the desk and began to decipher the coded message in the scroll, using the page from the Bible as the key. The blacksmith had not decoded a message in almost a decade, and his eyes were no longer as sharp as they once had been, but he still remembered the old craft. After checking his work three times, he silently read the message. His hand shook as he laid down the quill. For a moment, he was quiet, and then he turned to his daughter.

"It is he, Wynne. Thank the Lord, he has returned."

She sank down beside his chair. "Father, how can you know?" she whispered. "You said yourself that the Table died with the Pendragon. How could this man have survived?"

Aeddan stood and walked to the door of the room and then looked over his shoulder at Wynne.

"Tell Connor to come to your old room."

Wynne ran to the door and called to her husband before following her father down the hall to the room that had been hers before she married. After she and Connor entered the room, Aeddan walked over to the bed in the corner of the small, tidy room and said quietly, "You had a bad fever when you were eight years old."

"I remember, father," Wynne said.

"Aye, but what you may not remember is that when you were near death, the Knight, Sir Percival, learned of your sickness, and he came to this house. I was one of his captains in the Legion of the Marches. Your mother had passed, so you were all I had. He came to your bedside and knelt on the floor, here," Aeddan said, pointing to a spot at the foot of the bed.

"The floor . . . it was dirt back then. He said to me, 'Come, Captain, kneel with me, for I intend to pray for God's mercy until either your child is well or has passed into heaven.'"

Aeddan's voice broke when he said the last word, but after a moment, he cleared his throat and continued, his eyes fixed on the floor. "And so we prayed together, side by side, a common blacksmith and a Knight of the Table, until the morn." He looked up at his daughter.

"Your fever broke, and Sir Percival left to rejoin the legion. From that day to this, thank the Lord, you haven't been sick a day, Wynne, not a day. So . . . so you say, how do I know?"

He lifted the deciphered message, tears streaming down his face, and read in a halting voice, "Captain Aeddan, I pray that this message finds you and the child, Wynne, safe and in God's grace. It has been many years since our parting, but I remember, as if it was yesterday, our time of prayer together, and the child's smile when she woke, having cast off her ague."

Wynne raised her hand to her mouth and spoke in whisper. "Father, I remember . . . the tall man, with dark hair . . . he was kneeling beside you when I woke."

Aeddan wrapped his arms around his daughter and hugged her tightly. "Aye, lass, he surely was. And now, he has returned."

The Marches

As Aeddan the Broad walked up the road toward the stone meeting-house, the feeling of disquiet within steadily grew. After receiving the message from Sir Percival, he had sent a rider to the tower atop the hill to the north, with orders to light three fires on the stone roof—the signal for a general council of war. That signal had not been given in almost a decade.

The thirty war leaders and their retainers gathered in the meeting-house above had hastened to answer the call. Each of the men represented one of the thirty towns or villages that formed the northwestern border, or the Marches, of what had once been the kingdom of Arthur Pendragon. If they found his reason for the call to arms to be wanting, their ire would be great indeed, and he would almost surely be deposed as the leader of his village.

In truth, Aeddan did not fear the loss of his standing in the village, but rather that he would fail Sir Percival. He was not skilled in the use of words, like the younger and more ambitious Bran, the headman from the town of Cairn to the west. Bran had not served in the Legion of the Marches during the war with Morgana, and he rarely attended the training musters each spring. For Bran, coin was worth more than honor, so he would surely oppose the Knight's request.

Aeddan glanced over at Connor, walking beside him, and he was reassured by his calm demeanor. Although he had not asked him to do so, Aeddan knew Wynne's husband had met with some of the younger headmen before the meeting. Had Aeddan been walking into a hornet's nest, Connor would have let him know. As Wynne had confided in him before her marriage to Connor, "He's not the strongest or the handsomest man in the village, but he is surely the cleverest."

Connor caught Aeddan's glance and looked over at him.

"All will be well, Aeddan. You shall see."

"Aye, I pray that it is so, but I fear they won't remember the debt that is owed."

The two men walked on in silence for a while, and then Aeddan gestured toward the meetinghouse above. "You see, the affairs of the south have always been distant from us. Oh, we swore fealty to the rule of the Pendragon, but in truth, we knew that the new King, like Uther before him, would leave our cold, green hills and poor homesteads alone for the most part. And so it was. The King didn't take much in taxes, and he didn't give much in protection. We were expected to take care of our own, and well, we had always been able to do that. But . . . there was a time when that was not so."

Aeddan stopped walking, pulled out a leather flask from his cloak, and took a long drink. Then he offered it to Connor, who smiled and shook his head.

"Wynne always knows when I've had a taste, and I don't want to be scolded tonight."

"Aye, that she does," Aeddan said with a nod. After taking another drink and restoring the flask to his pocket, the older man raised a fist in quiet frustration.

"I . . . I fear that the men up there won't remember the fell times, when the witch Morgana unleashed her raiders against the Marches. It was so many years ago. At first . . . well, we thought the raids, which were bigger and came more often, might be the work of a new Pict war leader . . . someone out to prove his mettle, but then we came to know otherwise. We came to know that these new and fearsome bands of Picts, Norse, and Saxons were sellswords—warriors paid with Morgana's gold."

A roar of laughter from the meetinghouse, now just a hundred paces distant, drew Aeddan's attention for a moment, and then he continued.

"The witch was clever. She knew that if she burned enough of our towns and villages, and killed enough of our people, the Pendragon would have to send forces north, weakening his center. And so kill and burn she did aplenty; those that were not killed in a raid were sold into slavery. In time, the Pendragon did send forces to help, but they moved too slowly, and they always returned to their quarters farther south, leaving us at the mercy of her raiders all over again."

Aeddan paused for a moment and looked down at the field below, where he and the men of the village trained during the spring and summer months.

"And then, Sir Percival came. At first, we had no faith in him. Aye, we knew he be a doughty fighter, but what could he know of fighting raiders and brigands who struck without warning and then ran off? We were wrong. He'd fought an enemy like that before—the seawolves. He knew what he was about, he did indeed. He ordered a part of the royal garrison to come north with him, and he had them build fortified camps outside each village. He moved into one of the empty houses in the village and lived and ate with the rest of us."

Aeddan turned and reluctantly started up the road again, gesturing with his hands as he walked.

"Then the Knight had each village form a core of one hundred and twenty fighting men, men who would train and take the field of battle together, under an elected commander they trusted. There was plenty of grumbling, but we did as he said, and . . . well, then he taught us to fight together like Romans."

Connor nodded. Aeddan knew the younger man had heard the story before. Every child in the Marches had.

"We learned to form ranks in an instant and to attack and retreat in close order, instead of running at the enemy in a mad rush. He had us build lookout and signal towers along the entire length of the Marches, to prepare ambushes, to patrol our lands, and to use our coin to buy spies among the enemy. In time, the Legion of the Marches—that's what we called ourselves—killed so many raiders that Morgana decided this root was not worth the digging, and so she left us alone. But, as I say, that was a long time ago. Half of the men waiting for us in there tonight were too young to even hold a sword during those fell times. They won't remember."

Connor smiled a knowing smile. "We'll see, Aeddan."

The two guards waiting outside the meetinghouse pushed open the door, and Aeddan and Connor walked into a cavernous stone room. The crowd of men in the room were dressed in an array of outfits, ranging from animal skins to the plain leather jerkins, wool leggings, and leather boots worn by Aeddan and Connor. Most of the men were younger than Aeddan, but a few like Fferog, the war leader from the next village to the north and the master of the council, had served with Aeddan during the fell times.

As Aeddan and Connor walked toward the dais at the far end of the large, candlelit hall, the tide of voices in the room began to ebb and then fell silent as Aeddan stepped into the speaker's circle. The blacksmith was mystified and somewhat unnerved by the silence. Meetings of the Council of the Marches were typically raucous affairs that had to be brought to order by shouts and threats.

As he scanned the hard, weather-worn faces of the men waiting for him to speak, his disquiet grew. *Can they know of the message? Have they spoken of the matter beforehand and decided to deny my request? Well, so be it. I will say my piece and march south alone, if that's the way of it.*

Aeddan stepped to the edge of the circle closest to the crowd and spoke in a loud but measured voice.

"Welcome, my friends. I have called this council together to hear great tidings and to answer a call to war."

Aeddan paused for a moment, his eyes roving over the crowd of men in front of him, before continuing. Most of the men gave him a respectful nod. The only man who ignored him was a short, stout man with a bushy beard and a balding head—Bran. He was talking to one of his retainers, a scowl on his face.

"Four days ago," he began, "a royal messenger came to my home with a message." Aeddan paused for a long moment and then said, "Sir Percival has returned."

For a moment, there was a shocked silence. Then the room exploded into a cacophony of sound. Fferog, a giant of a man wearing a ceremonial grey robe, walked onto the wooden dais and pounded a great staff against the floor, bringing the hall back to order.

He turned to Aeddan and spoke in a loud voice. "We all would hear what you have to say about this matter, Aeddan the Broad."

The blacksmith gave his old friend a nod of thanks, and then his eyes returned to the men before him.

"The messenger brought a scroll that bore the seal of Queen Guinevere." Aeddan held up the scroll. "I have it here. It's written in the old code. The man who wrote the message is Sir Percival, for he spoke of things that were between he and I, alone."

"I don't believe it," Bran called out. "The Knights of the Table are all dead." Aeddan turned toward Bran and said coldly, "He lives."

"And what does Sir Percival seek from the council?" Fferog called out, cutting off Bran's response.

Aeddan's gaze left Bran and returned to the older leaders in the center of the room. "The Knight has slain Hengst the Butcher and retaken Londinium from the Norse."

The room exploded in a roar of cheers. After Fferog had restored order to the meeting hall, Aeddan continued.

"The Norse and Morgana have raised an army. They will try to retake Londinium. Sir Percival is marching to the city's aid with a great force. He asks that we send him as many men from the legion as we can spare."

"I don't believe—" Bran began, only to be cut off by a roar from Fferog.

"You will be quiet, Bran of Cairn!"

"I will not!" Bran bellowed in defiance as he pushed his way to the front of the room, his ruddy face a mask of scorn. "Show me this royal messenger! He is a charlatan who has played Aeddan the Broad for a fool. I will not march a single furlong for a dead knight."

The room was silent for an instant. Then it was rocked by roars of rage and condemnation.

CHAPTER 29

NOVIOMAGUS REGINORUM

Morgana's tent was set up a short distance from the crest of a hill, just outside the ruins of the Roman settlement of Noviomagus Reginorum. Nearly a thousand Saxons, Picts, and a motley assortment of local brigands and outlaws were camped below her in a broad, uneven crescent. As she looked down on the dirty, foul-smelling men who were eating, sleeping, and dicing in disparate groups, a wave of anger washed over the Roman princess.

A decade ago, the emperor's gold had paid for the force she had led against the Pendragon at Camlann, an army that was tenfold the size of this one. This time, it was Morgana's own horde of silver flowing into the pockets of the scum below. She intended to make Sir Percival, his army, and his precious Queen repay that outlay in both coin and blood, in full measure.

She started toward her incense-laden tent, hoping to escape the stench wafting up from below, when a shout drew her attention. One of the Saxons standing on the shore of the estuary pointed toward the sea. As she watched, a line of dragonships with their sails furled rowed into the estuary and began to land in the muddy flats below. Ivarr the Red and Sveinn the Reaver had arrived.

Morgana watched the incoming ships for a moment and then turned and looked to the right, where Lord Aeron's tent stood alone, a half furlong distant from hers. His black charger was tethered to a stake behind it. The knight wasn't visible, but the flap to his tent was open, and she knew he would be watching the approach of the men who had killed his brother Knights at Camlann. From this point on, she would have to watch him closely. If he wavered in his fealty to his promise, she would have the Saxons kill him.

The sound of hoofbeats approaching from the north drew Morgana's attention away from Lord Aeron's tent, to a rider she recognized as one of her spies. The small man quickly dismounted from his sweat-lathered horse and bowed to Morgana, a fearful look in his eyes.

"Speak," Morgana said impatiently.

"Sir Percival marches south at speed, with an army of at least a thousand, Milady."

Morgana was momentarily taken aback by the tidings. Merlin's web of spies was more formidable than she suspected, and this Sir Percival was more decisive than she'd anticipated. She had hoped the Knight of the Table would not learn of the invasion until Ivarr and Sveinn had landed. This would have forced the Knight and his peasant army to make a series of brutal forced marches in order to intercept the invaders before they reached Londinium, leaving his soldiers exhausted before the final battle.

"Where? Where is he now?"

The messenger cowered as he answered. "I don't know, Milady. I am the fourth rider in the chain, and all I was told is that he marches south."

In her fury, Morgana reached for the jeweled dagger at her belt, but then she hesitated. She needed the fool.

"Do you know where the first rider in the chain came from?" Morgana snapped.

"Yes . . . yes, Milady, Isca, on the Sabrina River."

She drew a handful of silver coins from a silken purse hidden within her cloak and dropped them at the man's feet.

"You have done well. Buy a new horse and ride to Calleva. Tell the messenger there that he is to ride to Corinium. Once there, he must find out where Sir Percival's force is camped and send word to me. Now go!"

"Yes, Milady," the messenger said as he backed away.

Morgana walked to the ruins of a nearby Roman wall and unrolled a map across the top of it. The map showed the old Roman roads that ran throughout Albion. Abbey Cwm Hir was between sixty and seventy leagues to the north. If the Knight and his forces had left the abbey three days ago, and he'd pushed his men, they could have covered as much as twenty, perhaps even thirty leagues.

She suspected that the Knight had marched south from the abbey to Isca and crossed the Sabrina River using local ships and barges. From there, he would make for Corinium and then Calleva. From there, the Roman road east would bring him directly to Londinium.

Morgana looked down at the Saxon and Pict forces below, and those of the Norse disembarking from their ships. Their combined army would number close to two thousand five hundred men, and the Norse, although unruly, were seasoned fighters. Sir Percival's army would likely be made up of farmers and tradesmen. If she could intercept the Knight before he obtained reinforcements from Londinium, she could destroy his army and then take Londinium at her leisure. She looked down at the Norse again. They would need to move quickly.

NOVIOMAGUS REGINORUM

Lord Aeron watched Ivarr the Red and a giant of a man with a mane of reddish-brown hair walk up the hill from the estuary to where Morgana was waiting. The two Norse leaders were accompanied by fifty warriors. Morgana was accompanied by Garr, the leader of her Saxon sellswords, and an equal number of Saxon warriors.

As he watched the Norse and the Saxons warily approach each other, the Knight considered attacking the Norse in the hope of precipitating a battle between the two suspicious groups, but then he rejected the idea. Morgana would have anticipated this possibility and assigned one or more archers in her camp to kill his horse if he made the attempt. She would also take great pleasure in sending one of her assassins to kill Guinevere in retribution.

When Lord Aeron had overheard one of the Saxons tell another warrior, two nights earlier, that they were all going to get rich sacking Londinium, he had discounted the comment. Morgana did not have enough men to take the city, and if that had been her objective, she could have marched directly there from her castle. It was only when he learned that she was meeting a large force of Norse warriors at this precise location that he grasped her plan.

Londinium would be the target of their combined attack, but it would also be the bait. Morgana knew his brother Knight would march south to defend the city, and her army, when combined with that of the Norse, would be large enough to crush his smaller force. Although Lord Aeron desperately wanted to forewarn his brother Knight, he knew he couldn't leave the camp without his absence being noticed. At this point, all he could do was hope that fate would intervene and offer him an opportunity to save his friend and the kingdom—before the disaster he foresaw came to fruition.

The Camp of the Queen's Army, North of Calleva

Percival looked out upon the near-perfect rows of tents and the wooden fortifications encircling the perimeter of the army's camp with feelings of pride and trepidation in equal measure. From this distance, the disparate group of volunteers now called the Queen's Army looked as if it had been forged into a disciplined and well-trained army. Percival knew the reality to be otherwise.

The men below were enthusiastic and committed to the cause, but many of them had never wielded a sword in battle. Such men couldn't take on the Saxon and Norse warriors, at least not on even terms, and prevail. He would need more men-at-arms to gain victory in the coming battle, and those men-at-arms were not yet at hand.

The messengers he had sent racing to the north, seeking aid from the Legion of Marches, had not yet returned, and he was still waiting for Cynric and the mayor of Londinium to answer his call to arms. If his messages had been received, and if the forces requested marched without delay, then victory was possible. If not, he could be leading these men to their doom.

"Do I sense there is a measure of unease in your thoughts, Knight?" Capussa said as he strode up the hill toward Percival, followed by Merlin. Percival ignored the question and gestured to the camp below.

"You have done well with the army, Capussa."

"We have done well," Capussa said, placing one hand on Percival's shoulder and a second on Merlin's, "and I would also cede acclaim to the hundreds of veterans from the Pendragon's army who have joined the ranks in recent days. But you avoid my question, Knight," Capussa said.

"Yes, I have concerns," Percival said, "Morgana, Ivarr, and this Sveinn lead a formidable force of hardened fighters. Our men—"

"Fight for their homes, for their Queen, and . . . they fight for you, Knight," Capussa said. "As long as you lead, they will follow. They have what you call faith."

"In truth, they believe you are invincible," Merlin said quietly.

"As Capussa well knows," Percival said, glancing over at his friend, "I am not. On many a day in the arena, his blade saved my life."

"And, thank the gods, your blade saved mine as well," Capussa reminded him.

"As for their faith," Percival said, his gaze returning to the men below, "they need to place that in God, not in me, for divine intervention will be sorely needed in the days to come. And although I have prayed for it a thousand times on my own behalf, and I will continue to do so, it has rarely come to my aid."

"Has it not?" Merlin said, arching his grey brows. "Yes, it is true that you have borne more trials and tribulations than any man I have ever known, and surely, any man who has endured so much would have every reason to believe his prayers for relief went unanswered. But I would ask you this: What man could have survived what you have endured without divine intervention—and that on a near daily basis?"

When Percival didn't answer, Merlin continued.

"My answer would be few, maybe none. And I would ask you an even graver question. Could the Sir Percival who embarked on that ship a decade ago have done the things you have done upon your return? Could he have struck down Hengst the Butcher? Could he have inspired this army of volunteers to follow him?" Merlin said, gesturing to the army below. "And could he have accomplished all these things, as well as those that I believe are to come, without the assistance of a Numidian general who is a master of the art of war?" Merlin shook his head and smiled. "You see, I believe the Lord did answer your prayers, Sir Percival, and Albion's as well. This land needed a sword forged in the hottest of fires to regain what was lost . . . and you are that sword."

Percival looked at Merlin in silence for a moment, unsettled by the old Roman's words. Then his eyes returned to the camp, and he spoke in a quiet voice. "If you are right, then I shall pray all the harder that I am worthy of this burden. God save me."

"God save us all," Merlin said.

"Well then 'amen,' as you Christians say," Capussa said gravely.

Merlin and Percival looked at the Numidian in surprise and then burst into laughter.

"Is that not correct?" Capussa said gruffly.

The sound of approaching footsteps interrupted the three men, and Percival turned to see Keil jogging up the hill, dressed in the livery of the Queen's Guard.

"Sir Percival, the Queen would see you," Keil said with a gasp.

Percival restrained a smile. The young archer had earned his position by outrunning and outshooting all but three of the men who'd vied for a position as a member of the Queen's Guard, although he still needed work with the sword.

"Lead, the way, guardsman," Percival said, and followed the young man down the slope.

As he strode down the hill, he heard Merlin say to Capussa, "Come, my friend. Let us have that cup of mead. Sir Percival, in spite of himself, shouldn't have to bear all the night's merriment."

Percival glanced up the hill for a moment, confused—merriment?

* * *

GUINEVERE, CADWYN, AND Sister Aranwen had taken up residence on the fourth floor of the royal waystation outside the town of Calleva. The circular stone tower stood on a rise at the edge of the encampment, surrounded by a stone wall. Percival, Capussa, Merlin, and the Queen's Guard were quartered in the floors below.

As Percival walked up the rise toward the stone structure, his attention was drawn by the music playing in the grassy area just outside the waystation's northern wall. Long tables of food had been set up, and a circle of grass set aside in the middle for dancing. When he stopped to look down at the feast and the festivities being prepared, young Keil walked over, his face alight.

"It's Michaelmas, Sir Percival. The Queen ordered Merlin and Capussa to allow the men to celebrate. Why, I suspect the women in every nearby town and village will be coming here tonight."

"You do, do you?" Percival said with amusement.

"Yes, sir. I mean, who wouldn't want to dance with the men of the Queen's Army? But don't worry, sir, General Capussa is rotating the men in and out by company, so folks won't have too much to drink, and the lines will always be defended."

Percival smiled as he spoke, "Well, who am I to argue with the Queen?" When Keil turned and started toward the waystation again, Percival hesitated a moment and said in a whisper, "And God knows we'll need the Archangel on our side in the coming days."

When Percival and Keil reached the door to Guinevere's chambers, the Knight nodded to the two guards on duty, and one of them turned and knocked respectfully. Cadwyn opened the door, resplendent in a long, yellow dress that flowed nearly to the floor, and gestured for Percival to come in.

"Sir Percival, please come. The Queen awaits."

"Thank you, Lady Cadwyn. Please, after you."

Percival followed the young woman to a large candlelit room at the end of a stone corridor, where Guinevere was seated at a wooden table covered by a white tablecloth. An array of plates filled with cheese, meat, and fruit were laid out in front of the two place settings at the table.

Cadwyn curtsied to Guinevere and disappeared into the next room. The Queen gestured to the seat across from her.

"Welcome, Sir Percival. Please, sit. It has been a long day's march, and since tonight is Michaelmas, we should say a prayer of thanks and celebrate with a modest feast."

Percival bowed, and spoke hesitantly. "Will Lady Cadwyn and Sister Aranwen be . . . joining our table tonight?"

"No, they have already eaten. It shall be just the two of us. Is that acceptable to you?" Guinevere said with the hint of a smile.

"Why yes, yes, of course, my Queen. It is always my privilege to dine with Your Highness," Percival said quickly.

"And hopefully, your pleasure as well," Guinevere said as she poured wine into the goblet in front of him.

"Always, my Queen," Percival said, his eyes meeting hers.

"That pleases me, Sir Percival. Now, would you say a prayer for us tonight that is fitting for the occasion?"

"Yes, my Queen," Percival said. Then he bowed his head, clasping his hands together.

"We thank you, Lord, for this bounty, of which we gratefully partake, and I fervently pray, on this feast day, that you grant the Queen and this kingdom the protection of the Archangel's mighty shield and sword in the trials to come."

"Amen," finished Guinevere, nodding her approval.

The two ate and drank for several moments in awkward silence, and then Guinevere leaned back in her chair, her eyes meeting Percival's. As the Knight looked at the Queen, her face seemed more beautiful and her eyes more alluring than he remembered from their last meeting. He reached for the wine glass in front of him, his throat suddenly parched, and took a drink.

"Sir Percival, I have watched you and General Capussa, and yes, Merlin as well, engage in quite lively conversation when you are together."

"You have? I mean, yes, my Queen, at times we do talk thus," Percival answered.

"And I have watched you laugh and smile with those men, and with the men in the camp as well."

"Yes, that is also true," Percival said, his brow furrowing in confusion.

"Then why, Sir Percival," Guinevere said, with a smile in her voice, "do you find no occasion for mirth and joy when we talk? Since you do not converse thus with me, should I fear that you find me dull and dreary?"

Percival's eyes widened, and for a moment, he was at a loss for words. "No, my Queen," he said at last. "You are not dull or dreary in the least. In truth, I have never met a more interesting woman," he said, struggling with each word. "It's just that you are the Queen, and they—those you speak of—are my friends and brethren-in-arms."

"Then I shall do away with that difference, with a royal command."

"A command, my Queen?"

"Yes, tonight you shall address me, see me, and think of me, in all ways, as if I was just Guinevere—the daughter of the mayor of the local town yonder, or even that of a farmer, baker, or cooper. I would have us talk together . . . as we did on those morning rides so long ago."

"But, my Queen—"

"Guinevere—just Guinevere," she corrected, lifting a finger in a delicate remonstrance. "And you, you are just Percival, for the remainder of this night."

Percival stared at the Queen for a moment in silence and then smiled. "Yes . . . Guinevere."

"Now, Percival, I saw you, Merlin, and General Capussa laughing together today at the midday meal. Please do tell me what was so amusing that we might laugh together as well."

Percival's brow furrowed as he recalled the moment, and then a look of amusement came to his face.

"I was in the nearby town with General Capussa today, buying supplies, and one of the men from the town, a man who was as cruel as he was ugly, took it upon himself to bully one of our wagon drivers, young James. He told the lad that Morgana was a witch and that James had better run home to his mother before Morgana turned him into a frog.

"Well, General Capussa and I happened to hear this as we walked past the wagons to mount our horses, and Capussa," Percival said with a smile, "is not, let us say, a man to suffer fools quietly. The general turned to young James and said, 'I wouldn't worry about that frog spell, James. Merlin says it does not work. But keep an eye out for the one that turns a man into a toad.' Young James turned to the general, his eyes as wide as the eggs of robin, and said, 'Does that one work, General?' The general pointed to the bully and said, 'Alas, it does James, and as you can see, Morgana used it on this man.'"

Guinevere burst into laughter, and Percival laughed along with her. Thereafter, the two of them talked and laughed together without reticence, reminiscing over happier times shared in the past. During a lull in their conversation, a lively tune from the celebration below could be heard. The Queen stood and walked over to the window, opening the shutters to reveal the dancing going on below.

"Come, Sir Knight," she said, gesturing to the place beside her at the window.

Percival shook his head in mock sadness. "Alas, I cannot. My Queen has commanded me to only answer to the name Percival."

Guinevere laughed. "Percival, then."

As they stood by the window, watching the revelry below, the bard and the musicians began to play an old ballad that had been popular at court long ago, a song that would always fill the dance floor. Couples began to fill the grass square below set aside for dancing.

"Do you remember this song?" Guinevere said.

Percival hesitated and then nodded, remembering a distant night as if it were yesterday.

"Yes, I do," he said. "It was played at one of the balls I attended at court."

"And do you remember dancing to this tune?" Guinevere said with a smile.

"Yes . . . yes, indeed I do. Two ladies of the court insisted that I dance with them. Thankfully, I was able to do so without making too much of a fool of myself."

"That would have been Ladies Evelynn and Isfair," she said. "And as I recall, you danced quite well."

Percival turned and his eyes met hers. "You watched—"

"I did," she said quietly. "I wished that I might have danced in their places."

"You—"

"Yes. So, must I also, as you say, 'insist' that you dance this ballad with me, Percival."

"My—"

"Guinevere."

She stepped away from the window and made a formal curtsy that was the prelude to the dance, and Percival, after a moment's hesitation, stepped forward and made the required formal bow. And then they were dancing . . . stiffly at first, but gradually they both returned to a faraway place where they had both danced before, although not with one another.

Although the ballad was long, when it came to an end, and each of them gave their ending curtsy and bow, a part of Percival wished the song could have played on forever.

"Thank you, Guinevere. I . . . I shall never forget that dance," Percival said.

"Nor shall I, and I fervently pray it is not our last," Guinevere said softly.

"And I as well," he said. They stood in silence looking at each other, neither willing to break the spell. Then Percival bowed. "I fear it is late, Milady, and I must see that the men are ready to march in the morning."

"Yes, I understand," Guinevere said, and he could hear the regret in her voice.

Percival bowed and walked to the door. Her words reached him just before he pulled open the door and stepped into the stone corridor.

"Did you ever . . . reminisce about the rides we took together in the mornings and the things we spoke of so long ago, when you were in that distant land?"

Percival turned and looked at Guinevere, and for a moment, he was once again standing in a cold stone cell gazing at the stars through a small barred window—stars he knew a woman with beautiful blue eyes and golden tresses could see in the skies over Albion as well.

"Yes, I do. Those memories . . . and the thought that someday I would see you again are what kept me alive in the arena. Good night, Guinevere."

* * *

CADWYN WAS LEANING halfway out the window of the storage room next to the Queen's chambers when Sister Aranwen, who'd just arisen from a nap, looked into the room.

"Cadwyn!" she whispered. "What are you doing?"

The young woman jumped down and strolled over to the next window, her hands clasped behind her back.

"Oh, just enjoying the air. It is such a beautiful night, don't you think?"

"You can't fool me, Cadwyn Hydwell. You've been eavesdropping on the Queen and Sir Percival!" Sister Aranwen whispered, glancing over her shoulder.

"I have not! Well, yes I have, and it's wonderful! I think she's in love with him, and he with her. I knew it would come to be!"

The nun turned around and started out of the room. "God save us. I swear, you will yet send me to an early grave."

Cadwyn ran past the nun, blocking her path. "I'm right, and you know it," she whispered insistently, hands on her hips.

Sister Aranwen looked away for a moment, and then she walked over and sat down on a small wooden bench. Cadwyn put a hand to her mouth and whispered, "You knew. You have always known."

The older woman nodded silently, answering in a quiet, resigned voice. "I have. You cannot serve a woman for so many years and not know of things such as these."

"Tell me, please!" Cadwyn whispered, sitting down by the older nun.

"Oh, Cadwyn Hydwell, you are quite the scoundrel!" she sighed, and then gave the younger woman a tired smile. "But you are a true friend to the Queen, and when I am gone, she will need all of your strength and love."

"You're not leaving, are you Sister Aranwen?" Cadwyn said, a look of concern coming to her face.

Sister Aranwen smiled. "Not yet, my dear, but in due time. So, yes, I will tell you things of yesteryear that may aid you when the time comes, but," she continued sternly, "only if you pledge upon the blood of the Christ to keep them secret. Do you so pledge?"

Cadwyn's eyes widened, and she hesitated. Then she made the sign of the cross and said, "Yes, pledge I do."

"A woman of Guinevere's station, a woman whose father was a man of great wealth and power, is merely a shiny jewel to be bought and sold in a world such as this, and so she was."

"But Arthur—" Cadwyn interjected.

"Was a good and noble man, or he became such over time, and yes, he cared for Guinevere, and she . . . she adored him, but her adoration was that of a young woman for a man who is a mighty king; it was not love. Later—and you must remember that Arthur and Guinevere were only together for five short years—she came to respect Arthur's desire to bequeath peace and justice to the people of this land." The sister shook her head in regret. "Alas, that was beyond even his power. So you see, the Queen has never had the gift of true love."

"But what of Sir Percival and Guinevere? You said—"

"Patience, patience," Sister Aranwen said, clasping her hands together in her lap. "At Camelot, the Queen and her guards would ride every morning at the break of dawn before . . . before it became too dangerous. Since Arthur insisted that a Knight of the Table attend the Queen on these rides, Sir Percival rode with her on many a morning. At first, he was merely a guardian, but over time, they began to talk and share things with one another, and the Queen's admiration for him grew. She said that he was the most interesting man she had ever met, and, I have to say, when she told me of their conversations, I, too, was intrigued. Well, with each passing day, their feelings for each other grew, and then one day . . . he was gone."

"Gone?"

"Yes. When the people of the Marches begged for assistance, Percival volunteered for the assignment and left that same day."

"I don't understand. I thought you said he cared—"

The nun held up one hand, and Cadwyn closed her mouth. "He did, Cadwyn. I believe that's why he left. He is an honorable man, after all. Shortly after that, the Queen stopped going out for her rides. Oh, the threat of an attack was growing, but I also think that she couldn't bear the memories."

Sister Aranwen was silent for a moment, and then she continued, a distant look in her eyes.

"When she learned the King was going north to the River Tyne to meet a possible attack, she begged him to let her come along. At first, I couldn't understand why, but when I learned Sir Percival had been ordered to march south from the Marches and to meet the King there, I knew."

Cadwyn sat down beside the nun, her eyes rapt with attention.

"Arthur allowed her to come, but alas, she did not get a chance to talk with Percival. Instead, she almost saw him die in that terrible battle on the Aelius Bridge. That's . . . that's why Galahad has always been special to her. Percival would surely have died that day if Galahad hadn't come to his aid."

Sister Aranwen drew her black prayer beads out of her pocket and moved her fingers along the string in silence for a moment before continuing.

"A month later, Percival was sent to the Holy Land on that foolish Grail quest. The Queen tried to intercept him on the way, so she could at least say good-bye, but he was already boarding the ship when we reached the outskirts of the city. As we watched the ship disappear into the distance from a nearby hill, tears rolled down her face, but she never made a sound. So you see, they have been in love for a very long time."

Cadwyn stared at the older woman, confused by her internal turmoil. "Why do you fear the Queen's love for Sir Percival? Arthur is dead. I don't understand."

Sister Aranwen looked at the young woman, her eyes filled with apprehension.

"Cadwyn, I lived through Camlann. I saw Arthur and his legions march against Morgana once before. I fear that if . . . well, after having waited so long for him, he is lost that . . ." Sister Aranwen's voice trailed off, and she bowed her head in silent prayer.

Cadwyn reached over and took the Sister's hands in her own. "This time, it will be different, Sister Aranwen," she whispered.

The older woman lifted her head. "I pray that you are right, child, I pray with all my heart and soul that it will be so."

*   *   *

AFTER DRINKING TWO cups of mead with Capussa, Merlin returned to his quarters, intending to retire early, but he could not find the respite of sleep. The mystery posed by the note accompanying the wooden cup Jacob the Healer had given to Sir Percival consumed his thoughts. After an hour of lying awake in the dark, the old Roman arose, lit a candle from the glowing embers in the room's small hearth, and returned to the desk, where the missive was hidden. He drew out the scroll and again struggled to unlock its meaning.

Percival had been right. Much of the note had been written in an Aramaic dialect that had not been used in centuries, one he could neither read nor seem to translate. Although Merlin understood the Greek and Latin words randomly interspersed among the Aramaic script, these did not provide any clue as to the meaning of the Aramaic words.

At first, Merlin had ignored the Greek and Latin words in the text, assuming they were nothing more than the irrational digressions of a sick old man, and focused on the Aramaic script. Since these words were unknown to him, he tried to ascertain their meaning by seeking out similar words in related languages, such as Hebrew and Syriac. Alas, this had come to nothing.

After seemingly endless hours of futile struggle, Merlin had turned his attention back to the Greek and Roman words in desperation, and over time, he came to realize that the Aramaic was just a ruse. The message was in the Greek and Latin words; they simply had to be assembled together in the proper order. He intended to find that order tonight.

When at last the cock crowed, signaling the coming of dawn, Merlin stood and walked over to the window and watched the sun rise. He had solved the mystery. Percival had been right. The cup given to him by Jacob was not the Holy Grail, but it was a grail that was holy.

CHAPTER 30

THE ROAD FROM NOVIOMAGUS REGINORUM TO LONDINIUM

s she rode amidst her Saxon guard, Morgana fumed at the army's slow pace. Sveinn's men had stopped to raid almost every town and village along the road, and although Ivarr had initially restrained his men, in time, they too had joined in the pillaging. Now the Norse warriors were hours behind her, their horses slowed by the weight of the booty they carried. At this rate, the march to Londinium would take five days instead of three.

Unlike the Norse, the early reports from her spies said Sir Percival and his army were marching south at speed and in good order. Although this was a part of her plan, Morgana had been surprised by the rapidity of the Knight's approach and his army's discipline. Still, she had no fear of the eventual outcome of the approaching contest. Her force, when joined by those of Sveinn and Ivarr, was a third larger than Sir Percival's, and unlike the rabble led by the Knight, the Saxons and Norse were hardened warriors. Once the battle was joined, they would break the Knight's lines, and the slaughter would begin.

The only matter weighing on Morgana's mind, other than the Norsemen's laggardly pace, was the silence from her spies. Three days had passed since their last messages—a delay she vowed would be paid for in blood. Morgana turned to Garr, the Saxon war leader riding beside her.

"Call a halt for the midday meal. We can encamp in that field over there."

The tall, square warrior had served under Morgana's command in the last years of the war against the Pendragon and had proven himself to be a shrewd, if brutal, leader. He had also proven to be loyal, as long as he was timely paid his due in silver. The Saxon raised a fist, and the order was passed down the line by a mounted crier.

Morgana spurred her horse off the road and cantered up the slope of a knoll at the far end of the field, followed by Garr, three Saxon warriors, and two of her household retainers. Moments after she dismounted, Garr called out in his guttural voice, "Lady Morgana, a rider comes."

She turned and looked in the direction the Saxon was pointing. A Pict warrior approached from the north. It was Talorc. What was he doing here? He should have been at the Abbey Cwm Hir, awaiting the order to kill Guinevere. She seethed with rage as she watched the Pict ride through the Saxon lines at a leisurely pace, his eyes roving over the warriors with a mixture of amusement and scorn.

"I know this man. I will talk to him alone, Garr," Morgana said curtly.

The Saxon war leader watched the approaching Pict for a moment with distaste, his hand resting upon the pommel of his sword. Then he nodded and walked back to his men.

Talorc halted his reddish-brown horse several paces short of Morgana and dismounted.

"Roman Princess, I can see you—"

"What are you doing here, Pict?" Morgana hissed. "You should be seventy leagues north, watching the Pendragon's whore!"

Talorc's eyes narrowed, but he smiled, displaying his sharpened black teeth. "The Queen of the Britons is five of your Roman leagues from here . . . along with an army."

"You lie! My spies—"

"Are dead," the Pict finished with scorn. "The man whose skin is the color of the night and your fellow Roman, Merlin the Wise, have seen to that."

"What? There were—"

"Four. Now, there are none."

"Five leagues? Where? Wait—" Morgana looked around for Garr

and saw him watching the exchange, along with three Saxon warriors, ten paces away. She waved him imperiously over. The Saxon strode to her side and glared at the Pict. Talorc returned the glare, his hand resting upon the wicked-looking hunting knife sheathed at his waist.

Morgana gestured at Talorc. "This man brings tidings of great import. Listen."

As Talorc begrudgingly retold his story, she withdrew a map from a pocket in her traveling cloak and spread it out on the small wooden camp table nearby.

"We are here," Morgana said, pointing to the midpoint on the road that ran from Noviomagus to Londinium. "Where is the Knight and his army?"

Talorc slowly drew the hunting knife from his belt and walked over to the map. After staring at the map and then lifting his gaze to the surrounding hills and sky for several moments, he touched the sharpened tip of his blade to a spot to the north of their position—a point between their position and Londinium.

"This place. It is called the Vale of Ashes. The army—they call it the Queen's Army now—is camped there by a river."

Talorc's comment about the name of the army enraged Morgana, and she suspected that's why the Pict had said it.

Garr looked suspiciously at the man. "How do you know this, Pict?" he demanded.

"I have followed this army for many days, Saxon, and I know it comes for you and the Norse dogs marching behind you. I also know that the man who leads this army will not allow you to pass on to Londinium. On the morrow, Saxon, there will be blood," Talorc said with satisfaction in his voice.

"How many are they?" Morgana said.

The Pict reached for a stick lying on the ground and began to draw lines in the dirt. "For each line, a hundred soldiers," he said as he drew twenty separate lines.

"Why should I believe you?" Garr said in a low growl.

Talorc's eyes narrowed, and then he spoke in a terse whisper, his hand tightening on the knife in his hand. "I don't care what you believe, Saxon, but know this: If I wanted your head, I would take it myself. I would not wait for the army of the Pendragon's Queen to do that for me."

Garr started toward him, a snarl on his face, but Morgana cut him off.

"Garr, send riders to Ivarr and Sveinn. Tell them the enemy is less than a day's march away. Tell them that if they're not here before night-fall, I will march away and let them fight the Britons on their own."

The Saxon reluctantly shoved his partially drawn sword back into its sheath, glared at the Pict, and then walked across the field to where two of his men were currying their horses. Morgana turned to Talorc and spoke in a cold, hard voice.

"Where is the Pendragon's whore?"

"You mean the Queen of the Britons," he said with a small smile.

"She is the queen of nothing, Pict," Morgana hissed.

"No, Roman Princess? Then why is it that so many men have flocked to her banner and marched to war without the promise of gold or sil-ver?" Talorc said in quiet contempt.

"If her men are stupid enough to fight for food, then she is welcome to them. Now where is she?" she said, stabbing a finger into the map.

The Pict touched the map with the tip of his knife. "Here, in a villa, five miles north of the army. She is guarded by one hundred men. The Knight of the Table is with her."

"Tomorrow, you will kill her, but not," Morgana said, turning to look across the camp at where Lord Aeron was sitting on a rock honing his sword, "until Sir Percival has left for the battlefield."

"What will you gain from this killing, Roman?" Talorc growled.

"That's not your affair, Pict!" Morgana snapped. "I have your blood oath, and you will honor it."

For an instant, rage flared in the man's eyes, and then it faded. The Pict smiled and backed away from Morgana, sheathing his knife. After mounting his horse, Talorc looked over at Morgana and said in a hard, flat whisper she could not hear, "Yes, I shall keep my oath, Roman, and you will keep yours, or you will follow the Queen of the Britons into the grave."

*   *   *

AT FIRST, LORD Aeron didn't recognize the Pict warrior when he rode into the camp from the north, then he saw the blue fletching on the arrows, just visible over the top of the deerskin quiver strapped across his back. This was the same warrior Morgana had secretly met in the forest many months ago. Lord Aeron watched the rider for another moment and then turned away, feigning a lack of interest. He continued to hone the blade of his sword with a well-worn whetstone, but he could still see Morgana from the corner of his eye.

The tense exchange between the Pict, Morgana, and Garr did not make any sense to him until Morgana drew a parchment role from her cloak—a map. Then he knew: The Pict must have brought word of Sir Percival and his army. When Garr left the meeting and sent two messengers racing south, he felt certain that the army led by his brother Knight must be close by. It seemed Sir Percival was moving faster than Morgana had anticipated. A battle would come soon, maybe even on the morrow.

The knight continued to hone the sword blade, waiting for the rumors to race around the camp, as he knew they would. An hour later, he stood up, sheathed his sword, and walked his horse across the camp to the creek on the far side. As he crossed the field, he passed by a lean old man clad in a motley collection of animal skins that marked him as a local hunter. The man was sitting alone, fitting an iron point to the tip of a wooden arrow he had whittled from a piece of hardwood. Lord Aeron drew his horse to a halt next to the man, using the animal's body to hide him from Morgana's sight.

"Hunter, I'm told that the enemy is near."

The hunter nodded without looking up.

"So the Pict says. Don't trust him. After dark, I'll go and see for myself."

When Lord Aeron didn't move, the hunter looked up at him in

silence and then spoke quietly. "Saw you kill that Saxon the other day. A bad one, he was. Killed a woman in one of the villages the Norse sacked on their way in. I knew the lass's father . . . a good man. There was no cause for him to do that. So I guess I'm thanking you for doing something . . . something I should have done."

"Why are you telling me this, hunter?" Lord Aeron said quietly.

The old man's eyes returned to his work when spoke. "I served the Pendragon as a scout in the last years of the war. My son . . . he was proud of me. He's gone now. I remember those days. So let's just say that we were both someone else, a long time ago, and leave it at that."

For a moment, the two men's eyes met, and then Lord Aeron glanced back at Morgana's camp on the knoll. She was still immersed in conversation with Garr.

"The Pict said the Queen was with the army," the hunter said in a whisper as he returned to his work.

For a moment, the breath caught in Lord Aeron's throat. "The Pict said this?" he asked in a hoarse tone.

"Aye, he was dead sure. She's staying at a villa behind the lines. I've been there before. Might just visit there tonight."

"I'd like to ride along with you, if you don't mind," Lord Aeron said.

"I'll be at that big oak at the top of yon hill, two hours after dark. Can't wait long."

"Understood," the knight said, and continued walking his horse across the camp to the stream on the far side.

North of the Vale of Ashes

After bathing in a spring a mile from the manor where the Queen was staying, Percival dressed in silence. The sun had passed below the horizon moments earlier, and although it was still early in the fall, the Knight could feel the chill in the air on his bare skin.

As he donned his leather jerkin, he sensed someone watching him from the other side of the small clearing and reached for his sword.

"You have no need of that. I've only come to talk with an old friend."

Percival eased his hand away from the sword. He had not heard that voice in nearly a decade, and yet he recognized it immediately. And yet the voice was different. It lacked the irrepressible mirth and passion he remembered.

"Galahad," he said in disbelief as he watched his brother Knight emerge from the shadows, dressed in a long, black cloak. "I . . . feared you perished at Camlann, brother. You cannot know how it gladdens my heart to see you alive," Percival said, a depth of feeling in his voice as he walked over to his friend and embraced him.

When the two men separated, Galahad looked at him and said, in a voice laden with regret, "Maybe the man that you knew did perish at Camlann."

Percival could only see the outline of Galahad's face in the dark, but the certainty in his voice disturbed him.

"How did you know that I would be here?"

"Oh, I remember your obsession with bathing, and I knew there would be no time for it in the morning. Your mother . . . you said she insisted upon it when you were a boy, as I recall."

"I did, didn't I?" Percival said, the hint of a smile coming to his face.

"Come, sit," Galahad said, gesturing to two large stones in the clearing, alongside the remains of a past fire. A small stack of branches lay beside the ashes. "We can start a fire and drink a toast or two to a world that is no more."

Percival walked over to one of the stones and sat down as Galahad adeptly lit a small fire, using a striking steel and stone.

"Why, I don't think I've ever seen you light a fire before, brother. You are quite the woodsman now."

"Alas, how the mighty have fallen," Galahad said with a sad smile as he sat down on the rock and drew a skin of wine from his traveling cloak.

As the light from the flames grew, Percival could see the cruel scar that marred the right side of the other man's face and the second scar across his forehead. Although the wounds shocked him, it was the flat-dead look in Galahad's blue eyes that shook him to the core.

"Oh, don't grieve for me, brother," Galahad said, misunderstanding Percival's look. "From what I saw when you walked out of that spring, fate has dealt you a far crueler throw of the dice than I."

"It was God's will," Percival said as he threw a branch into the fire.

"If it's all the same to the Almighty, I'll take a different path and drink from a very different barrel of ale the next time around," Galahad said.

"That might be difficult. From what I remember, you have already sampled just about every cask, barrel, and keg in the land."

The two men laughed together, and for a moment, they returned to a different time and place.

"Let us drink a toast to what once was," Galahad said as he filled two simple wooden cups with wine and handed one to Percival. He raised his cup. "To the Table, the Pendragon, and Queen Guinevere."

"So say we all," Percival said, raising his cup.

Then both men drank a long draught and stared into the fire in silence.

Percival looked over at his friend, questions swirling through his mind. Where had he been all these years? Had any of the other members of the Table survived? Had he come to join with him in the battle against Morgana?

"How is she?" Galahad asked, interrupting Percival's thoughts.

"The Queen is well. She is less than a league from here. You must come and see her. We can ride there together. I will seek an audience," Percival said, standing up. "We can talk on the way. I have many—"

Galahad stood up and threw his wooden cup into the fire. "There's no time," Galahad said, shaking his head. "I only came to honor a promise that I made to Lancelot."

Percival looked at Galahad in confusion.

His brother Knight looked down at the fire and spoke in a tired voice, as though he were watching a painful but all too familiar tragedy unfold.

"At Camlann . . . just before the final charge, Lancelot asked for my forgiveness, and he asked . . . that I seek your forgiveness on his behalf, as well, if you ever returned. I think . . . he knew he was going to die."

Percival looked into the night sky, remembering Lancelot's stern countenance, their arguments over strategy and tactics, and the older Knight's rage when he had raised his concerns directly with the King at a meeting of the Table. Lancelot had taken Percival's breach of protocol as a personal affront and had never spoken to him directly again. After that day, he had been excluded from all strategy sessions with the King and had been assigned the least favorable duties. His ostracism had been one of the reasons he had volunteered to serve in the Marches, although it had not been the most important reason.

"There's nothing to forgive," Percival said. "We disagreed on how to fight the war against Morgana, and he was surely a hard taskmaster, but I believe that his heart was true. However, I grant him my forgiveness, whether needed or not."

Galahad nodded and squatted down by the fire, his eyes distant.

"He sent me to hold the left flank, before the final charge was made, so I didn't see it, but I am told that he was magnificent. The charge and the savage melee that followed broke the enemy's lines and carried the day, leaving the Pendragon the master of the field . . . a field of dead. The King died from his wounds, and the Table died with him. Oh, Sir Dinadan and I lived, but not for long. Sir Dinadan recovered from his wounds . . . only to later die by the blade of Hengst the Butcher."

Galahad was silent for moment and then looked over at Percival, a smile on his face. "But then, you put that right, brother. I wish I had been there to see you strike the Butcher down."

Galahad's smile slowly faded, and when he continued, his voice was filled with both anger and regret.

"All that blood . . . and that for a people who couldn't even rouse themselves to fight by our side . . . to fight for their own survival. Well, they have reaped in full measure the misery of that cowardly choice. Instead of living under the King's peace, they now slave under the Norse lash."

"What are you saying?" Percival said in confusion.

"Criers went out in the days before Camlann, calling on anyone who could bear arms to join the ranks. The response was feeble." The anger drained from Galahad's voice as he finished, as if he were too tired to carry its weight. "Less than a thousand men came, and they were a miserable lot."

Percival shook his head in frustration. "You can't ask farmers and other men that ply the peaceful trades to take the field as soldiers on the morrow with the call of a battle horn. It takes time, training, leadership. That's what I tried to tell Lancelot, and later, the King, before I left for the Marches. We needed to raise levies from the peasants, to organize them, train them, to let them pick their own leaders. Lancelot wouldn't hear of it. In his mind, cavalry and archers won wars, not a peasant infantry, and he had the King's ear."

"He was right," Galahad said, anger returning to his voice. "As I said, the few who came broke and ran."

"Galahad, the Roman cavalry didn't conquer most of the known world, the Roman infantry did. The men who filled those ranks weren't Knights of the Table or master bowmen. They were tradesmen, farmers, fishermen, and stable boys. The difference was they were trained to be soldiers on the Field of Mars and on hundreds of other practice fields throughout the empire," Percival said.

Galahad looked in the direction of Morgana's encampment to the south and shook his head. "You're wrong, and you will see that on the morrow, if you take the field. You must take the Queen and leave this place. Morgana may want a battle, but the Norse do not. They seek the riches of Londinium. Let them pass, and you will avoid a slaughter."

"And the people of Londinium? What of them? Should I leave them to be spitted on the swords of the Norse?"

"Yes!" Galahad answered, his voice rising. "That's what they deserve! Haven't your spies told you? The mayor of Londinium and his council rejected your call for reinforcements. The cowards will stay within their walls and allow you and your army to be annihilated, in the hope that this will leave fewer men to besiege their city."

"No, that cannot be," Percival said, shaking his head.

"It is. It will be Camlann all over again. Morgana will win the day. You must retreat," he said with desperate intensity.

"I will not."

"Then you and your army of peasants will die, and when the carrion are picking at your bones, what will happen to the Queen? Will you leave her to be enslaved as a Norse pet or to face Morgana's knife!" Galahad said in a cold, hard voice.

"That will not happen!" Percival said, raising a clenched fist. "You and I, the last of the Table, will fight together on the morrow, with the Queen's Army, and we will defeat Morgana and the Norse."

"Those days are gone. I am no longer a Knight of the Table."

"You will always be a Knight of the Table."

Galahad shook his head and spoke in a voice bereft of hope. "No. A promise was made, a bargain struck. What has been done cannot be undone. The price would be too high."

Percival crossed to his side and laid one hand upon his shoulder. "I don't know what you have promised or what you've done, but I know you are a man of honor, and I know we need your sword—"

Galahad stepped away from him, and the Knight's hand fell away. "Good-bye, Percival," he said and walked toward the forest wall. Just before he entered the darkened wood, he turned. "We were both cursed, brother," he said, "to fall in love with the one woman we couldn't have. When you came to know this, you did the honorable thing. You took the farthest posting from Camelot, the defense of the Marches, and I believe you agreed to undertake the Grail quest for the same reason— to stay away from her. I took a different path. I buried my pain in drink and in the arms of other women. If . . . if you truly love her, you must take her away from this place."

"I will pray for you, my friend," Percival said.

"Pray instead for yourself, and for the Queen, for on the morrow, I fear it will be you in need of God's mercy," he said and then disappeared into the forest.

CHAPTER 31

Guinevere's Quarters,
North of the Vale of Ashes

When the knock came on the outer door to her chambers, Guinevere placed her hand on her chest, in the vain hope of slowing the beat of her pounding heart. Arthur had come to her on the night before he left for the battle of Camlann. She remembered his tired and worn face, a face that had aged twenty years in the last months under the weight of a thousand burdens. Although he'd told her all would be well, in her heart, she'd known otherwise. She'd somehow known that it would be their last parting. Now she faced that prospect again.

She rose from the chair beside the small writing desk in her chambers, on the second floor of the old manor house, and walked to the window. The dark horizon to the south was ablaze with hundreds of small fires, marking the site of an encamped army preparing to go to war—her army. A moment later, she heard a soft knock at the door. After taking a last look at the distant lights, she walked over and opened the door.

"Good evening, Lady Cadwyn, Sister Aranwen. Do we have a guest?" Guinevere asked, forcing a smile.

"Yes, my Queen, Sir Percival is here," Cadwyn said.

"Then let's not keep him waiting." Guinevere gestured for the women to lead the way. She followed them into the main room, where Sir Percival was waiting by the door. Her eyes widened when she saw him. The Knight wore a white tabard, with the seal of the Table on the chest, over a heavy mail shirt.

Greaves were strapped to his lower legs, and gleaming gauntlets covered his hands and forearms. In the crook of his arm, he held a blackened steel helm with a long, square nosepiece and spiked crest that seemed to bristle with restrained ferocity.

Percival bowed. "My Queen, I must join the army. We will engage the enemy in the morning, and the last dispositions must be made."

"Yes, of course," Guinevere said, nodding, unable to speak for a moment.

Percival bowed again and turned to leave, and Guinevere called after him. "Wait, Percival."

She turned to Cadwyn and Sister Aranwen. "Lady Cadwyn, Sister, would you please wait for me in my chambers."

After the two women had left the room, Guinevere stared at the waiting Knight for a long moment, endeavoring to find the right words. "Percival, the royal command of last night stands."

"I understand . . . Guinevere."

"I . . . I have made a parting such as this once before . . ."

Percival's eyes met hers, and she knew he could sense the terrible fear weighing upon her soul. After a long moment, he placed the helm under his arm on the table by the door, drew off his gauntlets, and held out his hands. Guinevere took a step toward him and placed her hands in his, and he clasped them tightly. She closed her eyes for a moment, comforted by both the power and the love she felt in his touch.

"It will not be thus. I shall return," Percival said.

She opened her eyes and smiled. "I will wait for you and . . . when you return, I would have you speak to me not as your Queen . . . but as a woman."

"I will, Guinevere," Percival said. Then he released his grip on her hands, retrieved his helm and gauntlets, and departed.

THE ROAD FROM NOVIOMAGUS REGINORUM TO LONDINIUM

As Morgana watched Sveinn form his men into ranks on her left, she smiled in quiet scorn. The Norse warlord had fallen into the trap she and Ivarr had laid for him. Just as anticipated, the arrogant fool had insisted upon being in overall command of the army, citing his greater experience and fearsome reputation. Although Morgana and Ivarr had feigned resistance, in the end, they had accepted the demand, knowing this would place Sveinn's men in the center of the line.

If, as Morgana expected, the fighting in the center was the fiercest, then much of Sveinn's strength would be spent by the end of the victorious battle, leaving Ivarr and Morgana's forces well positioned to annihilate the Norse leader and his men in a surprise attack after the battle, as planned. With that done, the two allies would then march on Londinium alone and split the spoils when the city was sacked.

Alas, as with any plan, there were pitfalls as well. Although the three of them had agreed the army should march before dawn to force the enemy to fight on the ground of their choosing, Sveinn had ignored this agreement. Instead, he and his men had drunk themselves into a stupor, as they did every night, making them slow to rise. Now, they would be forced to fight on the ground chosen by Sir Percival and his Numidian friend and to fight that battle on their terms.

The Knight's army was arrayed at the northern end of a narrow valley an hour's march away. The valley was bordered on the north, east, and west sides by steep slopes. Morgana and the Norse would be forced to march into the valley through the southern end and to fight on a narrow front, where only six hundred men could fight abreast in a line.

Sir Percival's choice of a battle site was both wise and foolhardy. The ground would offset Morgana's advantage in numbers, but it would also leave his army trapped in a pocket at the northern end, if he failed to carry the day. Sir Percival was forcing his army to choose between victory or annihilation.

The Knight's strategy is an act of desperation, she thought. *He knows his allies in Londinium have deserted him, so he intends to try to survive by fighting a defensive battle of attrition.*

A cruel smile played across Morgana's face as she envisioned the scene described by her spies in Londinium. The lord mayor and the council had voted to hide behind their walls rather than march out and join the force that had nobly marched to the city's relief. When Cynric the Archer had threatened to kill the mayor after the vote, he and his formidable bowmen had been dragged off to prison. That was fortuitous. The archers in the ranks of the Norse and Saxon could not compete with the archers in this land.

Morgana spoke in a whisper, "Alas, Sir Percival, only a fool puts his faith in the honor of other men. Today, you will now learn that only gold and the sword can be trusted."

"Milady?"

Morgana turned to Garr, who had ridden up on his horse from the rear.

"Sveinn is ready to march."

Morgana looked with disdain at the line of Norse warriors, now clad in their armor and beginning to march in a line of roughly three men abreast.

"Give the order to move out," she said coldly. "We certainly don't want to keep our ally waiting, do we?"

The Saxon nodded, wheeled his horse, and bellowed out commands to the line of men behind her. Far to her right, Morgana could see Lord Aeron clad in battle armor, standing alone by his black destrier. The spy she had assigned to watch him last night had disappeared, which troubled her. Lord Aeron had one more role to play before she had him killed—a role that would force him to choose between his precious Queen and his brother Knight. As she watched the knight mount his horse, Morgana experienced something that was alien to her—a moment of regret.

You are as foolish as you once were handsome, Sir Galahad. Did you really think that I would honor my promise?

Guinevere's Quarters,
North of the Vale of Ashes

Guinevere stared at the open Bible on her lap and then slowly turned yet another page, not having read a word of the sacred text. Thoughts flitted through her mind like butterflies in a tempest, each gaining only a whisper of contemplation before being swept away by the next gust of wind. In one instant, she would be struggling to find peace through the words in the Book of Psalms, and in the next, she would be drawn into the maelstrom of violence raging two leagues distant by the blast of the battle horn. From there, her thoughts would race back through time to a darkened room in a distant castle, where a younger woman waited to hear the tidings of another terrible battle. Each minute seemed an hour, each hour a day.

After futilely struggling to read another line, Guinevere raised her head and looked across the room at Sister Aranwen. The nun was sitting in a chair, silently praying with her eyes closed. Her eyes strayed to Cadwyn. The young woman was sitting restlessly in another chair holding a map of the battlefield that Keil had drawn for her earlier in the day. Guinevere knew the young woman had just returned from yet another visit to the guard station near the front wall, where she had once again sought tidings of the battle.

As she looked around the ancient stone sitting room, she wondered how many other women had waited in this room in centuries past and prayed for victory, or just for survival. How many had felt the agony of a loss too great to bear when the battle was over?

Guinevere shook off the morbid thought and once again tried to read the words in front of her, but another strident burst from a distant battle horn drew her attention. She laid the open Bible down on a nearby table and walked over to the window that looked to the south, where the battle was raging. There was nothing to see. The fields surrounding the villa were empty, and the forested hills beyond were still, just as they had been an hour earlier.

* * *

Talorc watched the second-floor window from behind the trunk of an oak tree, just outside the low wall that encircled the stone manor. It had taken him over an hour to crawl to the spot, and he was covered in dirt and sweat.

He didn't fear discovery by the Queen's uniformed guards, but he did fear the sharp eyes of the hunter called Torn. The hunter had discovered

Talorc's tracks in the hills outside the Abbey Cwm Hir, despite the care
he had taken to avoid detection. From that day forward, the hunter and
his dogs had relentlessly pursued his trail, forcing him to spy on the
Queen from a greater distance.

Talorc glanced up at the sky. It was over four hours past sunrise, and
he knew a patrol would pass by the tree at around noon. If the Queen
didn't show herself within the next few minutes, he would have to make
the slow, perilous crawl back to the forest and then attempt to return
later in the afternoon.

As the Pict reached up to unstring his bow, he heard a distant blast
of horns from the battle raging to the south. Glancing up, he saw the
Queen appear at the manor's second-floor window. She stared in the
direction of the sound, her beautiful face filled with subdued apprehension. Talorc dipped the tip of an arrow into the small pot of black
poison Morgana had given him the day before, nocked the arrow in his
bow, and stepped out from behind the tree for his shot.

As he was releasing the arrow, a second arrow slammed into the tree
an inch from his face, causing the Pict to move his bow ever so slightly.
The movement saved Guinevere from a kill shot. Instead of plunging
into the Queen's chest, Talorc's arrow flew to the right, grazing her
right arm, just below the shoulder.

Talorc turned and ran toward the forest line to the south, frantically dodging to the left and the right, in a desperate effort to avoid the
arrows flying past him like angry bees. As soon as he reached the cover
of the forest, the Pict glanced back and saw the tall, lean hunter who'd
been his nemesis for the past month sprinting after him, followed at a
distance by three armed men on horseback. Talorc raced down the far
side of the hill, leaped upon his horse, and galloped south.

*　*　*

GUINEVERE LOOKED DOWN, stunned to see blood running freely
down her arm. A moment later, Cadwyn's scream suddenly shattered the
room's peace and quiet. The young woman ran to her side and pulled
her away from the window. Sister Aranwen sat frozen for a moment in

shock and then sprang from her chair and ran to the Queen. She pulled the white linen cloth from around her own neck and pressed it against the wound as she guided the Queen to a small bed on the other side of the room. Then she turned to Cadwyn and said with desperate urgency, "Cadwyn, run and find Merlin! Go!"

Cadwyn ran to the door and yanked it open, only to find her way blocked by the two guards pressing into the room with their swords drawn. The soldiers froze in the doorway, staring aghast at the Queen's blood-soaked arm.

"Get out of the way!" Cadwyn screamed as she shoved her way past the two men. "The Queen has been wounded! I have to find Merlin."

As Guinevere sat down on the bed, she gave Sister Aranwen a reassuring smile. "It is only a small wound, Sister. Merlin will see to it."

Moments later, she began to shiver, despite the warmth of the day, and her breathing became more labored.

"Sister, I am going to lie down, I feel . . . cold," she said.

As she lay back, she felt as if every ounce of strength was draining from her body, like blood from a fatal wound. Sister Aranwen nodded and eased her back against the two pillows. Guinevere saw the fear in the other woman's face, despite her effort to hide it.

Moments later, Cadwyn reentered the room with Merlin close behind.

The old Roman stepped past the guards carrying a black wooden box under his arm, and knelt by Guinevere's side. He slowly eased the linen cloth from her wound. As he did so, his nostrils flared, and he spoke in a whisper, "Wolfsbane."

Sister Aranwen's eyes widened, and Guinevere, feeling her strength steadily ebbing away, looked up at Merlin and said, "Tell me."

Merlin opened the black box and drew out two white cloths and a vial of a pale yellow liquid.

"I believe the arrow was tipped with wolfsbane . . . a poison, my Queen, and . . . something else that I haven't smelled in a long time. A potion from the east."

"What does that mean?" Cadwyn said, tears pouring down her face, her eyes frantic.

"It means we clean and bind the wound, and then we wait," Merlin said quietly, his face grim.

Merlin poured the yellow liquid on one of the white cloths, quickly cleaned the wound, and then bound it with the second cloth. Guinevere was surprised when she did not feel any pain from his ministrations. All she felt was a growing coldness within.

After binding the wound, Merlin drew a blanket over the Queen.

"Rest, my Queen. All will be well," Merlin said with calm assurance as he stood. He glanced over at Cadwyn's stricken face and pointed to the small pitcher on a nearby table and said, "Cadwyn, please take the pitcher and get the Queen some fresh, cool water from the well."

Cadwyn grabbed the vessel and raced out the door.

Guinevere drew the woolen blanket tighter around her as another shiver wracked her body, and shut her eyes for a moment. As she struggled against the growing pain within, she could hear Sister Aranwen and Merlin talking in whispers.

"Can you save her?" Sister Aranwen asked.

"Not without a miracle," Merlin whispered.

"Then we shall pray for that with all our hearts," the nun said.

Guinevere opened her eyes and spoke with difficulty. "Merlin . . . the look on your face tells me that you have no cure for the poison that even now I can feel taking my life."

Merlin's silence was all the answer Guinevere needed. She looked over at Sister Aranwen.

"Sister, please bring a parchment and quill. I would have you write a message for me."

CHAPTER 32

THE VALE OF ASHES

Torn's face had been raked and scored by low-hanging branches as he galloped through the forest in his relentless pursuit of the Pict warrior. An errant rivulet of blood flowed into his left eye, but he ignored it and drove his heels into the horse's sides yet again, in spite of the animal's labored breathing. He was almost within bowshot.

The Pict's horse raced out of the forest ahead of him and galloped along the eastern rim of the valley, where the two armies were locked in combat below. Torn's horse emerged from the forest moments later. As the gap between the horses closed, Torn could see the Pict's objective—a trail that led down the slope to Morgana's encampment. Six Saxon warriors were galloping up the trail to meet him. The Pict was Morgana's assassin.

Torn glanced over his shoulder, knowing he could not take on the Saxons and the Pict alone. The two guardsmen riding after him had not yet emerged from the forest. This left him only one choice. The hunter pulled his horse up short and leaped off, bow in hand. Ignoring the pounding of his heart and the blood partly obscuring his vision, he nocked an arrow and drew the bowstring. The moment he released the shaft, Torn knew the shot was true. The arrow raced toward the center of Pict's back.

As if sensing the threat, the Pict wheeled his horse to the right an instant before the arrow struck. The shaft flew past him, striking one of the approaching Saxons in the arm, drawing a scream of pain and rage. For a moment, Torn was sure the enraged Saxons would charge him, but they did not. They formed a circle around the Pict and escorted him back down the hill to the safety of Morgana's camp.

A moment later, the other two members of the Queen's Guard galloped over to Torn and dismounted with their bows at the ready. Torn glanced over at the two younger men, Devyn and Leith.

"He's gone," Torn said quietly. "The Saxons took him to Morgana's camp."

Leith looked over at Torn. "A prisoner?"

"No . . . no. They were sent to protect him. He was surely sent by Morgana, may the devil take her soul," Torn said in a voice filled with rage and regret.

A roar from the battle raging on the valley floor below drew Torn's attention to the contest that would determine Albion's fate. Two lines of infantry were locked in combat on the floor of the narrow valley. The army of Norse and Saxons arrayed on the south side of the valley was visibly larger than the Queen's Army on the north, and the Britons were hard pressed, but they could not back up. The north wall of the valley behind them barred further retreat.

As the hunter and the other two guardsmen watched the battle, mesmerized, a group of six giant Norse warriors furiously attacked the Queen's shield wall on the right flank, driving the Britons back. Just when it seemed as if the line would break, Sir Percival raced up on his black charger, dismounted, and waded into the Norse attackers with his sword.

The Knight's ferocity and skill shocked the hunter. Two of the Norse giants were cut down in seconds, and a third was sorely wounded. The rest of the warriors stepped back and took up a defensive position, unwilling to take on their attacker. As soon as the flank was stabilized, the Knight once again mounted his horse and rode behind men calling out encouragement and looking for new threats.

Torn wheeled around when he heard the sound of hooves pounding toward him from the rear. It was Lewyn, one of the guards assigned to the Queen's quarters. The guardsman pulled up his horse a pace away, a desperate look on his face.

"Torn . . . the Queen," Lewyn gasped, "she is near death. The Pict's arrow was poisoned."

"Cannot Merlin save her?" Torn said in a tortured voice.

Lewyn shook his head, his eyes filled with grief. "It is a thing beyond even his skill."

"God forgive me, I have failed her," Torn whispered. Then he walked over and mounted his horse.

Torn turned to the other men. "Return to the manor. I will be joining the battle line below."

"What? Your duty is—" Lewyn started.

"To protect the Queen, and I have failed. Now . . . I will kill her enemies until I am spent. The rest of you will return to the manor and protect Lady Cadwyn and Sister Aranwen."

* * *

MORGANA SCANNED THE length of Sir Percival's hard-pressed lines from the slope of the hill that bordered her right flank and smiled in satisfaction. After four hours of hard fighting, the greater weight of the Norse and Saxon forces had pushed the Queen's Army, step by step, deeper and deeper into the valley, leaving it backed up against a steep, circular slope from which escape would be all but impossible.

The cost had been far higher than she'd anticipated. Sir Percival's infantry had made the Norse and Saxons pay in blood for every inch of ground, and Cynric the Archer and his men had wreaked havoc with their longbows. Apparently the lord mayor's prison in Londinium was not as secure as he thought. Still, the end was near. They just needed to make one more massed attack on the center of the line, and it would collapse—an attack she had called for three times, without seeing any movement from Sveinn's force.

"Garr, why is there no attack on the center? I told that fool—"

"There will be no attack upon the center, Roman," a coarse, guttural voice growled from behind her.

Morgana wheeled her horse around and saw Canute, Sveinn's second in command. The giant Norseman's blond hair was matted with sweat, and blood from a scalp wound flowed down the right side of his neck.

"What do you mean? That is the weakest point!"

"So you say, but we have tried to break the Britons' shield wall there before. Each time the Knight with the raven hair has cut down our strongest warriors and rallied his men. Now, Sveinn and Ivarr the Red have agreed that it is time for you and your Saxon sellswords to bleed."

Morgana's eyes narrowed. She should have anticipated this. When Sveinn had refused to press the attack, Ivarr had inveighed against her by suggesting her forces had not carried their share of the burden in the battle. Although the charge was not wholly false, an attack by her force at this point would be foolhardy.

The ground in front of her line sloped sharply upward, giving the enemy a defensive advantage, where the ground in front of Sveinn and Ivarr's men was level. That advantage would give Sir Percival time to join the fight, as he had over and over again throughout the day, and then it would be a slaughter. She had never seen a man fight with such skill and ferocity other than Lord Aeron.

Morgana smiled. The time had come to use the knight's lethal blade one last time. She would demand that he challenge Sir Percival to single combat. In return, she would promise to spare the Queen's life and free him from his pledge of service—if he prevailed. The noble fool would have no choice but to consent, and no matter how the contest ended, she would be the winner. Either Lord Aeron would kill Sir Percival, or Sir Percival would kill him. If Percival prevailed, he would die a moment later by one of Talorc's poisoned arrows.

Once their hero was dead, the Britons would break and run, and she, Morgana, would kill a second army of Britons in her lifetime.

THE VALE OF ASHES

For the past four hours, Sir Percival had ridden behind the army's right flank and the center, shoring up near breaks in the line. Capussa had played the same role for the left flank, while at the same time directing the overall battle. As Percival moved out of the line, after fending off yet another savage attack on the right, the Knight saw Torn walking toward him, bearing a sword and shield. He rode over to the hunter, assuming that Merlin or the Queen had sent a message, and dismounted.

Torn's face was a mask of despair.

"Forgive me, sir. I have failed the kingdom. The arrow of a Pict warrior has struck the Queen. It was a slight wound in the arm, but the arrow . . . it was poisoned."

Percival's face froze.

"The Queen . . . she—"

"She lies on her deathbed, I am told. Sir . . . I would take the line with your soldiers, if you will allow it."

Percival stared at the hunter, unwilling to accept his words. "An arrow . . . you are sure—"

Torn looked down at the ground. "I am sure, Sir Percival. An arrow with blue feathers. It was Morgana. The assassin rode straight for her camp after . . . after the Queen was struck. The Saxons . . . they recognized him."

Percival looked away for a moment, struggling to find cause to challenge the truth of what he had been told, but the look of pain and anguish on the hunter's face swept away any doubt. The Knight closed his eyes, and the din of the nearby battle faded into silence. He was left alone at the edge of an abyss as deep as the ocean and as dark as the night. As the dream that had almost become a reality faded, the agony of the despair within him became an unbearable and all-consuming fire.

It was then that the water from a spring in a faraway desert seemed to wash over him a second time, replenishing his reserves of hope and faith. When he opened his eyes, as he had on that day so long ago, he knew he could bear the pain. He also knew he would finish the task Guinevere had assigned to him.

Percival looked into the hunter's tormented eyes. "Torn, you bear no fault in this matter. The sin is Morgana's alone, and now . . . she will pay for it."

The cheers on the field behind him drew Percival's attention back to the battlefield. As he watched, the Norse and Saxon line moved back, and a figure on a mighty charger clad in black armor rode forward. The men fell quiet, and then the knight called out in the loud voice, "I, Lord Aeron, call upon Sir Percival to face my sword, alone!"

Sir Percival recognized the voice. "Galahad," he whispered. He'd heard the men in the ranks speak in hushed tones of the mysterious Lord Aeron: The black-clad knight who served at Morgana's beck and call—a warrior as unmerciful as he was reputedly invincible.

How could it be? How could his friend and brother in arms have agreed to serve under the banner of the Pendragon's enemy?

And then he remembered what Galahad had said the night before. "A promise was made, a bargain struck. What has been done cannot be undone. The price would be too high."

Percival mounted his horse and wheeled around to face the armored knight awaiting him in the middle of the field. As Percival slowly rode toward the line of men standing between him and the waiting knight, Capussa rode up, accompanied by Cynric the Archer.

"What are you doing? This is a trap," Capussa growled.

Percival turned to his friend and nodded. "It is. If I win, there will be an archer there ready to kill me, and if I lose, she will use the defeat to try to carry our lines."

"Then you won't accept the challenge?"

"No, I will accept, but I will not fight this knight. He will join us."

"What?" Capussa said, his dark eyes widening. "Have you lost your senses?"

"I . . . I have lost much this day, my friend, but not my reason. Trust my judgment in this," Percival said with certainty.

Then he turned to Cynric. "You and your best archers must be ready for the attack upon us. Watch, most of all, for a Pict whose arrows are painted blue."

"Who is this Lord Aeron?" Capussa said.

"He is a man of honor who has borne the yoke of the cruelest servitude in order to save the life of another. Today, that bondage ends . . . and today, his master will pay the toll for her evil deeds," Percival said in a voice that held the promise of a harsh retribution.

The Knight rode forward, and the shield wall parted as he approached. Lord Aeron rode his horse forward and met Percival midway between the lines, and the two men stared at each other on a battlefield that was now as silent as death. Then Galahad spoke in a voice filled with regret. "Forgive me, brother. I have no choice."

"So be it, Galahad," Percival said, quietly staring into the blue eyes just visible through the eye slit in the knight's helm, "but join me in a prayer before we slaughter each other, a prayer for the Queen, for she dies as we speak."

Galahad's eyes grew wide. "Guinevere?" he said in a voice filled with disbelief. "Tell me of this!"

"She was struck by an assassin's arrow within the last hour, a poison arrow," Percival said quietly. "Even Merlin, with all his skill, cannot save her."

"An arrow . . . what color was this arrow?" Galahad asked, his voice suffused with rage.

"Blue."

For a moment, Galahad closed his eyes, and then he raised a mailed fist that shook with an uncontrolled rage. When he opened his blue eyes, the cold despair Percival had seen there the night before was gone. Now, they were filled with wrath. Galahad stared at Percival for a long moment and then said, "We shall fight on this day, brother, but not against each other. Today, we shall fight together, for the Queen!"

As the two lines of men to their front and rear watched in stunned silence, Galahad wheeled his black destrier around and backed it into place beside Percival's horse. For a moment, the Vale of Ashes was deathly quiet, and then the Queen's Army exploded in a triumphal roar.

CHAPTER 33

GUINEVERE'S QUARTERS, NORTH OF THE VALE OF ASHES

Merlin stepped away from the Queen's bed and walked over to the window, praying in silence. Then suddenly, he pulled up short, his eyes turning to Sister Aranwen, kneeling at Guinevere's side.

"Yes, a miracle . . ." Merlin whispered ". . . we need a miracle." Then he turned and ran out of the room. As he crossed the courtyard at a run, he passed Cadwyn, whose hands were shaking so badly the pitcher of water she was carrying was already half empty.

"Cadwyn, quickly, bring the pitcher to the sitting room, but do not let the Queen drink a drop until I return," Merlin said as he ran toward his quarters.

"Merlin, what is it? Can you save her?" Cadwyn cried, desperation in her voice.

"I cannot, but a miracle can," Merlin said over his shoulder.

"A miracle?" Cadwyn said incredulously.

Merlin ran up the stairs to his small quarters on the second floor, pulled a wooden box from underneath his bed, and gently withdrew the wooden cup that Jacob the Healer had given to Percival. Then he raced down the stairs and across the courtyard.

When he ran through the door to Guinevere's quarters, Sister Aranwen and Cadwyn were kneeling beside the Queen, holding her hand and praying. Tears ran freely down their faces. Merlin walked over to the pitcher of water Cadwyn had placed on a nearby table and poured the water into the ancient wooden cup he held in his hand. He looked at the unimposing vessel for a moment, said a quiet prayer, and then walked over to the bed. Cadwyn and Sister Aranwen moved aside, giving him room to kneel by the Queen.

The Queen's face was ashen, and her shallow gasps for breath told him that she only had minutes to live. "Drink," Merlin whispered urgently. She silently shook her head as she writhed in pain.

Merlin leaned closer and whispered in her ear, "Guinevere, if you drink from this cup, you will live . . . you will live to see Percival again."

Guinevere's eyes opened, and she nodded weakly. Merlin lifted her shoulders and raised the cup to her lips. She took a long drink and swallowed. After gasping for breath, she took another drink and lay back again, spent. As Merlin and the two women watched, Guinevere's breathing steadily became more regular, and her fair skin began to regain its normal hue.

Cadwyn put her hand to her mouth and whispered, "Merlin, your potion has saved her!"

Merlin bowed his head in silence for a moment, overcome with emotion, before rising and walking over to a chair and sitting down. He idly looked over at the book that lay open on the table beside chair. It was the Bible. He shook his head as he read the words of the Psalm: "For you have delivered my soul from death, my eyes from tears, my feet from stumbling; I will walk before the Lord in the land of the living."

Merlin looked down at the empty cup in his hand and then placed it in the pocket of his cloak. When he withdrew his hand, it was shaking so badly that he had to clasp both hands together in his lap to stay the tremor. He looked across the room to where Cadwyn and Sister Aranwen were kneeling beside Guinevere. The Queen was smiling. She was truly saved.

Merlin stood, walked to the window, and pushed open the shutters the guards had closed after the attack, and the sun poured into the darkened room. The old Roman stared to the south in silence, until Sister Aranwen walked over and said in a whisper, "Was it the potion," she whispered, "or was it the cup?"

A smile came to Merlin's face. "Why Sister, it was neither. It was the miracle you prayed for."

Sister Aranwen raised a questioning eyebrow and returned to Guinevere's side.

Moments later, Guinevere sat up on the bed. She looked tired, but her color had returned, and the pain in her eyes had been replaced by the quiet strength he remembered.

"My Queen, you should rest," Sister Aranwen said, concern in her voice.

Guinevere smiled and shook her head. "Thank you, Sister, but I am quite well. More, I . . . I feel as young as the day that we first met. Forgive me, my friends, but I must speak to Merlin alone for a moment."

After the two women left the room, Guinevere gestured to a chair across from the bed. "Merlin, please, sit for a moment. It appears you have saved my life yet again."

Merlin walked over to the chair and sat down, shaking his head. "No, my Queen, it was not I."

"There was no potion in that cup?" she said.

"No."

"Tell me."

Merlin clasped his shaking hands together on his lap.

"Jacob the Healer of Alexandria died while Sir Percival was in prison, serving in the stead of Jacob's son, Joshua. When Percival returned, Joshua told him that Jacob had left the Knight a cup and a written message, along with a substantial sum of gold for the passage home. Neither Percival nor Joshua had been able to make any sense of the message, for it was written in an ancient form of Aramaic, and yet words from the Roman and Greek tongues were interspersed in the message as well. Joshua told Percival that his father had been very sick during his last days and could well have lost his senses. As for the cup, all his father had told him, and these words were spoken in the throes of a fever, was that the cup was not the grail Percival sought, but it was one that had served."

"One that had served?" Guinevere repeated in confusion.

Merlin nodded. "When Percival told me the story, I couldn't believe that a man as wise as Jacob the Healer would have simply left a wooden cup of no moment for the man who'd saved the life of his only son, let alone wasted his last breaths speaking of such a cup. I pondered this for a time and then, many weeks ago, I asked the Knight if I might see the cup and the note."

The old Roman drew in a breath and slowly exhaled in an effort to calm his racing heart before continuing.

"I have spent nearly every night in the past month struggling to translate the note. Two nights ago, I broke the code, but I couldn't be sure that I was right about the translation until you drank from the cup and were saved."

Guinevere's eyes widened. "But if it is not the Holy Grail, then how . . ."

"Jacob's note said that this cup," Merlin said, drawing the ancient wooden vessel from his cloak, "is the cup that Christ drank from at the supper where they celebrated the resurrection of Lazarus from the dead. Martha of Bethany, Lazarus's sister, kept the cup to remember the miracle, and through the centuries, it was passed down to Jacob of Alexandria." He stared at the simple wooden cup for several moments before continuing.

"We . . . we have always believed that the Holy Grail . . . the cup the Christ drank from at the last supper somehow had miraculous powers, but why . . . why just that cup? Christ would have consecrated the food and wine that he and his followers ate and drank before every meal, and he would have drunk from many a grail, so why would not these other vessels also have the miraculous powers conveyed by his blessing?"

Guinevere smiled and spoke in a whisper, "Why not, indeed, Merlin the Wise. You will keep this cup safe and not speak of it," she said. "It is a holy relic that must be preserved for all time, for it may be the only grail that survives, and Sir Percival surely paid a most heavy toll for its recovery."

The pounding of a heavy fist on the outside door to Guinevere's quarters interrupted Merlin's answer. He rose and walked quickly to the door, pulling it open. Keil stood there, breathless.

"Your Highness, an army comes!"

"My God, our lines must have been broken!" Guinevere said in anguish.

"No, my Queen," Keil said, bowing, a broad smile coming to his face. "This army is from the Marches. They come to fight for Sir Percival, and they are over a thousand strong!"

The Vale of Ashes

Cynric and his archers focused their fire on the men within striking distance of the two knights in an effort to weaken the line around them to the breaking point. As he drew his bowstring back and targeted a Norse warrior on Sir Percival's right, Cynric saw an arrow flash across the battlefield and strike Lord Aeron in the shoulder, finding a gap in his armor—an arrow with blue feathers. Cynric traced the path of the arrow back to its source, and he saw a Pict warrior standing just clear of the melee surrounding the two knights. As he watched, the Pict warrior smiled and nocked a second blue arrow, an arrow that Cynric knew was meant for Sir Percival.

"You have shot your last arrow, Pict," Cynric whispered as he centered his aim on the Pict's chest, drew the string of his five-foot bow back to its fullest extent in one smooth movement, and released his arrow. The shaft flew across the field, swift and true, striking the Pict full in the chest. The man stood there for a moment, in shock. His eyes lifted to meet those of the tall archer. Then he fell facedown in the dirt.

Percival was unaware Galahad had been wounded, until he saw him slipping from his saddle to the ground. He charged forward on his mount, driving back the Norse warriors who pressed forward, intending to kill the stricken knight. He leaped from his horse and fought his way to Galahad's side. As he threw Galahad's arm over his shoulder and prepared to fight his way back to the safety of his own lines, Sveinn the Reaver shoved aside his fellow Norseman and stepped forward.

"I shall take pleasure in hanging your head from the mast of my ship, Knight," the giant Norseman said with a growl as he moved toward Percival.

At that moment, Capussa moved in front of Sir Percival, accompanied by two soldiers. "Your fight is with me today, Norseman," he said, "and I will keep my head, thank you."

Sveinn roared and leaped forward, his sword striking downward in a deadly arc at Capussa's head. The Numidian sprang toward him, dropping to one knee. He guided the onrushing blade away from him with a glancing blow from his buckler shield and at the same time drove his own sword into the Norseman's exposed thigh. Then he sprang back to his starting place.

The giant screamed in rage as his leg collapsed beneath him, and he fell to the ground. Sveinn's men raced forward to drag their warlord back within their shield wall, giving Capussa and Sir Percival the seconds needed to drag the wounded Galahad back within the protection of their lines.

When Percival moved to assist the men who ran over with a litter, Galahad seized his arm and said, "Do not worry about me, brother; the wound is not fatal. Morgana knows your men are near to the breaking point, and she will attack again. You must stay in line, or she will carry the day."

"He's right. She will make one final push," Capussa said.

Percival reluctantly nodded, and the litter bearing Galahad was taken to the command tent. As he started back toward the shield wall, a man dressed in the uniform of one of Guinevere's guards ran over to him, gasping for breath. The man's face was so covered in dust that at first Percival didn't recognize him.

"Guardsman, what is it . . . Keil?"

"Yes . . . Sir . . . here's . . . a message from . . ." Keil gasped as he handed a small piece of parchment to Percival and then fell to his knees in a spasm of coughing.

Percival read the note twice and then closed his mailed fist over the parchment. A moment later, he turned to Capussa. "Have the herald blow the horn and raise the truce flag. I would have words with Morgana." Then he turned to Keil and said, "I must ask you to deliver two more messages today."

* * *

MORGANA, WITH IVARR the Red on her right, waited in the space that had been made between the lines for the parley, as Capussa and Sir Percival rode forward. They stopped four paces away. For a minute, the two parties just looked at each other, and then Morgana spoke, in a voice laden with scorn.

"So, has the invincible Sir Percival and his Numidian companion come to surrender to the Queen's Army?"

"We have not," Percival said in a calm voice.

"No?" Morgana said with a cold laugh. "Are you going to die in a last charge, Sir Percival, like the Pendragon and your fellow knights did at Camlann?"

When Percival didn't answer, Morgana rode forward to within a pace of the Knight and spoke in a venomous tone, "I killed your King and your brother Knights at Camlann, and today, I have killed your Queen and that noble fool Galahad—oh yes, Sir Percival, your fellow knight will die in agony before the day is done, from the poison arrow that felled him. All that remains is this—you can surrender and spare the army of peasants that you so foolishly led into this trap, or you can watch every one of them die—for no quarter will be given. As for you and the Numidian, know this before you choose: if you fight on, I will crucify you both if there is even one breath left in your broken bodies when I take this field."

A cruel smile played across Ivarr the Red's face as he listened to the exchange.

Percival stared at Morgana in silence for a moment, and then he spoke in a voice that was as unyielding as the finest steel sword.

"This is not Camlann, Morgana. It is the Vale of Ashes, and yes, it is a trap, but it is one that we led you into. General Capussa, would you introduce Morgana and Ivarr the Red to the might of Londinium."

Capussa smiled and slowly raised his left fist above his head. Moments later, a thousand men armed with swords, spears, axes, pikes, and clubs ran to the rim of the slope that bordered the east side of the battlefield and roared out their defiance.

Morgana and Ivarr the Red looked up in shock at the mass of armed men ready to plunge down the slope into their right flank. Morgana's eyes narrowed, and the smile on Ivarr the Red's face vanished.

"The lord mayor and Cynric put on a show for your spies, Morgana," Percival said. "They were always coming to this fight. Now, General Capussa, would you introduce Morgana to the Legion of the Marches."

Then Capussa lowered his left fist and raised his right.

"Look behind you," Percival said.

Morgana and Ivarr the Red wheeled their horses around and stared in shock as ten formations of one hundred men marched, with the precision of a Roman legion, into the entrance of the valley behind them, cutting off their escape route.

When Morgana and Ivarr the Red faced Percival again, both bore defiant looks, but their eyes betrayed them. Percival sensed their fear. They knew they were facing annihilation. He rode his horse a pace closer to Morgana and spoke in a voice that was as cold as death.

"Queen Guinevere of the Britons is not dead. She is alive, Morgana, and on this field of battle, and on this day, it is you, not I, who will choose to yield or die."

THE VALE OF ASHES

Percival sat astride his horse and surveyed the battlefield. The bloody trial was over. The surviving Norse and Saxon soldiers were sitting, kneeling, or lying down in the center of field, surrounded by a thousand men at the ready on each side. Their arms were stacked in a great pile outside the ring. The armies of Morgana, Ivarr the Red, and Sveinn the Reaver were beaten, but the cost of victory had been heavy. Litter bearers were still running throughout the field gathering up the dead and wounded.

As he watched two men pick up the body of a young man, a Briton, and carry it over to the grassy area set aside for the dead, Capussa rode up alongside of him.

"Most of the dead you see are the Norse and Saxons, not Britons," Capussa said, gesturing to the bodies lying unmoving on the field. "Once

Morgana set off that explosion, the bowmen from Londinium on the hill, they . . ."

"Sought vengeance for five years of subjugation and pain," the Knight finished.

Capussa nodded.

Percival watched another black pall of smoke drift across the field from the fire still burning in the square that had once been Morgana's tent and shook his head.

"It is a fire that will not die."

"Merlin told me of this," Capussa said. "It is a weapon from the City of Constantine known as Greek fire. Few know how to mix this fiery potion. Morgana must have brought it with her. Water will not quench its flames, only dirt, and, as you can see," Capussa said, nodding to the men shoveling dirt on the flames, "it resists to the very last."

"I was fool to give her the time to ponder the surrender offer," Percival said in quiet regret. "That gave her the opportunity to set the fire and . . . to escape. Now, we shall have to fight her another day."

"Bah. You think too much, Knight," the Numidian said dismissively. "Had you demanded an immediate surrender, she would have refused and the battle would have been joined again. More men would still have died. Whether the witch would have escaped or not is a matter in the hands of the gods. Today, we have won a great victory. We must honor the dead by celebrating what we have gained."

Percival looked over at Capussa and nodded. "Yes, we must."

A mounted messenger rode over to Percival. "Sir Percival, a member of the Queen's Guard has come with a message. The Queen, she comes."

Percival looked at the man, surprised. "She comes to the battlefield?"

"Yes, she is on her way. And . . . there is another matter. You must come to the command tent. Lord Aeron . . . I mean, Sir Galahad . . . he is ill unto death."

The look on the messenger's face shook Percival to the core. He wheeled his horse around and galloped over to the large tent at the most northern end of the field, dismounted, and walked into the candlelit interior. His brother Knight lay on a long wooden table, his head resting upon a worn blanket.

The healers had removed Galahad's armor and bandaged his right shoulder with a clean cloth. This had staunched the blood from his wound, but it had not remedied whatever ailed him within. His face was ashen, his breath labored, and his blue eyes were clouded in pain.

"The battle?" he said in a hoarse voice.

Percival walked over to his wounded brethren, and the two men gripped forearms. "It is won, brother. The day is ours."

"What of Morgana?"

"She escaped, with a small force, but be assured, she will be hunted down."

"You have done it. Camlann is avenged," Galahad gasped as he released Percival's forearm and closed a trembling fist in triumph.

Percival shook his head. "Not I, brother; we have done it. All of us, and you most of all."

"Morgana told you of my pledge?" he asked, his voice filled with quiet regret.

"No. She did not have to. I knew there was only one price that would have induced you to serve under her banner—the Queen's life."

Galahad nodded and pushed himself up with his good arm. A wave of pain crossed his face. Percival moved to gently push him back down, but Galahad shook his head and gasped, "I must tell you of this. My time is short. Yes . . . that was the price . . . it had to be done. At Camlann, I was struck in the face with an arrow in the last minutes of the day. When I awakened, I was Morgana's prisoner. She told me that she could kill the Queen at will . . . she had assassins everywhere, and Guinevere . . . there was no one left to protect her. But in the end, I still could not save—"

"Galahad, she lives."

Galahad looked at Percival, his eyes desperately seeking confirmation of the spoken words. "The Queen?"

"Yes. She is well. When we met on the battlefield, I had been told that the poison from the Pict's arrow would take her life within the hour. Later, I received a second message. Merlin saved her life." Percival grasped his friend's hand. "Galahad, the Queen will be here in a moment with Merlin. He will attend to your wound."

Galahad lowered his head back to the blanket beneath him and drew in a ragged breath. There was a smile on his face.

"Thank the Lord," he whispered. "After I have passed, you must tell her, brother. I would have her know that I honored my oath to the King and to the Table."

"Galahad, she knows of your great sacrifice. I sent a messenger after you were wounded," Percival said.

Shouts of "All hail Queen Guinevere!" could be heard from outside the tent. Galahad squeezed the Knight's hand as hundreds of voices took up the cry. Moments later, Keil and another guard drew back the tent flaps and Guinevere walked in, followed by Merlin.

Percival bowed, and Galahad made an effort to sit up, but Guinevere raised a hand as she walked over, staying his effort.

"Rest, Sir Galahad. Merlin will attend you."

"My Queen—"

"Shhh," Guinevere said softly, gently taking Galahad's feverish hand in hers, "brave knight. It is I who should bow to you, for I know of your sacrifice. I am, and I shall always be, in your debt."

Merlin walked around to the other side of the table and looked at the bandage on the knight's shoulder and nodded his approval.

"Do you have the arrow that struck him?"

Galahad answered in voice almost too soft to hear. "It is there, on the table."

Merlin walked over to the blue fletched arrow lying on a nearby table and sniffed the point.

His face was grim when he laid it down.

"It carries the same poison as the arrow that struck you, my Queen."

"No!" Guinevere cried, her face turning pale.

Galahad's breath grew more labored, and he closed his eyes in pain.

"Merlin, the cup! Do you have it with you?" Guinevere said, her eyes frantic with anxiety.

Merlin looked at Guinevere in confusion for an instant, then he plunged his hand into the pocket of his cloak. "I think . . . yes, in the rush, yes, it is here." He ran to the pitcher of water resting on a nearby table, filled the small wooden cup, and returned to Galahad's side.

"Drink, Sir Galahad, drink!" Merlin whispered urgently.

"My time is at an end," the knight whispered, his face a rictus of pain.

"Galahad, please, I ask this of you," Guinevere pleaded softly.

Galahad opened his eyes and looked at Guinevere for a long moment. Then he reached for the cup. His hand was shaking so badly that she had to guide the cup to his lips. After swallowing the water, Galahad lay back, exhausted, his eyes closed once more.

Merlin poured the rest of the water in the cup onto a white cloth and bathed the knight's fevered brow and cheeks. For what seemed like an eternity, nothing happened, and then the look of pain on Galahad's face faded, his labored breathing steadied, and the striated muscles in his neck and jaw relaxed. After several moments, Galahad opened his eyes, and his gaze moved from Merlin to Guinevere and finally to Percival, eyes that were as blue as the sky and free of pain.

"Do not grieve for me," Galahad said with a serene smile, "for I am forgiven." Then he closed his eyes and was still.

Merlin stepped forward and placed his finger against the side of Galahad's neck. After several long moments he withdrew his hand and said, "He is dead," in a voice filled with sorrow.

"No!" Guinevere gasped. "The cup . . . Merlin, it saved my life from the poison. Why not Sir Galahad?"

"Look at his face," Merlin said softly.

"It cannot be," Percival said, his voice filled with wonder as he stared down at his friend.

"The scars . . . they're gone!" Guinevere gasped. "Why then does he not live?"

"I believe," Merlin said, "that Galahad died a hundred deaths in the service of Morgana. In the end, he sought forgiveness and heaven's peace from the Almighty, not life, and I believe that is the gift he received."

Sir Percival knelt beside the body of his brother Knight, in prayer. A moment later, Guinevere, tears running down her face, knelt as well. Merlin reached for a white shroud lying on a nearby table and slowly drew it over the knight's body. Then he knelt and joined Percival and Guinevere in prayer.

CHAPTER 34

LONDINIUM, THREE WEEKS LATER

ercival stood on a hill just outside the walls of Londinium staring down at the Tamesis River, where a galley made its way seaward on a path of white gold laid down by the morning sun. The day he embarked for the Holy Land on a similar ship had been one such as this, and for an instant, he returned to that place in time, recalling the sorrow, frustration, and confusion of the parting. The memory faded as the ship sailed out of sight.

Merlin was right. The man who had left ten years before was not the man who had returned, and yet in one respect they were same. The Percival of yesteryear, like the Percival of today, was in love with Guinevere, and both men carried no small measure of guilt for feeling thus. Although Arthur was long dead and Guinevere free to marry, the feeling persisted.

"I fear that I look upon a man who is vexed to the core of his being."

Percival turned, surprised to see Merlin standing behind him.

"Is this book so easy to read?"

"No, just this particular chapter."

"And what, sage, vexes my soul?"

Merlin joined Percival at the crest of the hill and gazed out at the scene below in silence before answering.

"Percival, you are a disciple of honor, carrying both her virtues and burdens. You always have been. On some days I wish that I could infect you with at least some of the mores of the scoundrel, but alas, I have yet to find such a potion."

The Knight's eyes grew distant for a moment. "Trust me, Merlin, I have done my share of wrongdoing. The line of dead men who would attest to that is long, indeed."

"And the line of those who would say otherwise is far longer."

The two men fell silent, and then Merlin answered Percival's question.

"As to your question, what vexes your soul, Sir Percival of the Round Table, is your need for the blessing of a King who is dead, before you take the hand of the woman who was once his Queen."

Percival glanced over at Merlin. "I would not have Guinevere know of this."

"She does not, but she knows that you are troubled, and . . . since she is in love with you, it distresses her."

"Then I will bury my qualms, since what I seek cannot be found."

"That may be, or you could be looking in the wrong places."

The Knight turned to face the old Roman, a question in his eyes.

"Percival," Merlin said, clasping his hands behind his back, "in the last three days, you have visited almost every church in Londinium and come to this hill nearly every morning. If Arthur's spirit is to be found in this world, I do not believe that you will find it in these places."

Percival's gaze returned to the Tamesis River flowing below. "I would pray at the foot of Arthur's grave, but I am told you are the only one who knows of his resting place, and you have refused to divulge that secret to anyone, including Guinevere."

"That is true. Nor would I divulge it to you. That was Arthur's command, and it was a wise one. Excalibur lies with him, anchored in a sacred stone, and evil men in the pursuit of that great talisman would do terrible things to learn of its whereabouts. He wanted to protect Guinevere from that danger. So I alone carry this secret."

"Then, as I said, I will consider the matter at an end."

"Do not be so hasty, Knight. If any part of Arthur's spirit remains in this world, I do not believe it would have stayed in that bier, far to the north. No, it would be in a vale, a half days ride from here, where Lady Alona is buried."

"Lady Alona?"

Merlin walked over to Percival and stood by his side. "Nearly two decades ago, Arthur married a young noblewoman named Alona. I attended the wedding. It was a rare thing. They married solely for love, not for gain or position." He paused for a moment, and then he continued, his voice filled with sadness. "There was . . . a magic between them, a love like I have never seen before. Alas, a year later, she died in childbirth, and the child with her. Arthur was so fraught with grief, I feared he would take his own life. Over time, he learned to bear the pain, but he never forgot her. As I say, if his spirit remains in this world, it will be with her."

Percival stared at Merlin for a long time, and then his gaze returned to the river below.

"Merlin, I would ask that you take me to this place, that I might say a prayer beside this woman's grave."

Merlin smiled. "Then so you shall, Sir Percival."

Two hours later, Percival and Merlin dismounted from their horses outside a small chapel on the edge of a forest, north of Londinium. Merlin led his horse down a crude stone path that circled to the rear of the chapel and disappeared into the wood. Percival followed.

"We are watched," Percival said quietly.

"Indeed we are," Merlin said, "and I can assure you that we would proceed no further if Father Gildas and his minions didn't recognize me. Few know of this place, but it is never without guardians. Come, the grave is ahead."

The two men tied their horses to a tree behind the chapel.

"Our horses will be safe here. The grave is just ahead," Merlin said.

The older man led the way down a narrow path into the wood. With each step, the light overhead receded, leaving them walking in shadow through a grove lined with oak trees that were as ancient as they were massive. Just when it seemed that they had walked past the mightiest of these wooden giants, a circle of trees appeared ahead that was mightier still. Merlin walked between two of these coal black sentinels into a vale that was bathed in the light of the midday sun, and Percival followed.

"These trees must have been planted here, in this way, a long time ago," Percival said.

"Yes, by my estimate, over two thousand years ago. I cannot say by whom, or why they were planted in a circle around this vale, but I believe this was a holy place then, as it is now." He motioned toward the north. "Lady Alona's ancestral home is a half league distant. She told Arthur that she had once become lost in these woods as a child and spent the night within this vale. The trees . . . she said they kept her safe. When she was dying, she asked Arthur to bury her here, and so he did. She lies over here."

Percival followed Merlin to the center of the vale. A low wall, with a gate at one end, encircled a gravestone hewn from a giant white rock. A simple but beautiful cross had been carved into the gravestone. The words *Alona, beloved of Arthur* were carved beneath it. A stone bench stood a pace away from the gravestone.

Merlin gestured toward the grave and said quietly, "This is where she is buried. I will leave you alone here."

Percival opened the gate in the wall and knelt down beside the gravestone and prayed in silence. When he rose sometime later and made the sign of the cross, he was surprised to see that the sun was long past midday.

Percival turned, hearing footsteps approaching from the path behind him, and saw Merlin open the gate in the wall. He walked past Percival to the gravestone, knelt down, and drew a ring from his right pocket. For a long moment, he looked at the ring, and then he placed it underneath a rock at the base of the grave and stood up. After making the sign of the cross, he walked over to Percival.

"May I ask what you have left there?" Percival said.

"The ring that Arthur gave her . . . Alona's wedding ring."

"You kept it safe all of these years?"

Percival looked over at the smaller man, but he sensed that Merlin wouldn't speak of the matter further.

"We should leave," Merlin said.

Percival nodded and followed the smaller man to the path that led back to the chapel. The Knight slowed as he reached the end of the vale and turned to look upon the grave again. His breath caught in his throat as he saw two ghostly figures in the waning afternoon sun—a man and a woman.

The woman was sitting on the bench with her back to Percival. Her lithe, young body was resplendent in a shimmering white dress that strikingly contrasted with the cascade of raven hair flowing down her back. The man kneeling beside the woman was partially hidden by her body, but Percival could see he was placing something on her finger—a ring.

Percival took a step forward and then froze as the man stood and looked across the vale directly at him. At first, the Knight didn't recognize the ghostly figure, and then he realized—it was Arthur—a young Arthur, one whose face no longer bore the burdens of time and the weight of responsibility, but only the blessing of contentment.

Percival dropped to one knee and bowed his head. When he looked up again, Arthur raised his right hand and slowly made the sign of the cross. Then he smiled, turned to the woman, and took her hands in his, and then they were gone.

The Knight knelt there for a moment, in silence, and prayed he was worthy of the hand he now had been granted leave to seek. As the vale descended into shadow, he stood and followed Merlin up the trail.

LONDINIUM

Percival looked out the first-floor window of the stone mansion in the heart of Londinium, serving as the temporary royal quarters. Six lines of young men were practicing rudimentary sword craft in the courtyard under the watchful eye of a cadre of older soldiers. Although the royal forces were growing by the day in size and skill, Percival knew that an invasion in force by the Saxons, Norse, or Franks could imperil the struggling kingdom. If they could just obtain a few months' respite while the army's foundation was being laid, they might yet have a chance to bring a measure of peace and security to the land.

"Are you musing about the dangers posed by the morrow again?" Capussa said as he walked into the room.

"Something like that," he answered.

"A year ago, you and I would rise each day knowing that we faced death in the arena. Now, we can rise each day with at least a measure of doubt on that score. I think even you would concede, my friend, that we are at least sailing in the right direction."

Percival smiled.

"Well there is that."

"Good!" Capussa said, "Now that I have lifted a burden from your shoulders, you can attend the Queen with a smile instead of a frown. She has sent for you."

"I will tell her of your noble deed," Percival said with a small smile as he turned toward the door.

"Do that. Now, what is that man doing with that sword?" Capussa said as he stared out the window at a young Briton wielding a wooden practice sword. "You there," he called out to the man, "that's a sword, not a club."

Capussa was still scolding the soldier when Percival walked out of the room. His smile faded as he walked up the stairs to the second floor, where Guinevere and her now larger royal court were quartered. The anxiety Capussa had professed to have banished was the lesser of the two that vexed him this morning.

Percival nodded to Keil, standing outside the door, dressed in a spotless royal guard's uniform.

"Guardsman Keil, your service in bringing the message to me on the day of the battle with such haste. It was a noble effort, and it saved many a life. I will not forget it."

"Thank . . . thank you, Sir Percival."

"No, Guardsman Keil, thank you." Percival raised his hand to knock on the door, but Cadwyn opened it first.

"Lady Cadwyn, I hope all is well with you today."

"Why thank you, Sir Percival, all is quite wonderful. The Queen is expecting you. Please come in."

As Percival followed Cadwyn down the broad hallway to the second-floor hearth room, he noted that the young woman's lavender dress was more formal than the dress she'd worn in his past visits. The room, like the rest of the royal quarters, was decorated with the rugs, wall tapestries, and fine furniture donated by the citizens of the grateful City of Londinium, a city that was once again bustling with life. The more visible trappings of the Queen's royal status increased the trepidation the Knight felt as he walked into the large palatial room.

Percival walked by the fire burning in the hearth to the window that overlooked a formal garden that had been left untended for years. The neat rows of bushes and hedges were overgrown, the flowerbeds were bereft of color, and the rose trellis in the center waited in vain for the red and white blooms that should have come with spring. Yet, despite the years of neglect, nature had not withheld all of its blessings. The majestic plumes of the trees that encircled the garden were painted with the soft red, yellow, and gold hues of early fall, giving the vista a stately, if worn, splendor.

"It's beautiful in its own way, is it not?" Guinevere said from the door.

Percival turned quickly and stared at the Queen in silence, taking in the golden braid encircling her head, the silver diadem, and the cascade of golden hair flowing like a river over her shoulder and down the back of her resplendent indigo-blue dress. When she smiled at him, the spell holding him in place was broken, and he quickly bowed. "My Queen, forgive me, I . . . I didn't hear you."

"I would have you call me Guinevere, as you did the night we dined . . . and danced together."

"Yes . . . Guinevere, and yes, it is a beautiful garden."

She walked across the room and stood beside Percival at the window and looked down at the garden below. A distant look came to her eyes.

"I used to walk alone in the forest near my father's castle on days like this, when the leaves were just turning and the sun was still warm. It was one of my most favorite things to do. Did you ever walk in the woods thus when you were a boy, just for the joy of it?"

"Yes. On many a day. It was a habit that my father was not fond of," Percival said with a wry smile.

"Oh, I cannot imagine an errant Sir Percival," Guinevere said with a laugh. "Tell me of your favorite place there. I should like to visit."

Percival looked into the distance and then spoke in a soft voice.

"There is a vale two leagues or so from my home that is surrounded by a stand of oaks . . . trees that are as mighty as they are old. When times were hard and I sought a measure of peace, I would go there and watch the rays of sunlight break through the clouds and touch the ground, and then disappear. It . . . was as if I were watching a window to heaven open and close. As a boy, I believed that if I were lucky enough to be standing in the spot where the light touched the earth, I . . . I would receive a gift from heaven."

Guinevere looked up at Percival. "And what do you believe that gift would be, if that came to pass?" she said.

Percival turned and faced Guinevere, who was now but a step away from him.

"It has come to pass, and that gift, Guinevere, was you."

A tear rolled down her cheek. "Percival," Guinevere whispered, gazing into the Knight's eyes. "Arthur Pendragon asked for my hand, and that was given, but he never asked for my heart."

Percival slowly knelt down on one knee and took the Queen's hands, his eyes meeting hers.

"I am not worthy, my Queen, but I . . . I would have both your heart and your hand if you would have me as your husband."

A smile as radiant as the beams of sunlight Percival remembered from that distant vale lit Guinevere's face. "Then they are yours," she said, "and you are mine."

CHAPTER 35

PEN DINAS

Keil, Torn, and four of the Queen's guardsmen raced to the top of Pen Dinas in the last hour of the day, their horses lathered with sweat.

"Make haste, Keil," Torn said. "We will lose the sun in moments!"

Keil dismounted and opened the parchment map Sister Aranwen and Cadwyn had painstakingly drawn for him a week earlier. His hands were shaking as he recalled the testy exchange between the two women that day.

"It . . . it was so long ago, Cadwyn! Wait . . . wait, I do remember. We were staying at Pen Dinas. It was a moonlit night . . . the Queen didn't know I was watching. She walked down to the wall, the one that encircles the tower. She put something behind a rock. It must be the ring. Yes! It is in the wall."

"In the wall? Sister, there are a thousand rocks in that wall. We have to know which one," Cadwyn had said with exasperation.

"Patience, child. It is coming back to me. The Queen . . . she stopped at the rock on the hill . . . the big one, and then walked straight down from the rock to the wall. She walked with some care, as if—"

"—she was marking the spot! The ring is there!"

Keil scanned the hill below the old tower and spied the large rock embedded in the earth ten paces from the wall marked on the map. He ran down the hill, glancing at the fading sun as he did so. After circling to the side of the rock facing the wall, he walked down the hill in a straight line and knelt beside the wall.

The mortar holding the rocks in place was crumbling and much of it was covered with moss, but there was nothing there to give him a clue as to which of the hundreds of stones could be the right one. The guardsman reached for a square stone and tried to pull it free. It would not move. He tried another and another. All were still held fast by mason's mortar. Then his eyes fixed on a rock farther to the right, a rock with a slight discoloration in the center. He reached for the rock and gave it a tentative push. It moved.

The guardsman drew in a breath as he placed both hands on the rock and pulled. It came free. He reached into the space behind the rock, and his trembling hand closed on a small wooden box. He drew the box from its hiding place and opened it. There was a golden ring within.

Keil gently closed the box and stood. He turned to Torn and the other guardsmen waiting on the hill above.

"We have done it!"

The taciturn Torn gave him a rare smile and then glanced at the sun, just passing below the horizon.

"Replace the stone, Guardsman Keil, and make haste! We don't want to be late for the wedding, do we?"

Abbey Cwm Hir

As Percival stood at the altar beside Capussa, waiting for the Queen to emerge from the sacristy, he glanced out the window across from him. Thousands of tents covered nearly every patch of open grass within a half league of the abbey, ranging from the grand and stately shelters erected for the wealthier nobles and knights, to the modest shelters cobbled together by farmers and herdsmen. All desired to gain just a glimpse of the royal couple and to be able to say to their children and grandchildren that they were there on that historic fall day.

Although the church could only hold a fraction of the people desirous of attending the ceremony, the first row had been set aside to honor the members of a departed brotherhood. Thirty gleaming swords anchored in blocks of stone stood in the pew, each engraved with the name of a deceased Knight of the Table.

When Guinevere emerged from the sacristy with the bishop,

followed by Sister Aranwen and Lady Cadwyn, the quiet murmur in the church fell silent, and Percival and Capussa dropped to one knee. The Queen, resplendent in a magnificent white dress, walked over to the two men, a radiant smile on her face.

"Please rise," Guinevere said and extended her hand to her betrothed.

Percival took her hand, and the couple walked over to the waiting bishop. When the marriage vows had been said, Capussa, standing beside Sir Percival, handed the Knight the wedding ring. Guinevere's eyes widened as Percival slipped the golden ring on her finger, and for a moment, she stared at it, remembering a wish made long ago, one that now had been granted. She glanced over at Sister Aranwen and Cadwyn, seated two paces away, and smiled, a look of profound gratitude on her face.

Guinevere turned to Percival and the couple kissed. When they parted, the Queen and the Knight stared into each other's eyes in silence, as if willing the moment to last forever. Then the royal couple turned and faced the assembled notables in the church, and they were met with a thunder of applause that shook the very walls of the old chapel.

As Sir Percival waited for the joyous clamor to die down, he looked over at the line of swords standing in the front pew, silently witnessing the ceremony, and for a moment, they were standing there—all of them. His gaze moved from Lancelot to Kay, to Tristan and Gawain, and each of the others, until at last, it came to rest upon the knight at the end of the pew—the knight with the rogue's smile and the devil-may-care look he would never forget.

Then, in a heartbeat, the Knights disappeared. As he stared at the line of steel sentinels left behind, Percival said a silent prayer for his departed brethren and asked for their prayers as well, for he knew he would need them in the days to come.

Guinevere saw the look on his face and whispered, "Percival, what is it?"

The Knight looked down at his beautiful wife and Queen and smiled. "I was just saying good-bye to my brothers."

THE END

EPILOGUE

organa stood on the crest of a hill a half a league distant from the abbey and watched Guinevere and Percival emerge from the church. Rage flared in her eyes at the applause of thousands of nobles, knights, soldiers, and peasants waiting outside. As the sound of trumpets and cheers reached a crescendo, Morgana turned to a woman waiting a pace behind her, dressed in the habit of a nun. She handed the woman a tiny glass bottle.

"A drop is all that is necessary. You will wait until I give the word."

Reading Group Guide

Percival's character unfolds before our eyes throughout the story. What do we know about him at the onset of his journey? How does that view change as the story progresses?

Arthur Pendragon and all but two of the Knights of the Round Table have perished before *The Return of Sir Percival* begins. What role does Arthur play in the story in spite of his physical absence? How important is that role to the outcome?

During a typical "hero's journey," the main character is often helped along their quest by a guide. Who plays that role for Percival?

We eventually learn that Bishop Verdino is actually Merlin the Wise. Early in the story Bishop Verdino's character is painted as being dishonest, a trickster, and possibly even as stealing from the Queen. Cadwyn describes the bishop as a "pompous old thief." In what ways are the Bishop's acts misrepresented? And how does he redeem himself?

Sir Percival and Queen Guinevere's relationship blossoms over the course of the novel. What are some clues early on of Percival and Guinevere's feelings for each other?

How does Percival's guilt over King Arthur's absence affect his feelings and actions toward Queen Guinevere? Do you think Sir Percival was returning to Queen Guinevere all along?

We see two different versions of Lord Aeron over the course of the story. What are these two different identities and how do they differ? Is Lord Aeron's ending a happy one?

Morgana is an interesting and powerful character. What are her motives and what is her ultimate goal? For example, is she simply seeking vengeance or is it power she desires?

How is the theme of identity woven into the story? How are Sir Percival and Lord Aeron both symbolic of the quest to define and understand one's identity?

Did Sir Percival's recounting of his time in the land of the Moors surprise you? In what ways?

Cadwyn, Queen Guinevere's handmaiden, and Aranwen, Queen Guinevere's spiritual attendant, have an interesting and often humorous relationship. How does this relationship move the plot forward?

What is the significance of Sir Percival's story about Princess Sumayya? How does that story affect Sir Percival's story?

How does Jacob the Healer aid Sir Percival in his quest for the Holy Grail? And how does Jacob the Healer affect the lives of Lord Aeron and Queen Guinevere?

Author Q & A

Q: Can you share what inspired you to write an Arthurian legend? For example, how did you become interested in this genre and what are some of your favorite books?

A: I have been fascinated by myths and legends since I was a little boy. *Bullfinch's Mythology* was a fixture in my personal library, and I made a trip to the library almost weekly, for years, seeking new material on this subject. After reading every book I could find on ancient Greek myths, I moved on to Norse myths and Celtic myths, and finally arrived at the legends and myths unique to Britain. The Arthurian legend is the most prominent and fascinating in the latter genre.

As far as favorite books within the Arthurian genre, I enjoyed Thomas Malory's *Le Morte D'Arthur*, which I read decades ago, and I also enjoyed Geoffrey of Monmouth's *History of Kings of Britain*, which I read just before writing *The Return of Sir Percival*.

Q: You take a very different approach to your tale. What inspired you to begin your story after the fall of Arthur Pendragon?

A: The central themes at the heart of this tale could only come to life in an Albion where Arthur and all but one of the Knights of the Round Table have died and Camelot has fallen. Moreover, this time frame allows Guinevere, Percival, Capussa, Merlin, and Lord Aeron to take center stage and fulfill the roles assigned to them, without being over-shadowed by Arthur.

The timing of the story also gave me the flexibility to let each character look back upon the lost magic that was Camelot through a series of flashbacks. These periodic reminiscences tell the story of yesteryear through the eyes of each character, thereby deepening the reader's insight into, and connection with, each character's persona. They also forge the links that tie the past to the travails of the present.

Q: This telling of the Arthurian legend seems to have more history and less magic. What inspired you to go that route rather than the potions-and-wands approach, as other authors in this genre tend to do?

A: The real Arthur achieved fame struggling to defend the Celtic Britons from Saxon invasions. His story is the story of a people's fight for survival. To the extent possible, I wanted this same existential struggle to be at the heart of the tale told in *The Return of Sir Percival.* Insofar as magic is concerned, I think readers will find that magic and mystery have been woven throughout *The Return of Sir Percival*, both human and divine, in ample measure.

Q: Your knowledge of the time period seems significant. Did that knowledge lead you to the story, or did the story lead you to that knowledge?

A: I am an obsessive history buff, and I have a particular passion for Roman and post-Roman Britain. However, the historical threads that appear in *The Return of Sir Percival* are only there to enrich the story and to enhance and provide depth to the backgrounds of the characters (such as the dynastic struggle in Constantinople). They were not the inspiration for the tale.

In truth, the story came to me when I was recovering from an eye operation. The idea became such an obsession that I set aside another book that I was three quarters of the way through (a second thriller) and started writing *The Return of Sir Percival*.

Q: Geography plays a major role in this story. What kind of research did you do while writing the novel? Did you encounter the map during your research, or is it something you were inspired to create as a result of your findings?

A: I love geography. The room where I sit and write is full of maps, both historical and modern, and I spent a good deal of time trying to place Sir Percival's journey across the Land of the Britons within a viable historical reality. One of the key sources that I used as a reference was *Roman Roads In Britain*, by Ivan D. Margary. The references and maps in *Oxford Illustrated History of Roman Britain*, by Peter Salway, were also helpful.

Some of the other books that I read while writing the book were *Foundation*, by Peter Ackroyd; *History of Britain*, by Simon Schama; *A Brief History of Roman Britain*, by Joan P. Alcock; *History of The English People*, by Paul Johnson; *Empire of Gold: A History of The Byzantine Empire*, by Thomas F. Malden; *The Ruins of The Roman Empire*, by James J. O'Donnell; *How Rome Fell*, by Adrian Goldsworthy; and *The Fall of the Roman Empire: A New History of Rome and the Barbarians*, by Peter Heather.

All of these were fascinating and informative reads, and they provided great insight into the Roman and post-Roman reality that existed in Britain. However, the seventh-century universe that I used in the story is entirely fictional, with certain limited exceptions. For example, the roads Percival travels in the story are Roman roads, and, where possible, I used historical landmarks to add context and color, such as the site of Walton Castle in Felixstowe (this was originally built by the Romans as a Saxon coastal fort and now lies in the ocean), and the Roman signal station at Filey (which is just ruins now).

Q: What was your favorite chapter to write in *The Return of Sir Percival* and why? And on the other side of the spectrum, were there any chapters that were particularly challenging for you to write? If so, can you share what it was about these parts of the story that challenged you?

A: The chapter where Sir Percival walks into the arena in Londinium was great fun to write, as was the scene where Cadwyn bursts into Guinevere's quarter's pantomiming a sword fight. The most challenging chapters were those where Guinevere returns to the past, in a series of conversations with young Cadwyn, or where she returns to the past alone, in a series of solitary reveries. Each reminiscence is intended to give the reader an empathetic insight into the personality of this intelligent, complicated, and fascinating woman, so it was critical to get them right.

Q: Do you have a favorite character in the story? If so, what is it about this character that you most appreciate?

A: Yes. That would be Capussa, the Numidian mercenary. He is older than Percival, and in many ways wiser. He sees the world as it is—a Hobbesian universe where life is truly "nasty, brutish and short." (quoted from *Leviathan*, Thomas Hobbes). And yet, this realization does not suborn Capussa's innate goodness or his patient and positive outlook on life, nor does it dull his wonderful sense of humor.

Lord Aeron also has a special place in my pantheon of magnificent characters. In the story, Lord Aeron, as the magnificent young Galahad, is the most handsome man at court and the life of every party. Although these antics often place his loyal friend and fellow knight Percival in the awkward position of having to explain his early morning absences, Percival nonetheless holds his roguish brethren in the highest regard.

After the disaster at Camlann these two men travel very down different paths, but both are forced to endure cruel hardships and carry terrible burdens in the service of their King and Queen. In the end, these two knights come to epitomize, in different ways, what was most noble about the brotherhood of the Knights of the Round Table.

Q: In a similar regard, which character in *The Return of Sir Percival* do you most personally identify with and why?

A: Cynric the Archer. He is a man who rises each day and "gets the job done," without complaint, despite the setbacks and tragedies he has endured during his life. He is also a man who is not afraid to resist what may be a noble, but foolhardy venture. Yet, once the decision is made to attempt the near impossible, he steps across the proverbial line in the sand along with everyone else.

I identify with Cynric on account of his quiet perseverance and exceptional, but hard-earned skills. In my humble estimation, the world rides on the backs of men and women who have these characteristics.

Q: How do you get in the mood to write? Is there anything in particular that helps you stay focused? Do you have any writing rituals, for example?

A: Due in part to vision problems, I try to write early in the morning. This is the time when my mind is clear, my eyes are fresh, and when the constant harassment inherent in the practice of law is least intrusive.

I also try to write every day. Writing a book is somewhat like climbing a mountain. When you stand at the bottom, the idea of climbing to the top seems daunting, even irrational. However, with each step, the end goal seems more attainable. If I write every day, then the internal "you are never going to get there" voice becomes less persuasive with each sitting.

Q: *The Return of Sir Percival* ends with quite a cliffhanger. Did you know how this first book in the series would end when you started to write it? Or did the ending come to you as you were working on the book?

A: Unlike other books that I have written, or that I am currently working on, I had a pretty clear vision of where the road was going when I sat down to write *The Return of Sir Percival*. There were many side roads, diversionary paths, and secondary characters who were conjured into existence as the tapestry was woven, but I knew the destination from the beginning. I wish every book came to me with that singular clarity.

Q: And lastly, because readers will be curious about what your next book holds, can you share what readers can expect from Sir Percival and Guinevere in their next adventure?

A: I am working on the prequel. It will capture Sir Percival's early life and adventures as a Knight of the Round Table before the fall and his travails and trials in the Holy Land. It will also chronicle Guinevere's life in the last years before the fall and provide a window into the Camelot that was lost. Then, I will write Book II.

About the Author

S. ALEXANDER O'KEEFE was born in Providence, Rhode Island. He is a graduate of Dartmouth College and Fordham University School of Law, and he practices law in Newport Beach, California. Mr. O'Keefe and his wife, Cathy, who live in Irvine, California, have three children. *The Return of Sir Percival: Guinevere's Prayer* is Mr. O'Keefe's second novel.